A Death for a Dilettante

...

A Death for a Dietitian

Robert Forsythe 5 and 6

DUET

A Death for a Dilettante

...

A Death for a Dietitian

E. X. Giroux

FELONY & MAYHEM PRESS • NEW YORK

All the characters and events portrayed in this work are fictitious.

A DEATH FOR A DILETTANTE/A DEATH FOR A DIETITIAN

Robert Forsythe 5 and 6

A Felony & Mayhem mystery

PRINTING HISTORY
A Death for a Dilettante
First edition (St. Martin's): 1987
A Death for a Dietitian
First edition (St. Martin's): 1988

Felony & Mayhem Duet edition: 2025

Copyright © 1987 and © 1988 by E. X. Giroux

All rights reserved

ISBN: 978-1-63194-332-4 (paperback)
978-1-63194-333-1 (ebook)

Manufactured in the United States of America

Cataloging-in-Publication information for this book
is available from the Library of Congress.

The icon above says you're holding a book in the Felony & Mayhem "British" category. These books are set in or around the UK, and feature the highly literate, often witty prose that fans of British mystery demand. If you enjoy this book, you may well like other "British" titles from Felony & Mayhem Press.

For information about British titles or to learn more about Felony & Mayhem Press, please visit us online at:

www.FelonyAndMayhem.com

Other "British" titles from

FELONY&MAYHEM

MICHAEL DAVID ANTHONY
The Becket Factor
Midnight Come
Dark Provenance

ROBERT BARNARD
Corpse in a Gilded Cage
Death and the Chaste Apprentice
The Skeleton in the Grass
Out of the Blackout

SIMON BRETT
Blotto, Twinks and the
*   Ex-King's Daughter*
Blotto, Twinks and the
*   Dead Dowager Duchess*
Blotto, Twinks and the
*   Rodents of the Riviera*
Blotto, Twinks and the
*   Bootlegger's Moll*

ELIZABETH IRONSIDE
The Accomplice
The Art of Deception
Death in the Garden
A Very Private Enterprise

MAGGIE JOEL
The Second-Last Woman in England
The Past and Other Lies

SHEILA RADLEY
Death in the Morning
The Chief Inspector's Daughter
A Talent for Destruction
Fate Worse than Death

LESLIE THOMAS
Dangerous Davies:
*   The Last Detective*

L.C. TYLER
The Herring Seller's Apprentice
Ten Little Herrings
The Herring in the Library
Herring on the Nile
Crooked Herring

E.X. FERRARS
Something Wicked
Root of All Evil
The Crime and the Crystal
The Other Devil's Name
A Murder Too Many
Smoke Without Fire
A Hobby of Murder
A Choice of Evils
Last Will and Testament
Frog in the Throat
Thinner Than Water
Death of a Minor Character
I Met Murder
Woman Slaughter

This book is for Betty and Harold Windover
and for days of auld lang syne

A Death for a Dilettante

Prologue

Winslow Maxwell Penndragon was a dilettante in the true sense of the word. One of his nicer traits, and he had a number, was his acceptance of his lifestyle. No pretense was ever made that he cared for work or had any intention whatsoever of engaging in anything so demeaning. Luckily his father and his grandfather had labored industriously enough that their heir could do as he chose. What Winslow Penndragon chose to do was to gratify his every whim. Upon inheriting the Penndragon estate, he immediately liquidated the various business concerns so carefully nurtured by his sires, profitably invested the proceeds, and turned his attention to a varied and colorful life.

As was shortly apparent, Penndragon didn't confuse idleness with indolence. Many of his fads and pursuits were more exhausting and, at times, hazardous, than daily toil ever could have been. He roamed the world, finding and delighting in exotic places and dangerous situations. If his courage was ever in doubt, those doubts were laid to rest when Britain entered the lists against Germany in 1939. Penndragon had missed the First World War, but he wasn't about to miss this one. He

1

returned to his country, took a commission in the Royal Air Force, and threw himself with enthusiasm and valor into the Battle of Britain. His was a charmed life. He was shot down over Germany, interned in a POW camp, promptly engineered a brilliant escape, made his way back to England, and became a legend in his own time.

Because of his rather girlish beauty, his meticulous grooming, and a penchant for outlandish vests, Penndragon was often suspected of being effeminate, perhaps homosexual. Actually he was robustly and lustily male. He was introduced to sex at the tender age of eleven by his mother's parlor maid. She was barely five years his senior, short and plump, apple-cheeked and dark of hair, and delightfully experienced. For the remainder of his life, Penndragon showed a decided preference for deliciously plump, dark-haired girls of the working class.

The years rolled by, wonderful years, thoroughly enjoyed by the dilettante. In his early sixties, he became interested in writing and turned out a number of adventure novels—lightly fictionalized with each hero bearing a striking resemblance to the author—that were fairly well received but certainly not best-sellers. Worldwide fame arrived when he decided to spurn fiction and write a factual book with the unwieldly title of *How to Enjoy the Art of Dilettantism*. Recounting his own life proved to be juicy, exciting, violent, and, at times, outrageously funny. Penndragon was plunged into a new role, that of successful author, and took to it with his usual aplomb. He lectured to learned societies, gave informal talks, signed autographs, appeared on panel shows, and proved as gifted with the spoken word as the written one. He promptly wrote a second best-seller, this one called *The Diligent Dilettante*.

By the time Winslow Penndragon reached a hale and hearty seventy-one, his life was as rich and enjoyable as it had ever been. His health was excellent; he delighted in fine food; and his physical beauty survived the years; and in every way he was a happy, fulfilled man.

Then, without warning, the first ominous cloud appeared in the sunny heavens of Penndragon's private world. Astounded and completely nonplussed, he still had recourse to his favorite maxim—"Only the best will serve." With this in mind, he sought counsel from his godson, Chief Inspector Adam Kepesake of New Scotland Yard.

Chapter One

Whether Chief Inspector Kepesake was the best is debatable. He was one of the better-looking inspectors, certainly the best-dressed, and he was fortunate in having the most able detective sergeant at the Yard. Sergeant Brummell, christened Charles but known to all as Beau, was hard working, intuitive, and, for reasons many found mystifying, devoted to his superior officer. In appearance he was Kepesake's direct opposite. Brummell had the ability to make a new suit of clothes look like something picked up at a rummage sale; a freshly shaved face look as though it had rarely seen a razor; and a thick head of hair defy any comb ever manufactured. He also had tenacity, and that was evident as he slid a sheaf of forms into the in-basket on Kepesake's handsome desk.

"The superintendent says he has to have these today, Chief."

"Put him off. Tell him I'm up to my ears."

"I tried but he said—"

"I can guess what he said." Scowling, Kepesake inserted a fresh cigarette in his jade holder. "Chap's a ruddy slave driver. Well, let's get at it." He glanced up. "What is it, Helm?"

"A visitor, sir," the young constable told him.

"Make an appointment or have someone else handle it."

"Says it has to be you, sir. Sent his card in."

The chief inspector looked at the card and beamed. "Why didn't you say so? Bring him right in."

To Brummell's surprise, Kepesake, who rarely stirred from his office chair, sprang up and rushed to meet his visitor. Wonder whether he's a relative, Brummell thought, watching the men embrace. Sure dresses like the chief. Not that vest though! Even the chief wouldn't go that far.

Waiting until Kepesake had the other man ensconced in the most comfortable chair his office offered, Brummell asked, "Want I should leave?"

"No. Beau, I'd like you to meet Uncle Winslow. My sergeant, Uncle. Beau, you've heard of Winslow Penndragon."

"That I have. Recognized you right away, sir. Saw you the other night on television—that panel show. Liked how you managed to corner the psychologist."

Penndragon gave him the smile that was rapidly becoming famous. "It didn't take much effort. The man is a buffoon."

The sergeant swung on his superior. "You never told me that Mr. Penndragon is your uncle."

"Only a courtesy term, Beau."

"Adam is my godson," Penndragon explained. His glance flickered over Brummell's wrinkled suit, and he turned to Kepesake. "It's been…how long has it been since I've seen you?"

"Too long." Waving his holder, Kepesake peered through a cloud of smoke. "Nettie Kimshaw's garden party, last August. How's the family?"

"Bunny's fine. The amazing Grace is still as exasperating as ever. And your mother and father? In good health, I trust."

While Penndragon and Kepesake exchanged news, Brummell watched the older man with something approaching awe. To think he'd just shaken the hand of Winslow Penndragon. Wait until he told the wife about this. Penndragon was as handsome in the flesh as on telly or in photos, with a mane of silver hair worn a bit long but suiting that face. Tall, slender, and well built, he had hardly a wrinkle and skin like a baby. Clothes—a beautifully tailored suit that had cost a mint, gray silk tie the same shade as the suit, and a brocaded vest with swirls of lavender and rose and pale green against a silver-blue background. Have to have a lot of confidence to wear a vest like that. Fascinated, the sergeant watched as Penndragon extracted a cigar case and helped himself to a cheroot. Before the case was open, Kepesake was around the desk, flicking his lighter.

The two men had now worked through relatives and were catching up on tidbits about friends and acquaintances. Rather disconsolately, Brummell eyed the in-basket. Looked as though the superintendent was going to be raising hell about that stuff. Penndragon, who hadn't appeared to notice anything but his godson and his cheroot, followed Brummell's eyes. "Looks as though I caught you at a bad time, Adam."

Kepesake waved a dismissive hand. "It will wait. Must get one's priorities right. We'll have lunch at the club—"

"Sorry, this isn't a social visit."

"Do you mean you require our professional services?"

"Not the Yard's. Simply some advice."

Brummell started to rise. "Perhaps I'd better…"

"No." Penndragon waved him back. "You might be able to help."

"Tell us what we can do," Kepesake said earnestly.

For the first time since he'd entered the office, Penndragon seemed a trifle uncertain. "I have a spot of bother that needs looking into. A personal matter that demands discretion. I was wondering whether you could recommend a…I suppose a private inquiry agent is what I'm looking for."

"Oh." It was Kepesake's turn to look uncertain. "I imagine I can suggest several." He raised a brow at his sergeant. "What about Reynolds and that agency he started?"

"Depends on what Mr. Penndragon has in mind, Chief. Reynolds is reliable, but he's a bit of a rough diamond."

Grinding out his cheroot, Penndragon frowned. "A rough diamond is scarcely what I need. Specifically, the person I employ must be a gentleman or at least be able to act the part. This person will be required to enter my house and pose as a friend or acquaintance. He must be intelligent, capable, personable, and above all, discreet."

Kepesake smiled. "A tall order, Uncle Winslow. Most investigators are hardly the paragon that you're describing."

"I'm aware of that." Resting his snowy head against the chair back, Penndragon closed his eyes. Brummell had been unable to believe that this man was over seventy, but suddenly he looked his age. His delicate features were weary and incredibly fragile. He murmured, "Adam, I'm desperate. This is serious and could be…I think there is an urgency."

Kepesake lost his smile. He gazed at his godfather and then at his sergeant. "Any ideas, Beau?"

"One. But it's a long shot, Chief. We do know someone who fills the bill but—"

"For heaven's sake, Beau, spit it out!"

"The Farquson case. That business in Maddersley-on-Mead."

"Forsythe!" Penndragon's eyes snapped open and he sat up. "Robert Forsythe. Perfect!"

Kepesake raised his brows. "You know Forsythe?"

"We met once, but mainly I know him through newspaper accounts of his exploits. Amazing man."

"The reporters think so." Kepesake sighed. "As you know, he's a barrister and quite reluctant to being pulled into anything resembling detection. I doubt very much—"

"You've worked with him, Adam. Surely if you put a word in, he would consent to help me."

Brummell was shaking his shaggy head. "The chief's right, sir. Mr. Forsythe only helped us out because he had no choice. I don't think he'd budge on our say-so."

"But you can speak with him. At least ask him to see me. Once I talk to him I'm certain he can be persuaded."

"Of course I will," Kepesake assured. "I'll do all I can. I'll ring up immediately. When would you like to see him?"

"As soon as I can, if possible this afternoon." Penndragon reached for his cigar case. "This woman whose name is always linked with Forsythe. Just who is she?"

"Abigail Sanderson?" Kepesake busied himself lighting his godfather's cheroot. "Forsythe's secretary."

"I'm aware of that. But what is their relationship? Their names are always coupled."

Throwing back his head, Kepesake laughed. "If you're wondering whether it's romantic, I must disappoint you, Uncle. Miss Sanderson's not only old enough to be Forsythe's mother but she's acted like one ever since the death of his own mother. She was his father's secretary too and practically raised the boy."

"How old is she?"

"That's a secret." Brummell was laughing too. "Miss Sanderson is touchy about her age. Better keep that in mind. At a guess I'd say well into her fifties."

"And her employer?"

"Mid-thirties. Thought you'd met him."

"A number of years ago and at the time I barely noticed him." Penndragon stretched his slender frame. "Well, that's settled."

"Hardly," his godson told him. "You still have to persuade Forsythe."

"Adam, I have exceptional powers of persuasion." Penndragon flashed the famous smile. "Also, I have a habit of getting what I want. Devoted a lifetime to just that."

Brummell's first thought was that Penndragon was going to need all the persuasion at his command to sway Robert Forsythe. His second was that something was giving the man hell to make him so shaken and worried.

Chapter Two

Resisting the impulse to slam the door behind her, Miss Sanderson closed it softly and regarded the barrister with a blend of affection, anxiety, and exasperation. The affection was habitual. The anxiety and exasperation were emotions that had steadily been building since Forsythe's return from a disastrous fortnight in Switzerland. He slouched in the leather chair inherited from his father, one leg propped up on a hassock, his expression morose as he regarded the walking cast on that leg.

"What do you want?" he demanded.

"To straighten this room up. Mrs. Sutter said you wouldn't let the cleaner in here this morning."

"Couldn't stand the woman fussing about. And that goes for you, too."

She calmly continued wielding the feather duster. "Sorry to interrupt your work, but this place looks like a pigsty." Circling behind his chair, she attacked the bookshelves.

"*What* work?"

"Good question. A bit slow, isn't it? Young Peters is winding up the Herald case and Vincent has the Montrose one well in hand. How are you feeling?"

"Nice of you to ask. I didn't think anyone gave a damn."

She paused and looked at the back of his long head. "Feeling sorry for ourselves, are we? Wallowing in self-pity?"

"Might as well. Obviously you haven't a shred of sympathy."

"I did warn you."

"I knew it! Now we get to the 'I told you so' lecture."

Taking a last flick at the books, she moved the duster along the wainscoting. When she didn't answer, he snapped, "Get on with it."

"I wouldn't stoop so low. Little late for it anyway. Anyone asinine enough to try to ski with a wonky knee like yours asks for a broken ankle."

"What was I supposed to do? Sit by the fire like an old man while everyone else was out on the slopes?" She shrugged and he bellowed, "Will you get out of here and leave me in peace!"

"As soon as I'm finished." Putting down the duster, she began emptying ashtrays. "Be a good boy and I'll bring you a mug of nice hot broth."

"I don't want broth. I want whiskey."

"Not with those painkillers you're gulping. Give them up or give up whiskey."

"Sandy, you're a hard woman."

She swung on him. "Look, I tried to persuade you to go down to the house in Sussex and relax until that ankle heals."

"And who would look after this practice?"

"The ones who are doing it now. Peters and Vincent and Mrs. Sutter."

"But—"

"No buts. You're like a bear with a sore paw—completely unreasonable. If I pay attention to you, I'm fussing. If I don't, I'm a heartless fiend." She took a deep breath. "All you're doing by staying on in chambers is making us as miserable as *you* are."

He raised a hand. "You've made your point, Sandy, and you're right. I was a fool to try to ski and I've been driving the staff mad. I suppose I should go down to Sussex, but Mrs.

Meeks would drive *me* mad with her infernal coddling." He shifted his leg and winced. "I'm bored. Too much time on my hands and nothing on my mind."

She sank into one of the visitor's chairs. "I know it's irksome, and that knee must be hellishly painful too. Robby, you need a hobby."

"I have hobbies."

"Ah, but none you can manage at present." She ran a hand over her beautifully styled gray hair. "Why don't you go to Spanish classes with me?"

"I've no desire to speak Spanish. Besides, you've been toddling off to them for weeks and what have you learned?"

She cut loose with a torrent of Spanish and he grinned. "Sounds impressive, but what does it mean?"

"I asked, 'How much is it?' and then I said, 'That's too much.' I proceeded to tell you to do unspeakable things to either your mother or sister. My instructor tells me that such an expression would get one decapitated in a Spanish-speaking country. Then—"

"Sandy! What kind of teacher *is* this man?"

"Young and handsome and madly sexy, also amusing. You really should join Lino's class."

"I've no avid desire to be decapitated in Spain. Doesn't Lino teach you anything practical?"

"Certainly." She waved both arms and spat out more Spanish.

"The translation?"

"I just announced to all and sundry my desperate need for a bathroom. That practical enough?"

He nodded but was gazing past her shoulder with an abstracted expression. "I've been wondering whether what Sir Hilary said about me a number of years ago is the truth."

"And what is that?"

"We were involved with the Calvert case and Sir Hilary told Melissa Calvert that I've a devious mind, more suited to detection than to law. I wonder whether he meant it."

"Only way to find out now would be to hold a séance. Sir Hilary, bless his rowdy soul, has been dead for years. What made you think of that? Tired of being a barrister?"

"Most of the time I wouldn't exchange law for anything else. But sometimes...right now..." He shifted his leg again. "Sandy, do you think crime detection could become addictive?"

She shook her head violently. "Not for me. Not after that grisly business in Maddersley-on-Mead." She eyed him with shrewd eyes. "Feel like you need a fix? Some nice juicy case with bodies bleeding all over the place?"

He avoided her eyes and she immediately started tapping her thumbnail against her front teeth. "Will you *stop* that?" he roared.

"Helps me think."

"That's the most infuriating habit. What are you thinking?"

"About coincidences. Mrs. Sutter mentioned Adam Kepesake rang you up shortly before I came in and now you're raving on about detection being addictive. Methinks I smell a rat."

He stared at her. Such an austere face, he thought, such a deceptively austere face. Such a greyhound figure. Such an ability to look past his defenses with those cool blue eyes and expose any thoughts he had. He threw up his hands. "What's the use? No wonder I've never married."

"A number of times you've come close. What was the trouble? Afraid you'd never find a woman like me?"

"Afraid I would."

The cool eyes steadily regarded him. "Don't try to throw me off the scent. What did the rat want this time? Trying to drag you into solving another case for him?"

"This has nothing to do with the Yard. Kepesake merely wants me to speak to his godfather—"

"Who no doubt has any number of bodies bleeding all over *his* floor. Just who is Kepesake's godfather?"

"You'd never guess," Forsythe told her smugly.

"I'm not trying to."

"None other than the famous Winslow Maxwell Penndragon."

She jerked forward, a slow flush working up her thin face. "Blimey!"

"Thought that would shake you. Know anything about him?"

"After those books of his, I shouldn't think there are many who don't. Dilettante, wealthy, brilliant war record…" She grinned. "Sounds as though Penndragon practically held off the Luftwaffe singlehandedly. Been everywhere and done everything. I've a copy of his latest book in my desk—fabulously interesting. Must ask him to autograph it."

Forsythe smiled at her excitement. "I take it you aren't adverse to meeting this gentleman."

"I'm practically panting. But what does he want to speak with you about? Can't be legal expertise. Penndragon must have a battery of his own lads to keep up with the libel suits he has every time one of his candid books hits the market."

"I haven't a clue and neither did Adam Kepesake. But Kepesake did stress the necessity for discretion. I gather he dotes on his illustrious godfather."

"And so would I," Miss Sanderson said fervently. "What time may we expect him?"

Forsythe glanced at the ormolu clock on the mantelpiece. "If he's punctual, any moment now."

"Good Lord!" Her hands flew to her hair. "You could have told me sooner. I must look a fright."

"You look fine, Sandy. Calm down. I've seldom seen you acting so feminine."

"At least I managed to get this room tidied. Poor Mrs. Sutter, she'll have a fit."

"Mrs. Sutter wouldn't quiver an eyebrow if she ushered in the Prince of Wales. Ah, Mrs. Sutter…"

For the first time since she'd joined the staff, Mrs. Sutter opened the barrister's door without knocking. Her normally stolid face was glowing. In a hushed voice she said, "Mr. Penndragon."

Forsythe started to push himself up and Penndragon told him genially, "No, stay where you are. Accident?"

"Skiing." He glanced past his visitor. Mrs. Sutter was posted in the doorway, staring at Penndragon as though transfixed. "Thank you," Forsythe said and she backed out of the room, leaving the door ajar. She had to return to close it.

Penndragon shook his head. "Seems a nervous lady."

"Hardly. Your effect. Sandy, please bring up a chair. Mr. Penndragon, my secretary, Miss Sanderson."

The dilettante gave a courtly bow, gently pushed Miss Sanderson aside, and slid the chair up himself. Miss Sanderson, as transfixed as Mrs. Sutter had been, fumbled for her own chair. Penndragon gallantly seated her before sinking into his. "We've met before," he told the younger man. "You may not remember..."

"At a dinner party given by...I forget the name, but it was around Christmas—about four years ago. I remember you well. You were recounting a trip to Tibet."

"You've a remarkable memory." Penndragon regarded the leg encased in the cast. "I had thought to ask your advice and help with a personal matter, but Adam didn't tell me you're immobilized."

"I doubt he's heard about my accident. I haven't seen him for months. As for being immobilized—" Forsythe waved an airy hand. "No difficulty in moving around. Simply a small bone broken."

His secretary wrenched her eyes from their visitor and glowered at Forsythe. After days of rushing around cosseting him—blimey, what a phony!

"Well, that *is* a relief. I'm counting on you and when I saw you I thought, well that's out." Penndragon smiled at the barrister and let the tail end of that smile drift over his secretary. Miss Sanderson promptly beamed back. "I hardly know where to begin. I suppose I must be blunt, but this is going to sound dreadfully dramatic. In the last week my life has been...Mr. Forsythe, two attempts have been made to kill me."

Miss Sanderson made a muffled sound and Forsythe raised his brows. "In London?"

"At my family home in Warwickshire. When I'm not traveling, I spend most of my time there. I maintain a pied-à-terre in the city, but I rarely use it. And that is the reason why this investigation must be discreet. I'm forced to face the fact that a member of my family or one of my servants is responsible." Penndragon shook a baffled head. "I simply can't believe that."

"You'd better give us the details," the barrister told him.

"The first attempt involved my car. It's a vintage Bentley, a car I'm extremely fond of. Five days ago I was going to drive to Coventry on a business matter. I'm a wretched driver and generally my nephew handles that chore, but that day he had a backlog of work—Bunny acts as my secretary—and I decided to drive myself."

"Were the members of your household aware of this?"

"Yes. I had mentioned it the previous evening at dinner." Penndragon glanced down at his hands. They were long, slender, graceful, and at that moment were twisting together in his lap. He reached for his cigar case, courteously raised an inquiring brow at Miss Sanderson, and when she nodded, lit a cheroot. "The Bentley had been in for servicing and my man Evans went into the garage early that morning to pick it up. While I was breakfasting, he brought it back and parked it in front of the main door. Evans assures me that the car was operating perfectly at the time. As soon as I had finished my breakfast, I paused in the hall for my overcoat and briefcase and then went directly to the Bentley."

With his eyes fixed on the glowing end of his cheroot, Penndragon said softly, "I find this most painful. Would you be kind enough…may I have a drink?"

Miss Sanderson poured a generous whiskey and soda for their guest, another for herself, and, ignoring Forsythe's imploring gesture, handed him a glass of soda. Penndragon took a long swig and continued, "The driveway is rather twisting, but nearer the road it straightens out into a steep slope. I've been told by my nephew that I have a habit of 'riding the brakes.' As I neared the gates, I braked sharply and discovered they didn't respond. Luckily

I didn't panic. I steered the car, at quite a speed, between the gate-posts and across the road, crashing into the embankment."

"Were you hurt?" Miss Sanderson asked in a hushed voice.

This time the smile was all for her. Penndragon stretched his long body and touched an arm and one hip. "Shaken and badly bruised but—" The smile vanished and his lips set. "The Bentley was badly damaged. The horrifying part is that if I hadn't braked at that time, I probably would have been killed. From my property the land falls in a steep and treacherous hill into the village, and there's no way I could have avoided a bad accident. In fact, if there had been another vehicle traveling along the road at that moment...well, I wouldn't be here telling you all this."

"You had the brakes checked," Forsythe said, and it wasn't a question.

"Of course. A capable mechanic has serviced my cars for years. He told me that after the Bentley left his garage that morning the brake connection must have been loosened. He found a spot where the car had been parked on the driveway that was drenched with brake fluid. I have sworn him to secrecy." Penndragon held up his hand. "I know what your next question is. It would have been fast and simple to do this. And the only time it could have been done was while I was breakfasting."

"Evans had an excellent chance to do it," Miss Sanderson said.

"Impossible! Evans and his sister have been in my employ for over twenty years." Penndragon gave a shaky laugh and held out his glass. Miss Sanderson refilled it, then her own, and took the one Forsythe was hopefully extending and splashed soda in it. Giving it a disgusted look, he pushed it away. Penndragon shook his head ruefully. "You're probably wondering whether I drink this much habitually. I don't. I suppose it's the strain. I have to consider that a member of my household wants me dead. Quite frankly, I can't believe it."

"Sadly enough the majority of murders are committed by a member of the family," the barrister told him. "Now, the second attempt."

"It happened two days after I smashed up the Bentley. I was still stiff and sore, but it was the one day a week that I work on the gardens. For early spring it was a fine day and I wanted to get some pruning done. I put on my gardening clothes and stopped at the tennis court on my way to the shed where I keep the rest of my gear—gloves, gardening hat, and so forth. A spirited game of singles was in progress and I sat down on a bench to watch. Evans and my sister-in-law had come out of the house to watch and we cheered the players on.

"When the set was finished I went to the shed, put my hand on the knob, and was about to open the door when a guest, Susan Vandervoort, called to me. As I stepped back, I must have shoved the door. Something came plummeting down and there was a loud thud. Susan ran up and…" Penndragon paused and took a sip of his drink. "A piece of statuary that once had been part of a fountain had been stored on the floor at the rear of the shed. It had been chipped and I planned to have it restored but hadn't gotten around to it. A charming little piece of a small girl holding a seashell. Someone had balanced the statue on a narrow ledge above the door so that when the door was opened it would fall on whomever was underneath. I hardly need to tell you what the result would have been."

Miss Sanderson frowned. "Surely the person who put it up there would have been trapped in the shed."

"The shed has a sizable window at the rear. That window was open."

Templing his fingers, Forsythe regarded them. "So…nip in and lift the statue into place. Clamber through the window and away. Again fast and simple." He glanced up. "Why did your guest call to you?"

"Susan had just discovered a clump of daffodils that was in full bloom in a sheltered spot and wanted me to have a look. Unusual in March. Susan and the daffodils saved my life. Odd. Friends have always insisted that I have a cat's nine lives and I think I've believed it. I went through the war unscathed and I've been in positions where I *should* have died, and yet I lived through them. Certainly I've had mishaps—a fall and a broken leg in the Austrian Alps." He waved a negligent hand at Forsythe's cast. "A dislocated shoulder in Tunis and…all minor mishaps. I fear I've always taken life for granted. Fortunately I've a strong constitution and my physician tells me I'm in marvelous shape. I *enjoy* life and am looking forward to about another thirty—"

"*Thirty*," Miss Sanderson blurted.

Again she was bathed in his wonderful smile. She was practically purring as he told her, "Yes, thirty. I come from a long-lived line. When my grandfather died he was over a hundred and my father was eighty and in excellent health when he was killed in an accident. If that hadn't happened I imagine father would have exceeded the hundred mark. Yes, Miss Sanderson, at seventy-one I'm looking forward to many more years. And no one is taking them away from *me*."

"In that case we'd better narrow down the lists of suspects." Forsythe pushed his glass toward his secretary. "Sandy, I took my last medication almost four hours ago. Fill that up and I don't mean with soda."

This time Miss Sanderson knew better than to argue.

Chapter Three

Winslow Penndragon waited until Forsythe had his drink and then he said slowly, "From here on it might be best if you questioned."

"My first question concerns the time element. You've pinpointed the time available to loosen the brake connection in the first attempt. Have you any idea about the second?"

"I can give you the precise amount of time. My gardener Jarvis was able to confirm that. It appears he entered the shed to get some tools shortly before I tried. At that point, the statue was in its usual place."

"And this was?"

"About half an hour before. From the shed you can see the tennis court, and Jarvis noticed me coming out the rear door of the house and pausing by the court. Then, of course, I became interested and sat down on the bench with my sister-in-law and Evans. As soon as the set was over, I went directly to the shed. So the statue had to have been lifted into place while I was sitting there."

"And again, the members of the household were aware you were gardening that morning?"

"Yes."

"Hmm." Forsythe stroked his chin. "This should make it simpler. All we seem to have to do is eliminate the people who were with you during breakfast and the ones at the tennis court."

Penndragon shook his head. "That's where this whole affair becomes bizarre. In the breakfast room with me were two young guests—"

"I think," the barrister interrupted, "we'd better have the number of people in the house and their names."

"My staff consists of six including the gardener. There are two maids, but they're very young and have only been with us for a few months. Their names are Dolly and Geneva Morris and they're nieces of Evans and his sister Linda. The cook…Mrs. Krugger is out of the question."

"You mentioned Evans and his sister have been with you over twenty years."

"Close to twenty-one now. When they came to me, Evans was in his late twenties and Linda is much younger than he."

"How much?"

"At that time she was only sixteen. A lovely girl. Unfortunately her plumpness has disappeared under rolls of fat. Too bad. Little Dolly looks much the same now as her aunt did at the same age. Geneva is quite plain."

Flipping open her notebook, Miss Sanderson wrote down Evans and Linda Evans. On the other side of the page she put down Dolly and Geneva Morris, Mrs. Krugger, and Jarvis. "Then there is Grace Penndragon," Penndragon said, "the widow of my only brother. Gerald was much younger than I, but Grace is about my age. Gerald piloted a fighter plane too and was killed in 1945. His son was born after his death—about four months if I remember correctly—and I took the boy and his mother in. Gerald's son was named after me; it was his father's wish and Grace honored it, but he's always been called Bunny. Silly name, but somehow it suits him. I raised Bunny as my son and saw to his education. After he came down from Oxford, he decided to remain with me as companion and secretary. It was his decision. I certainly didn't pressure, but I was delighted to have him with me. Bunny's extremely competent, wonderful at details about visas and traveling arrangements and so on."

Miss Sanderson added Grace and Winslow Maxwell II to her list. After the man's name she jotted down Bunny. She waited for the other names and when Penndragon didn't speak, she glanced up. Again his hands were twisting together in his lap. She lifted a brow at the barrister and he prompted. "Your guests?"

"Susan Vandervoort, Jason Cooper, and Leslie Hobbs."

"Are these people related to you?"

Penndragon crossed his long legs at the ankles, uncrossed them, smoothed down his flamboyant vest, and finally said, "Yes, but it's a bit complicated. May we leave this for later?"

"You said they were young," Forsythe persisted. "How young?"

"Young to me. Susan's thirty-one and Leslie and Jason a few months short of that age."

After she wrote the three names down, Miss Sanderson put a large question mark beside them. They waited and when Penndragon remained silent Forsythe said, "We'll return to the morning of the accident with the Bentley. You said two of your guests breakfasted with you."

"Susan and Leslie. Bunny finished his meal and left the room a few moments after I sat down. He had to put the necessary papers in my briefcase for my appointment in Coventry. Linda had cooked that morning as our cook was indisposed again—" Breaking off, he chuckled. "If Mrs. Krugger hadn't been enjoying ill health, I would have breakfasted in my own quarters. Mrs. Krugger is not only a confirmed hypochondriac but is the world's worst cook. Boils *everything*. Linda as well as being a fine housekeeper is also an adequate cook. She takes her meals with the family, so she'd arranged the food on hot plates and took her breakfast with us. Evans was bringing the Bentley and Jason had gone out for an early walk. Grace was still in bed. She rarely stirs before ten."

Miss Sanderson looked up from her notebook. "So Susan Vandervoort, Leslie Hobbs, and Linda Evans couldn't have touched the car. Which leaves Jason Cooper, your sister-in-law, nephew, and Evans."

"Precisely."

The barrister eased his injured leg off the hassock, winced, and reached for his glass. As he drained it, he glanced at his secretary, appeared to reconsider a demand for more whiskey, and told the older man, "You said Evans and Mrs. Penndragon were with you at the tennis court. Who were the players?"

"My nephew and Jason Cooper. Now, do you understand how bizarre this is?"

Miss Sanderson glanced down at her notes. "The ones who could have fixed the brakes couldn't have touched the statue."

Springing up, Penndragon strode around the room. "I refuse to believe *two* people are trying to kill me! And what about motive? No member of my household has reason to want me dead. It has to be a maniac."

"Maybe two maniacs," Miss Sanderson muttered.

Forsythe followed the older man's movements. "It does seem farfetched, but the brakes were interfered with and that little statue didn't climb up over the door by itself. Let's begin with the most common motive—money. Who would gain financially by your death?"

"Bunny is my heir. There's a small income for life for Grace, several bequests to charitable institutions, a scholarship in my brother's name, and legacies for the servants. That's the way my will stands at present."

"Present?" Forsythe arched his brows. "You're considering changing the terms of your will?"

"Yes."

"Is your nephew aware of this?"

"He is. And of the reason for the change. But Bunny was right in sight while the statue was moved. Anyway, you'd have to know my nephew. He's not only incapable of violence but totally devoted to me."

"And Bunny couldn't have been working with his mother," Miss Sanderson pointed out. "Grace Penndragon was a spectator at the tennis game. Either of them could have drained the brake fluid, but neither could have made the second attempt." She frowned and added, "Linda Evans could have made the second attempt, but not the first. Her brother...vice versa. None of the guests could have done both."

"And none of these young people are mentioned in the current will." Forsythe said crisply, "I think you must tell us about your guests. You say they're all related to you?"

"Closely, the closest possible relationships." Penndragon stopped pacing and leaned against the back of his chair. "This is one reason why discretion is essential. Susan is my daughter; Leslie and Jason are my sons."

Miss Sanderson's mouth fell open. "But...I've read your books. You never married."

"Several times I considered it, but—" He flashed his warm smile. "Many people would accuse me of selfish motives in remaining a bachelor. And they're right. There's been no place in my life for a wife or children. But there was another reason, not quite as selfish. Until recently I've spent little time in England. I couldn't sentence a woman to a husband who rarely would have been with her or the children."

"What about your nephew and your brother's widow?" Miss Sanderson asked.

"Even when Bunny was in school, he spent his holidays wherever I happened to be at the time. As I mentioned, he's been my companion ever since he finished his education. As for the amazing Grace—"

"Why do you call her amazing?" Miss Sanderson asked.

"When you meet her, you'll see why. During the war Grace had a most responsible job. She worked in the decoding department, quite hush-hush, and I understand she was one of their best cryptographers. Even now she's called to London when they have a knotty problem. Yet this woman, who's a wizard at codes, hardly knows what day it is. Spends most of her time working at word puzzles. As for neglecting Grace...well, frankly, we've never gotten along. I opposed her marriage to Gerald. Not only was she much older than my brother but completely unattractive—a scraggly looking woman without even the compensation of a nice personality."

"Yet she and her son did come to live with you," Forsythe remarked.

"Grace made clear that was only for Bunny's sake. My father left the bulk of his estate to me—Gerald was virtually penniless. I saw to my brother's needs during his lifetime and, of course, have looked after his family for forty years."

"Let's get back to your daughter and sons," Forsythe told him.

With a deep sigh, Penndragon sat down again. "I know this is necessary, but I'm finding it incredibly embarrassing. Very well. My three children are...my grandfather would have said they were born on the wrong side of the blanket. They're illegitimate. I can read your faces. You're thinking not only are they all roughly the same age but I must have been forty when they were conceived. I'll explain, but do keep in mind that I'm making no attempt to defend myself."

A slender hand stroked silvery hair away from his brow. "I'm a man of strong appetites. My sexual appetite operates with a specific type of woman. Another reason I've never married is that I'm drawn only to females I could never consider making my wife. These infatuations have always been brief. The only women I desire are very young ones, under twenty, and of similar physical characteristics—short plump girls with round faces and dark hair. And of the working class—shopgirls, wait-resses, domestic workers. There, I've bared my breast to you."

"In complete confidence," Forsythe assured.

This mention of confidence seemed to give Penndragon some.

"Over thirty years ago, to my complete shock, I found I had gotten three girls pregnant at the same time. Sally, Joyce, and Susan. Sally was a waitress in a café in Leeds; Joyce worked in a bookshop in a tiny village called Mousehole on the Channel; Susan in a women's clothing shop in London. I was candid with all three. From the beginning they knew I would never marry them, but as a man of honor that I certainly wouldn't desert them if they became pregnant. When I learned the situation, I immediately consulted with my solicitor—"

"Did these girls know about the others?" Forsythe interrupted.

"Of course not! They'd not the slightest suspicion they weren't the sole object of my interest. As I was saying, I consulted my solicitor and followed his advice. I settled an amount of money on each, had them sign statements agreeing they had no further claim on me, and told them they could take any course they wished. It was their decision whether they terminated their pregnancies or not. All three decided to have their babies."

Miss Sanderson was regarding him as though he'd just arrived from another planet. Forsythe looked at her uneasily. His secretary had a notoriously sharp tongue. But she simply asked, "Were there difficulties in persuading them to sign the statements?"

"Not really. Although they looked very much alike, they possessed very different natures. Sally—she was Leslie's mother—was a survivor, a pretty little piece but hard as nails. All she objected to was the amount of the cash settlement. Claimed it should have been more and had the temerity to threaten me with a paternity suit. I told her to sue and be damned, and quite sensibly she raised no further objections.

"Jason's mother—Joyce—was somewhat different, just as calculating but much more clever than Sally in concealing it. To my surprise, Joyce flared up and told me her only interest in me had been my money. I'd always thought she loved me. Not only was she insulting but she enjoyed every minute of it. Told me she hated men and would be most happy to raise her child by herself. She signed the statement, took the money, and booted me out."

Even after thirty years the memory still rankled. Penndragon was flushed and indignant. Hiding a grin, Forsythe said, "And the third girl, that would be Susan Vandervoort's mother."

"At the time she was Susan Miller. Susan was the youngest of the girls, barely sixteen and gentle, modest, and affectionate. Susan had shown no interest in expensive gifts; all she wanted was me. My interview with her was a painful ordeal for both of us. She made no mention of marriage, but she begged me to let her have some small corner in my life. Finally I convinced her it was over. She wept and clung to me and refused to take money. For the sake of her unborn child, I convinced her she must accept the settlement. She meekly signed the statement and we said goodbye. Of the three girls, only Susan loved me. After this was accomplished, I put them from my mind."

"But not their children," Miss Sanderson said hopefully.

"I could lie and give you the answer you'd like to hear, but the truth is that I forgot the children completely—until last October. As one grows older, there is a tendency to look backward in time. I'd never done this before, but on my birthday—I was on a lecture tour in New York—I suddenly realized I was seventy-one and my only relatives were a nephew and a sister-in-law whom I detest. I began to hunger for someone closer and regretted that I'd never married.

"My life has been devoted to my own gratification and I've always gotten exactly what I wanted. While I was feeling sorry for myself, I realized that I *could* have what I wanted. Somewhere I did have a family; somewhere I had three children."

"A case of having your cake and eating it too," Miss Sanderson muttered.

He lifted an ironic brow. "Exactly. Once I make a decision, I move rapidly. Before I returned to England, I had engaged a private agency to quietly undertake the task of finding my children and compiling histories of their lives. When I returned to England in mid-December, the information was on my desk. Before Christmas I had looked up all three and spoken with them."

His secretary seemed speechless and Forsythe asked, "Were you planning on adopting them?"

"No. My plan was this. I would meet them, persuade them to visit in my home for a month, and select one of them. I knew there might be some resentment toward me, but I hoped one might prove compatible and with that one I would share my life." Penndragon gave the barrister a shrewd look. "As the reports showed that my daughter and both my sons were in financial trouble, I sweetened the pot by offering each of them five thousand pounds for that month. I also hinted to all three that if we hit it off, he or she might be my heir."

"Blimey," Miss Sanderson breathed. "Did you tell them three people were competing?"

"Definitely not."

Forsythe tapped a finger against the edge of his desk. "You met them before Christmas. Did they immediately come to your home?"

"They arrived the first and second day of this month. I'd hoped to have them gathered in January, but…I think it best to explain just what happened when I met each of them."

Glancing at the clock, Forsythe said, "Time for tea. Sandy, would you do the honors?"

As the door closed behind her, Penndragon gave Forsythe a conspiratorial wink. "I hope I haven't shocked your secretary."

"Never fear. Sandy's appearance is deceptive. She's virtually shockproof."

"And the world condones this type of behavior now. Women boast about having children out of wedlock and no one seems to worry about marriage vows. Thirty years ago, society was much more narrow-minded and stern."

The men chatted about the changes in moral values until Miss Sanderson bustled in with a tray. With some amusement, Forsythe noted she'd outdone herself. She'd brought out the fine china and had managed to obtain dainty sandwiches and a profusion of small cakes. Penndragon's earlier reticence appeared to have vanished and between sips and bites he spoke freely.

"Leslie Hobbs was the first one I approached. He looks much like his mother, Sally—short, plump, and dark-haired. Sally turned out to be a shrewd businesswoman, but Leslie didn't inherit the trait. This was what had put him in trouble financially.

"Before his birth, Sally had used her settlement to buy the café where she worked and promptly married the cook, a man named Hobbs. The café proved to be a success, but her hasty marriage was a disaster. Hobbs was a heavy drinker and somewhat of a brute. He resented the baby and took every opportunity to punish him. Sally put up with it for six years, but then Hobbs beat the child badly, breaking Leslie's leg in two places, and when Sally tried to intervene, the man turned on her. She kicked Hobbs out and he died several years later.

"In time she set up other cafés in Leeds until she had a chain of five. From the time Leslie was old enough to act as a busboy, he was taught the business while his mother ran it. About two years ago, Sally was killed by a lorry while crossing a street and Leslie took control. Instead of carrying on with the cafés, he sold them out and came to London to open a rather pretentious restaurant. He decorated lavishly and hired a staff, including a Spanish maître d' and hostess, and a noted French chef. He overextended badly and also fell in love with his hostess Lola, who proved to be an expensive young lady. By the time I looked him up, he was terribly in debt. Not only is he in danger of losing the business but also Lola."

Miss Sanderson refilled the cups and nudged the cake plate closer to their guest. "What was your reception from Leslie Hobbs?"

"The second coming of Christ," he said dryly. "Sally had never made any secret about the boy's natural father. I got the impression both mother and son were proud of it, and I think both hoped I would re-enter their lives. To prove I was his parent, I took along the statement signed by his mother, but it wasn't necessary. Leslie was only too eager to go home with me at once, but I put him off. I did advance some funds to cover his more pressing debts. Then I sought out my daughter."

He selected a cake, put it on his plate, and looked dreamily past the barrister's shoulder. "Susan Miller had married too. She'd used her settlement to purchase a tiny dress shop, but she wasn't a good businesswoman. The shop didn't prosper and by the time her daughter was a toddler, Susan was in trouble. An admirer came to her rescue and put his savings into the business. Amos Vandervoort was much older than Susan; in fact, he's my senior by about ten years. They were married. Vandervoort adopted little Susan, and her mother and he eked out a living and raised the child. Apparently Vandervoort was devoted to both Susans. When my daughter was eighteen, Susan died and between Amos and young Susan, they managed to run the shop. Four years ago, he had a heart attack and then a stroke and Susan was forced to put him in a nursing home. She chose an expensive one and was unable to finance it from their tiny business income, so she sold it and took a position as a buyer with a large store. But even with a fair salary, she couldn't meet her stepfather's expenses. Susan is devoted to the man and, according to the report from the agency, lives frugally and cuts every corner to keep Vandervoort in his nursing home. But it isn't working."

"Your daughter must have been delighted when you went to her," Forsythe said.

"Delighted...no. I'd thought she would be anxious, perhaps depressed about her situation, but she seemed care-free and happy. She knew nothing about me and I had to show her the statement signed by her mother before she believed that I was her father. She didn't seem to resent it; in fact, she seemed...amused."

Miss Sanderson cocked her gray head. "Does Susan resemble her mother too?"

"Susan is a feminine version of me at the same age—similar bone structure and coloring. I was charmed. It was like looking into a mirror. I'd been disappointed in Leslie, but Susan...I pressed her to go home with me, but she simply laughed and said she would have to give it some thought. I hoped the cash

offer would sway her, but she laughed at that too. Finally she
said she would let me know her decision. I had to settle for that."

Her duties as hostess completed, Miss Sanderson leaned
back and selected a cigarette; Penndragon hastened to extend
his lighter. She blew a smoke ring, regarded it, and said,
"Sounds as though you've made your choice."

Penndragon nodded. "I was impressed by my daughter. Her
flat was tiny, but she'd made a bright and attractive home. Her
mother's and stepfather's wedding picture was on the mantel
with a bowl of small roses beside it. When I was there, she was
decorating her Christmas tree and told me it had a theme. Her
mother had collected little dolls in national dress from many
countries, and Susan was hanging them on the tree. Little girls
and boys from all over the world. Christmas carols were playing
and it was so homey. I hated to leave without some commitment
from her, but I didn't dare press. From her flat, I went to look
up Jason Cooper. I admit I was of two minds on seeing the boy."

"Why?" Miss Sanderson asked.

"First, let me tell you Jason's history. Sally and Susan had
both stuck with what they knew best—cafés and dress shops.
Joyce did too. With her settlement, she bought the bookshop in
Mousehole, but she never married. She raised her son by herself.
In Joyce's world, there was room only for Jason and I think she
must have devoured the boy. No chance of a normal life for
Jason or even another relationship. Toward the end, Joyce developed leukemia and was bedridden. She urged the boy to sell the
shop in Mousehole and relocate in London. Still trying to run
his life, of course. As usual, Jason obeyed and for the first time
in his life he was parted from his mother. He came to London,
spent six weeks locating a flat and a suitable location for his
bookshop, and was called back to Mousehole about three weeks
before I met him. I thought Joyce might…she might maliciously
interfere with my plans for Jason.

"It took courage to enter her hospital room and face her.
I didn't recognize her. She was so wasted and incredibly small.
But her mind was still clear and much to my surprise, she

seemed glad to see me. Jason was at her bedside and she introduced us in such a way that there was little awkwardness. Then
she asked to speak privately with me, and Jason left us. Joyce
said that even though she had renounced all legal claim on me,
I must help our son. She told me their troubles, but I already
knew that the new shop would be financially difficult to handle.
I assured her that if Jason would visit me for a month, I would
see that he had ample funds to get started, and she promised she
would see that he did. But, as I soon found out, she hadn't really
softened. She proceeded to tell me exactly what she thought of
me. She still hated me and called me callous, selfish, a satyr. She
ordered me to do the right thing by her boy or she would come
back and haunt me." Penndragon laughed. "If anyone is capable
of that, Joyce was."

"She must have kept her promise," Miss Sanderson said.

"She did. A few days later she died and after her funeral,
Jason rang me up and told me he was at my disposal. His mother
had extracted a deathbed promise from the boy."

The secretary made no effort to hide her curiosity. "What
is Jason Cooper like?"

"In appearance, he's a combination of Joyce and me. He
has my height and build and his mother's coloring—brown eyes
and hair and olive skin. Jason has been living in my home for
almost two weeks and I still know nothing about him. Joyce was
a dominant woman and perhaps the boy simply never developed
a strong personality. He's…I suppose the word is inscrutable—
like a wooden Indian."

Tapping a thumbnail against her front teeth, Miss
Sanderson pondered. It was Forsythe who said, "Both Leslie
and Jason were willing to come whenever you asked. What was
the delay?"

"Who rather than what. Susan was the delay. At Christmas,
I selected some porcelain figures of children for her tree and
had them delivered. I thought she'd be in touch to thank me
and agree to my request, but I heard nothing from her. In early
January, I became impatient and rang up her flat. The caretaker

told me that she'd moved suddenly, just before the new year, and had left no forwarding address. Then I rang up the store where she worked and was told she'd taken a leave of absence and hadn't left a number where she could be reached. I thought of getting in touch with her stepfather's nursing home, but decided against it. In the meantime"—Penndragon's lips twisted— "Leslie Hobbs was driving me frantic. He kept ringing up and asking when. I put him off.

"By the middle of February, I was rapidly losing patience and was about to resort to the private agency again when my daughter finally rang me up. Susan said her stepfather had suffered another stroke and that she'd taken a room close to the nursing home to be near him. But his condition had stabilized and she was willing, if I still wanted her, to come to Penndragon on the first day of March. I urged her to come immediately, but she said she hadn't been feeling well herself and we settled on the date she'd selected. When Evans brought her from the station, I was dismayed. She was thinner, washed-out, ill looking. Her high spirits had vanished and she was abstracted and depressed. She explained that the doctors thought Amos Vandervoort might die at any time."

"What were the reactions of your children when they met?" Forsythe asked.

"Not quite what I had expected. Leslie arrived the day before Jason and Susan. He drove up from London in an expensive sports car. The following morning, Jason arrived by the early train and that evening Susan by the late one. Leslie put on a great show of being overjoyed to learn that he had a brother and sister, but Susan and Jason seemed completely indifferent not only to Leslie but to each other. Of course, Jason is grieving for his mother and Susan is worried and anxious about her stepfather."

Miss Sanderson frowned. "I would have sworn there would have been fireworks—three people who never knew their father and were suddenly faced not only with that father but with brothers and a sister. How did the other members of your family react?"

"Much to my surprise, Grace, who seldom bothers with anyone, seemed to take a fancy to Susan. Bunny is pleasant to both my sons, but it's obvious he's smitten with my daughter."

"And your children's reactions to their aunt and cousin?"

"Again, Leslie acts overjoyed. Immediately started calling them Cousin Bunny and Aunt Grace. Susan and Jason?" Penndragon shrugged an elegant shoulder. "As far as they're concerned, Grace and Bunny could be pieces of furniture." He spread his hands. "And that, Mr. Forsythe, is about all I can tell you."

"Not quite. I've a hunch you can tell us the murderer's name."

Penndragon's eyes widened. "It would appear I've chosen wisely. You *are* a detective."

Chapter Four

Miss Sanderson sat tensely, her eyes wandering from the barrister's face to Winslow Penndragon's. Again, the older man's hands were twisting together, but that was the only sign of agitation. "Yes, Mr. Forsythe, I've thought this through and have been forced to conclude that the danger to me arrived with my three children. I believe Susan Vandervoort, Jason Cooper, or Leslie Hobbs has twice tried to kill me."

"They couldn't have," Miss Sanderson blurted. "You've proven that none of them could have made *both* attempts."

"One of them could have a confederate," Penndragon said gravely, "someone not connected with my home, a stranger who crept onto my grounds and ruined the brakes or put the statue above the shed door at the direction of one of my children."

Miss Sanderson's chin jutted. "That would be incredibly stupid! Any chance of inheriting or even a prospect of future financial help would be gone with you dead."

"Sandy," Forsythe said, "there are other reasons for murder besides gain."

"Revenge or hatred or fear," Penndragon said somberly. "Yet, I can't believe any of them feels those emotions for me."

"You did desert their mothers," Miss Sanderson pointed out.

"After providing for them. Sally, Susan, and Joyce possibly had better lives than they would have if they'd never known me. As for their children…all three had decent homes, ample funds, devoted mothers."

"Leslie's home wasn't so decent," Miss Sanderson reminded. "A drunken brute of a stepfather who broke his leg in two places."

"By the time Leslie was six, his stepfather was gone. Anyway, Hobbs was Sally's choice, not mine." Turning abruptly away from the secretary, Penndragon faced the barrister. "Do you agree with my reasoning?"

"Some of it. However, you did ask for advice. You have two courses. For your own safety you could leave your home, possibly leave England. Or—"

"I will not run," Penndragon snapped.

"—or get to the bottom of this."

"That I intend to do. Will you help me?"

Forsythe didn't hesitate. "Yes. But I must make it clear that I could fail. Twice your life has been in jeopardy. This is a determined and possibly clever person. I'm unable to give you my guarantee that I can prevent a third attempt."

"I ask for no guarantees. I make only one condition. When—I won't say if—you discover the identity of this person, your work is done. I won't tolerate interference from the police."

"But—"

"On this point I'm adamant. I'll deal with him or her myself."

"I'll not be a party to personal vengeance."

"There'll be no vengeance. That I promise. I'll simply clip a wing so that no further effort to harm me will ever be made."

"You won't take the law into your own hands or use violence?"

"You have my word."

"Very well. I'll do my best."

Penndragon made no effort to shake hands to seal the bargain. A complacent man, Miss Sanderson thought, never for a moment considering Robby might have refused to investigate.

A man who'd always gotten what he wanted and fully expected to have the person responsible for two efforts to kill him delivered into his hands.

Forsythe cleared his throat. "Now for details. I'll have to come to your home, of course. How will you pass me off?"

"As a friend...no, that won't wash. Neither Grace nor Bunny would believe that. Hmm." Penndragon plucked at his lower lip. "I think your father was a member of one of my clubs."

"Which one?" Penndragon named the club and the barrister nodded. "Father was a member and so am I, although I rarely use it."

"Right, a club member, merely an acquaintance, having sticky problems with an injured ankle and in need of a rest in the country. And the clincher...have you ever done any writing, Mr. Forsythe? Come to think of it, we should be on first name basis from here on, Robert."

"Some," Forsythe said modestly. "I've been working on a treatise on criminal law begun by my father—"

"Intermittently," Miss Sanderson said scathingly, "and for years."

Penndragon paid no attention to the interruption. "That makes it even more plausible. Gives you the excuse to bring Miss Sanderson—"

"Abigail," the secretary said rather coyly.

"Abigail with you. As a fellow writer it's only natural I would extend the invitation to both of you."

"I was wondering whether you wanted me," Miss Sanderson said, and added smugly, "Winslow."

He turned to her employer. "I'll be driving home tomorrow and would be delighted to take you and your charming secretary with me."

Forsythe didn't look delighted. "You drove down?"

"Hardly, not after my last experience behind a wheel. I came by train, but I'm hiring a car and driver to return to Penndragon, so you needn't worry. The car won't have been interfered with and the driver is an expert. What time can you be ready?"

They settled on a time and then Penndragon rose, tugged his garish vest into place, and asked, "Any further questions?"

"One," Miss Sanderson said, "that description of your cook. Why on earth did you employ her and why keep her on? Has she been with you for years and you hate to discard her?"

"Mrs. Krugger is a rather recent addition. She came to us about...perhaps four years ago. My sister-in-law hired her. Apparently she hit it off with the woman and as Grace hardly knows what she's eating, she seems satisfied with the cook. I generally cook for myself in my own quarters. I feel sorry for Bunny and often have him in for a decent meal. And, as I mentioned, Mrs. Krugger has imaginary illnesses that frequently lay her low and Linda takes over."

"I still don't understand why you don't get rid of her. From your books, I assume you're something of a gourmet."

"I am and that's precisely why I put up with Mrs. Krugger. In one area, I've never met her equal. She serves the most appalling boiled messes and yet she's a superb baker—her bread, cakes, pastry...*heavenly*. Unfortunately, she's temperamental, only bakes when *she* wishes to. Once each year she makes a divine cake—brandy-swathed and filled with cherries. She refuses to serve it until it's reached the peak." He smiled at Miss Sanderson. "We're about due for one of them and you may have a chance to taste it. Then you'll understand why Mrs. Krugger remains in my house. Now, Robert, do you have any questions?"

"Yes. Sandy and I...we've received a certain amount of publicity. There must be many people who know that we've been connected with other murder cases. After two attempts on your life, don't you think the members of your household will suspect why you're bringing us to Penndragon?"

This time Penndragon's smile was complacent. "If they knew about the attempts, yes."

"But they must know."

"I carefully concealed both from them. The car accident was easily explained away—simply my atrocious driving, which all of them accepted."

"But Miss Vandervoort was right there when the statue nearly fell on you."

"Susan is convinced that was an accident. I told her that I'd asked my gardener to move the statue to provide more floor space in the shed and that Jarvis had foolishly put it on the ledge."

"And she believed that?"

"Jarvis is quite old and doddering, and I pretended great indignation at his stupidity. Yes, Susan believed me. So, you needn't worry. Not one of them suspects a thing."

Miss Sanderson said crisply, "With the exception of the person or people who made the attempts."

"Of course."

After a moment, Forsythe nodded. "We've covered everything we can at this time."

"Until tomorrow, then." Penndragon moved toward the door and Miss Sanderson hurriedly rose to show him out. There was no necessity. Mrs. Sutter, blushing furiously, was posted outside the door. Putting one possessive hand on his arm, she escorted him to the front door. Shutting the door, the secretary said hotly, "Robby, she had no business to do that! *La perra!*"

"Careful, Sandy. *That* I understood. Your Lino seems to specialize in curses."

Remorsefully, she gazed down at the tea tray. "I really shouldn't have called her a bitch."

"That's true. You've a nasty tongue at times and I was on pins and needles fearing you'd use it on Penndragon."

"Why on earth should I have?"

He grinned. "I've seen you cut people to shreds on less provocation than our professional dilettante gave you. Sit down and let's run over this business."

"It's late. Aggie will have dinner ready and then I'll catch it. What a dictator! I've the nerve to ask Winslow why he doesn't get rid of his cook and *mine* tells me when to get up, when to go to bed, and to be sure and eat my carrots."

"Aggie will have to wait. Blame it on me." His secretary shrugged and perched on the chair recently occupied by their illustrious guest. "Now, what do you think of our friend Penndragon?"

"Not a friend. We're simply useful in clearing up the trifling matter of who's trying to knock him off. What do I honestly think of him?" She said dreamily, "*Magnífico.*"

"In basic English, Sandy."

"In basic English, the man is an unmitigated snob. Couldn't possibly marry a girl from 'the working class.' Also—what was it Joyce Cooper called him? A satyr. Sowed copious amounts of wild oats with mere children. He should be despicable, but he isn't. Somehow ordinary rules don't apply to him. I should loathe everything he stands for and yet…" She looked sheepishly at the barrister. "I find I'm yearning to be under twenty, chubby, and dark-haired, perhaps a barmaid. I must be getting senile."

He looked fondly at her. "Then so am I. He had somewhat the same effect on me. *Cojeamos del mismo pie, compadre.*"

Her pale blue eyes widened. "That's Spanish. You never let on—"

"Only a few phrases, Sandy."

"What did you say?"

"We both have the same weakness, friend. As for the spell Penndragon casts, its content is probably twofold. One part is charisma—"

"He does ooze charm."

"The other is that he's a member of a rare species. Ever met a true dilettante before?"

"Never."

"I doubt we ever will again. The man is well worth keeping alive."

She was tapping her nail against a front tooth; Forsythe winced, but said nothing. Finally she said slowly, "That may not be possible. He's wearing blinders."

"And those blinders are made of sheer vanity. Penndragon refuses to believe that a servant in his employ might want him dead. He refuses to believe that a nephew threatened with disinheritance might kill him."

She bobbed her gray head. "Or that a sister-in-law who has reason to hate his guts might try to knock him off. But he was right about one thing. No one could have made both tries."

"He was right about another thing. There has to be a confederate, but not necessarily an outsider. There are any number of combinations."

"Agreed. One of the established household working with one of the prodigal children. Two of the children working together. Revenge, hatred, fear, gain…so many possible motives."

With an effort, Forsythe hoisted himself up and reached for his canes. "When we get to Penndragon, perhaps we can untangle them."

Miss Sanderson rose and their eyes met. "He should run for it."

"What was that famous quote from the war years? 'Never have so many owed so much to so few.' Sandy, Penndragon was one of the gallant few." As he hobbled toward the door, he said soberly, "He'll never run."

Chapter Five

Winslow Penndragon did things with flair. The hired car proved to be a limousine chauffeured by a strapping young man in a trim uniform. Brushing protests aside, Penndragon insisted on sitting in front to allow maximum room for his guests. Considering the circumstances, Forsythe was as comfortable as he could be. He stretched out on the wide cushioned seat, his injured leg supported on a jump seat. His secretary huddled in a corner, gazing sometimes through the window at the passing countryside and at other times through the thick pane of glass at the back of Penndragon's snowy head and tweed-clad shoulders. The tweeds were suitable for a country home, but with them he wore another startling vest, this one of daffodil-colored suede. The man certainly had a penchant for outlandish vests. She turned to share this thought with her companion, but Forsythe had closed his eyes and appeared to be dozing. She regarded him anxiously. Although he had made no complaint, she sensed he was in pain. As she watched him, his eyelids quivered and his eyes opened. "Must be nearly there, Sandy."

"Can't be much farther. How are you feeling?"

"Bearing up."

"When did you last take a pill?"

"Haven't had any today. When we get to Penndragon, I plan to down several whiskeys. Seem to be more effective than those painkillers."

"Down too many and you'll probably fall and break your other leg." Miss Sanderson peered out of her window. "For your information we're going through a village and I see the beginning of what looks like that steep hill Winslow mentioned."

The limousine glided to the top of the hill and turned smoothly between the gateposts. For a time, the driveway rose steeply and then leveled out, zigzagging between low stone walls that balanced terra-cotta urns holding neatly trimmed shrubs. Beyond them stretched the gardens. "Nice layout," Miss Sanderson said. Then she blurted, "My God! Robby, sit up and take a look at the house."

He struggled up. "To put it mildly—eccentric."

Penndragon was a substantial and quite undistinguished manor house, but what riveted the eye was the edifice tacked to one side of it. A tower, built of yellowish rock and a great deal of glass, reared up over the slate roof of the main house. It might have looked at home as a castle keep, but here it looked unsightly and ridiculous. Their host had swung around and was smiling broadly at their expressions. He pushed aside the glass panel. "Shocking, isn't it?"

"Worse than that," Miss Sanderson said bluntly. "Wished on you by an ancestor who took leave of his senses?"

"My own doing and completely sane. I find Grace trying to live with, so when Bunny was a small chap, I had my own quarters built."

"But a *tower*?"

"I'd always wanted to live in a tower. Wait until you see the interior."

The car drew to a stop before the massive door of the manor house and Miss Sanderson scrambled out and stretched. Penndragon and the chauffeur assisted Forsythe. While their host proceeded to give directions about luggage, Miss Sanderson had a second shock. She nudged Forsythe. "What is *that*?"

That proved to be a scarecrow wandering along the driveway. As it drew closer, they could see it was an elderly woman wearing high rubber boots, a brown skirt with the hem dripping down, a matching jacket bereft of buttons and secured with countless safety pins, and a straw hat anchored under a sharp chin by a bright scarf. She carried a string shopping bag stuffed with newspapers, magazines, and a single Argyle sock.

"*Alice Through the Looking Glass*," muttered Miss Sanderson. "A twin for the White Queen."

Forsythe chuckled. "Beau Brummell's female counterpart."

"A New York bag lady," Penndragon told them. "Otherwise known as the amazing Grace." He raised his voice. "Grace!"

The apparition paid no attention and seemed to be about to wander on. Taking two long strides, Penndragon tapped her shoulder and pointed at the highest safety pin. She nodded and fumbled inside the jacket. "Will you stop doing *that*!" he bellowed. He lowered his voice. "She turns off her hearing aid at the damndest times."

"Don't shout," his sister-in-law snapped. "I can hear you loud and clear."

"Our guests, Grace—"

"*Your* guests."

Penndragon shot an embarrassed glance at Forsythe and Miss Sanderson and proceeded to introduce them. Grace pushed horn-rimmed glasses up on her short nose and peered at the barrister. "Another writer, huh?" She turned her attention to his secretary. "You look like a useful person. Have something in common with Bunny. He fetches and carries for a writer too." She turned away and then, perhaps feeling she must make an additional effort, called, "*Try* to have a nice time." From her expression, it seemed she considered that impossible.

Her brother-in-law spread expressive hands. "I said you had to meet her."

Miss Sanderson watched Grace Penndragon disappear around the corner of the house and then jerked to attention. Another person was approaching, this time from the opposite direction. A woman, but that was all she had in common with the scarecrow. She was a willowy young woman dressed modishly in tight pants, a gray silk Russian blouse, and one of those berets worn by painters to keep paint out of their hair slanting over an eye. The straight flaxen hair that cascaded over her shoulders was worth protecting. Her resemblance to their host was uncanny. Penndragon's dove gray eyes, fine features, and flawless skin were framed by those shimmering sheaves of hair. But her cheeks contained no trace of the peach bloom that colored her father's face. The girl was chalky.

"Susan," her father called, "please give our guests a warmer welcome than your aunt just did."

Their welcome from Susan Vandervoort, while certainly not warm, was polite. She asked all the correct questions and made all the correct responses, but her voice was flat and disinterested. Her father was regarding her with worried eyes. "It's cool, my dear; shouldn't you be wearing a jacket?"

"I'm quite warm enough, Winnie."

"Please don't call me that."

She lifted mocking eyes. "I thought we decided Mr. Penndragon was too formal."

"I asked you to call me Winslow."

"I prefer Winnie." She turned to the barrister. "I understand you're a writer like Winnie."

"Hardly. Certainly not in the same league as your father—"

"Winnie is not my father. *My* father is in a nursing home and very ill."

With this curt remark, Susan seemed to feel that she had discharged her social duties. She nodded at Forsythe and his secretary, turned away, and followed Grace's route around the house. Penndragon shook his head. "Sorry. You're not receiving much of a welcome. Grace is always impossible and Susan…she's a bit thorny."

"Not to worry," Forsythe reassured. "But I really should get off this leg."

"Again sorry. Come in and we'll get you settled." Penndragon led the way up the shallow steps and Forsythe, with the help of his canes, hobbled along behind. The entrance hall was spacious and had a soaring ceiling. Doors opened off of it, but Forsythe was gazing forlornly at the curving staircase. Taking his arm, Penndragon guided him to a bronze grill set into the far wall. "This will make it easier for you. A lift—installed by my father. Not for himself. Father delighted in racing up and down stairs, but Mother was rather frail and she used it."

As he reached for the grill, the door opened and a short woman bounced out. Definitely bounced, Miss Sanderson thought. She was shaped like a rubber ball with a round head balanced on plump shoulders. Her dark hair was close-cropped and the round face nestled on a series of chins. "Where is your brother?" Penndragon asked. "The driver needs help with the bags."

"In the pantry washing decanters."

"And why aren't you in your kitchen making dinner?"

A shoulder moved in a ponderous shrug. "It's no longer *my* kitchen. Mrs. Krugger is on her feet again and booted me out."

Penndragon groaned. "Just my luck. I'm dining with you tonight. The sacrifices one must make."

"Never mind, Mr. Penndragon," she consoled. "Mrs. Krugger is complaining of lower-back pain."

"Thank the dear Lord for that. Linda, I'd like you to meet our guests. Miss Sanderson and Mr. Forsythe. Robert, Abigail, Linda Evans."

The housekeeper offered them a plump hand and a warm smile. "I'll take you up to your rooms." She glanced at Forsythe's cast. "You'll have time to rest before dinner and, if you wish, I'll have it taken up to you."

"Robert will join us for dinner," her employer told her. "He must meet the rest of the menagerie."

"Menagerie? I take it he's already met Mrs. Penndragon."

"That he has." Penndragon turned to his guests. "You're in good hands. I'll see you at dinner or at least at what Mrs. Krugger considers dinner."

They were indeed in good hands with Linda Evans. The lift wafted them up to the next floor and she led the way along the hall, tossing bits of information over her shoulder. "Only a few steps. I made up Mr. Penndragon's father's suite for you." She opened a door. "Your room, Mr. Forsythe. Miss Sanderson, yours is through there. Bathroom between." She made a sweeping gesture. "This was a study and when we converted it to a bedroom, we decided to leave some bookshelves and many of the books. Bedroom area here, sitting area near the windows. There's a desk for you, Mr. Forsythe, and I had my brother move in a reclining chair so that you can pamper your leg a bit. If you need anything, ring. Geneva will look after it." She paused by the door. "Your luggage will be up directly."

As soon as she left, Forsythe headed to the recliner and eased his leg up. He glanced around approvingly. The room was huge and the sitting area furnished with chairs and side tables as well as a desk. A small bar was squeezed between bookshelves, and it looked well stocked. There were thoughtful touches—an excellent reading lamp at his elbow, a vase of pink carnations on the desk, a row of filled bowls on the bar.

As Miss Sanderson made her way back through the bathroom, she echoed his thoughts. "Penndragons live well, Robby. My room's as nice as this one. Doesn't have a bar, though. Care for a small libation?"

"I thought you'd never ask. Make that a large whiskey if the supplies run to it."

She investigated the row of decanters. "Anything your little heart desires, including a wee fridge with ice." Ignoring ice, she poured two whiskies.

Forsythe took a long drink and sighed with satisfaction. "What's in the bowls?"

She lifted the glass tops. "Salted nuts, crisps, dried fruit. From the sound of Mrs. Krugger's dinner, better have some."

The barrister munched nuts and finished his drink. "Any impressions?"

"This would be a dandy spot to vacation if our host wasn't a target for a killer." She bit noisily into a crisp. "The amazing Grace seems to be a dingbat and Susan Vandervoort looks like a ghost and obviously isn't trying to curry favor with her wealthy papa. Linda Evans…odd attitude for a servant. Shows familiarity with her boss and has a decidedly proprietary attitude toward this house. '*We decided*' and so on."

"Well, at least she's a jolly woman."

"Must have been a pretty girl. Her skin's nice and she has gorgeous eyes. Hmm." Miss Sanderson munched another crisp. "Sixteen and short and plump…I wonder."

"Don't jump to conclusions."

"What I'm going to jump into is the shower and some fresh clothes. Aren't you planning to change?"

"They'll have to make allowances for my invalidism."

She snorted. "That's not the way I heard it." She tried to imitate his voice. "No difficulty in moving around at all. *Boñiga!*"

He grinned. "You certainly picked up some nasty Spanish words. When we meet the family around the dining table, try not to use any."

They met yet another family member before they reached the dining table. They were walking toward the lift when an Irish retriever came bounding up to them, stopped and sniffed at Forsythe's trousers, and proceeded to gnaw at one of his canes.

"Easy boy!" Grasping the collar, Miss Sanderson hauled the animal back. She glanced at the man approaching them. "Lively dog."

"Behave yourself, Helter," the man commanded. "Yes, he's a bit rough, but he has an even temperament. Not like his mate here." He pointed down at the retriever at his heels. "Skelter's in a delicate condition and tends to be somewhat aggressive at the best of times. No, don't touch her. She nips."

Miss Sanderson hastily pulled back her hand. It was obvious from the sagging chestnut belly that Skelter was in quite a delicate condition. Showing a fine set of teeth, the bitch backed away from the strangers. Her owner extended a friendly hand. "Miss Sanderson and Mr. Forsythe, I'm Bunny Penndragon."

"Another useful person," Miss Sanderson told him and shook hands.

"Ah, you've met Mother." He grinned. "Has a fixation that all secretaries do is fetch and carry. We know better, don't we?"

Forsythe smiled at him. "I do anyway. Sandy is like another hand."

Bunny glanced down at the cast. "Looks as though you could use an extra hand now. I'll shoot you down in the lift and take the dogs down the stairs. Meet you in the hall and we'll get you off that leg."

When the grill slid back, Bunny was waiting. Both dogs were sprawled in front of double doors to the left. He waved a hand. "Uncle's domain. The mutts seem to feel called on to guard it, and Uncle Winslow can't stand dogs."

Bunny looks a little like a dog himself, Miss Sanderson decided. A nice dog with an equable disposition. He was as tall as his uncle, but with a heavier build. His hair was lightly dusted with gray and his eyes slanted down at the outside corners. Folds of skin below those eyes gave an appearance of sadness, but there was a twinkle in those brown doggy eyes and lines of humor around his lips. "On to the drawing room," he told them cheerfully. "We have a little drinking session before dinner. Always sherry. Some sort of tradition."

He ushered them into the drawing room, found comfortable chairs, and waved at his uncle who was presiding at the drink table. Penndragon poured sherry and gave the glasses and orders to his nephew. "Introduce our guests around. They've already met Susan and Linda."

Bunny took sherry and two young men over. "Jason Cooper and Leslie Hobbs," he announced and then wandered away toward Susan Vandervoort.

The taller man, Cooper, gave them a curt nod, but the shorter man was more expansive. Hobbs gave them wide smiles, warm and somewhat moist handclasps, and offered solicitous inquiries as to the condition of Forsythe's leg. Then they too wandered away. Jason returned to a chair near the hearth; Leslie posted himself near the drink table and his father. Penndragon paid no attention to his son. He was glancing around the room with an expression of vexation. "Bunny," he called. "Your mother isn't down. Has she turned off that blasted hearing aid again and didn't hear the dinner bell?"

"I'll check," Bunny said and started toward the door. "Ah, here she is now."

"Indeed I am," Grace Penndragon said. "As for turning off that blasted hearing aid, I feel no need to. As you'll notice, Winslow, I'm also wearing my glasses." She accepted a glass from her son and steered a course toward the new arrivals. "My brother-in-law thinks it strange that occasionally I neither wish to hear nor see too clearly—"

"Clearly!" Penndragon grimaced. "We have to shout at you and you bumble into furniture."

Ignoring him, she confided, "I find it a blessing to be short-sighted and hard of hearing. Makes the world easier to bear." She took a sip and continued, "But lately things are so interesting I feel no need to resort to silence and blurred outlines." She set her glass down violently. "Why always sherry? I *hate* sherry."

Grace had dressed for dinner. She wore a clinging tea gown that had seen better days and the hearing aid control was looped over a corsage of bedraggled artificial violets on one shoulder. Without the hat, she proved to have an unruly mop of salt-and-pepper hair cut into a Dutch bob. Directly over one eye another bunch of violets bobbed in her hair. As she perched on a chair between Forsythe and his secretary, Grace fell into silence. Miss Sanderson followed the older woman's intent gaze. Bunny was now seated at Susan's side on an ornate love seat. He'd thrown a casual arm over the back and one hand brushed her shapely shoulder. The girl hadn't fussed over her dinner costume. She'd merely exchanged tight pants for a silk skirt and removed the artist's tam. She wore neither makeup nor jewelry, but with that face and hair, she needed no adornment.

As Miss Sanderson watched, Susan turned to Bunny and gave him a wan smile. Bunny whispered something and the smile widened into a laugh. Faint color stained her cheeks. She was amazingly lovely. Winslow Penndragon, Miss Sanderson noted, was watching the young people as intently as Grace and she, and with no evidence of pleasure.

"Bunny's good for her," Grace murmured and then said, "Poor child." Whether she was referring to her son or her niece wasn't clear. Grace raised her voice. "Observe Linda playing hostess."

Linda Evans had moved over to the hearth and was carrying on what seemed a one-sided conversation with Jason Cooper. He listened and occasionally nodded, which seemed his only contributions. "Like talking to the Sphinx," Grace told Miss Sanderson. The secretary silently agreed. Jason was a good-looking chap, but his father's description had been accurate. On that olive-skinned face was no trace of animation or expression. His half-brother more than made up for his lack of gregariousness. Leslie Hobbs was not only talkative but positively garrulous. As he rattled on, he waved his hands and occasionally both arms. The object of his attentions was Winslow Penndragon. The older man made a gesture similar to that of shooing away a bumptious puppy and strolled across the room toward his daughter. Before he reached her, dinner was announced by a manservant.

He must be Linda's older brother, Miss Sanderson thought, uncle to the maids she had yet to see. There was no family resemblance between brother and sister. Evans was as tall as Linda was short, as gaunt as she was chubby, as formal in manner as she was chummy. An odd couple, Miss Sanderson thought, as she followed Linda and Penndragon down the hall—the housekeeper acting like a member of the family and the majordomo obviously keeping his place.

The dining room was similar to the other rooms at Penndragon—huge and smelling simultaneously of furniture polish, the fragrance from the floral centerpiece, and mildew. Evans and a plump little maid served a rather limp salad.

Dolly—it had to be her because she was pretty—had a mass of dark curls and her uniform strained over a voluptuous figure. Winslow Penndragon seemed to be paying more attention to those swaying hips than he was to his salad. Examining the contents of her plate, Miss Sanderson didn't blame him. The only people doing justice to the first course were Jason, on her right, and Grace. Jason was chewing methodically and Grace as though she had no comprehension of taste or texture. Miss Sanderson concentrated on the wine, which was excellent. As Jason was making no effort to converse, she turned to the left, but Leslie, in a light shrill voice, was talking to Grace.

"—and so, Aunt Grace, I'm seriously considering having my name legally changed to Penndragon."

The woman's fork clattered to her plate and she directed the gleaming lenses of her glasses at the young man. "Really? Making a rather belated effort to legitimize yourself?"

"Of course not! As you well know, I am legitimate. But in my profession, Penndragon makes a better sounding surname. Can you imagine a restaurateur called Hobbs? Perfectly ghastly!"

"Hobbs *is* a ghastly name but I must admit it does suit *you*."

"Aunt Grace!"

Penndragon called, "Having trouble, Leslie?"

"Aunt Grace is being…she's frightfully rude to me."

"She's frightfully rude to everyone. Grace, do behave yourself." Grace made no response and her brother-in-law sighed. "She's turned off her hearing aid again. What's the use!"

Bunny remarked placidly, "Mother likes to have the last word."

"Unfair." Leslie turned to Miss Sanderson. "Don't you feel it *unfair*?"

Miss Sanderson was at a loss. She'd enjoyed the brief exchange and had a hunch Grace had taken the only course possible with Leslie. She hadn't really taken to him. Not only were his palms damp but beads of perspiration glistened on his brow. He was a compulsive talker and proceeded to regale her with a detailed description of his restaurant. "Miss Sanderson, my decorator knew instinctively the effect I sought—subdued elegance. A great deal of rich deep ruby velvet and dark wood. We used teak most effectively and…"

She heartily wished she had a hearing aid to switch off as his words continued to wash over her. Dolly and Evans served the next course—boiled mutton, boiled potatoes, and boiled cabbage. Blimey, she thought, and noticed both the host and Forsythe were helping themselves liberally to bread. She followed their example and tasted the wine Evans had just poured. Both wine and bread were first rate. A loaf of bread, a jug of wine, and thou…She wished fervently that Leslie Hobbs would shut up. He had exhausted his decor and was now working on his staff. "And my chef is French," he shrilled. "I'm certainly not a snob and didn't employ André because of that, but he is a *marvel*. I had to tempt him away from a *divine* little bistro on the Left Bank and…"

Frantically she tried to disassociate herself not only from that voice but her unappetizing plate. She caught snatches of conversation. Forsythe was chatting with a vivacious Linda; Bunny was engrossed with his lovely cousin; and Winslow Penndragon was odd man out. Susan had turned away from him to Bunny, and Jason, on Penndragon's left, was stolidly and silently addressing himself to a plate of boiled mutton. Leslie prattled on relentlessly, "One of André's specialties is Beef Richelieu. *Superb!* The Madeira sauce with just a soupçon of truffles…"

Practically salivating, Miss Sanderson reached hastily for a slice of bread. Surcease, she silently cried, help! I'm starving and this idiot is driving me bonkers. Help arrived from an unexpected source. A glowering Penndragon bent toward his daughter. "*Susan*, I've spoken to you twice. You're acting as deaf as your aunt."

Flaxen hair rippled across gray silk as she turned her head. "I'm sorry, Winnie—"

"That," Leslie blurted, "is not a proper way to address your father. Why can't you call him Daddy as I do?"

Penndragon's icy gray eyes fastened on Leslie's round face. "I like that term no better than Winnie." Having squelched his son, he said to Susan, "I was going to suggest you try a drop of this Chablis. It's quite distinctive."

"I don't drink."

"But surely a bit of wine…"

Eyes as gray and cold as his own locked with his. "You told me that before you approached us you had our backgrounds investigated. Surely you know *why* I don't drink."

"Your mother?"

"My mother was an…I could use the word alcoholic but, bluntly, she was a lush. Systematically and quite horribly, she drank herself to death. From my earliest memories, she was a zombie. Unkempt and hiding bottles and staggering—"

"My dear child, I wasn't suggesting—"

"The alcoholism was only a symptom of a deep-rooted illness. The illness was *you*. You used my mother as a toy and then threw her aside; she never got over you and spent her life drowning herself in drink. Father did his best and, as I grew older, I tried to help, but she slipped away from us. By the time she died I think we both were relieved to see her go. She put herself and us through hell."

"I had no idea," Penndragon muttered. "She married—"

"She married simply for father's support—someone to look after us. The second time, mother made a better choice of men. My father is—"

"Susan! Amos Vandervoort is doubtless an admirable man, but he's *not* your father. I am your father. It's a bit late, but I fully intend to be your father. Please let me."

She laughed harshly. This time the laugh didn't increase her beauty. Her features were contorted, almost ugly. "*You.* You've not the slightest comprehension of fatherhood. You haven't the faintest comprehension of *love*. You've no idea what it is to love only once as my mother did."

Penndragon reached to take her hand, but she pulled away and sprang to her feet. "Being a father isn't only a biological act.

Being a father is being *there*. My father was. He looked after me, kissed my bruises, played with me, let me help him put up the Christmas tree, went without in order to give to me." She stared down at Penndragon with open contempt. "After thirty years, you're trying to buy your children—with money. I don't know how Jason feels or even Leslie, but there's no price tag on me. I *have* a father and I don't want *you*." She dropped her napkin on the food congealing on her plate and bolted from the room.

Penndragon's face was as chalky as his daughter's had been. He pushed back his chair. "I'd better go after her."

"No," Bunny said firmly. "It would hardly be tactful. I'll settle her down." Throwing down his own napkin, he left the room.

Grace must have turned on her hearing aid, as she nodded her head until the violets bobbed up and down and said approvingly, "Really well done. Couldn't have done better myself."

"Aunt Grace!" Leslie protested. "Daddy, please don't be upset. Susan was perfectly horrid. She owes you an apology. Of all the ungrateful, *spiteful* girls!"

"Look, Hobbs or whatever your name is now," Grace rasped, "try not to be such a blithering idiot."

Leslie wailed, "Daddy!"

"It's seldom your aunt and I agree on anything, my boy. But right at present we do. Better take her advice." Penndragon turned to his other son. "We've heard from your sister and brother. What is your opinion, Jason?"

Jason shrugged. "She has a right to her opinion." His voice was deep and rich, but about as expressive as his face.

"I asked for yours."

"You're well aware of why I'm here."

"Indeed I am. Well, Leslie, it would appear you're my sole supporter."

"And a firm one, Daddy. I really admire you."

"Blithering idiot," Grace said succinctly and then, "I want dessert."

"Evans," her brother-in-law asked, "what delicacy is Mrs. Krugger regaling us with for a sweet?"

"Bread pudding, sir."

"Ye gods!" Penndragon rose with lithe grace. "Any who wish may remain and partake of Mrs. Krugger's pudding. For those who don't, coffee will be served in the drawing room." Belatedly, Penndragon remembered his newest guests. He spoke to Forsythe. "I should imagine you'll wish to retire. I'll walk you to the lift."

With the exception of Grace, there was a mass exodus. Linda Evans, chattering steadily with Jason, led the way. Penndragon followed, flanked by Forsythe and his secretary. Leslie trailed his father as closely as the retrievers had Bunny. When they reached the hall, Penndragon, with a weary but charming smile, said, "Rather a trying introduction, but it may be better tomorrow. Dinner was atrocious and if you wish I'll have Linda take up a snack for you."

"I had rather a lot of bread," Forsythe confessed. "And you were correct. Mrs. Krugger is quite a baker."

"Linda reports Mrs. Krugger's back is bothering her. If we're fortunate, she will take to her bed again. But regardless of that, I'll cook dinner for you tomorrow. Just a small group—"

"I'd love to taste your cooking, Daddy," Leslie chimed in.

"And you will—at a later date. Dinner tomorrow will be for Abigail and Robert and perhaps Bunny. We'll be discussing writing and you wouldn't be interested, my boy. Goodnight and sleep well." Penndragon took a couple of steps and halted. "Leslie, find Bunny and have those dogs detached from my door."

Helter and Skelter were still sprawled out on the threshold of Penndragon's tower. The male seemed to be dozing, but the bitch rolled her eyes and drew lips back from gleaming fangs.

"You don't care for dogs?" Forsythe asked.

"Not those two."

"Daddy," Leslie said eagerly, "I'll shoo them away."

"Go ahead and try," a voice said behind them. It was Grace, who must have finished her pudding at breakneck speed. "I'd love to see it, Hobbs. That bitch will have your arm." She paused beside her brother-in-law and peered up at him. "Winslow, I think you'd better speak to Bunny. He's paying too much attention to Susan."

"Do you want me to forbid him to associate with his cousin?"

"He certainly won't listen to *me*. And you know how I feel about cousins."

"Ah, yes—your Aunt Eunice." Chuckling, Penndragon told Forsythe and Miss Sanderson, "Grace's aunt married her cousin—"

"Laugh if you want, but their poor child—a congenital idiot!"

"How terrible," Leslie said. "Aunt Grace, I certainly do *not* approve of marriages between blood kin."

She spun around and glared at him. "If I didn't know better, I'd swear your parents were blood kin. If ever there was a congenital idiot, it's you."

His mouth snapped open, but she reached for her hearing control. As the lift door closed behind them, Miss Sanderson sighed with relief. "The end of a perfect day."

Later Miss Sanderson, attired in a flannel robe and a nest of hair rollers, checked on her employer. Forsythe was in bed with a heating pad draped across his bad knee. She adjusted the blankets and noticed how drawn his face was. "Anything I can get for you, Robby?"

"A whiskey is called for."

"You had rather a lot of wine with dinner."

"So did you."

"I'll make that two."

She handed him a glass, drew up a chair, and took a sip. "I hope Mrs. Krugger does take to her bed. If she doesn't, I'm going to be existing on bread. I wonder whether it's possible to get an overdose of starch."

"Let's have your impressions, Sandy."

She waved a hand. "Oodles. Jason seems a surly cuss. No, I take it back. Rather, he's completely self-contained. Susan's a stunner and Bunny, who looks like a nice doggy, is taken with her. Not that I blame him. But she looks ill and obviously hates her 'daddy's' intestines. As does the amazing Grace."

"Leslie Hobbs?"

"He's a...one moment, Robby. I'm thinking of the proper word." She poked at a roller and then smiled. "Leslie is a lickspittle."

"That does fit. I find I rather like Grace Penndragon."

"She has style and a tongue that makes mine sound kindly."

He drained his glass and handed it to her. "Tomorrow we go to work. We've seven principal suspects. I'll take three and because you're more mobile than I, you take the other four." He listed names and she made a face. "What's the problem?"

"Why did you stick me with Leslie Hobbs?"

"You were getting along famously at dinner, talking a mile a minute."

"Leslie was." She stood up. "Any instructions?"

"Proceed cautiously."

She laughed. "You try *that* with the amazing Grace."

Forsythe reached for the lamp. "I'll have her eating out of my hand."

"Want to make a bet?" Miss Sanderson asked as the light blinked off.

Chapter Six

The morning room at Penndragon proved to be more cheerful than the dining room. The paneling was washed in white and a pot of purple hyacinths sat on the breakfast table in a shower of weak but welcome sunlight. Grace Penndragon, clad in her dilapidated brown suit, and Susan Vandervoort, wearing a corduroy jumpsuit, were breakfasting when Forsythe and his secretary came down. The girl greeted them politely and Grace raised her head long enough to see who they were and then lowered it over a bowl of porridge.

"I'll get your plate," Miss Sanderson told her employer as he eased himself into a chair and propped his canes beside it.

Susan waved at the buffet. "Mrs. Krugger is still on her feet and the menu is a bit Spartan."

"I find it more than adequate." Pushing away her bowl, Grace neatly sliced the top of an egg. "Porridge and a boiled egg are a good way to start the day."

"The porridge is lumpy and the eggs are cold," Susan warned. "But the croissants are freshly baked and yummy."

Ignoring the other food, Miss Sanderson piled croissants on two plates and poured coffee. "I'm still wondering whether one can overdose on starch."

"I haven't," Susan assured her. "And I've been here for a fortnight. Of course, Linda was cooking part of that time."

"You young people," Grace said disdainfully, "always complaining. As for you, Susan, you only pick at your food even when the incomparable Linda is cooking." She turned her attention to Miss Sanderson. "Somewhat of a celebrity, aren't you? Newspapers full of you last November—those mass murders in Maddersley-on-Mead."

Miss Sanderson was spreading marmalade and her hands abruptly stilled. "If you don't mind, I'd rather not discuss that."

"Sandy had a bad time," Forsythe explained.

"I suppose so. Probably quite different reading about it than living it. But you were quite a heroine, saving the child's life and all." Grace dug out a last fragment of egg. "But surely you can tell us how the little girl is now. What was her name? Lucinda Foster?"

"Little Lucy," Miss Sanderson said fondly. "She's coming along splendidly. Her uncle and aunt adopted her. They're fine people and have a girl and two boys of their own."

"Do you think you did Lucy a favor? Saving her life, I mean," Susan ventured.

Forsythe and Miss Sanderson stared at the girl. "I don't take your meaning," Forsythe said.

"I put it badly. What I meant was that Lucy Foster is only an infant now—"

"Thirteen months," Miss Sanderson said crisply.

"She'll grow older and when she does…think what a horror awaits her when she finds out what happened to her family. Sooner or later, she'll have to know."

The secretary was regarding the blond girl in an unfriendly way. "You think it would have been better to let a maniac hack her to pieces?"

"Of course not! I was thinking of the trauma the poor child will experience when she finds—"

"I think I know how Susan feels," Grace interrupted. She waved a hand. "This awful world! Full of bombs and unrest and terrorists killing innocent people. What a world for children to inherit. What a mess to bring them into."

The barrister arched his brows. "If people waited for a perfect time in history to have children, I fear the human race would have vanished centuries ago."

"Not a pleasant subject for breakfast," Susan said and rose. She said to Miss Sanderson, "I'm afraid I've offended you, but Grace is right. I was thinking along those lines." As she brushed past Forsythe's chair, she added, "I wonder whether the disappearance of our race would be such a bad idea."

He waited until the door closed and then he muttered, "She's awfully young to be so bitter."

"Not bitter," Grace said, "simply young and afraid and facing the death of a loved one. Death is not easy for the young to live with, Mr. Forsythe."

Neither is that girl's negative attitude, Miss Sanderson thought hotly. The barrister caught her eyes and jerked his head. She took the hint, drained her cup, and left him to Grace Penndragon. Forsythe found shortly that she was not going to be easy prey. She reached under her chair, found her string bag, and extracted the *Times*. Folding it at the crossword, she began, with remarkable speed, to fill it in. She used a pen and her printing was small and clear.

"I'm fond of puzzles too," Forsythe hazarded.

"Indeed? Then why don't you go and do one?"

"I'm strictly an amateur, but I can see you're an expert."

Heavy black brows drew together above the horn-rims. "Buttering me up, eh? The question is why. I'm very fond of *all* types of puzzles." She filled in more spaces and then the pen stilled. "You present no puzzle to me. You wish to interrogate me. Go ahead, it might be amusing."

"Why should I wish to interrogate you?"

"Come now. I may be old, but I'm not senile. Simply because I dress oddly and act oddly, people believe I'm dotty. The moment Winslow rang up from London and announced he'd be bringing you home, I knew his reasons. It's Forsythe

the detective he wants, not Forsythe the eminent barrister and budding author. Wants you to save his miserable life, doesn't he?"

"Winslow and I *do* belong to the same club. I *am* writing a treatise on criminal law."

"And I'm the queen of the May. Posh! Don't insult my intelligence. My brother-in-law's had two narrow squeaks and, much to my delight, for the first time in his life feels what other mortals do—fear."

There seemed no sense in being evasive with this woman. Settling back, Forsythe charged his pipe and lit it. "What was the first?"

"When he smacked the Bentley into the embankment across the road. The second was when he narrowly escaped being beaned by that statue in the gardening shed. Nice tries, but he's tough to kill." The pen moved rapidly, filling in more spaces. "You're wondering how I know. Winslow covered up well and probably fooled the others, but I've time on my hands and I'm observant."

"The Bentley could have been an accident."

"Bullshivers! Winslow should never be allowed behind a wheel and I never drive with him. Evans is a dour devil, but if I need to go out, he's the one who drives. But even Winslow is not *that* inept."

"It could have been a mechanical failure, Mrs. Penndragon."

"If it had been, my brother-in-law would have fired his mechanic instead of turning the Bentley back to him for repairs. Anyway, Ed—he's the mechanic—spent far too long peering at the driveway in front of the door. When Ed left, I went out and found a damp area. I'd say it was brake fluid."

"Extremely discerning."

"Simple observation. The second attempt was rather risky. Poor old Jarvis might have gotten beaned with the statue instead of Winslow."

"Who told you about that?"

"Susan. Winslow has her convinced that it was Jarvis's carelessness. Jarvis is like me, old but still bright. Winslow swore him to silence, but I cornered him and he told me all about when he'd last entered the shed and so on. From there, it was simple to figure time and opportunity." She frowned thoughtfully. "A wonderfully complex puzzle. It will take more thought before I solve it."

She filled the last square and threw the paper on the floor. Forsythe picked it up and his eyes widened. "You *really* are the amazing Grace!"

"After the work I did during the war, that's mere child's play." She fished in her bag. "How would you like this?"

She held up the Argyle sock. Forsythe stared at the gaudy object. "*One* sock?"

She pointed at his cast. "Be a while before you can wear two. I made this for Bunny as a Christmas gift, but when I had the first sock done, I realized it was too small. Instead of unraveling it, I hung on to it."

He laughed. "Hoping to find a one-legged man?"

"A one-footed man." She waved it. "Pure wool and warm."

Taking it from her, he folded it and tucked it into his pocket. "I'm honored."

"Wear it in good health. If you solve this murder—"

"Attempted murder."

"—I'll knit the other one for you."

"Then you must help me."

She stroked her long upper lip. "I know I'm a suspect and I'm sure you'll want to know my motive. My motive is an emotion that surpasses hatred. I can't think of a word to describe my feelings for Winslow Maxwell Penndragon. It far transcends mere loathing. To understand, you'd first have to understand him. The image he presents to the world is that of a devil-may-care, charming, daring man. And that is partly true. The other part, and this is carefully concealed, is that he's left a trail of victims behind him."

"You're thinking of the mothers of the three young people in this house."

"Sally and Joyce and Susan. Yes, and many others like them. Children, overawed at being seduced by this distinguished man. I'm also thinking of his comrades in the war, members of his squadron who attempted to emulate his daring and lost their lives—"

"Come now! Fighter pilots were always in danger. You can't blame Winslow for their deaths."

"Ah, but I do." She passed a hand over her rumpled hair. "Mr. Forsythe, you didn't live through that war. You haven't the slightest conception of what a group of high-spirited young men, full of competitive spirit to be the bravest and most courageous, can be like. I know. My husband was one of them. Because of Winslow, his brother Gerald died. He was younger and had a case of hero worship for his older brother that was obsessive. Anything Winslow tried, Gerald had to have a go at. Winslow was a superb pilot; my husband barely competent. Winslow was well aware of this. He could have talked Gerald into enlisting in another branch of the service. He didn't bother. Gerald died. Winslow lived."

Her head drooped and Forsythe said softly, "The fortunes of war."

"No!" Her head snapped up. "Gerald was a *victim*. I am a victim. When he was killed, we'd been married barely six months. Winslow tried to prevent our marriage. Couldn't understand that his brother wanted an older, unpretty woman. But Gerald and I had something Winslow could never understand. We were deeply in love. I lost him forty years ago and I still love my boy husband. Forty years…alone."

"You have his son."

"Winslow has his son. Bunny not only looks like his father, but he's like him in other ways. He worships his uncle. Bunny has lived in my brother-in-law's shadow—no life of his own. No relationship even with his mother. Bunny is also a victim."

"Winslow led me to understand it was Bunny's choice to stay with him."

"He had no choice. Winslow raised him…conditioned him. And now Winslow, on a whim, plans to disinherit him. Wouldn't you say I have an excellent motive to destroy this monster?"

"You've also given one for your son."

She stood up. "Bunny is as capable of harming a hair on his idol's head as he is—" She halted and then thumped the crossword puzzle. "And Bunny is hopeless at puzzles." She stepped up to the buffet and tucked a couple of croissants into her bag. When she turned, she gave the barrister a brilliant smile.

He pulled himself up on his canes. "Mrs. Penndragon, will you help Sandy and me?"

"In what way?"

"Tell us about the rest of the household."

"No. I'll tell you only about myself."

"You don't want to prevent a third attempt?"

"I devoutly hope it will be a success. But I will tell you this." She opened the door. "If I'm your mysterious murderer, you'll not prevent my brother-in-law's death and you'll also never solve it. Mr. Forsythe, I'm very good at this sort of thing."

"And I, Mrs. Penndragon, am also very good at this sort of thing."

"You're a worthy adversary. My, but this is an exciting time! Haven't enjoyed myself as much in years. Now, get to work and earn that other sock."

The door closed. After a moment Forsythe pulled out the sock and thoughtfully looked down at it.

As she abandoned Forsythe to the mercies of Grace Penndragon, Miss Sanderson mulled over the four suspects that her employer had allotted to her. She decided to confront the least appetizing first and tracked down Leslie Hobbs. He was in the library, perched on a swivel chair behind an imposing desk. His dark eyes were roving around the room. With a great deal of dark wood and windows curtained in crimson velvet, the decor seemed to epitomize his idea of subdued luxury. When his eyes lighted on Miss Sanderson, he made no move to rise, but did make an inviting gesture at the chair opposite him. "Good morning," he said cheerfully. "Having a tour of Penndragon?"

"Looking around, yes. Your ancestors certainly built on a massive scale."

"They liked space and I inherited that from them. My restaurant—"

"You described it at dinner last evening."

"So I did. You know, I feel much at home here. Took to Penndragon immediately. Odd, because I've no background for a house like this. Mother and I always lived in rooms either behind or over our cafés."

"You seem to have taken to your father too. Was it a shock finding out about him?"

"In a way, it was traumatic meeting him. But ever since I can remember, Mother had told me all about him. We'd watch him on television or see a picture of him in a paper and Mother would say, 'He is your *father*.'" Leslie smiled and Miss Sanderson noticed a dimple in one cheek. He really wasn't a bad-looking man—short and pudgy and inclined to perspire readily, but he had nice eyes and an easy smile. He was also inclined to talk, and she settled back. It was soon apparent that Mother had not only told all about her romance with the dilettante but had built up hopes in her son of an eventual reconciliation.

"Mother would say," Leslie rattled on, "'Mark my words, one of these days your father will come looking for you. He never married and although he won't want me, I'm sure he'll want his son.' She was right, although she didn't live to witness it."

Miss Sanderson lit a cigarette. "Of course your mother had no idea that Winslow had other children."

"That came as a *shock*. Even when I arrived here, Daddy didn't let on about Jason and Susan. The next day, Jason arrived and Daddy introduced us and then to Susan when she arrived."

"Were Susan and your brother as surprised as you were?"

"I've no idea. At that point, I wasn't noticing anything but my own reaction. I felt strongly that Daddy should have told us before we got down here. Keeping us in the dark was unfair."

Unfair seemed to be Leslie's favorite word, but this time Miss Sanderson agreed with him. Not only unfair, she decided, but callous. Leslie had relapsed into a brooding silence, his full lips drawn into a pout. The secretary prompted, "And the three of you found you had a ready-made family."

"A father, a brother, a sister, an aunt, and a cousin. It was infernally awkward, but I made the best of it. I've done all I can to be agreeable to them. Jason and Susan ignore me—"

"Winslow told me about Jason's mother and Susan's stepfather."

"I guess you can hardly expect either of them to be overflowing with joie de vivre, but there's Aunt Grace. Every time I speak to her she says something incredibly insulting. Daddy says she's like that with everyone, but she isn't. She doesn't pick on Jason and she's nice to Susan."

"Your cousin seems a nice chap."

"He is. I get along like a house afire with Cousin Bunny, but he's not around much—always closed up in the tower with Daddy." The pout became more pronounced. "Do you know that I've been at Penndragon for a fortnight and not once has Daddy invited me into his quarters. He's had Jason and Susan in and tonight he's having you and Mr. Forsythe. Not *me*."

Before he could announce how unfair this was, Miss Sanderson hastened to say, "No doubt getting acquainted with his children one at a time. Your turn will come."

Leslie brightened and the words bubbled out. "Certainly it will! I'm simply nervy. You'd be too. Looking around at all this—" he made a sweeping gesture "—and not knowing if it will be mine or Susan's or Jason's." Bending forward, he said in a hoarse whisper, "Between you and me and the gatepost, I figure I've got the inside track. Jason doesn't even bother talking to Daddy and Susan—well, *you* heard her. That's no way to become Daddy's heir. Now, what I do is agree with everything he says, try to do little things for him. Show I'm *really* his son. I deserve to be his heir. Makes me see red when I think of what I've missed out on."

"Winslow said you'd had a normal childhood."

"*Normal!*" He spat the single word. "Being beaten by a drunken old bastard—sorry, Miss Sanderson, slipped out."

"Your father also said your stepfather was out of your life when you were six."

"Six years too late. He broke my leg, you see—in two places. Didn't heal properly. When I see Mr. Forsythe on those canes, I wince. Even now I limp when I'm tired. That sound like a normal childhood?" Without waiting for a response, he raced on. "Didn't get a proper education. Mother had me out of school at sixteen to work in her damn cafés—"

"You're still in the restaurant business."

"*Restaurant.* Not cheap little greasy spoons serving chips and fish, chips and steak, chips and eggs. A fine dining room with only the best food. No chips in my restaurant. And while I was growing up, Bunny was going to private schools, calling Penndragon home, traveling all over the world with *my* father. Wasn't that unfair?"

"Winslow seems to be trying to make amends."

"Sure. Giving us a little cash to get us here to decide which one *he* wants. Dangling us like puppets—" Leslie broke off abruptly and, apparently regretting his frankness, said quickly, "Don't get the wrong idea, Miss Sanderson. I'd appreciate it if you wouldn't mention any of this to Daddy. It's just that I'm so—"

"Nervy." Standing up, Miss Sanderson smoothed down her skirt. "Never fear, Leslie; I certainly won't repeat any of this to Winslow."

Only to Robby, she thought, as she left the library.

Forsythe glanced into the drawing room but didn't see his quarry. As yet his search for Susan had been unfruitful. He'd stopped Linda Evans, but she knew no more about the girl's whereabouts than he did. He had better luck with Linda's niece. "Saw Miss Vandervoort putting her coat on, sir, about ten minutes ago," Dolly told him. "Said she was going out."

As Forsythe donned his own coat, he decided Dolly Morris really was an attractive little thing. She had her aunt's eyes and radiant smile. She was also a flirt and the sway of her hips looked rather deliberate.

He stepped out and found that although it was sunny, the breeze was cool and brisk. He hoped Susan hadn't wandered far and, to his relief, found her on a bench near a well-tended maze. She had an open book on her lap but was gazing off into space. As he hobbled toward her, her eyes focused, and she gave him a wan smile. "Braving the elements too, Mr. Forsythe?"

"A breath of fresh air seems in order. I can't walk far, but I wanted to get out for a time. May I join you or—" He pointed a cane at her book.

She closed it. "By all means."

He sank down beside her, propped his canes, and turned so he could read the printing on the cover. *The Collected Works of William Shakespeare*. "Ah, another admirer of the Bard."

"Admirer? I suppose in a way. The man scares me half to death. He has captured every human emotion in words."

"This scares you?"

She was wearing a fur jacket over her jumpsuit. Pulling the collar up around her slender neck, she said somberly, "'For I am sick and capable of fears. Oppressed with wrongs, and therefore full of fears.' A few words written so long ago and yet expressing exactly how I feel at this moment."

"Your father?" Forsythe asked gently.

"After breakfast this morning, I rang up the home. He's no worse, but they can offer no hope." A sheen of tears made her gray eyes brilliant. "Strange, one never associates death with a person as vital as Father. When he had his first stroke I felt…betrayed—as though he'd done something cruel to me. When he began to feel better, he had to comfort *me*. I clung to him and wept and he held me as though I were a child again. Now, I don't even have that." A single tear ran down an exquisite cheekbone. "He doesn't recognize me and he can't speak…" She fumbled in a pocket, came up empty-handed, and accepted Forsythe's handkerchief. She dabbed at her eyes. "Sorry, I've no right to burden you with my problems."

"There are times when all of us need comfort." He hesitated and then asked, "Don't you feel a measure of comfort from your family?"

"A new family and all complete strangers. Bunny's rather a dear, but I've known him only a short time. Jason…what's your impression of him?"

"He seems aloof."

"He is. Completely remote. Only here because of a deathbed promise. How does Leslie strike you?"

"'Sweet words, low-crookèd curtsies, and base spaniel fawning,'" the barrister quoted solemnly and then thought, by George, I'm attempting to impress this young woman.

She laughed and warm color tinged her cheeks. "I told you Shakespeare said it all. I shouldn't poke fun at my half-brother, but he's so eager to win Winnie's approval and all he manages to do is irritate his dear daddy."

"There's also your aunt and Winslow."

"I find Grace somewhat…sinister. That sounds odd, doesn't it? But despite those clothes and mannerisms she's formidable. One feels Grace is always one jump ahead."

Remembering his recent interview with the lady, Forsythe nodded. "And Winslow?"

"How tactful you barristers are," she mocked. "Careful not to call him my father. Last evening you heard my outburst and that's the way I feel about him. Well, perhaps I wasn't entirely truthful." She turned the heavy book over in her hands, hands the same shape and only slightly smaller than Penndragon's. "Winnie really isn't responsible for my mother's addiction. Her parents and her grandparents were all heavy drinkers. It was an inherited weakness. Even if Winnie hadn't treated her so shabbily, Mother might have drowned herself in alcohol just the same. But he brings out the worst in me. Winnie seems so sure he'll get what he wants."

"And he wants you?"

"I think so. He seems to have no feeling for Jason, and Leslie…well, Winnie seems to despise the man. But I feel he's gradually moving in on me—trying to control, to *force* me to love him." She lifted a haughty chin. "I refuse to love him and he can't buy me."

"Which may be the reason for his attraction."

She laughed again. "The unattainable. If Leslie was brighter, he'd act the same way and then Winnie might want *him*." A gust of wind lifted her long hair and she shivered. "I'm getting chilled. Are you?"

"Teeth chattering."

She rose, handed him a cane, and retained the other. "Lean on me. I'll help you into the house."

She did, supporting him with a strength surprising for her lithe frame. Forsythe was glad of her help, enjoying the feel of her fur-clad arm, the smell of clover in her blowing hair. At the same time, he felt a stirring of anger. Treats me as though I'm her doddering grandfather, he thought, and I'm not much older than she. Of course, with this damn leg and halting gait I'm probably acting the part. She hung their coats in the entrance hall, gave him his other cane and a lingering smile, and then walked down the hall. Despite her feelings about Winslow Penndragon, she not only looked like him but moved with his exquisite grace.

Words came to the barrister and he murmured aloud, "'Thy hyacinth hair, thy classic face, thy Naiad airs have brought me—'"

"Quoting again, are we?" Miss Sanderson rasped from behind him. "You've the same idiotic expression Bunny has when he's gazing on that fair maiden."

"I fail to see anything idiotic about admiring pure beauty."

She gave him an impish smile. "'Beauty is but a flower which wrinkles will devour.'"

"Not true in Susan's case. Bone structure. Must remember her father is far from young and still makes *you* drool."

"I'll ignore that. Now, Robby, you've had quite enough gadding around. Into the lift and collapse in that recliner. I'll take our lunches up in a bit."

She steered him toward the lift with Forsythe protesting. "I haven't finished my list yet."

"Neither have I. Whom do you have left?"

"Bunny, and I may be able to catch him at the luncheon table."

She held back the grill. "Your work is done for now. Bunny and his uncle are closed up in the mysterious tower. Linda says they lunch there and apparently even the effervescent housekeeper doesn't dare disturb them at work."

Forsythe found he was glad to reach his room and put his leg up. When Miss Sanderson joined him, she was empty-handed. "Met Geneva in the kitchen and she's trotting the tray up."

"What's she like?"

"When Winslow called her plain, he was being kind. Geneva looks like her uncle—built like a plank and with a slight cast in one eye." She chuckled. "That's one working girl who's safe from the master of the house. How did you make out with the amazing Grace?"

Pulling out the sock, he held it up. "She gave me this. If and when we solve her brother-in-law's eagerly awaited murder, she's promised its mate."

"An unusual gauntlet. She's tumbled to us?"

"Had it figured out before we arrived. She's convinced another attempt will be made on Penndragon and hopes this one will be successful. Warned me that if she's the killer, we'll never catch her."

"And she's the lady you were going to have eating out of your hand."

A tap sounded on the door and Miss Sanderson went to collect their lunch. As the meal was spread on the table, he asked, "What in hell is this?"

She peered into the bowl. "For a moment I thought it was Bubble and Squeak, but this mess has obviously been boiled. Better down it. You need your strength."

He tasted it and grimaced. "Ugh! Penndragon must be out of his mind."

"Not so. Simply abysmally selfish. Stays in his tower stuffing down goodies while his family and guests face this slop. Have a roll."

Pushing the bowl aside, Forsythe spread butter lavishly. While he nibbled, he gave her the details on his talk with Grace. When he'd finished, she shook a baffled head. "Let's pray she isn't the culprit. I had a hunch she was more than weird clothes and weirder behavior. I also have a hunch that's merely an act to irritate her brother-in-law."

He nodded. "Susan called her aunt sinister." He filled her in on his conversation with Penndragon's lovely daughter. "Not much we didn't already know."

"Except that Susan's well aware of her father's tenacity. I could tell the way he was looking at her yesterday that he's made up his mind to have her, come hell or high water."

"It may not work, Sandy. Penndragon may have met his match."

Putting a dish in front of him, she ordered, "Eat your prunes. Now, my turn to tell all. Leslie Hobbs, bless his avaricious little heart."

When she'd recounted their conversation, her employer nodded. She flipped a hand. "So, Robby, you see I didn't get any more from Leslie than you did from his sister. He's rather slimy and practically taking inventory of his inheritance, but there's something rather pathetic about him."

"Also the fact that he actively resents being shut out of his father's life for so long."

"Much as I hate using the word, it does seem unfair."

"Unfair to all three children. Who's next on your list?"

"I couldn't get to Jason Cooper this morning. Linda said he'd been out for an early walk and then went to his room to read. I'll have a try for him now." She stood up and passed a hand over her gray hair. "You've stuck me with beauts, Robby. I've no idea how to approach Jason."

"You're resourceful. Tuck that afghan over my knees, please. Might as well have a nap."

"Nice to be an invalid." She arranged the colorful afghan. "How would you suggest I approach Evans and Linda? Bolt into the servants' quarters and yell, 'Hey, which one of you tried to knock off your boss?'"

Settling back comfortably, he closed his eyes. "Keep in mind that the Evanses could have a couple of good reasons."

"Linda and Dolly? Possibly. But Penndragon may be a bit beyond pursuing nubile maids."

"I'm inclined to doubt it. I can think of a couple of quotations—"

"No, you don't!"

She slammed the door behind her and Forsythe grinned.

Chapter Seven

Miss Sanderson decided to use the stairs instead of the lift. When she reached the bottom, she turned toward the rear of the house where the kitchen and various offices were located. She had come up with the skeleton of a plan, an excuse to speak to the majordomo and his sister on their own ground. She found Evans in the butler's pantry, perched on a high stool, his head bent over a tea service he was polishing. When he saw her he started to slide off the stool, but she waved him back. "No, don't interrupt your work, Evans. I was wondering whether you'd seen Mr. Cooper."

"Not since I served luncheon, miss. Mr. Cooper made no mention of his plans for this afternoon. He may be walking. A great gentleman for exercise is Mr. Cooper." He rubbed a chamois across the curve of a sugar bowl and added, "My sister might know his whereabouts. She spends a great deal of time talking to Mr. Cooper."

Or at him, Miss Sanderson said silently. She leaned against the counter. To draw Evans out, a compliment might be in order. "I'm amazed how you keep this place in such splendid shape with only a small staff."

"We manage, miss." Apparently feeling this too abrupt, he said, "We have cleaners in weekly, miss, and they handle the heavy work."

"It must be difficult finding maids, though. Girls generally prefer jobs in cities."

"Not like it once was." Setting down the bowl, he started on the creamer. "When I was a young man, girls were only too eager to enter service. Now they think themselves too good. Think they're a cut above us because they work in factories."

"Your nieces don't seem to feel that way."

He held the creamer up to the light and critically examined it. It looked fine to Miss Sanderson, but he spotted something and dabbed more polish across a handle. "That's my sister's doing, miss. Molly is determined that her girls will follow her into service. Begged Linda and me to get them started, see to it they're properly trained."

More compliments, Miss Sanderson decided. "You're doing a wonderful job with the girls. Both Dolly and Geneva are most efficient. When the girls leave, what will you do for maids?"

He rubbed vigorously and this time the creamer must have met his standards because he set it aside and began on the ornate teapot. "There're a couple of widows in the village who are willing to work here. Neither of them will ever see fifty again, but they know their job. Trained when girls were taught to work."

Great. All she'd done so far was get a quick course on the old versus the new. She tried a different tack. "How long have you been at Penndragon?"

Setting the pot down, he scratched at thinning hair. "Let's see…twenty-one years on the first of August, miss."

"A long time in one place. My, you must have been very young."

"Not that young, miss. This was my third position—and the best. Mr. Penndragon is a good employer. Never orders, always asks politely. He's away a lot too. That makes it easier. Only Miss Grace around most of the time and she's no trouble.

Only time guests are here is when Mr. Penndragon and Mr. Bunny are home."

A lonely life for Grace, Miss Sanderson thought. Spending so much time rattling around this place with only a few servants for company. She was about to prod Evans with more questions when he spoke first. "This was my sister's first position. Only a young girl Linda was, but she took to it right away. Of course, service runs in the family. Our dad was a butler and our mum a cook. All of us—I've four sisters—followed in their footsteps. Molly—she's the mother of Geneva and Dolly—is housekeeper for a family in Glasgow. Should have found a position for both girls there. Too much responsibility for Linda and me, seeing to the girls."

From what Miss Sanderson had seen of the curvaceous Dolly, she was inclined to agree. But there was nothing for her here but the history of the Evanses. The majordomo appeared to have lost interest in his polishing and before he could start reminiscing again, she said hastily, "Perhaps Linda knows where Mr. Cooper is."

He glanced at his watch. "By now Jarvis will have brought in the flowers. You'll find Linda in the plant room. Straight down the hall, miss, second door to the left."

She thanked him and went in search of his sister. The housekeeper was setting pink-and-white carnations into a crystal bowl. She flashed her cheerful smile and asked, "What brings you here, Miss Sanderson?"

"Trying to find Jason Cooper. We haven't had a chance to get acquainted."

"Lots of luck." Linda trilled with laughter. "He seems rather left out and I've tried to talk to him, but he hasn't much to say."

"Some people are naturally shy."

"And ill at ease. But Jason seems quite relaxed. Maybe quiet by nature."

"He must find it tedious here, time hanging on his hands."

"Jason seems to fill it. Does a great amount of walking and reads a lot. He plays billiards with Leslie and is always trying to corner Bunny for a set of tennis. Too bad Bunny's so busy with

Mr. Penndragon. Jason plays chess too. The night he dined in the tower, I understand he had a game with his father."

I'm running out of conversation, Miss Sanderson thought. "Your centerpiece is lovely."

The housekeeper looked as critically at the flowers as her brother had at the silver. "Not much choice right now. Only these and daffodils. Bad time of year for hothouse flowers. Jarvis tries, but he's getting on and the grounds take time." She positioned the last carnation and glanced up at her companion. "This is for Mr. Penndragon's table and it must be perfect. I understand you're dining with him tonight."

"Robby and I are looking forward to it."

Laughter tinkled again. "After your dinner here last night, that doesn't surprise me. You'll find Mr. Penndragon an inspired cook. Oh, by the by, he's requested all of us to turn up for tea."

"Mrs. Krugger's tea?" Miss Sanderson asked dubiously.

"Special treat. Can't tell because I'm sworn to silence. Happens only once a year and Mrs. Krugger and Mr. Penndragon make quite a ceremony of it. All that's lacking is pipers to usher them in." Miss Sanderson moved toward the hall and Linda called, "Might as well use the rear door. Jason is probably hanging around the tennis court hoping Bunny will show up. He's out of luck. Mr. Penndragon and his nephew are hard at it."

"Is Winslow working on another book?"

"That's a secret too, but I rather think he is. Be sure to slip something warm on. The wind's nippy. If you like, you can borrow my cape. Doesn't look like much, but it's comfy. Hanging on the peg by the door."

Linda's cape proved to be a voluminous garment fashioned of houndstooth check. As Miss Sanderson stepped into the wind, she pulled the hood up over her head. The tennis court was only a few yards from the rear door and her quarry was leaning against the back of a wooden bench. Although he was wearing a heavy red and black cardigan, Jason was bareheaded. As the door banged shut, he looked up hopefully. "Haven't seen Bunny, have you?"

She shook her head and he grunted, "Probably still closed up in the tower. Do you play?"

"Not well and certainly not in this weather." She spread her arms and the cape ballooned around her spare figure. "A bit awkward in this getup anyway."

He scowled. "Well, might as well walk." Without issuing an invitation for her company, he set off briskly along a path.

Curt, bordering on rude, but she couldn't afford sensitive feelings. She trotted to catch up and adjusted her steps to his long strides. Jason evinced no pleasure in her company, but she doggedly set out to make conversation. "Linda tells me you're a great man for exercise."

"Tennis and walking. I don't jog and certainly don't do pushups and that sort of rubbish."

They were passing the gardening shed and she would have liked to have slowed for a closer look, but Jason was setting a hectic pace. "What do you do in the winter when tennis is out?"

"I keep busy."

"How?"

He stopped abruptly and looked down at her. His eyes, she noticed, were the same shade of brown as his wiry hair. His brow, high-bridged nose, and jaw were shaped much like his father's. "Look, Miss Sanderson, are you actually interested or just babbling?"

Her cool blue eyes met his. "I don't *babble*. If I wasn't interested, I wouldn't ask."

"I suppose I should say sorry, but most people prattle on as though they're scared stiff of a lull." He started off again, but this time his strides were shorter. "In the winter, I read and play chess and pore over my stamp and coin collections. Mama played chess and approved of the reading and collecting because they're solitary pursuits. She didn't approve of my playing tennis or joining the billiard club, but I did anyway."

"Approve? Surely you're old enough to do as you wish."

"As long as Mama was alive, I never got beyond short pants. Not in her eyes."

Jason made no effort to conceal the bitterness he obviously felt. Grieving for Mama? He sounded more resentful than sorrowful. "Your mother must have found it difficult raising a boy alone."

He snapped at the bait. "She loved every minute of it. You may have met women like her—wants a child, but not the bother of a husband." He gave a barking laugh. "I think when Mr. Penndragon bolted, he did her a favor. In all those years she never once mentioned my father, who he was, where he was."

His heavy brows drew together and the olive-skinned face was tight and closed. I'm losing him, she thought. "It's none of my business—"

"When people say that, you can be damn sure they're about to stick their noses into *your* business."

Enough was enough. Stopping short, Miss Sanderson wheeled, and marched back toward the house. To hell with Jason Cooper! Robby could have him! A powerful grip on her arm halted her and swung her around. "Kindly take your hand off my *nosy* arm!"

"Arms can't be nosy," he told her, and for a moment he reminded her of Robby. It was something he might have said. "This time I *am* going to apologize. You seem not a bad sort and I've bitten your head off for no reason except...I suppose I'm a loner, Miss Sanderson. All I've ever had was work in the shop and a few hobbies."

"And Mama." She softened and said gently, "Many of us don't like our parents."

"I didn't like her, but I did love her. When her illness was diagnosed, I was frantic. I couldn't picture life without her. Oh, I knew what she did to me, what she'd made of me, but what would I do without her? Without someone to tell me what to wear, what to eat..."

This is more like it, Miss Sanderson thought happily. "Winslow mentioned that you did leave her."

"At her insistence. She knew she was dying and wanted to see me set up. Her dream had always been of having a good-size bookshop in London. In a way she was an ambitious woman, but I was her only ambition. So, at her urging, I went to the city to scout a location." At the memory, the impassive mask fell from his fine features and they glowed. "It was like being set free from a prison and I rebelled. Everything Mama didn't approve of I did. I drank a bit, not a great deal, but some. Mama would never let me eat veal. Claimed it was too hard on my digestion. For three nights in a row I had veal." He laughed. "Mama was right. I had indigestion that I shudder to think about. But the freedom, the wonderful freedom!" He sobered. "Then I was called back to Mousehole. Mama was dying."

"And you met your father."

"I met a famous man who claimed to be my father. He'll always be Mr. Penndragon to me."

"You're here."

"I'm here only because of Mama. I kept my promise because it was her last wish. I said she was ambitious for me. She wanted me to have a London shop, to have support from a wealthy father. I want neither a father nor a London shop."

"You said you liked London."

"No. I said I liked the freedom. I have that freedom now. As soon as this interminable month is over, I'll go home."

"To Mousehole?"

"It's the only home I've ever had. I'm comfortable there."

"And you hate your father?"

"Worse than that. Hate is a hot emotion. I feel nothing for Mr. Penndragon and want nothing from him."

She waved a hand. "Not even this?"

His dark head shook. "Not even this. Let Leslie have it."

A hand touched Miss Sanderson's arm and she jumped and looked down. Grace Penndragon had noiselessly approached and was standing at her elbow. She wore the straw hat tied under her chin and was attired in an old Burberry several sizes too large. The shoulders sagged, the too long sleeves were folded back, exposing a ragged lining, and the hem drooped over rubber boots. The hand clutching Miss Sanderson's arm wore a large red mitten; the other hand, this one bare, clutched a half-eaten banana. "Charming place to pick for a tête-à-tête," Grace said jovially.

"Cold," Miss Sanderson said, and shivered.

"Miss Sanderson is chilled," Jason said. "Better see her back to the house." He strode away from them.

"Unsociable chap," Grace said. "Noticed you'd softened him up some. Talking a blue streak. Some terribly reticent people do that when the right button is pushed. Dig up any dirt?"

"I'm freezing." The secretary set off toward the house. Grace tagged along and this time Miss Sanderson found it was she who had to shorten her stride to accommodate the older woman's gait.

"Being a Sphinx yourself, eh? Come on, loosen up. What did you learn from the lad?"

"I learned Jason Cooper has had one hell of a life."

"Lot of that going around. Mine's been no picnic. Where's the head honcho?"

"Honcho?"

"The boss. The great detective."

"Napping."

"In a warm room while you'd doing the cold spadework."

"Mrs. Penndragon, where did you pick up these expressions?"

"You can call me Grace. Might as well. We've got a lot in common." Grace pushed the glasses up on her short nose. "Had a wonderful time adding those words to my vocabulary—during the war, from a strapping marine corporal. Built like a god, but with nothing between his ears but space. That was before I met Gerald." Her mouth quirked up. "It was a gas." She finished the banana, regarded the skin dubiously, and poked it down into her bag. "Care for a banana?"

"No, thanks."

"That's good. None left." She rummaged in the bag. "Ah, an apple." She bit into the fruit.

"I've been wondering where you got the Burberry."

"From a rubbish bin. It was Bunny's. Boy's horrible extravagant. Still a lot of wear in it, so I took it. Grew up in a poor family. Can't stand waste."

Miss Sanderson grinned. "I'll wager it's not waste you were thinking of but annoying your brother-in-law."

"Told you we had a lot in common. You're right. Every time Winslow sees me in this coat, smoke comes out of his ears. People may start to think his sister-in-law has to rummage in dustbins." The apple core followed the banana peel into the bag. "Winslow would dearly love to turf me out of his house."

"Turf? Honcho? I'd say your slang is more modern than the forties."

"Right again. Winslow can't abide slang."

"There's no need to ask what your favorite hobby is."

Grace laughed. "Bearbaiting or, in this case, Winslow-baiting."

Changing the subject, the secretary said, "I understand tea is a special event today. Do you know why?"

"Cherry brandy cake. One of the reasons Winslow keeps Mrs. Krugger on. A yearly ritual and he looks forward to it."

"There has to be *some* other reason."

Grace tilted her head back and, behind the thick lenses, her eyes looked sad. "Mrs. Krugger is all I have. When Bunny and Winslow are away, there're only servants for company. I can't abide Linda, and Evans is remarkably like Jason—another Sphinx. But Mrs. Krugger is sociable and it's pleasant to sit down with her for a cuppa and some chat."

Lonely, Miss Sanderson mused, so many desperately lonely people. Jason Cooper, who calls his father Mr. Penndragon…her thoughts veered to the Evanses. Odd siblings. Linda tossing off Christian names, Evans using only titles. Yet Linda always referred to her employer as "mister." Perhaps her hunch about their relationship was wrong.

"Hurry up," Grace urged. "Wouldn't want to miss tea."

Chapter Eight

With the exception of Linda Evans, the entire household was gathered for tea. Forsythe, looking better rested, sat beside his secretary on the love seat. Behind the tea table, Penndragon was flanked by his daughter and Jason. Grace perched on a hassock and Bunny and Leslie Hobbs occupied opposite ends of a sofa.

Miss Sanderson muttered, "It's been ten minutes and my stomach's rumbling. Where's tea?"

"Methinks it's arriving," Forsythe told her.

Tea was arriving and the housekeeper had been correct. This was a ritual. Evans led the procession, solemnly bearing the gleaming tea service. At his heels was Dolly, dimpling over a silver cake plate. Miss Sanderson avidly checked the plate's contents. Only a small pile of tarts on one side. Hopefully she regarded the next person, but all Linda had to offer was a cake knife and a rather derisive smile. The last member of the procession was a middle-aged woman, pink and wide and comfortable, wearing a starched apron and balancing a pottery plate holding a rectangular object swathed in cheesecloth.

Evans deposited the tea service before his master, stepped back to a wall, and folded his arms. Lowering the cake plate,

Dolly flashed a radiant smile at Penndragon. His hand rose as though to pat her enticing rump and then hastily pulled back. His housekeeper, losing her smile, dropped the knife with a clatter and thumped down between Leslie and Bunny.

Penndragon beamed up at the cook. "At this time, Mrs. Krugger generally says a few words. Mrs. Krugger?"

Turning even pinker, she cleared her throat. "Mr. Penndragon sets great store by this treat. Many's the time he's begged for the recipe, but it was my mum's and her mum's before her and, you might say, I have to keep it in the family."

Miss Sanderson's stomach rumbled audibly and she thought, get on with it and let's eat. The cook seemed in no rush. "This is a cherry cake and some might think that common, but I'm here to tell you this is no ordinary cake—"

"Hear, hear!" Penndragon enthused.

"Takes a lot of fussing and then it must wait. Take it too soon and it's mild, take it too late and it's gotten too strong." She tapped her bulging chest. "I know when it's just *right*!" She gazed around as though awaiting applause.

When none was forthcoming, her employer said genially, "Perhaps, Mrs. Krugger, you could unveil your treat."

Delicately she pulled back layer after layer of the mummy's wrapping. As the cake came into view, a strong odor of brandy wafted across the room. Mrs. Krugger reached for the knife, cut off a sliver, deposited it on a side dish, and with a flourish, handed it to her master. He took his time, first peering at it, then holding it to his nose and inhaling. The cook handed him a fork and he lifted a morsel to his lips. He appeared to be rolling it around in his mouth. Rather like a wine-tasting ceremony, Miss Sanderson decided. Mrs. Krugger seemed to be holding her breath. Then he beamed. "You've outdone yourself! There are no words!" Wreathed in smiles, the cook commenced slicing the cake and arranging it on the silver plate.

When she had finished, she stood back, her hands folded under her apron. Impatiently, Miss Sanderson waited for the cake to be served, but Penndragon was regarding the cook with open concern. "Linda tells me your back is acting up again."

"Indeed it is, sir. Agony I've had for two days!" A wide pink hand clasped her lower back.

"We certainly can't have that. You must go to bed immediately and put heat on it."

"Who will tend to dinner, sir?"

"Linda, you can cope, can't you?"

The housekeeper admitted she could and Mrs. Krugger said happily, "Good of you, sir. As I tell anyone willing to listen, Mr. Penndragon is a grand gentleman."

"Dolly, be good enough to help Mrs. Krugger to her room and see that she's made comfortable."

As the cook, leaning heavily on the maid's arm, departed, Miss Sanderson thought for a moment that the family would break into the round of applause the speech hadn't inspired. Penndragon swept an understanding look around the circle of bright faces. "That should take care of your stomachs for a few days. Now, my dear, will you hand around the cake while I pour?"

Linda jumped to her feet, but Penndragon was looking at his daughter. The housekeeper muttered and sank back. Susan, appearing unconscious of the honor just bestowed, handed the cake around. She took the plate first to Grace, who quickly snatched three slices, earning a glare from her brother-in-law. Linda, still looking like a thundercloud, took one small piece and Miss Sanderson, restraining herself, took two and a tart. After serving Bunny, Forsythe, and Leslie, Susan moved gracefully back to the table and placed the plate in front of her other brother. Jason reached for the side closest and took a couple of tarts. Penndragon deftly handed around cups and napkins and sank back into his chair. As he helped himself, he glanced at Jason's plate. "Jason, do have a slice of cake. I've no idea why those tarts were brought out. This is an occasion!"

His son swallowed and took a sip of tea. "Looks lovely, sir, but I'm afraid I can't have any. I'm allergic to cherries. Always have been. Break out in bumps."

"But you've had cherries since you've been here. I distinctly remember Linda serving an excellent cherry cobbler—"

"That was the day before Jason arrived," his housekeeper told him.

"So it was. What a shame."

Silence fell as they applied themselves to the treat. Lifting her fork, Miss Sanderson wondered what all the fuss was about. It looked like the cherry pound cake frequently baked by her Aggie. She tasted it and promptly changed her mind. Penndragon was regarding her quizzically. "Abigail, can you find a word?"

"Ambrosia," she breathed.

"Robert?"

"Definitely food for the gods."

Penndragon turned to his right. "And you, Susan?"

She put down her fork. "Too rich," she said flatly.

"Daddy," Leslie burbled, "my chef, André, could never match *this*."

For once he'd hit on target. His father gave a nod of approval and announced, "Anyone who wondered why Mrs. Krugger is at Penndragon now has the answer. Grace! What are you up to now?"

What his sister-in-law was up to was wrapping her last slice of cake in a tattered bit of paper. He glared at her. "You don't have to *steal* food!"

"Save, not steal." Giving a gamine grin, Grace stuck the package in her bag between the banana peel and the apple core. Then she minced toward the door, calling back, "Can you guess where the rest of the cake will end up, folks? First in the tower and then in Winslow's tummy."

"That woman!" Penndragon transferred enraged eyes from Grace to her son. "Your mother is the most…the *most* infuriating person I've ever known. At times, I think she should be certified."

Bunny told him mildly, "If you didn't react, she would stop doing it."

Penndragon relaxed and turned to the love seat. "Robert and Abigail, dinner will be served at eight, but please come at seven-thirty. Visitors are generally given a tour of the tower. Bunny will show you around, as I'll be busy in the kitchen."

As Forsythe and Miss Sanderson headed toward the lift, she told him, "If our host doesn't give us a hearty meal, I'm going to have to sneak down to the village. I'm desperate."

He laughed. "You're luckier than I am. I can't move well enough to sneak anywhere."

"Try raiding Grace's string bag."

"Cores and peels don't tempt me and I had sufficient cherry cake."

"Don't underestimate the lady. She could have a full-course meal tucked in there." As they walked toward their rooms, she said brightly, "Maybe Grace is trying to kill our dilettante with a stroke of apoplexy."

"I wouldn't put it past her." Forsythe added darkly, "In fact, I wouldn't put anything past Grace Penndragon."

When they returned to the entrance hall, they found Bunny, his dogs sprawled at his feet, lounging against the double doors. Skelter gave them her usual welcome, an ominous growl and bared teeth, but Helter didn't stir. Bunny glanced at his watch. "Right on the dot. Can't wait to see Uncle's domain, eh?"

"Can't wait to sample Uncle's cooking," Miss Sanderson retorted. "Penndragon would make a dandy clinic for weight reduction."

Bunny pushed open a door and then gazed raptly past their shoulders. They turned and saw Susan rounding the curve of the staircase. She moved in a drift of palest green and her lustrous hair was piled high on her head. No longer was her face chalky. Her cheeks glowed with color. Either she was feeling better or had resorted to makeup.

Bunny whispered, "'She walks in Beauty, like the night—'"

"Blimey!" Miss Sanderson pushed past him. "Another quoter."

Forsythe followed and Bunny hastened to catch up. The double doors led into a narrow hall that, in turn, led to another door. Bunny opened it, bowed, and ushered them into a circular area. Doors opened from it and a spiral staircase wound upward. The handrail was hung with charming bronze lamps.

"Main floor," Bunny said with an expansive gesture and then, like an elevator operator in a department store, announced, "Lounge, dining room, kitchen."

Forsythe steadied himself on his canes. "And this is the limit of my tour. I'll never make those steps."

"Not so. Over here, we have another lift, for the convenience of guests unwilling or unable to mount three floors on narrow steps."

"But not for the master," Forsythe said, hobbling into the lift.

"Perish the thought. Uncle, like his father before him, races up and down those steps like a mere lad. Next floor—mainly offices and a small art gallery. I'll give you a peek at the offices—unadorned working places." He threw open a door. "Mine."

"Oodles of the latest equipment," Miss Sanderson said enviously.

Forsythe pointed at a good-size computer. "Is all this necessary for writing?"

"Some of it, but writing is only a part of the work. My grandfather and great-grandfather bought up mines and textile mills and such, but Uncle Winslow, without expending any effort, has increased his inheritance many-fold."

"How?" Forsythe asked.

"Investing—an uncanny ability to know what to buy, when to sell. He's a financial genius."

Miss Sanderson lifted her brows. "With your help."

"He's the brains; I'm only the workhorse. Now, on to the gallery—a small collection but worth seeing." He opened another door, disclosing a hall-like area. Pictures hung on the walls, well spaced and with a light beaming down on each frame. Both Forsythe and his secretary took deep breaths. The barrister said, "If I'm not mistaken, that's a Picasso."

Stepping closer to the painting, Miss Sanderson studied the acrobats depicted. "Circa 1905, his rose period."

Bunny's doggy eyes widened. "An expert, by Jove!"

"Hardly. When I was a slip of a girl, too poor to lunch out, in bad weather, I took my ham rolls to art galleries. While munching, I soaked up bits of information."

"Which she is more than willing to share," Forsythe said dryly. "Winslow really has catholic taste. Modern artists cheek by jowl with old masters." He halted before a large canvas. "Marvelous! The dappling of light across those shoulders—"

"Renoir," his secretary said smugly. "Circa—"

"Sandy!"

"I hate to cut this short," Bunny said, "but we must get on. If we're late, Uncle will be furious."

When they were back in the lift, Forsythe asked, "About security—"

"An alarm system on all the windows."

"What about all the doors?"

Bunny pushed back the grill and they stepped out again into the circular area. Here the staircase, in a shower of bronze lamps, ended. "Only one door into the tower, Mr. Forsythe, the one we entered from the main house. But not to worry. When Uncle's not in residence, his treasures are tucked away in a bank vault." He led them toward the only door opening on the round hall. "This floor has bedroom, bath, and dressing room—all fit for an emperor. Observe, Chinese Chippendale and trifles from all over the world."

The bedroom was indeed large enough for an emperor and, in keeping with the furnishings, the upholstery and walls glowed vibrantly in jewel tones. Looking at the crimsons, ambers, greens, and azure blues, Miss Sanderson thought them not dissimilar to Penndragon's vests. Bunny was leading her employer across an ancient silky rug toward a number of glass cases. "Uncle wants you to look at his jade. He said Adam Kepesake mentioned you collected."

"Nothing like this. I've only a few pieces." Forsythe pointed at a white jade camel. "Where did he get that?"

"Afghanistan. And this piece was from—" Bunny broke off and called, "Miss Sanderson, if jade isn't your cup of tea, do have a look at the cabinet of Meissen china."

"*This* is my cup of tea." She was standing beside the enormous bedstead. "Come look at these, Robby."

With obvious reluctance, he pulled himself away from the jade. His secretary was fingering a silver cherub on a pedestal by the bed. On the opposite side was another. Miss Sanderson's austere face was aglow with pleasure. "They look exactly like little Lucy!"

"They do a little—the ringlets, the dimples."

"A little! See the hands and those fat little feet." She lifted one cherub. "They're quite weighty. Look, Robby, one is standing, the other kneeling. Both the picture of little Lucy."

"With the exception of the wings, Sandy."

"Benvenuto Cellini," Bunny said with a grin. "Circa—"

"I don't care who made them or when. I *love* them. I covet them. I'm—"

"Hungry?" Bunny suggested. "Lady and gentleman, it is time. We've exactly three minutes to get to the table."

As they left the room, Miss Sanderson took a last look at the cherubim and sighed.

Winslow Penndragon's dining room was a dramatic contrast to the one in the main house. It was cozy, intimate, smelling only of carnations and the mouth-watering odors that wafted in each time the louvered door to the kitchen opened. Penndragon, with his nephew's help, handled the serving. The oval table was exquisite with candlelight gleaming on silver, crystal, and snowy linen, but Forsythe and Miss Sanderson reserved all their attention for the contents of their plates. As course after delicious course was served, little effort was made to converse. If Penndragon ever fell upon hard times, Miss Sanderson mused, he might well make a master chef.

It wasn't until they were having coffee in the lounge that she took time to observe their host. That evening he was wearing a sober black suit, a perfect foil for his choice of vests. This one was by far the most outrageous she had yet seen. All the colors of the spectrum were embroidered against scarlet silk.

Penndragon handed her a balloon glass. "I see you're admiring my vest."

"It goes well with the Chinese Chippendale. Should use it for a chair covering."

He laughed and his nephew said, "If Mother had said that, you'd be raging."

"Grace would have *tried* to be insulting. Abigail means it as a compliment."

Miss Sanderson hadn't meant it as a compliment, but she held her tongue. She could hardly insult a man who had just plied her with such a sumptuous meal. Striking a pose, Penndragon said, "I am now prepared to accept laudations."

Taking a sip of excellent brandy, she told him, "Tell you what. I'd swap both your Cellini cherubs for the recipe for that game pie."

"At times you *do* sound a bit like the amazing Grace. But not even for those treasures will you get the recipe. In confidence, I'll tell you this—be patient, purchase my forthcoming book and that recipe will be yours."

Her pale eyes widened. "You're writing a *cookbook*?"

He looked faintly chagrined. "Hardly that. Although this book does include my favorite recipes, each is accompanied by an amusing vignette of where and how I got it. It will be called *Delicacies for a Dilettante*." He turned to his nephew. "Remember the Sherpa village where we ate baked yak?"

"I would dearly like to forget it, but I must admit your version is delectable."

Miss Sanderson lit a cigarette. "I may pass on your book. Can't picture myself whipping around to my butcher for yak meat."

Penndragon sank into a chair beside her employer. "Robert, you're very quiet tonight."

"Hard to get a word in when Sandy gets going. But I would like to discuss your jade. You have a fantastic basket of fruit in three different jades…"

As Penndragon began to discourse learnedly on jade, Miss Sanderson's attention wandered. She glanced around the lounge. Apparently the dilettante reserved his flamboyance for his vests and his bedroom. This room, like the offices on the first floor, was merely functional. There were no ornaments, but the chairs were comfortable, a gas fire beamed heat, and on the mantel above was what appeared to be an enlarged snapshot in a silver frame. Setting down her glass, she wandered over for a closer look. It had faded to sepia, but was still quite clear in detail. Beside the fuselage of a Spitfire, two young men posed. They wore flying jackets with sheepskin collars and their hair was blowing back from their faces. The taller man's arm was looped affectionately over the other's shoulders. Except for short hair, the tall man could have been Susan Vandervoort in pilot's clothing. "Uncle and my father," a voice said near her ear.

"I can see your resemblance to your father, Bunny. You have eyes and a mouth like his. But Susan…it's uncanny."

"Their mouths are different. Hers is more…more vulnerable."

She touched the glass. "I suppose these tiny rows of planes are—"

"The ones Uncle shot down. Impressive, isn't it? He was the ace of his squadron."

"Odd name for a plane. Why did he choose it?"

"No idea. My father named his after a famous singer."

"Bunny," Penndragon called and they turned. "You've been hard at it all day. Better have some time for yourself."

Having dismissed his nephew, he was returning to his conversation with the barrister when Bunny interrupted. "Will you need me further tonight?"

"Hmm. Yes, you'd better check in later. Make it in an hour."

And that, Miss Sanderson thought wryly, is the time he's allocating to Robby and me.

"The call you want me to make to your editor?"

"That and a few other things."

Bunny paused in the doorway and Miss Sanderson saw him glance at his watch. Uncle was extremely punctual, she remembered. Penndragon refreshed their glasses and turned his attention to Forsythe. "At the risk of sounding impatient, I must ask about your progress."

Forsythe lifted his eyes to the older man's face. "I think we've decided that you're mistaken about one of your children being the culprit."

"I am seldom wrong. Tell me, what is your reasoning?"

"I spoke with your daughter; Sandy with both your sons. After tea, we discussed this thoroughly and agreed not one of them has a ghost of a motive. Leslie doesn't like your nephew being raised as a son while you ignored him, but it's clear he desperately needs your financial help."

"That I know only too well. And my death would cancel any hope he has for that. Jason?"

"He has no feeling for you one way or the other. And he has no plans for expanding his shop in Mousehole and no desire to have a larger one in the city. If Jason has reason for resentment, it's directed against his mother, not you."

"I told you Joyce was a possessive woman. Now, the most important one. After Susan's tantrum at dinner last evening, it's clear she blames me for her mother's drinking problem and possibly her death."

"Susan confessed to me that she was simply hitting out at you when she said that. Her mother, she's convinced, would have drunk anyway. It seems Susan Miller came from a line of alcoholics."

Penndragon fingered a brilliant embroidered peacock on his vest. "Susan may hate me because when she needed a father, I wasn't there."

"I think she thanks you for that. Sounds as though Amos Vandervoort was the best father a child could have."

Penndragon colored faintly, but all he said was, "That's a relief. I should hate to think of Susan trying to kill me."

No mention of how he would feel if it was either of his sons, Miss Sanderson noted. While their host was feeling relief, she rose and returned to the mantel. "Your plane had an intriguing name."

His silver head swung toward her. "The Pansy? I named it for my mother's parlor maid. The chaps in my squadron found the name hilarious."

"Pansy—the maid; I mean—she was another of your conquests?"

"The reverse. I was barely eleven when Pansy seduced me."

"Precocious lad, weren't you?"

"Enjoyed every minute of it."

"Winslow," the barrister said sharply. "We'd best make the most of the hour you've given us. Tell us about another servant—Linda Evans."

Penndragon's color deepened. "Ah, you know."

"Guessed. Why did you withhold this from us?"

"It was such a trifling matter."

"Trifling to seduce a sixteen-year-old child in your home with her brother working for you? She *was* sixteen, wasn't she?"

"Yes." Unabashed, Penndragon braced an arm on the mantel. "Linda was the reason I employed them. Evans did have good references, but Linda caught my eye. She was such a tempting morsel. I made no attempt to mislead her. Linda was only too eager to come to my bed, but before she did, I assured her there was no chance of marriage and that my infatuations were short-lived."

"How long did this one last?" Forsythe asked.

"I really can't recall. Perhaps about six months, no longer. I do tire of these little girls quickly." He treated Miss Sanderson to a brilliant smile but this time she made no response. Her expression was as cold and closed as Forsythe's. Her host made another effort. "These girls are not like you, Abigail. All body—no sparkling intellect." When this compliment fell flat, he spread his hands. "I suppose you consider me a cad. Are you judging me?"

"We're not here to judge," the barrister told him. "Your morals, except as a motive for murder, are not of the essence. To return to Linda Evans. After you were through with her, she stayed on. Explain."

"When we were finished with our little affair—"

"When you discarded her," Miss Sanderson said flatly.

"When I discarded her, I gave her a gift of money and told her she might leave if she wished. She begged to stay on. I cautioned her she must not have false hopes. If she stayed, she would be a servant and nothing else and must act like one. The only concession I made was that she could join family and guests for her meals. She's abided by the rules."

"And her brother stayed on too," Forsythe said. "What is his full name?"

"Roger Evans."

"Was Roger Evans aware of his sister's seduction?"

"I've no idea. I supposed he couldn't have helped but be." Penndragon made an impatient gesture. "This is ancient history. Neither Linda or Evans would wait over twenty years to take vengeance."

"Dolly Morris," Forsythe said tersely.

"I haven't touched Dolly! Well…"

"Details."

"It sounds rather sordid but…well, Dolly is like Linda before she put on all that blubber. Simply delicious! And it really wasn't my fault. It was Linda who—"

"Just the details. No excuses."

Penndragon's lips set. "Don't take that tone with me!"

"Do you want our help or not?"

After a moment, the older man shrugged. "A maid is sent into the tower each day to dust and generally straighten up. All Evans is required to do here is to act as valet and prepare my room for the night. When the Morris sisters arrived, it was Dolly to whom Linda gave the duty here. I came upon the girl when she was bending over the bed, putting fresh linen on. One thing led to another; Dolly was willing, and we ended up sprawling across the bed. I was merely kissing and cuddling the girl when Linda walked in." Pausing, Penndragon gave the barrister an indignant look. "She didn't even knock! There was a frightful scene and Linda slapped her niece's face and ordered her out of the tower. I was so angry that I almost gave Linda her notice on the spot, but I had second thoughts. She would be too hard to replace. So I calmed her down, explained that the reason for my attraction was Dolly's resemblance to her when she was a girl, and eventually Linda came around. Since then, she's done the work here herself and hasn't let me near her niece. In fact, she's sending Geneva and Dolly back to their mother at the end of this month." Penndragon's mouth drew down at the corners. "Linda watches me like a hawk."

"How sad," Miss Sanderson said insincerely.

The barrister was direct. "Excellent motive there for both Roger and Linda Evans. Now, about your sister-in-law—"

"Grace is scatty!"

"Grace happens to have a mind like a honed razor. If she's the one we're looking for, you're a dead man."

"I find that hard to swallow." One of Penndragon's shapely hands caressed his chin. "Mooching about in rags, practically eating from garbage bins…she does have reason to dislike me, though. I remember when she became engaged to Gerald—he was still in training at the time—she came to me and literally begged me to persuade my brother to give it up and enter another branch of the service. She mentioned ground crew." He laughed. "A Penndragon servicing planes. Ridiculous!"

"Was your brother a good pilot?"

"Gerald wasn't washed out in training, but no, his reflexes weren't the best and he took too many chances. Tried to be *too* daring. But it was Gerald's decision and that's what I told Grace."

Miss Sanderson's sharp chin jutted. "Another excellent motive."

"After forty years?"

"Hate has a tendency to grow. First you took her husband and then her son as your own."

"Bunny? The boy has always made his own decisions. I didn't *force* him to stay with me. Now that you've met my nephew, you'll agree he's the least likely of the lot."

"I wonder," Forsythe said softly. "Bunny is obviously in love with your daughter."

"Merely an infatuation. When I came to your chambers, I mentioned Bunny was smitten with Susan. It will pass."

"Would you welcome a marriage?"

"Certainly not."

"Because they're cousins?"

"Unlike Grace, I have no objection to cousins marrying. My great-uncle married a cousin and they had seven normal children. But I would never allow my daughter to marry Bunny."

"On what grounds would you oppose it?"

"Susan is *my* daughter. She will *never* be my nephew's wife."

Or anyone else's, Miss Sanderson thought hotly, if this man can prevent it. Aloud she asked, "Does Bunny know of your feelings?"

"We've never discussed it. I simply assumed…he's quite sensitive and would never oppose my wishes." Penndragon again stroked his chin, apparently lost in his own thoughts.

Forsythe's voice snapped him back. "When you first came to us, I had two suggestions—"

"Yes, and we decided to get to the bottom of this affair."

"I've come to the reluctant conclusion that that is impossible. I haven't the faintest idea who is trying to take your life. Now I must urge you to consider my second suggestion. Leave this house and get away from this group of people."

Stretching out a long hand, Penndragon tapped the silver picture frame. "I've endured much more; I'm not about to turn and run now."

"In that case, I'm afraid Sandy and I must leave you to take your chances alone."

"You can't do that! I won't *allow* you to."

To Miss Sanderson's delight, Forsythe said dryly, "You don't control *us*. Tomorrow we return to the city."

"Showing the yellow, eh?"

Color drained from the barrister's thin face until even his ears were white. Pulling himself to his feet, he drew his slender body up. His eyes locked with Penndragon's. "I'm no more a coward than you. But I do have more common sense. You don't need a detective. You need a bodyguard." A cane rapped against the cast. "Physically, I can't protect you."

Putting out a hand, Penndragon said penitently, "I spoke hastily and I apologize. Won't you reconsider?"

"No." Forsythe, with Miss Sanderson at his side, hobbled toward the door.

Winslow Penndragon called after them. "I'll have Bunny put a check in the mail."

Robert Forsythe told him stonily, "It will be returned."

When they reached the entrance hall of the main house, Miss Sanderson stepped over Helter and said, "Bravo! A pity Grace couldn't have been there. She'd have loved it. Penndragon must have a death wish. Closed up in this place with seven people, most of whom have well-earned reasons for finishing him off. Blimey!" As the lift moved upwards, she took a close look at her companion. He was still pallid and his mouth was pinched. "Can't figure myself out, Robby. Even after watching the charm and polish crumble, I'm still fascinated by that man. Must be reaching my dotage."

His mouth relaxed into a faint smile. "When we met him, you put it in a nutshell. Winslow Maxwell Penndragon can't be judged by ordinary standards."

"True." She added wistfully, "Maybe he still has a few of the cat's lives in reserve."

Chapter Nine

During the night, the weather turned blustery and now gusts of wind lashed icy rain against the windowpanes of the morning room. As though to make up for the weather, the buffet was laden with the bountiful breakfast that Linda Evans had prepared. With her at the stove, the culinary standards at Penndragon had risen appreciably.

Heaping plates at the buffet, Miss Sanderson felt content on two counts. Many of her favorite foods, hot and tempting, were spread before her and also she'd just completed arrangements for a hired car. She lifted a kidney and Forsythe called, "Whoa! Your eyes are bigger than my stomach."

Paying no attention, she added blueberry muffins and carried the food to the table. Leslie and Jason were bending over plates as well filled as the ones she carried and their sister was pushing kedgeree around. Beside her, Grace Penndragon sipped coffee and worked at another puzzle. As Miss Sanderson forked up scrambled eggs, Grace glanced at her over her glasses. "Evans tells me you've ordered a car. Bored with country life?"

Forsythe shrugged. "Duty calls. We've received a brief that my juniors can't handle."

"Odd. I wasn't aware a call had come through to you."

"Aunt Grace, a *few* things may happen that you don't hear about," Leslie snapped pettishly. His dimpled smile wasn't in evidence and his mouth was drawn in petulant lines.

"Not many, Hobbs. *You* received a call last night. From your accountant, I believe. Bad news?"

His mouth snapped open, but one of Grace's hands rose warningly toward the hearing control and he subsided, mumbling. She glanced at the mantel clock. "Wonder where Bunny is? Generally he's bolted his breakfast by now so he can wait on his lord and master. Linda's late in sitting down, too."

At that moment Linda appeared in the doorway, one fat hand clasping the jamb. Her face was the color of the table linen. "Winslow…" She took two steps and stopped, her heavy body swaying.

Jason and Leslie jumped to their feet, but before they could reach her, she moaned and slumped in a heap on the floor. Hopping up, Grace rounded the table. "Don't do that, Hobbs. Don't prop her head up. Get her feet up. Susan, ring for Evans. What in tarnation is wrong with the woman?"

"She's fainted," Leslie explained. "And she said something about Daddy."

"We can see she's fainted. Ah, Evans. Bring brandy and make it quick." Without any evidence of interest, Evans glanced down at his sister and backed out of the room. "In the meantime…" Seizing a pitcher of water, Grace dashed it over the housekeeper.

"That's enough." Miss Sanderson caught the older woman's arm. "Her eyes are opening."

As Grace bent over the woman, a voice said from the doorway, "Uncle Winslow's dead."

Bunny leaned against the doorjamb too and his face was as white as the housekeeper's. Leslie let out a wail, "*Daddy!*"

Grace took the situation in hand. "Bunny, sit down before you fall too. Jason, lift Linda into a chair. Evans, pour a good tot of that into your sister and give Mr. Bunny one too."

"Was it a heart attack?" Susan whispered.

"Murdered." Bunny collapsed into the nearest chair. Bracing his elbows on the table, he lowered his head into both hands.

"Brace up," his mother ordered. "Are you certain?"

"His head…his face…all battered…"

"With what?"

"One of the silver cherubim."

"God," Miss Sanderson whispered and then she felt Robby's arm around her shoulders.

Grace took over from Evans, who now seemed as shocked as the others. She poured brandy and passed it around. Miss Sanderson gulped hers. Bending over her son, Grace shook his shoulder none too gently. "Did you ring up the police?"

"Right after I told Linda."

"Then we may expect Inspector Davis. Winslow called him out here last winter for some vandalism on the grounds. Heavy florid man, nearing retirement, I should think." She tapped restless fingers against the table. "Colonel Blake will be ringing up the Yard for assistance—"

"You can't be certain of that," Forsythe said.

"You can bet your booties on it. Known the chief constable since he was a lad—great one for passing the buck. Winslow is—was—a public personage. Colonel Blake will take no chances. The boys from the Yard will be here. And that means Adam Kepesake."

"This time your guess is wrong," Forsythe told her decisively. "They won't allow him to become involved in this. Winslow was his godfather."

"I'm well aware of that. Known Adam since he was a lad too. Feels much the same about Winslow as Bunny does—hero worship. Take my word for it, Mr. Forsythe, the boy will be here."

Leslie was close to tears. "How can you be so cool? Don't you have any feelings, Aunt Grace?"

"Someone must keep their head, Hobbs. Now, we'd better plan strategy. Bunny, any idea of how long he's been dead? Feel his skin, test for rigor mortis?"

"Mother!" Bunny lifted his head and stared at his mother. "Please, don't be ghoulish."

"You're acting as idiotic as Hobbs." Her glasses swung around the room and the eyes behind those heavy lenses were serious. "Let me tell you a few facts. I know you're stunned, but the police won't be. Adam will be ripping this place and us apart. One of you is a murderer—"

"I disagree." Jason's deep voice cut across hers. "That tower is full of valuable objects. Mr. Penndragon was probably killed during a burglary attempt."

"And how did the burglar get in?"

"Through a door or window."

Forsythe shook his head. "Grace is right. The only door to the tower is the one from the entrance hall. No stranger could have gotten past those dogs." He swung around to the majordomo. "Were the doors and windows locked in the main house, Evans?"

"They were, sir. Last thing I do before I retire."

"What about the windows in the tower?" Jason asked.

Bunny sat up straighter. He said slowly, "An alarm system is attached to all the windows. Once triggered, it sounds not only in the tower but on every floor in this house."

"Maybe we slept through it," Leslie suggested.

Grace glared down at him. "I heard it tested. Have to be deaf not to hear it."

"And *you* are," Leslie said maliciously.

"There's nothing wrong with your hearing or anyone else's. Face it. It's one of us. Better get your alibis ready."

"I haven't an alibi," Leslie said. "I was in bed asleep."

"How do you know that, Hobbs? We've no idea when Winslow was murdered. Mr. Forsythe, do you agree?"

"It might be wise." The barrister glanced around the table. "Think back and try to recall where you were last evening, whom you were with, what you were doing. Times...that sort of thing."

Leslie turned on him. "What right have *you* to advise us? You were in this house too. You or your secretary could have murdered Daddy."

Putting a hand on his pudgy arm, Grace told him not unkindly, "You really are an ass, aren't you." The glasses turned toward Forsythe. "Time for truth telling. Miss Sanderson and Mr. Forsythe are the only people who are not under suspicion. They came here, at Winslow's request, to try to prevent exactly what has—"

"Mother!" Bunny pulled himself to his feet. "*What* are you talking about?"

"Two previous attempts on your uncle's life." There was a storm of protests and Grace lifted a majestic hand. "Mr. Forsythe."

"Robby," Miss Sanderson whispered. "Do you think this is the right time to—"

"Grace is right, Sandy." He gave her a reassuring smile. "No reason to conceal this any longer. Winslow did retain me to look into this affair. I see no harm in telling you about the attempts." He outlined the car crash and the incident at the gardening shed. As he talked, his secretary watched the faces of his attentive audience. Grace looked smug, her son baffled. As usual, Jason was inscrutable and Leslie outraged. Behind her, Evans leaned against the wall and Miss Sanderson couldn't see him, but his sister looked dazed. Susan's head was bent and her flaxen hair veiled her face.

When Forsythe had finished, Grace nodded approvingly. "Well put. All the facts and no conjecture. Now I think all of you realize the gravity of this situation."

Leslie jabbed a finger at the barrister. "Spies!"

"Brought in by your dear daddy," Grace reminded. The doorbell pealed and she said, "Evans, you stay here. I'll admit the police. Too soon for Adam, so that will be Inspector Davis and his boys." With a dignity strange in such a scarecrow figure, she marched into the hall.

Her son looked after her. "I can't believe it. Never seen her act like this. So...so competent."

"I doubt that you ever really saw your mother clearly before now," Forsythe told him gravely.

Sounds drifted down the hall, the piping of Grace's voice, deeper male tones, and then a storm of growls and barks. Bunny leaped up and ran into the hall. Grace returned first, rubbing her hands together, and looking gratified. "Dogs took exception to the invasion of the tower. Had at old Dr. Hawes—he's the medical examiner—and nearly took a chunk out of him. Bunny and a constable are taking the mutts out to the kennel." She posted herself at the door and beckoned to Miss Sanderson. "Come and watch. Quite a sight."

Nothing like a murder to brighten up a dull life, Forsythe thought with grim amusement. He'd seen it all too often—the police, plain-clothed and uniformed, the scene-of-the-crime men, the medical examiner with his bulging bag, most of them bored and jaded by crime, but efficient, knowing their jobs. How the dilettante would have hated it—strangers in his cherished tower, pawing over his personal effects, stripping his body, poking and prying… But then he was beyond caring, beyond anything.

Forsythe glanced around. Most of the others were watching Sandy and Grace. The exceptions were Susan and the housekeeper. Soaked to the skin, Linda was trying to dry her hair and the front of her dress with napkins. Susan's head was still bent, her glorious locks still concealing her face. The barrister suddenly noticed he was now sitting apart from the rest of the household. Those closest to him had discreetly edged their chairs away. No longer were Sandy and he guests. Sliding down beside him, his secretary echoed his thoughts. "Spies and pariahs, Robby."

"Yes."

"And probably flaming nuisances to the county constabulary."

He made no answer. That remained to be seen. Time passed, the minutes ticking by ponderously. A more subdued Grace returned to her chair and patted Susan's wrist. Throwing back her hair, the girl gave her a weak smile. No one spoke. The only sounds were the shifting of feet, Evans changing position against the wall, the clink of a cup against a saucer. Bunny came back and silently took up a post near the majordomo.

Finally Leslie jumped to his feet and blurted, "No one's told us we have to stay in here. I'm damn well going up to my room." He was soon back, looking slightly sheepish. "Constable by the door asked us to remain in here until they can take what he called 'preliminary statements.' If you ask me, it's awfully high-handed!"

"No one asked you," Grace said wearily.

Sitting down, Leslie proceeded to sulk. After a time, he muttered, "Hope they take me first. Like to get it over with."

He didn't get his wish. Miss Sanderson and the barrister were called first. They followed the constable down the hall to the stately library, where Inspector Davis had set up headquarters. He was seated behind the desk and a constable had cleared a side table and was laying out notebooks and pencils. Davis fit Grace's description—heavy and florid—and looked old enough for retirement. Score one point for the amazing Grace, Forsythe thought. Inspector Davis was hearty. "Glad to meet you. The chief constable has called on the Yard and I was speaking with Chief Inspector Kepesake. He'll be here to take charge and he advised me to talk to you first. Told me you might be able to throw some light on this tragic affair."

Score two and three for the amazing Grace—the Yard and Adam Kepesake. Forsythe cleared his throat and told Davis all he knew. He spoke tersely, but he left nothing out from the moment Winslow Penndragon had entered his chambers until the conversation with him in the tower the previous evening. Davis nodded his big head a number of times, looked scandalized when he heard of the dilettante's three illegitimate children, disapproving about Linda Evans and Dolly Morris, and when the barrister had finished, completely relieved.

"I'll tell you frankly, Mr. Forsythe, I'm happy Colonel Blake called on the Yard. At the time I figured he was jumping the gun but..." He turned his head and spoke to the constable. "See that this is typed up and ready for the chaps from Central Bureau. Thank you, Mr. Forsythe; you've been most helpful."

Forsythe picked up his canes. "Any objection if we wait in our bedrooms, Inspector?"

"Probably be a good idea. Shouldn't imagine the family is very welcoming now that they know why you came here."

"Pariahs," Miss Sanderson muttered again. Forsythe asked, "Isn't it irregular to send a relative of the deceased to head an investigation?"

"Highly." Davis chuckled. "But, according to Colonel Blake, the chief inspector threatened to resign if he wasn't allowed to come." Sobering, he patted his sizable paunch. "Not a sound idea. Too close to the deceased to think clearly."

"Would you mind giving us a few details about Mr. Penndragon's death?"

Davis silently debated and then said slowly, "I see no harm in it. Chief Inspector Kepesake will tell you anyway. Haven't much yet, Mr. Forsythe. Medical examiner puts time of death shortly after one A.M. Be able to pin it down better when he gets the autopsy done. Cause of death—blows to the head with a silver figurine."

"The Cellini cherub," Miss Sanderson said softly. "Which one?"

"Huh? Oh, one on the right side of the bed. The one kind of kneeling. Murderer left it propped up on the dead man's chest. Macabre touch."

Forsythe frowned. "Blows. Any idea of how many blows?"

"Quite a number. Smashed his head and face in. Dr. Hawes says it was overkill. With an object that heavy, one blow would have done it. No sign of a struggle. Body was tucked up and even the pillows weren't disarranged. Must have been sound asleep."

"Any fingerprints on the cherub?"

"Smudges. A surface like that doesn't take clear ones. And the killer could have worn gloves."

"There would have been a great quantity of blood."

"Lab boys are checking that now. Going through the bedrooms and so on. That's why we're keeping the household in the morning room. Of course, the killer could have had time to get rid of bloodstained clothes. Anything else, Mr. Forsythe?"

Forsythe said there wasn't and thanked him. As they moved down the hall, they met Bunny trailed by a constable. He averted his face as they passed him, but his mother, posted in the doorway of the morning room, waved jauntily and held something up.

Miss Sanderson pushed back the grill. "Knitting needles?"

"The other sock—a challenge."

"Blimey! Adam is going to tear our hides off."

"Mine, Sandy. And this time with some reason. His godfather was battered to death with me right in the house."

At his secretary's insistence, he lay down on his bed. He had thought he couldn't rest, but fell immediately into a deep sleep. When Miss Sanderson woke him, the room was shadowed and wind still gusted against the windows. Pushing himself up on an elbow, he switched on the bed lamp. Before he could ask, she said, "Nearly six. I went down to the kitchen and loaded a tray."

He swung his legs over the side of the bed. "I'm not hungry."

"Eat. You're going to need strength."

"I take it the Yard has arrived."

"Full contingent." She waved at a window. "I've been posted there. Adam and Beau and two uniforms. One of the uniforms looks familiar—that nice-looking chap from Adam's office."

"P. C. Helm." Forsythe bit into a sandwich. He chewed, swallowed, and said, "Maybe he'll leave us to last."

"And there are snowballs in hell. He'll want us first."

She was partially right. The summons arrived by Helm, looking solemn and distinctly nervous. But when Miss Sanderson tried to accompany the barrister, the young man shook his head. "Only Mr. Forsythe for now, Miss Sanderson."

Forsythe gave her a wintry smile. "Don't look downcast, Sandy. Your turn will come."

On the way down to the library, P. C. Helm spoke only once. "The chief inspector's pretty upset, sir."

What he means, Forsythe thought, is brace yourself, you're about to catch hell. Helm ushered him into the library, stepped in, and braced his wide shoulders against the door. Every lamp blazed and the light pitilessly exposed Kepesake's face. Lines were graven in that face that the barrister had never noticed before; the eyes were rimmed with red, the mouth set in a tight line. Even Kepesake's stance had altered. Generally he lounged back, his jade holder clasped between long fingers, smoke wreathing his head. Now he sat erect, his shoulders squared. No smoke drifted through the room and the cigarette holder wasn't in sight. Close beside him was Sergeant Brummell, and another, older constable sat at a side table, a notebook spread before him. On the blotter in front of Kepesake was a stack of typewritten pages, the edges neatly aligned.

The chief inspector started mildly enough with an inquiry about Forsythe's leg and an invitation to be seated. Then he brought his fist down sharply. "So that was my godfather's problem. Two attempts on his life! And I sent him to *you*. You stood by and let him be butchered!"

"Chief!" Brummell protested.

"No." Forsythe propped his canes against the desk. "Let him get it off his chest."

Kepesake's shoulders sagged and he fumbled in a pocket and pulled out the jade holder. "He gave me this. For a birthday. He gave me so much. Not only gifts. When I was a boy and visiting this house, he'd tell Bunny and me stories by the hour—where he'd been, what he'd done. To us he wasn't a man; he was a…a god. Larger than life, fearless…"

"I'm sorry, Adam," Forsythe said gently. "Sorry I couldn't save him." He touched his cast. "Helpless to protect him. But I tried—"

"I know. It's in your statement. I know you did all you could."

"He wouldn't leave here. He refused to listen."

"He couldn't. It wasn't in him." Pulling out a cigarette case, Kepesake inserted a white tube into his godfather's present.

Brummell leaned forward with a lighter and Kepesake said brokenly, "At first I couldn't believe it. Couldn't picture him dead. Do you agree with the abolishment of the death penalty?"

Forsythe hesitated and then said, "Most of the time. Once in a while…"

"I'd like it reinstated. When I find the…the person who did this, I want him or her executed. I want him drawn and quartered. By God! I'm willing to do it myself."

"Chief," Brummell said again, "the superintendent was right. You shouldn't have come."

"It's the last thing I can do for him." Kepesake made a visible effort for control. "One shock after another. That statement of yours. I had no idea my godfather had fathered children—"

"No one did. Including two of those children."

"I didn't know he played around with teenage girls. It…it *tarnishes* him."

"That shouldn't diminish the man—his courage, his life, his accomplishments. Sandy says quite rightly that Winslow Maxwell Penndragon can't be judged by ordinary standards."

After a time, Kepesake nodded. "She put it well." He glanced at the constable seated at the side table, pencil flying over the notebook. "Krimshaw! Don't be a bloody fool. Tear that up!"

Krimshaw flushed scarlet and hastened to obey. Brummell eyed him and said mildly, "I'll tell you when to start, Krimshaw." His bright blue eyes turned with open appeal to the barrister. "I've been trying to persuade the chief to let me take care of the household, leastways the ones he's close to."

"It's a sound idea," Forsythe approved.

Kepesake nibbled at his lower lip. "It will be awkward with Bunny and Aunt Grace. Bunny…well, we've grown apart, but when we were boys, we were close as most brothers. And I'm fond of Aunt Grace. She may act strange at times, but she's a kind woman. Always had sweets for us in her bag."

"A string bag?"

"No, then she had a cloth bag. Shabby affair, always bulging with odds and ends." Kepesake smiled slightly. "Quite a woman. She nearly drove Uncle Winslow mad at times." He added, "Aunt Grace will miss him."

Forsythe started. Then he thought that perhaps Kepesake might be right. After the excitement of her brother-in-law's murder had died down, Grace might well miss him. For forty years her spice of life had been annoying him. Old habits die hard.

Kepesake was staring off into space and Brummell was anxiously watching him. "Chief?"

Dragging himself to his feet, Kepesake tucked his holder in a vest pocket, and tried to smile. "I'll take your advice. I'm exhausted. You start the interviews, Beau. I'll be on deck in the morning."

"Helm," Brummell ordered, "find out which room the chief's been given."

The constable turned to obey, but Kepesake stopped him. "Same room I always have at Penndragon. Beside Bunny's. Beau, you'll be quartered in the one next to mine." On the threshold, he paused. "Robert." It was seldom he used the barrister's given name. "You'll help us, won't you?"

"Do you need to ask?"

"No."

Brummell watched the chief inspector leave and then he moved into the big chair just vacated. "After a night's sleep, the chief will be fine, Mr. Forsythe. He's badly shaken, that's all."

"Quite understandable," Forsythe agreed.

The sergeant riffled through the sheets on the blotter. "Any suggestion on who to start with?"

"You want me to sit in?"

"The chief asked for your help, sir, and so do I. Stay and ask any questions you want to."

"In that case, I suggest you have Mrs. Grace Penndragon in. As Sandy says, get the worst over first."

"Hard lady to get talking?"

"Hard lady to stop. A word of warning—don't let her clothes or eccentric behavior mislead you."

Glancing down at his rumpled suit, Brummell grinned. "Don't judge a book by its cover, eh? Helm, snap to it and bring in Mrs. Penndragon." He turned to look at the other constable. "As for you, Krimshaw, start your shorthand as soon as she opens her mouth. And if you're hot for a promotion, *never* do that again."

Krimshaw flushed again and his chin jutted. "Thought I was supposed to get it all down, Sergeant."

"Not when the chief's talking off the cuff." He got to his feet. "Mrs. Penndragon, please be seated. I'm Sergeant Brummell—"

"I know who you are. Asked your name when you arrived." She sat down and smiled broadly. "Saw Adam going upstairs. Well, if you can't stand the heat, you shouldn't go into the kitchen."

It was Brummell's turn to redden. His mouth snapped open, but she was still talking. "Can't really blame the boy. Winslow filled his head with the same rubbish he did Bunny's. Boy's wasting his time grieving."

Giving Forsythe a wicked grin, Grace reached into her bag and took out steel knitting needles and a ball of emerald wool. Expertly, she began casting on stitches. "Little job I have to do, Sergeant. Don't fret. As Mr. Forsythe will tell you I can handle two things at one time. Now, on with the inquisition. I gave vital statistics to Inspector Davis. Want them again?"

"For the record, Mrs.—"

"Name, Grace Lillian Penndragon née Atkins. Age, seventy-one. Relation to deceased, sister-in-law, widow of Gerald Richard Penndragon. Length of residence in this house, forty years. Reaction to Winslow's death—immense satisfaction." She paused to watch Krimshaw's flying pencil and added, "No sense in asking whether I killed him. If I say no, you'll think I'm lying. Yes, and you'll think me mad. Carry on, Sergeant."

Valiantly, Brummell tried to carry on. "About the first attempt on Mr. Penndragon's life. Where—"

"Sound asleep in my bed. I'm not an early riser. Can't prove it." She bestowed her wicked grin on the sergeant. "Of course,

I could have snuck down the back stairs, out the rear door, and diddled the brakes of the Bentley."

Brummell held out a sketch. "Could you point out the location of your bedroom?"

A needle tapped. "Here, beside the rear staircase, next to my son's—east wing. Same wing Mr. Forsythe and his secretary are in. Adam's room is next to Bunny's and you'll be here, Sergeant. My niece and nephews are in the west wing." The needle rose and stabbed at the younger constable. "You'll be in the servants' quarters. Better watch out for the pretty maid. Dolly is a looker and likes men, and you're a strapping lad."

Helm blushed to the roots of his fair hair and Forsythe said, "You mentioned that you're a late riser and yet for the last couple of mornings, you've been up before I was."

"That's because life started getting interesting. No sense in staying in bed when things are happening." Her glasses swung on Brummell. "Second attempt—I was on the same bench as Winslow, watching the tennis match. Not beside him. Never got too close to my brother-in-law. Evans was sitting between us."

Running a hand through his unruly hair, Brummell made another attempt. "If you'll give us a rundown on your movements—"

"—last night. Right." The needles flew and so did her tongue. "Linda Evans cooked dinner and everyone stayed at the table for pudding and coffee. Dolly and Evans served. We were five. My niece, my nephews, and Linda Evans. Jason and Hobbs left the dining room first—"

"Mr. Leslie Hobbs and Mr. Jason Cooper?"

"Right. The blithering idiot and the Sphinx. Said something about a game of billiards. Soon after, Linda left. Susan stayed on and we had a second cup of coffee. I had brandy too, but she never touches alcohol. Afterward—"

"Do you know the time you left the dining room?"

For the first time since she'd entered the room she hesitated. "Dinner was served at eight. It had to be after nine. I'm not certain how long."

Looking rather pleased at her hesitancy, Brummell asked, "Did you and Miss Vandervoort stay together?"

"For a time. We went directly to the morning room. I like that room and spend most of my time there. I was working on a puzzle and Susan went to the drawing room and brought back a book—Shakespeare. I'm rather knowledgeable on the Bard and we exchanged quotations. Susan's were rather morbid. She frets about her father—actually he's her stepfather—and after a time, I suggested she might better ring up the nursing home the old gentleman's in. She left and when she didn't return, I thought, poor child, the news couldn't have been good. I worked at my puzzle for a while and then I got bored and decided on bed—"

"Time?" Brummell asked.

"Before I left the room, I glanced at the mantel clock. It was eleven minutes after ten. I generally use the rear stairs, so I wandered down the hall toward them and met Evans and Hobbs. Evans was walking, but Hobbs was in a hurry. I'm curious, Sergeant, like to know what's going on. So I stopped Evans and asked what Hobbs' rush was. Evans said a call from his accountant in London had come in for him. I thought, more bad news, and then I went to bed."

"Directly?"

"Fast as I could." She held up a hand. "No, I heard nothing during the night. I'm a sound sleeper and I take this thing off when I retire." A needle flipped at the cord of her hearing aid. "Anything else?"

Brummell assured her there wasn't and thanked her.

Grinning at the barrister, Grace waved her knitting needles. An inch of sock dangled. She said jovially, "Our wager's still on."

As Helm closed the door behind her, Brummell asked, "What was *that* about?"

Forsythe told him and the sergeant shook a gloomy head. "Is her son anything like her?"

The barrister grinned. "Have him in and find out."

"Helm," the sergeant ordered. "Ask Mr. Winslow Penndragon to step in."

Chapter Ten

Bunny Penndragon proved as impassive as his cousin Jason and about as talkative. Ignoring the barrister, he gave his name, age, and relationship to the deceased in an unemotional voice.

The sergeant shuffled papers. "Would you be good enough to fill us in on your movements while your uncle breakfasted before the accident with his car."

As his uncle sat down, Bunny said that he'd left the table and had gone to his office in the tower. He put the papers his uncle required in a briefcase, took the case down to the entrance hall, and left it on the table there. Brummell selected a sketch and held it out. "I notice that from the windows in your office there's a clear view of the driveway directly in front of the main door. Did you notice the Bentley parked there?"

"I didn't go near either window. I was in a bit of a rush to get my uncle's papers ready. He hated to be kept waiting."

"And after you left his briefcase in the hall?"

"I went back to my office. I was typing the second chapter of his latest book, and he expected it to be done when he returned from Coventry."

"Were you surprised to hear of the accident?"

"Concerned about him, yes, but not surprised." Bunny smiled faintly. "There was a long-standing family joke about his driving ability. Uncle Winslow used to laugh about it himself. Said it was strange that such a superb pilot couldn't handle a car."

"You knew nothing about the previous murder attempts, sir?"

The young man glanced at Forsythe and then quickly away. "Not until my mother blurted it out this morning."

"Could you give us your movements last evening?"

"Mr. Forsythe has probably told you about the early part of the evening. I left the tower at twenty-six minutes after nine—"

"You're precise."

"Anyone dealing with my uncle had to be. When he asked me to return in an hour, he meant sixty minutes. I wandered down the hall, heard voices from the billiard room, and went in. Jason and Leslie were having a game. They're both good players and evenly matched, so I hung around and watched. They had some beer and I took a glass.

"Leslie won the game and Jason insisted on a rematch. At eight minutes past ten, Evans came in and told Leslie there was a call for him from London. Leslie hurried out and I stayed chatting with Jason until ten twenty-four. Then I returned to the tower. Mr. Forsythe and Miss Sanderson had left and Uncle Winslow was still in the lounge having a brandy. He gave instructions on a telephone call that I was to make to his editor and details on a couple of letters. When it was all clear, I said goodnight and left the lounge."

"And the tower?"

"No. I hadn't reached the doors that lead into the main house when my uncle called me back. He was in the central hall—"

"One moment." Brummell consulted another sketch. "That's where the spiral staircase is. Yes, go on."

The younger Penndragon had been speaking rapidly, but now he hesitated, cast a sidelong look at Forsythe, and said slowly, "The conversation we had has no bearing on this investigation."

Folding his hands over his stomach, Brummell said stolidly, "Let us be the judge of that, sir."

"It concerned Miss Vandervoort. My uncle asked me what my intentions were toward his daughter. Sounded like a line from one of those old melodramas and I was taken back, but I told him the truth."

Bunny was hesitating again but Brummell didn't prod. After a few moments, the young man spoke. "I'm in love with Miss Vandervoort and I've proposed to her. Uncle Winslow asked whether she had accepted and I said she hadn't said yes, but then again she hadn't said no. He asked for details and I told him Susan—Miss Vandervoort—had told me that we hadn't known each other long enough to consider anything as serious as marriage. She also said she was too upset about her father's— her stepfather's—illness to think clearly."

"What was your uncle's reaction?" Forsythe asked.

Bunny didn't look away from the policeman and he did answer. "He was enraged. He told me I was a fool and to stay away from his daughter and to give up any idea of marrying her. I thought he must be joking and I…I'm afraid I laughed. Then he got really ugly. He said if I disobeyed, I could leave his house and he'd change his will and disinherit me. He said he would prevent our marriage no matter what steps he had to take."

"Did you lose your temper?" Brummell asked.

"Not at that point. I was stunned. My uncle had always been like a father to me and never in my life had he spoken to me like that. I asked him his reason and he said he'd his own plans for Susan and I had no part in them. Then I did become angry. I told him I was over forty and I would do as I damn well pleased. He gave me my notice—"

"Just like that?" the barrister asked.

This time Bunny's doggy eyes turned directly on Forsythe. "Just like that. Two weeks and I was to be out. Then he topped it by telling me I could take my 'insane mother' with me. That tore it and I fired back. I said all the things one says at a time like that. Told him neither Mother nor I had been charity cases, that I'd earned every penny for our support. It went on and on…accusations and counteraccusations."

"There were no witnesses to this?" Brummell asked.

"No. Well, there could have been one. While we were in the lounge, Evans had come in and Uncle gave him instructions—the usual, laying out clothes for the next day, drawing a bath, checking for clothes to be cleaned. While we were arguing, Evans was on the floor above."

"Could he have heard you?"

Bunny shrugged. "He might have caught some of it. We were speaking loudly, at times shouting. And the stairwell acts rather like a sound tunnel." His eyes were still fixed on the barrister. "Evans was the one who put a stop to our argument. He came down the steps carrying a couple of suits and a vest, and Uncle controlled himself and looked them over. He told Evans to have them cleaned and then he dismissed me. He said, 'That will be all' as though I was a servant, and I turned on my heel and followed Evans out."

"And then?" Brummell prompted.

"Another scene followed." Bunny's lips twisted and he looked even sadder than usual. "My cousin was waiting in the entrance hall of the main house and—"

"Which cousin?"

"Leslie Hobbs. He was as upset as I was. Said he must speak to his father at once. I tried to stop him, but he pushed past me and ran down the hall to the central core of the tower. My uncle was going up the stairs and he turned around." Bunny shook his head. "He was as brutal and ruthless with the poor chap as he'd been with me. Leslie tried to tell him about a call he'd just received from his accountant and Uncle cut him right off. Told Leslie no one ever entered his quarters without an invitation. He said Leslie would never be his heir." Bowing his head, Bunny looked down at his big hands. "Uncle told Leslie he would not give him any further financial help and he hoped…he hoped Leslie would lose his restaurant and everything else he valued. Then he ordered us out."

"And you went."

"We did. Leslie was thunderstruck and I had to take his arm and pull him back into the entrance hall. He tripped over Skelter, one of my dogs, and she nipped at him. The poor devil was in tears. I tried to console him, telling him to wait and catch his father in a better mood, that maybe he would reconsider."

Forsythe leaned forward. "Do you think he would have?"

"No."

"About you?"

"Uncle never changed his mind about anything. He meant every word he said to both of us."

The sergeant rustled papers. "What did you do then?"

"I went upstairs."

"To your room?"

"To the west wing and Susan." Bunny gave a twisted grin. "To pour out my woes. She had ample of her own. She'd rung through to check on her father and his condition had worsened. I begged her to leave this house with me and we'd both go to him, but she said she couldn't. She said Winslow Penndragon had bought a month and she knew he wouldn't release her from her promise. I blurted out…I proposed again and she repeated what she'd said before. Then I tried to embrace her—"

"Tried?" Forsythe asked.

"Susan doesn't seem…she doesn't like being touched. She was gentle and kind, but she said there was probably nothing for us and I should try to make it up with my uncle. I told her it was too late for that and then we said goodnight. I went to the east wing and to bed. I thought I wouldn't sleep, but I must have been exhausted. I fell into a deep sleep and…that covers it."

The barrister had been stuffing tobacco into the bowl of his pipe. Striking a match, he said, "Yet this morning you returned to the tower and your daily routine."

"I was forced to. Uncle had given me two weeks' notice and, frankly, I needed the salary. I've no savings and with Mother to provide for…"

Sergeant Brummell said briskly, "Tell us exactly what happened this morning."

"I followed my usual routine. At seven-thirty, I was at my desk. I opened some of the mail, took my uncle's personal letters and put them on the desk in his office, and then went down to the kitchen on the ground floor. At eight, I took a tray with tea and a roll up to his bedroom—"

"You did this every morning, sir?"

"Unless I was told otherwise. I found him and—"

"No need to go through that again, sir." Opening a folder, Brummell took out several glossy prints and handed them to Forsythe.

He studied them. They were taken from different angles, but all showed Winslow Penndragon's baroque bed and its grisly burden. The only way he could identify the face on the blood-soaked pillow was by the mane of silvery hair. Both arms were folded over the duvet and one hand touched the Cellini cherub. The innocent beauty of that little figure made the crushed and battered head almost unbearable. Forsythe's brow wrinkled. "Bunny, these papers and the folder on the bed—scattered all over the duvet—know anything about them?"

Bunny rubbed at his own brow. "They were reports on a couple of companies that Uncle was thinking of buying stock in. There were two folders. Stock quotations, graphs, management, that sort of thing. You'll notice one of the folders on the bed table. The other was just thrown around on the bed. Before you and Miss Sanderson arrived for dinner last evening, Uncle told me to put them in a drawer in his bedroom."

"Was Winslow in the habit of taking work to bed with him?"

"He did often. He didn't sleep soundly or for long. He said he liked to keep busy."

"Could he have dozed off while he was reading them?"

"I doubt it. He never had before. Every morning the work that he'd been looking over was always placed neatly on the bed table. Uncle Winslow was meticulous and loathed disorder."

Forsythe continued studying the prints while Brummell asked more questions. "Mr. Penndragon, are you your uncle's principal heir?"

"I am."

"He couldn't have changed his will without your knowledge?"

"No, he would have had me ring up his solicitor."

"Even if he was cutting you out of it?"

"Particularly if he was."

"It's a sizable estate?"

"Yes. Investments, property, book royalties, a recent contract for the film rights on his first book."

Momentarily the sergeant was diverted. "Will they be using the original title?"

"I believe so."

Brummell seemed to be mulling over a film entitled *How to Enjoy the Art of Dilettantism*. Bunny shifted restlessly and Brummell said, "That will be all for now, sir. Thank you for your cooperation."

Pulling himself up, Bunny wearily moved out of the room. Forsythe piled up the prints and placed them on a corner of the desk. He muttered, "'Then felt I like some watcher of the skies/ When a new planet swims into his ken.'"

"What's that supposed to mean?"

"Discovery, Sergeant. A belated discovery by Bunny Penndragon that his idol wasn't perfect."

Brummell's snort was similar to Miss Sanderson's. "None of us are."

"Ah, but we don't try to give the impression of perfection. Winslow did. After forty years, his nephew finally saw him for what he was."

"Pretty heartless at that." Brummell darted a keen look at the younger man. "What do you suppose his plans were for his daughter?"

"Well, he was planning a clean sweep. With Grace and Bunny and Leslie Hobbs out of his life, there was only Jason

Cooper left. And Penndragon was aware Jason would leave as soon as he could." Templing his long fingers, Forsythe gazed at them. "He wanted Susan Vandervoort all to himself—a vassal."

"The day he came to see the chief…Mr. Penndragon boasted that he always got what he wanted. If he'd lived, do you think he would have gotten Miss Vandervoort?"

Forsythe's answer was a shrug and Brummell called to the constable at the door. "Leslie Hobbs now, lad." He grinned at the barrister. "Better sit up and take notice."

"You have information on Hobbs?"

"A nice lot."

"This sounds rather fast, Beau. You only came on the case this morning."

"This is rather a special case. Inspector Davis, who's sharp, told the chief he thought Mr. Hobbs was hiding something and every available officer was turned loose on checking out his background. Shortly after we got here the report was phoned in. With that and what Inspector Davis discovered at the inn in the village…well, we have some ammunition to fire at Mr. Leslie Hobbs."

The sergeant held his ammunition in reserve. His approach to Leslie was slow paced and mild voiced. Forsythe watched the man assessing his interviewer, noted Leslie's initial uneasiness change to disdain, and was vastly amused. He was making the same error many others had with Brummell, judging the sergeant by his clothing and supremely ordinary face, and neglecting the sharply intelligent eyes in that face.

Brummell had worked around to the morning of the second attempt on Penndragon's life. "You weren't with your father at the tennis court, Mr. Hobbs?"

"I'm not interested in the game." Leslie waited for the next question and when Brummell didn't speak, said, "I suppose you want to know where I was at that time. Sergeant, I'm going to be completely frank with you."

"Honesty is the best policy, sir." Brummell delivered the cliché guilelessly.

"I was in the tower." Leslie stared defiantly at the barrister. "*You* know how Daddy felt about his precious tower. One entered it only on his invitation. But I was curious…no, that's the wrong word. Meeting my father after thirty years and not really knowing what he was like…I thought if I could get a look at his quarters I would gain an understanding of him." Leslie's full lips drew into a pout. "And Daddy hadn't invited *me* to the tower. Susan dined with him and then Jason. Jason even played chess with him.

"That morning, I waited until Daddy had gone out to the garden and then, when I was certain the servants weren't in the tower, I slipped in." The pout disappeared and dark eyes glowed. "I'd only time for a quick look, but the *treasures*—paintings, collections of jade and china and antique silver—amazing!"

And all yours if you were to become his heir, Forsythe said silently. Brummell forged ahead. "Sir, kindly give us an account of your movements last night."

The memory of the treasures left Leslie's eyes. "A *terrible* evening. It started out not badly. For a change, dinner was palatable and afterward Jason and I played billiards. Jason *loves* games. I won the first game and Jason wanted to play another. Oh yes, Bunny joined us and watched and had some beer. We were setting up the table again when Evans came in and told me my accountant had rung up. I went to the nearest telephone, the one in the entrance hall, and met Aunt Grace wandering along the hall. She stopped Evans and I *knew* she would question him. Aunt Grace is incredibly nosy and I thought she might follow me and try to eavesdrop, but she didn't."

Perspiration was dewing Leslie's brow and he stopped to pull out a handkerchief and dab at it. Brummell was sitting back, his eyes half closed, looking as though he was dozing. Leslie rattled on. "Simply dreadful news. Floyd had been contacted by my bank manager—that man is *beastly*—and was told if I don't make payment on a loan in the next few days that the bank will take steps. *Steps.* They're going to foreclose on my restaurant!"

As though talking to himself, Leslie continued, "Everything I've worked for. My *life*. I knew there was only one hope—Daddy. But Bunny had said *you* were still with Daddy." He shot a hostile look in Forsythe's direction. "So I had to wait. I went back to the billiard room and tried to play. Jason became quite impatient with me because I couldn't keep my mind on the game. I tried to tell him about my problem, but he wasn't interested. I kept looking at my watch. Finally, I couldn't stand it any longer. I threw down my cue and *lunged* down the hall—"

"The time was?" Brummell asked sleepily.

"Exactly ten-fifty when I reached the entrance hall. Jason had said Cousin Bunny was going back to speak with Daddy, so I had to hang around for another ten minutes before Bunny came out. Evans was with him and he had some clothes over his arm. I grabbed Bunny's arm and told him that I *had* to see Daddy. He tried to stop me and I went simply *wild*. I thought if I could just get to Daddy, he'd help. *Help*. Let me tell you—"

"Your cousin already has. Now, Mr. Hobbs, after you spoke with your father…"

"After?" Leslie blinked. "Well, I simply couldn't stand being alone. Cousin Bunny was kind, but he seemed upset too. He advised that I wait until my father cooled down and also said if he could, he'd help me himself. And I *knew* he would. Bunny's the only person in this whole house who's been decent to me. He went upstairs and I went back to the billiard room. Jason had racked up the cues, covered the table, and was piling beer bottles and glasses on a tray. Jason is *so* neat—a real mama's boy. He carried the tray to the kitchen and I tagged along. Linda Evans was there, heating something on the stove. Jason was hungry and he took cold meat and things out of the refrigerator. I had coffee and had to *choke* it down. When Jason had eaten, we went up to our bedrooms."

Brummell stirred and slid a sketch over. "Kindly point out your room, sir."

"This one—in the west wing—down the hall from Jason. We said goodnight and I went along to my room. I couldn't settle down. I felt so alone. Not one of my relatives cared whether I was ruined."

"With the exception of Cousin Bunny," Forsythe pointed out.

Shooting an unpleasant look at him, Leslie turned back to the sergeant. "I don't mind police," he told that worthy, "but I simply despise *spies*. Coming here and pretending to be a friend and snooping!"

Brummell's eyes snapped open. "Mr. Forsythe is here at my request and you will consider him my colleague."

"In that case, I suppose I've no choice."

Forsythe hid a grin and said, "You were feeling alone in your room."

"I went back to Jason's door and knocked. He seemed grumpy and when I asked him for one of his sleeping capsules, he—"

"How did you know about those capsules?" the sergeant asked.

"I saw the bottle a couple of days after we'd arrived here. We were playing a game of billiards and Jason fumbled in his pocket for something and pulled out a bottle of yellow capsules. He said that after his mother's death, the doctor had more or less forced them on him. I asked him what they were for and when he said he was going to get rid of them, I advised him to hold onto them. Never know when something like that will come in handy."

Mopping at his damp brow, Leslie continued his grievances. "At first, Jason refused to let me have even one capsule. Said he didn't abide by drugs himself and didn't know how strong these were. Told me he doesn't believe people should pass around prescription drugs. I had to literally *beg* him before he opened the bottle and gave me one. I took it and…well, that's all."

"The sleeping capsule worked?" Brummell asked.

"Knocked me out like a light. This morning I felt pretty groggy, but it was worth it to get a good sleep."

Deciding the interview was concluded, Leslie took one last swipe at his brow, put his handkerchief away, and rose. Brummell waved him back. "Now, sir, if you'd tell me a bit about your restaurant." Leslie was only too eager to oblige. He was away in a flood of words about velvet and teak. Brummell shook his head. "Your staff, sir."

"Only the best, Sergeant. I'm like Daddy in that. The key positions are held by…well, André Marois is my chef. You may have heard the name. Widely known on the Continent…"

As Leslie chattered on, Brummell reached across the desk for a notebook. Flipping it open, he said, "You have a Spanish hostess and maître d'."

"Top notch. Lola Bianco and Cesar Guevarro. They—"

"They occupy the same flat, rather a lavish one."

"Nothing unusual about that, Sergeant, but in this case, not for the usual reasons. Cesar and Lola are cousins. And I do pay well."

"You're a frequent visitor to this flat, Mr. Hobbs."

"I am. Lola is my…I suppose you would say girl." Leslie considered and then added, "Mistress. If you could see her, you would understand. She's—"

"I haven't seen her, sir. But I understand Miss Bianco is a decorative young lady."

Leslie winked roguishly. "And a hot-blooded one, hot Spanish blood."

The sergeant didn't see the wink. He was consulting his notebook. "You give expensive gifts, Mr. Hobbs."

"With a beautiful creature like Lola, one must."

"What would a young lady like Miss Bianco want with a man's Rolex watch, expensive men's clothing—"

"I do buy a *few* things for myself."

Looking pointedly at the Patek on Leslie's plump wrist, the sergeant murmured, "Suits much too large for you. And—"

"This is none of *your* business." Leslie's upper lip now hung with drops of moisture.

The bright blue eyes snapped to the younger man's wet face. "In a case of this gravity, everything is *our* business. Another costly gift is a medallion, set with ruby and diamond chips forming the initials CG. Engraved on the reverse— 'Leslie, with undying love.'"

Leslie looked as though he were melting away. Perspiration streamed down pudgy cheeks and his lips were quivering. Finally, he groaned. "All right, Sergeant. Lola only fronts for Cesar and me."

"Even the staff at your restaurant believes that Lola is your mistress. Why the secrecy?"

"You think I'm going to run around shouting, 'I'm gay and my maître d' is my lover'?"

"I see no harm in that. Society is most permissive now."

His head drooped and a bead of water fell unheeded from his nose. "Daddy."

"You thought your father would disapprove?"

"I knew he would. Mother used to say, 'Do what you want, but for God's sake do it *quietly*. Winslow would never stand for a son like *you*.'" He mopped his face off and then declared, "What am I so upset about? It makes no difference now. Daddy is dead. And *why* in hell should you care?"

"Your sexual preference is not my concern, Mr. Hobbs, but there happens to be a guest registered at the inn in the village— a young Spanish gentleman named Cesar Guevarro."

"I brought him down with me and dropped him off at the inn."

"You've visited him there?"

"As often as I could make an excuse to leave this house. Try to understand my position. I was coming to strangers and I'm *very* sensitive. I needed Cesar's support. Sergeant, we're in love. If it had been Lola, you wouldn't be so…so censorious."

"I'm not censorious, Mr. Hobbs; I'm merely doing my duty. I understand it's possible to take a shortcut from the inn to this property. There's a footbridge and rather a steep climb, but it would take only twenty minutes to reach this house and—"

"No!" Leslie was on his feet. He shoved his chair with such force that it teetered. Helm moved up behind him, but Brummell waved the constable back. "You're trying to frame us! You're saying Cesar fixed those brakes while I breakfasted with my—No!"

"Mr. Hobbs," the sergeant said mildly. "Get a grip on yourself."

"Motive? What possible motive could we have? Daddy was our last hope to save the restaurant."

"Your cousin seems sympathetic and he's your father's heir."

"Bunny?" Leslie lurched and grasped at the back of the chair. "I can't take any more. Can I...please let me leave."

"By all means, Mr. Hobbs."

Leslie stumbled toward the door and then turned. "I can't stay on in this house. Can I go down to the inn and Cesar?"

Brummell gave this some thought and then said genially, "I see no reason to keep you here. Helm, ask either Atkins or Richards to escort Mr. Hobbs to the inn. And, Mr. Hobbs, do stay put."

"I will," Leslie promised, and followed Helm into the hall.

Forsythe grinned. "You know how to fire ammunition, Beau, and you were also most understanding with Leslie."

"Understanding but not foolish. A couple of Inspector Davis' boys are keeping an eye on Mr. Guevarro, and they can do the same with Mr. Hobbs." He glanced at his watch, a cheap one, not a Rolex or Patek. "Care for coffee?"

The barrister admitted it would hit the spot and when Helm returned, the sergeant sent him to rustle up coffee and biscuits. "On your way back, lad, ask Mr. Cooper to step in."

Helm shuffled his feet. "Sergeant..."

"Yes?"

"When I went for Mr. Hobbs, the young lady was looking pretty fagged. Like a ghost she was."

"In that case, bring Miss Vandervoort and better tell Mr. Cooper we won't need him until morning." Brummell grinned. "Mr. Forsythe, the age of chivalry is still lingering."

"With Miss Vandervoort, that ghostly appearance is not unusual."

"Good-looking girl, though. Any ideas stirring?"

"Early on, but yes—a few. You built a rather strong case against Leslie and the young Spaniard."

"In court, you'd be the first one to call it circumstantial." On blunt fingers, the sergeant rapidly ticked off points. "Mr. Guevarro made no effort to hide his identity, registered at the inn under his own name. The person who loosened that brake connection must have had some idea where the members of the household were. The gardener might have wandered around to the front of the house; someone could have looked out of a window or even come out. Seems foolhardy for a stranger to sneak onto the grounds and do it."

"True." Forsythe stroked his chin. "Winslow's bedclothes bother me—too neat. Beau, if a person was standing over you holding a blunt object and intent on murder, just what would you do?"

"Either jump up and grapple with him or roll to the other side of the bed. But Mr. Penndragon could have been attacked in his sleep."

"That doesn't square with what his nephew told us about Winslow's habits. And then, there's the murder weapon, the silver cherub. That bothers me too. It's such an awkward shape. Think how it would have to be held."

Swiveling his chair, Brummell looked searchingly at his companion. "It was handy, right beside the bed on a pedestal."

"Granted. But also in easy reach is a bookcase. If I remember correctly, it's used to display a silver collection. On the top is a pair of Georgian candlesticks—much easier objects to hold and swing."

While the sergeant was mulling this over, the door creaked open and Helm, wearing a smile and carrying a tray, solicitously ushered in Susan Vandervoort. Brummell gallantly seated her and hovered for a moment over her chair. Helm had been right. Susan was chalky and her dove gray eyes were deeply circled with dark shadows. Hollows showed under her cheekbones that Forsythe hadn't previously noticed.

Refusing coffee, she sat back, slender fingers fiddling with a gold chain belt. In a flat disinterested voice, she answered the preliminary questions. Brummell moved on to the attacks on the dilettante. "You breakfasted with your father on the morning of the car accident."

"Yes."

"And at the gardening shed, you called to him and saved his life."

"At the time, I had no idea I was saving his life. I simply wanted to call his attention to a clump of early blooming flowers."

"Didn't that whole affair strike you as strange?"

"Winnie explained that he'd asked the gardener to move the statue to make more room on the floor and quote 'The old fool had stuck it over the door' unquote. Winnie was so angry that I thought he'd probably discharge the poor old fellow."

"It's late, Miss Vandervoort, so we'll move on as quickly as we can. Tell me about last evening."

Susan told them much the same story as Grace Penndragon had. "I was thinking of phoning my father's nursing home and when Grace mentioned it, I decided to do it immediately. For privacy, I came here." She pointed to the telephone on the desk. "I was told my father's condition was deteriorating and the doctor only gives him a few more days." The girl's expression didn't change, but her fingers jerked at the gold links. "I had to be alone, so I went up to my room."

"You didn't consider appealing to Mr. Penndragon?"

A faint, ironic smile twitched at her pale lips. "Not for a moment, Sergeant."

"Why not?"

"Winnie was not a compassionate man. He'd paid for a month of my time and I knew he'd demand his pound of flesh."

"If you felt that way about him, why did you come here?"

"For five thousand pounds. I had to have the money to keep father in the home. He gets the best of care there."

Brummell nodded. "And once in your room?"

"I paced for a while and then got ready for bed."

"You had a visitor?"

"Bunny Penndragon—for only a few moments. I take it he's told you about it." Brummell nodded again. "I felt sorry for him. He's been kind to me and so has his mother. It took me only a short time to see what Winnie was, but after forty years, it was a terrible blow to my cousin. Bunny was shattered."

"You refused to leave this house when he suggested it."

"I'd made a promise and I keep promises."

"How do you feel about your cousin?"

"That is *my* business. Your business is my movements last night. After Bunny left, I went to bed."

"Did you see or hear anything further?"

Her fine brows drew together in thought. "I saw nothing, but I did hear a few things. Nothing that could help you."

"Tell me anyway."

"Bunny had left my door slightly ajar and I hadn't noticed this until my half-brothers came up. I was dozing, but their voices woke me. Jason's voice is deep and I couldn't hear what he said, but Leslie has a penetrating voice and I heard his every word. They said goodnight and then Jason's door closed—his room is across from mine. A few moments later so did Leslie's further down the hall. I was settling down again when a door banged open and someone started pounding. It was Leslie at Jason's door. He was demanding a sleeping capsule and even though I couldn't make out the words, I could tell Jason didn't want to give him one. I felt like shouting, 'For God's sake, let him have one so that we can *all* get some sleep.'"

"You don't care for Mr. Hobbs?"

A smile twitched at her lips again. "Grace has him pegged when she calls him a blithering idiot."

"Your feelings for Mr. Cooper?"

"At least he's quiet."

"Rather an odd reaction."

"Sergeant, try to put yourself in my place. Suddenly a father and aunt, a cousin, and two half-brothers are sprung on one—some bearable and others—people you wouldn't bother with if you'd casually met them. And don't lecture about blood being thicker than water. A trite expression and I've no idea *what* it means."

"You have a point, Miss Vandervoort. After that interruption, did you go to sleep?"

"For a time. I should have gotten up and closed the door because I was roused again, this time by running water. It sounded like the shower in the bath. I thought, that blithering ass doesn't care whom he wakes up."

"That was all?"

"Yes."

Reaching out, Brummell poured coffee for the barrister and then himself. Forsythe quietly asked, "Miss Vandervoort, have you any ideas concerning the murder of Mr. Penndragon?"

"None. To be brutally frank, I don't care. All I care about—" She appealed to the sergeant. "I must go to my father. He shouldn't...I can't let him die alone."

"I understand, miss."

"You've let Leslie leave. He stopped to tell Jason and me he was going."

"Only as far as the inn in the village. I haven't authority to let you return to London. But in the morning, I'll have a word with Chief Inspector Kepesake. I can't promise, but—"

"I'd appreciate it, Sergeant." She rose and bestowed a smile on him. This was no quick twitch, but Winslow Penndragon's brilliant, charming smile. She left the room with her father's lithe grace. Blood may not be thicker than water, Forsythe mused, but occasionally genes come through virtually intact.

"A troubled lady," Brummell muttered. "I'll speak to the chief."

"Sergeant." Ready color flooded into Helm's face. "I'd be willing to escort Miss Vandervoort to London."

"I'll bet you would, lad." Tilting back his chair, Brummell stretched his stocky frame. "That's all for tonight, Mr. Forsythe. We'll leave Mr. Cooper and the servants for the chief. No, not you, Krimshaw. Sit down and get to work. Get those notes typed up for the chief. Don't look glum, lad; you'll have help. Helm will give you a hand." He grinned at the good-looking constable. "Pretend Krimshaw is another maiden in distress. And, speaking of maidens, a word to the wise. Helm, that pretty maid bunking on the same floor as you happens to be sixteen."

"She looks older."

"Most girls do these days, but hands off."

"Miss Vandervoort has her outclassed, Sergeant."

"That's enough, Helm! Now, Mr. Forsythe, if you could point out my room."

They took the lift to the next floor and Brummell adjusted his steps to his companion's halting gait. Forsythe lifted a cane and pointed. "The last door is Grace's. The next is Bunny's and that will be Adam's. You're directly opposite." He swung open the door and found a switch. Jewel lights sprang up from shaded lamps.

Brummell gazed around. "My! Sure wish the wife could see *this*. Talk about how the other half lives. Funny, this is the first time I've ever stayed overnight in a house where we're investigating a crime."

"You may consider yourself fortunate, Beau. I've spent too many nights wondering whether a murderer is bunking in the next room. Little chilly fingers tracing a path up and down one's spine."

"I'd rather have stayed down at the inn. Think I'll lock the door. Goodnight, Mr. Forsythe."

Forsythe locked his own door, switched on the bathroom light, and hobbled across to his secretary's room. As he snapped the lock on her door, she called, "Who goes?"

"A burglar, Sandy."

Pushing up on an elbow, she switched on the bed lamp. Her head was a mass of plastic rollers bound in green chiffon.

Under this bright helmet, her face looked longer and thinner. Blinking, she patted the duvet. "Sit, burglar, and tell all."

"Your thirst for gory details will have to wait. I'm beat, bushed, and completely bewildered and I'm off to bed."

"I will *not* be ignored like this. I'll get into the library tomorrow even if I must disguise myself as one of the suspects. Grace, I think. Turn out a ragbag and I'll be her doppelgänger."

Chapter Eleven

The following morning, Forsythe was up, bathed, dressed, and on his way downstairs before his secretary stirred. It was shortly before seven and he didn't expect to see any of the household, but as he stepped out of the lift, Jason Cooper flung open the front door and came in. He wore a fawn raincoat and his dark hair and shoulders were drenched. Forsythe wondered what his reaction would be to the spy in their midst, but Jason was the same as usual. Flicking raindrops from his hair, he commented, "That wind has blown in a full-scale storm."

"Nasty morning for a walk."

"Have to have exercise no matter what the weather is like."

Jason brushed past Forsythe and headed toward the morning room. At a slower pace, Forsythe followed. He expected to find Brummell and the constables in the library, but a solitary figure was seated behind the desk, sleek head bent over a sheaf of papers. Kepesake lifted his head. "Didn't expect to see you so early. Leg giving problems?"

"Mainly the knee now. This infernal cast should be coming off shortly and that may make it more comfortable." Forsythe took a chair at the end of the desk. "Where's Beau?"

"Told him not to come down until eight. You worked late and Beau didn't sleep that well. Said it was the strange bed, but probably he was fretting about me. Like a mother hen, you know." Pulling out his holder, Kepesake stuck a cigarette in it. "And you can stop darting concerned glances at me, Forsythe. I was badly shaken yesterday, but I have myself in hand. Professionals have to, old boy. You amateurs have all the luck."

The barrister decided that the chief inspector was back to normal. Not only was he smoking heavily but he'd called Forsythe by his surname instead of the friendlier Robert and had also used the hated "old boy." Pulling out his pipe, Forsythe started scraping at the bowl with a penknife. "Have you had a chance to look over the interviews Beau did last night?"

"Was just finishing them when you came in. Beau left a note asking that I consider sending Miss Vandervoort to London and her stepfather. What are the details?" Forsythe outlined what the young woman had said and Kepesake nodded. "Compassionate grounds, eh? After I finish with Mr. Cooper and the staff, I'll give it some thought." His mouth set. "Beau has already allowed Mr. Hobbs to leave. Set a precedent that the others will try to use."

"Only to the village, and Beau had to come to an instant decision."

"He should have consulted me first. Well, at least Inspector Davis has the inn in hand."

Forsythe finished the small operation on his pipe and stuffed dark tobacco into its carved bowl. "Any results on the autopsy as yet?"

"One of Davis' lads brought it in a short time ago." Kepesake extracted a form and handed it across the desk.

Forsythe skipped over the first part. Description of Penndragon's general health, which appeared to have been remarkable for a man of his age. Winslow Penndragon might well have made it to one hundred. Cause of death…time of death, between one A.M. and two. He read on to the marks and abrasions on the body—fading bruises on the right upper arm and right hip. The car accident, he decided. He read the next item twice. "Marks on both shoulders?"

"Yes. According to the medical examiner, probably inflicted shortly before death."

Handing the form back, the barrister said, "That answers one important question."

"Which is?"

"Two people were involved."

"That we already knew."

"Surmised. Now we *know*. One person to hold him down, one to use the cherub. But the bedclothes should have been disarranged, kicking and so on. After the crime, the bed must have been straightened, the arms arranged, the cherub put on the victim's chest. Next question, any result from the search for bloodstained clothing?"

"I had that yesterday. Neglected to mention it to you." Forsythe's pipe clattered to the desk, spilling grains of tobacco. "Mind sharing it now?"

"The country constabulary located it. A decrepit old Burberry hanging from one of the pegs by the back door. It was—"

"—used by Grace Penndragon," Forsythe chimed in, remembering his secretary's description of that coat.

"Lab boys are working on it now. Cuffs and the front of the coat were bloodstained. More stains on the mittens found stuffed in a pocket of it—red wool with elastic cuffs. Knitted by Aunt Grace and large enough to fit most hands, unless they're paws like a gorilla."

"May be enlightening when the report is in on them."

Kepesake looked dour. "Don't get your hopes up. That Burberry was a...I suppose you'd call it a communal garment. It was originally Bunny's and when he discarded it, Aunt Grace took it for her wardrobe—to annoy Uncle Winslow, of course."

"There's still five people left."

"A hair from one of his children or one of the servants? Afraid not. Aunt Grace was generous with that coat, offered it to anyone who desired it." Holding up a hand, Kepesake counted off. "Mr. Cooper borrowed it one rainy day rather than go up to his room for his own. Another blustery day, Aunt Grace insisted Miss Vandervoort wear it as she hadn't packed rain gear. Evans has admitted he frequently threw it over his shoulders when he went out to bring wood in and so on."

"That leaves Leslie Hobbs and Linda Evans."

"Linda often hung her cape over the Burberry when the pegs were crowded. One of her hairs could easily be explained. And Aunt Grace, who has a warped sense of humor, forced Mr. Hobbs to put it on. He was quite indignant. Said she made him look a fool. And that," the chief inspector said flatly, "is that."

"The mittens?"

"A splinter of nail polish, a flake of skin? Aunt Grace, Miss Vandervoort, and Linda don't wear nail polish. We'll have to await the report for anything further, but, frankly, I've little hope." Kepesake fitted another cigarette into his holder. "Forsythe, we're up against clever people. Using that Burberry was an inspired idea."

Forsythe, trying to light his pipe, nodded. It took time and four matches before he could add to the smog his companion had created.

Drumming restless fingers against the desk, Kepesake muttered, "Ever noticed how little one really knows about a person one's close to? I thought I knew my godfather as well as I know myself, but that isn't true. This man…this person those people spoke about is a stranger."

It was then that the barrister noticed Kepesake's recovery was far from complete. He had a grip on himself, but pain lurked in his eyes and at the corners of his mouth. "You're thinking of Bunny Penndragon."

"He considered himself a son rather than a nephew. So did everyone else. How could Uncle Winslow turn on him like that? Forbid him to approach the girl he loves, order him from the only home he's known?"

"I think you must consider your godfather in a new light— human rather than a god. With human faults. A man who clearly loved only one person—himself. A man who would go to any lengths to achieve his own ends. He wanted domination over his daughter, and his nephew was expendable."

Crushing out his cigarette, Kepesake moved restlessly. "Looking back over the years…yes, there were signs. An old chauffeur who'd been with Uncle Winslow's father was thrown out because he dented the fender of a new car. I can remember Aunt Grace arguing, pleading with Uncle Winslow to let the man stay on. In vain.

"Later, there was a nasty business with the son of one of the maids. She was a widow and needed the work. Her son was older than Bunny and I and he was slightly retarded. He used to follow his mother from the village and sneak onto the grounds to play with us. He was a nice lad and we enjoyed playing with him, but when my godfather found out, he hit the roof. Said he wouldn't have a 'village idiot' associating with *his* nephew and godson. Ended up with the maid being sacked. The signs were there, but I was blinded to them. I suppose Bunny must have been too." The chief inspector pulled himself up short. "No sense in rehashing." The mantel clock chimed. "Eight. Beau will soon be with us. Ah, there you are. Right on the dot. Did you get any more sleep?"

"No, but I'm fine." Brummell, freshly shaved and wearing snowy linen, managed somehow to look as unkempt as ever. "Either of you had breakfast?"

The other men shook their heads and Kepesake said, "Have it served in here. Less awkward. See to the lads, eh?"

"Helm and Krimshaw have seen to themselves, Chief. Packing it away in the kitchen. The cook, Mrs. Krugger, is still in bed. Planning on talking to her this morning, Chief?"

"It would be a waste of time. The woman seems to spend most of her time in bed. We'll have Mr. Cooper in first, then the servants."

Brummell nodded and went in search of breakfast. When he returned, he was carrying a loaded tray and was accompanied by Dolly Morris bearing another tray and managing her enticing wriggle at one and the same time. Kepesake pointed at a side table and the maid deposited the tray and started on her way out. Kepesake called her back. "Miss Morris, I've only a few questions for you. Perhaps you could answer them now."

Without waiting for an invitation, Dolly perched on the chair opposite the chief inspector. Forsythe noted that although she was striving to be demure, her skirt was hiked up, exposing dimpled knees, and extravagant eyelashes were fluttering at Kepesake. If she was hoping for a prolonged interview, she was to be disappointed. Rapidly, Kepesake elicited details of the evening of the murder. Dolly, with the aid of Uncle Roger, had cleared the dinner table and tidied the kitchen. Then she and her sister Geneva had been sent by their uncle to the servants' quarters. No, they hadn't gone straight to their own room. Aunt Linda had a telly and the girls watched the shows with their aunt until ten. "Then she sent us to bed," Dolly told them. "Treats us like kids, she does."

"And you heard or saw nothing further that night?"

"No."

She was now showing Kepesake more charming dimples, these in her cheeks. They made no visible impression on the chief inspector and he dismissed her, took his plate from the sergeant, and applied himself to bacon and eggs. Beau was eating ravenously, but Forsythe took only toast and coffee. "Off your feed, sir?" Brummell asked.

"Not getting enough exercise," Forsythe told him.

Reaching for a rasher of bacon, Kepesake asked, "What about Helm, Beau? Any problem with him and that young hussy?"

"Not to worry. Sensible chap and I warned him off." The sergeant added ominously, "Better not be."

Forsythe recalled the good sergeant was the father of three children, two of them girls and pretty. Kepesake waited until Brummell had cleaned his plate for the second time and then told him, "Get this cleared away and tell Helm and Krimshaw to get in here. See whether Mr. Cooper's up."

"He's an early riser," Forsythe volunteered. "When I came down, I met him coming in from a walk."

❋ ❋ ❋

As usual, Jason Cooper was completely expressionless. The chief inspector didn't waste time with him. He fired questions and Jason fired back answers. Neither of them used any unnecessary words.

"The morning of the car accident," Kepesake said. "You were out for a walk."

"I was."

"Did you go around to the front of the house?"

"No."

"Where did your walk take you?"

"Out the rear door, past the tennis court, to a lookout point over the village."

"You take that path every morning?"

"Yes."

"A creature of habit, Mr. Cooper."

"Yes."

"Your movements the evening of the murder."

Jason's account of the evening was exactly the same as Leslie's had been but much terser. He had played billiards with his half-brother; Bunny had joined them for a time; Leslie had been called to the telephone. "When Leslie returned," Jason said, "his game was off. There was no point in continuing and I told him so. He left again. While I was tidying up the room and putting the glasses and bottles on a tray, he—"

"You're neat, Mr. Cooper."

"Compulsively—early training."

"Continue."

"I took the tray to the kitchen and Leslie tagged along. I had a snack and then went up and he followed me. While I was undressing, he came banging at my door. He wanted a sleeping capsule and I gave him one."

"After some argument."

"I don't care for drugs, not even headache tablets. Mama didn't—" Jason broke off and then said. "I don't approve of people doping themselves, but Leslie insisted and he seemed in bad shape. To get rid of him, I gave him one."

"And then?"

"I went to bed."

"And to sleep?"

"Not immediately. Usually I'm a sound sleeper, but that night I twisted and turned."

"Why?"

"I've no idea. Leslie was so jumpy maybe some of it rubbed off."

"You didn't leave your room for the balance of the night?"

"Once. I thought a hot shower might be relaxing and I went to the bathroom and took one. Then I was able to sleep."

"What time was this?"

"I don't know. Late."

Forsythe leaned forward. "Did you see Mr. Hobbs take the sleeping capsule?"

"No. I handed it to him and closed the door."

Kepesake, who had been sitting bolt upright in his chair, leaned back and relaxed. He lit another cigarette, taking his time. Forsythe's eyes shifted to Jason Cooper. The young man resembled the wooden Indian his father had likened him to. Since he had sat down, he hadn't moved once—no nervous mannerisms, no fidgeting. The only moving parts seemed to be his eyes and his lips. Yet he was a handsome man, a darker version of his father. The barrister had yet to see him smile. He found himself wondering whether Jason Cooper's smile had the charm and enveloping warmth of Winslow Penndragon's.

If the chief inspector was hoping to make the younger man nervous and more talkative, he wasn't successful. Jason simply waited patiently for the next question. Finally Kepesake asked it. This time his voice was different, softer and slower. "What were your relations with your father?"

"I had none."

"Could you enlarge on that."

"I came here because of a promise my mother had extracted. She was dying and I had to follow her wishes. I've simply waited for the month to end to return home."

"You weren't curious about your father?"

"No."

"What about the rest of your relatives?"

"The same applies to them."

"Surely not to your half-brother and -sister."

"Too little, too late."

Expelling a smoke ring, Kepesake regarded it. "A cold reaction, Mr. Cooper."

"Not when you consider the circumstances. Leslie, Susan, and I are over thirty. The only thing we have in common is that the same man sired us."

"And if you'd known of them earlier?"

"That would have made a difference." The wooden Indian suddenly showed emotion. Not in his face—that didn't change—but his voice roughened. "My life would be entirely different."

Forsythe tried to pin down the emotion in that voice. Fury…sadness…despair? Kepesake asked smoothly, "In what way, Mr. Cooper?"

"I can't see where this has any bearing on your investigation."

"Let me be the judge of that."

"Very well. I've had a restrictive life. An overly possessive mother. As a result, I'm almost a recluse—no friends, few acquaintances. Mr. Penndragon could have told our mothers about each other. At least, he could have taken the time to let each of his children know about the other ones—their names, their addresses." Jason's eyes shifted, gazing moodily beyond his interrogator. "Years ago I would have been overjoyed to know that I had a brother and a sister. But Mr. Penndragon left it too late."

"And then only for his own reasons?"

"Exactly. He wanted nothing from Leslie or me. From the moment his daughter walked into this house, I realized she was his objective. Leslie and I were…we were window dressing."

"You held this against your father?"

"Not his choosing his daughter. That was his concern. But I'll never forgive his selfishness in not telling us of the other children he'd fathered."

"Perhaps he relied on your mothers to tell you who your father was."

Jason's mouth moved and Forsythe finally saw his smile. This smile bore no resemblance to his sire's. It was simply a grimace, lips pulling back from even white teeth. Remarkably like the wolfish snarl of Bunny's female retriever. It was fleeting and all emotion was gone from Jason's voice as he said, "Mr. Penndragon knew my mother, knew Mama would never tell me his name. She didn't want to share. Leslie's mother was obviously looking, as he is, for financial gain. That was her reason for telling her son about his famous daddy."

"And Miss Vandervoort?"

"I can only guess. From what she said one night at dinner—" the dark eyes slid to the barrister "—it sounded as though her mother was too hurt and ill to ever broach that subject."

"So you put all the blame on your father."

"Wouldn't you?"

Kepesake said abruptly, "That will be all for now, Mr. Cooper."

The younger man didn't budge. "I should like to return to Mousehole. My shop is being looked after by an elderly clerk who's not terribly competent. I'm needed there."

"I understood you had sold that shop."

"I'd put it in the hands of an estate agency, but when mother died, I changed my mind and took it off the market."

"As soon as the inquest is held, you'll be free to leave."

"Leslie already has."

Darting a cold look at his sergeant, Kepesake said, "Only as far as the inn in the village. If you wish to join him there, you may."

"I'm not that desperate." Jason left his chair and the room.

Swiveling his chair, Kepesake grated. "Never again release a suspect without my permission!"

"I was doing my best, Chief. I saw no harm—"

"You've put me in an untenable position!" Kepesake sank back and massaged his brow. "Sorry, Beau, put it down to nerves and to that Cooper. Cold as ice."

"More repressed than cold," Forsythe said mildly.

Kepesake glared at the younger constable lounging against the door. "Helm! Stop dreaming about Dolly Morris and get the Evanses in here."

Helm, blushing furiously, snapped to attention. "Sir, I wasn't—"

"On the double!"

"Yes, sir. Both of them, sir?"

"That's what I said."

Forsythe hadn't seen Linda Evans since the morning after the murder. Then she had been sodden and dazed. She appeared to have recovered her high spirits and bounced in, her round face wreathed in a smile, followed by her gaunt brother. One hand was outstretched and she was talking. "Adam, my dear! Such a sad way to meet. It's been—"

"Miss Evans." Kepesake barely touched the plump hand. "As you know, I am heading the investigation into the death of your employer. Please be seated."

She dimpled at him as her niece had and with about as much effect. "Then it's Chief Inspector Kepesake, but I'll still think of you as Adam."

"Your thoughts are your own concern. Evans, do stop hovering and take a chair."

Evans lifted a chair over, placing it to one side and slightly behind his sister's. Crisply, Kepesake led them through the preliminaries. He spoke crisply to the majordomo. "After you delivered the Bentley the morning of the accident—did you enter the house?"

"Not immediately, sir. As instructed, I left the keys in the ignition and went around the house to the garage. As also instructed, I set out a number of traps there for mice."

"Is that one of your duties?"

"It certainly isn't," his sister said pertly. "Jarvis is supposed to take care of traps."

"Miss Evans, kindly bear in mind that I'm questioning your brother and I want his answers, *not* yours. Evans?"

"Jarvis usually attends to that sort of thing, sir. But Mr. Penndragon had noticed signs of vermin and asked me to look after it when I had brought back the Bentley."

"How long were you in the garage?"

"I really can't say, sir. When I entered the rear door, I found the house in turmoil. Mr. Penndragon was in the entrance hall and he was disheveled. Mr. Bunny wanted to send straight away for the doctor, but the master ordered him to ring up the garage."

"At that time, you had no suspicion the accident had been a murder attempt?"

"I do my job, sir, and don't pry." Evans looked fixedly at the back of his sister's head.

"Admirable." Kepesake's eyes coldly examined the house-keeper. "Miss Evans, while the tennis game was in progress, where were you?"

"I don't really remember. I suppose in the tower straightening up."

"We have evidence you weren't in the tower at that time."

The dimples were no longer in evidence and a faint flush worked up her round cheeks. Her brother cleared his throat. "Beg pardon, sir. I believe Linda was in the plant room. At least that's where she was when I came in after the game was finished."

"That's right, Roger. Jarvis had brought the flowers in earlier than usual and I was arranging them. You must remember, Adam—Chief Inspector Kepesake—one of my duties is flower arrangement."

"Did anyone enter the plant room?"

"Let me see...so hard to remember. No, Geneva was upstairs tidying the bedrooms. Dolly...she was turning out the china cabinet in the dining room. I recall she didn't want to do it and I had to speak sharply to her." The dimples flashed again.

"Mrs. Krugger, as Mr. Penndragon used to joke, was enjoying ill health and was in bed."

Kepesake shuffled papers, but it seemed only something to do with his hands. "Miss Evans, your movements the evening of murder from the time you left the dinner table."

She spoke as though she'd committed the details to memory. "As usual, Dolly and Roger cleared the table—"

"Your movements."

"All I was trying to say is that after dinner is finished, I go off duty. I went up to my room to watch television. Geneva and Dolly joined me and I let them watch a couple of shows and at ten sent them to bed. I'm very strict with my nieces. Another hour show came on and when it was over, I went down to the kitchen. I was heating milk for cocoa when Jason and Leslie came in. As soon as my drink was ready, I went up to my room, downed it, and went to bed."

"You saw or heard nothing through the night?"

"This is an old house, solidly built and sounds don't carry. Besides, I'm a sound sleeper."

Kepesake glanced over her head. "And you, Evans?"

"I'm on duty until dismissed by Mr. Penndragon. Dolly and I cleared the dinner table and tidied the kitchen. Then I sent my nieces to bed and started to lock up for the night. I checked all the doors and windows with the exception of the front door, which is left till last. I banked the fire in the drawing room and was going to do the same with the one in the morning room, but Miss Grace and Miss Vandervoort were in there. Then I returned to the kitchen to await Mr. Penndragon's summons. He rang for me at thirty-five minutes after ten—"

"You're a clock watcher?"

"In the evenings, sir. I'm getting on and my legs bother me—ankles swell. I went to the lounge in the tower and Mr. Penndragon gave me instructions—"

"Any that weren't usual?"

"Much the same as always, sir. It hardly seemed necessary to repeat them each evening, but the master did things his way. Mr. Bunny was in the lounge, getting his instructions for the following day. I went up to the next floor, turned back the bed, laid out night clothes, and started to run a bath. While the tub was filling, I looked over the wardrobe, found some clothing that needed cleaning, and later took them down for Mr. Penndragon's approval." A shade of expression crossed the dour features and Evans confided, "A stickler the master was for clothes, sir. Liked everything just so. Always looked a treat, he did."

"Yes," Kepesake said somberly. "While you went about your duties did you hear Mr. Penndragon and his nephew talking?"

Evans appeared to be debating and then he said slowly, "No use in dodging, sir. Yes, I heard them. Couldn't help it. They were both shouting."

"And you got the gist of their quarrel?"

"It was about Miss Vandervoort. The master was telling Mr. Bunny to leave her alone. Ended up with Mr. Penndragon yelling that Mr. Bunny was through and he could get out and take Miss Grace with him. Terrible it was. I couldn't believe my ears."

Kepesake was restlessly toying with his jade holder. "Evans, I want a straight answer on this. Did you tell Mrs. Penndragon what you'd heard?"

"Well…I'll admit I would have if she'd been downstairs, but by the time I bolted the front door, she'd gone up."

"Fond of her, are you?"

"Think we all are, sir. Jarvis thinks the world of her."

"I'm certainly not," Linda blurted. "The way she dresses and talks—it's disgraceful!"

"Seeing that you want to answer questions so badly, Miss Evans, I have a few for you. Exactly what was your relationship with the deceased?"

She drew her thick body up. "As you well know, I was his housekeeper."

Her brother directed a broad grin at the back of her head. "Better give it to him straight."

She swung around. "Shut your big mouth!"

"I would heed your brother's advice," Kepesake told her.

Linda eyed him warily and more color flooded into her face, making it look like a brick-red moon. "No decency," she muttered. "All that's past pulled out and stared at." She raised several of her chins and tried to look haughty. "For a short time after Roger and I came here, I was…I suppose you'd say I was Mr. Penndragon's mistress."

"When given a choice, you elected to remain on as a servant?"

"I jumped at the chance. He didn't love me anymore…I don't think he ever really did, but I adored him. I'd have stayed on if I'd had to be a scullery maid."

Ice-cold eyes sought her brother. "And you approved of this?"

Evans shrugged a narrow shoulder. "Didn't approve or disapprove, sir."

"A callous attitude toward a sixteen-year-old sister."

"To understand, sir, you'd have to know our family. Had four sisters, just like our mum. A regular tartar was our mum. She wore the pants in our house and neither Dad nor me had a chance. Nothing I say ever sways Linda."

"What about your niece? Same go for her?"

Linda gasped but Evans stolidly said, "Told Linda not to let Dolly come here. Then she sends the girl into the tower to work. Told her not to do that either. Told her if anyone knows— knew—what Mr. Penndragon was like, *she* should."

The red moon lifted toward Kepesake. "I thought he was…past it—too old."

"May have been getting on," Evans observed, "but he was still a man."

"I should have listened to Roger, Chief Inspector. That man went right after Dolly the same as he had me. I found them rolling around on his bed. He was pawing and slobbering all over her and Dolly was enjoying it. I slapped her and gave him a piece of my mind. He apologized and since then he didn't have a chance to get near the little flirt. I'm sending her back to her mother!"

"Could you have been jealous of your niece, Miss Evans?"

"No!" She hesitated and then said brokenly, "Yes, I guess I was. It brought back so many memories. And Dolly looks exactly like I did at her age."

Forsythe noticed Helm straightening at his post. The young constable was staring incredulously at the housekeeper's fat body overflowing her chair. He shook his head. Take a good look, Forsythe advised him silently, that's delicious Dolly in a few years.

The chief inspector was still toying with the jade. "You do know that under Mr. Penndragon's will both of you will be receiving sizable legacies."

Linda seemed to have lost all desire to talk and it was Roger Evans who answered. "The master told us, sir, said we'd be well looked after if anything happened to him. Very generous."

"Have you plans for the future? Will you stay on here?"

"I don't know whether Mr. Bunny will keep this house, sir, but I'm getting on and I've always wanted a place of my own...maybe in Brighton." His dour face was close to cheerful. "I've always liked fishing."

"And you, Miss Evans?"

"Don't know," she mumbled. "Can I...can we go?"

Kepesake dismissed them. Linda led the way, sagging rather than bouncing. Her brother lingered at the door long enough to turn and, surprisingly, lowered one eyelid in a roguish wink.

Sergeant Brummell grinned. "Chap enjoyed you cutting his sister down to size."

"That was a thorough job you did on her," Forsythe remarked.

Lifting his chin, Kepesake looked haughty without effort. "Long overdue. I've disliked her for years. She's far too familiar. Forgets her place."

Brummell winked at the barrister. "Never mind, Chief, doubt she'll even *think* of you as Adam from now on."

Chapter Twelve

Adam Kepesake stretched and then got to his feet. Restlessly, he paced the length of the library, pausing to glance at Krimshaw's notebook, stopping to gaze from a window. All that could be heard was the crackle of wood on the hearth, the lashing rain against the panes, Helm moving at his post by the door. Turning back from the dismal view, Kepesake said, "You can take a break, lads. Walk around and stretch your legs."

Krimshaw got up with alacrity and Helm looked at the mantel clock. "Nearly one, sir. All right to look up some lunch?"

"By all means. Have some sent into us."

As Kepesake leaned gracefully against the mantel, Forsythe decided that something about the man reminded him of Winslow Penndragon, not in his physical resemblance, but perhaps in his grooming and clothes—the well-cut suit, silk tie, a glimpse of matching silk above highly polished shoes, above all, an aura of arrogance.

The sergeant was watching Kepesake too and his eyes were fond. "Any ideas, Chief?"

"A number, and time to kick them around. Forsythe, do you have any thoughts?"

"Only the two I mentioned to Beau last night and one's been explained."

"The neatness of the bed?"

"Yes. Obviously it must have been straightened after the murder. But the murder weapon still puzzles me."

"I'm inclined to agree with Beau. The cherub was handy and the killer simply grabbed it."

"Perhaps. But still…"

Bending, Kepesake poked at the logs. A shower of sparks flew up. "Beau?"

"I've a fair idea now how the crime was committed. Mr. Penndragon was in bed, relaxing and looking over that material in the folder. It was some time after one A.M. Two people entered his room. Perhaps he was surprised but not alarmed. They walked over to the bed and one of them leaped on him and straddled his body, holding his shoulders down—"

"Why straddle? Surely that person could have circled the bed and grasped his shoulders?"

"Won't work, Chief. That's a wide bed. Awkward to try and stand on the far side and hold Mr. Penndragon down. Besides, for a man of your godfather's age, he was in good shape. A lot easier to pin him down by kneeling across his chest."

"That does make sense. Then?"

"The one wearing the Burberry and the mitts picked up the cherub and knocked the old gentleman out."

"Your reasoning?"

"The messiest job. Think of the amount of blood on that Burberry. The person holding him down could have leaned back and probably only the hands would have gotten spattered. Then the killer flailed at the head and face of the victim and when it was finished, they straightened up the bedclothes, put the cherub on his chest, went down to the main house, replaced the Burberry on a peg, and toddled quietly off to their rooms."

Kepesake nodded sagely and asked the barrister. "That agree with your reasoning?"

"Precisely."

"Mine too. Now, we need two people acting as partners. We have seven possibles. It could be Evans and his sister—"

Forsythe interrupted. "I don't get the impression they get along well enough to be partners at anything."

"Appearances can be deceiving. That could have been an act. Evans may well have resented his sister and young niece being used as…as conveniences. And there's Linda. That scene with Dolly could have well made her homicidal—the woman scorned, old boy. Then there're nice fat chunks of money coming as legacies. Worth considering?"

"It is, Chief."

Wandering back to the window, Kepesake gazed out. His voice was muffled. "I'm considering Aunt Grace."

"Don't think her son was her partner, Chief."

"Neither do I. There has never been a closeness between them. Anyway, both Aunt Grace and Bunny were at the tennis court. I was thinking of Jarvis."

"The gardener?" Forsythe asked.

"He's been here almost as long as Aunt Grace has. And Jarvis likes her. She potters around the grounds with him, chats with him. Took his side when Uncle Winslow found fault with his work. Look how Aunt Grace got the old fellow to talk after Uncle Winslow swore him to silence. Remember, Jarvis is also mentioned in the will."

Forsythe considered. An unlikely pair but possible. Kepesake turned back from the window. "Then there's Aunt Grace with another partner. I've been considering Miss Vandervoort. And her motive is clear—her mother's alcoholism and early death."

The barrister shook his head. "You've read what Miss Vandervoort told me about her mother's family. She didn't blame her father for that or for leaving her to be raised by a stepfather."

"She could have been lying, old boy." Kepesake added indulgently, "You do tend to be rather gullible when it comes to fair maidens."

"You've forgotten something, Chief. Miss Vandervoort saved her father's life at the gardening shed."

"True, Beau, that had slipped my mind." Kepesake frowned. "Very well, on to the next likely pair—Leslie Hobbs and Cesar Guevarro. Opportunity and motive there."

"Pretty foolish move on Guevarro's part," Brummell said flatly. "Fixing those brakes, I mean."

"We'll pass on. I'm trying to work Jason Cooper in."

"Not going to be easy," Brummell grunted. "Can't picture him working with anyone. He's a loner. Seems to me he'd do his killing alone."

"Maybe not. I'm thinking of him and his half-brother."

"Mr. Hobbs? I thought you just said Guevarro and—"

"Beau, I'm simply tossing ideas around. But think of it, two brothers, sharing a mutual hatred of a father. Hoping to gain more from Bunny than they could from that father. I've seen weaker motives for murder than that."

They all had. Again the silence was broken only by a gust of rain driven against the side of the house. Suddenly, the door was flung open. "Helm," Kepesake said, "with luncheon."

It wasn't Helm. Miss Sanderson carried the tray. Her face was pink and she darted a defiant look at the barrister. "I was in the kitchen when the constables came in. Linda isn't making lunch. She seemed distraught and went up to her room and the cook, of course, is still in bed. So I got something for Krimshaw and Helm and for us." She looked appealingly at Kepesake. "Mind if I lunch with you?"

"Not at all, Miss Sanderson. In fact, I'm delighted to see you." He gallantly took the tray from her and placed it on a table. "Keeping busy?"

"At what?" She made a face. "Spent most of the time lurking up in our rooms. When I did venture down it was sticky."

"People hostile?"

"People acting as though I'm the invisible woman. Looking through me. The only ones who talked to me were Grace and, oddly enough, the Sphinx." Kepesake looked his question and she smiled. "That's what Grace calls Jason Cooper."

"An apt name." He circled the desk to the swivel chair. "What do you have for us?"

"I remembered Beau likes beer." She put a bottle and glass down before the sergeant who gave her an appreciative smile. "Coffee for us, Adam. Milk for Robby."

"Sandy, I don't want milk."

"Don't be petulant. You've been living on whiskey, coffee, and painkillers."

"Dangerous diet," Kepesake agreed. "Be a good boy and drink your milk."

Forsythe glowered while Miss Sanderson lifted dishes onto the desk. "Pickles here, and a plate of sandwiches."

She held the plate out to the policemen. "Two kinds— salmon paste this side, egg salad over here."

Kepesake helped himself to two salmon triangles and two of egg salad. Brummell pondered and then reached for the egg salad. Twirling the plate, Abigail set it down in front of the barrister. He transferred his glower to the sandwiches. "Robby, stop sulking and eat. Adam, any chance of me having a peek at the reports thus far? I'm not being nosy…or maybe I am, but I'm completely in the dark."

"Welcome to the club," Kepesake said wryly. "That brings our membership to four. Forsythe is still brooding about the murder weapon; Beau is concentrating on the scene of the crime; and I'm grabbing at one pair for killers and then another. By all means look over what we have. Maybe you'll notice some-thing we've overlooked."

"That murky, eh? After lunch, I'll try my luck. Robby, you simply must eat and that's an order!"

Neither Brummell nor Kepesake bothered hiding their amusement. Miss Sanderson had spoken to Forsythe as though he were a small boy. With obvious reluctance he reached for a sandwich. He was lifting a triangle toward his mouth when he stopped, held it suspended, and frowned at it. Then he said slowly, "Sandy, do that again."

"Do what?"

"Hand around the plate."

"But—"

"Do it!"

She sighed, picked up the plate, and solemnly offered it first to the chief inspector, then to the sergeant. The men pantomimed taking sandwiches and then she turned, twirled the plate, and set it in front of Forsythe. "Salmon paste," he muttered and put down the sandwich untasted.

Brummell and Kepesake leaned forward, their eyes fastened on the barrister. Kepesake said, "Have you thought of—"

Forsythe held up his hand and the chief inspector broke off. No one moved or spoke and finally Forsythe lifted his head and regarded Kepesake. In that look, there was a trace of pity. "Adam, after what you've learned about your godfather…do you still feel the death penalty should be reinstated?"

"Nothing I've heard has changed my mind about that. He was brutally killed and no matter what his private life was, he didn't deserve that."

"You may change your mind."

"For God's sake, Forsythe, get on with it!"

"Part of this is conjecture, but some of it can be verified—"

"How does a salmon sandwich enter into it?"

"Hold on and I'll explain. The day after Sandy and I arrived, there was a special tea. Mrs. Krugger had baked a cake and—"

As he spoke, his listeners' expressions changed from eagerness to dismay and then to sick comprehension. All looked older and immeasurably saddened. Forsythe didn't speak quickly and his voice dragged; he hesitated frequently, but finally he finished. Kepesake bowed his head. "This sort of thing…it can't happen."

"I'm afraid it has," Forsythe muttered.

Brummell straightened his sagging shoulders. "One way to make sure." Without asking for Kepesake's permission, he pulled the telephone over and dialed. He spoke rapidly and then put a hand over the mouthpiece. "Mr. Forsythe, any idea about time?"

It was his secretary who said, "Late October or possibly early November of last year."

He relayed the information and rang off. "Now we wait."

They waited. Miss Sanderson cleared the desk, piling plates and cups on the tray. Adam Kepesake roamed around the room, lifting a log onto the grate, pulling back velvet curtains to peer out at the dreary day. The room darkened and he switched table lamps on. Helm stuck his head in the door and was told to get out. The sergeant sat stolidly, his eyes following the chief inspector, flicking toward the clock. It seemed a lifetime before the telephone rang. In time, it had been less than three hours.

Brummell took the call, jotted down a couple of notes, replaced the receiver. He said, "October the twenty-eighth. In London. Chief?"

Kepesake had halted by the window, his back toward the rest. He said softly, "Primitive feeling, vengeance. An eye for an eye, a tooth—Now I know vengeance *was* done and Winslow Penndragon got exactly what he had coming to him."

"Adam," Forsythe said sharply. "Don't swing too far the other way."

Kepesake spun around. "Tell me this. What would it have cost him? A few minutes of his precious time. But in his wonderful world, there was no time, no thought for anyone but himself." He walked back to the desk and sank heavily on the chair. "I take no pleasure in this."

"But it has to be done, Chief." Brummell touched the other man's shoulder. "Want the lads in now?"

"Yes."

As Brummell left to locate the constables, Miss Sanderson darted an imploring look at Forsythe. He started to push himself up. "Where are you going?" Kepesake asked.

"You no longer need us."

"I would like you to stay." He added, "Robert."

When Brummell returned with Krimshaw and Helm, the chief inspector said, "Helm, would you ask—"

A soft tap sounded on the door and Helm turned to open it. On the threshold stood Susan Vandervoort. No longer did she look like a ghost. Makeup discreetly brightened her cheeks and lips; rose-colored linen swirled around her slender figure. Girding her waist was a chain belt, silver this time. She glanced around the room and then fixed dove gray eyes on the chief inspector. "Sorry to intrude, but Sergeant Brummell said he would speak with you."

"About your father's condition." Kepesake rose. "Yes, he did mention it. Would you be seated, Miss Vandervoort."

She took the chair opposite him. "It would be a great kindness if you would let me go to him."

"You'll be leaving shortly. Helm, would you ask Mr. Cooper to step in."

She glanced over her shoulder. "What has Jason to do with my father?"

"Patience, Miss Vandervoort."

When Jason arrived and had accepted a chair drawn up beside his half-sister's, Kepesake nodded to his sergeant. Stepping forward, Brummell cleared his throat, and said gruffly, "Susan Barbara Vandervoort and Jason Jacob Cooper, you are charged with the murder of Winslow Maxwell Penndragon on the…"

As his voice droned on Miss Sanderson made a sound deep in her throat. Forsythe's eyes flew to her and he whispered, "Get out of here, Sandy. Find Grace and stay with her." She practically ran to the door, brushed past Helm, and disappeared.

Jason didn't move a muscle while Brummell spoke, but Susan started up. "Are you mad?"

Kepesake told her, "If you wish your solicitor present—"

"I asked whether you were mad."

Without taking his eyes off the chief inspector, Jason said, "Let's hear him out."

"Thank you, Mr. Cooper. We've established that on October the twenty-eighth of last year a civil ceremony was conducted in London uniting in the bonds of holy matrimony Susan Vandervoort, resident of that city, and Jason Cooper, resident of Mousehole, Cornwall. I'll ask you once more. Do you wish to have your solicitor present?"

Jason shook his head. After a moment, Susan whispered, "No."

"Would you like to make a statement?"

Again Jason's dark head moved in a negative gesture, but Susan said wearily, "Why not? The only reason we've tried to conceal this is because of my father. I wanted time to be with him when he dies."

"Whether you make a statement or not, Miss Vandervoort, you'll be escorted to your father. That I promise."

"In that case, we'll give you a statement. Jason, could you…"

He half turned toward her, sighed, and turned back to face Kepesake. "In a way, this will be a relief. Where will I start?"

"When you went to London last fall would be the best place."

"Very well. As you know, I went to London to make arrangements for a new shop. It was a totally new experience for me and for a time, I simply enjoyed the novelty of being on my own. Then I began to feel a bit guilty about my mother and, to salve my conscience, decided to buy her a gift. I went to the women's department of a large store and looked over their selection of bed jackets. I found one in her favorite color, but it was much too large. The clerk mentioned something about the buyer, left, and returned with a lovely blond girl—a Miss Susan Vandervoort. She assured me that she could order the jacket in Mother's size and I gave her the address for delivery and so on."

The young man had been speaking in his usual clipped way, but now his voice slowed. "I wasn't accustomed to talking to attractive girls. Mama disapproved of anything like that. But I looked across the counter at Susan, smiling at me with that soft blue jacket in her hands…something happened. When she started back to her office, I took my courage in both hands and followed. I didn't know what to say. I'm not glib and self-confident."

He looked sideways at Susan and she nodded. "He was certainly far from that. He stuttered and shuffled his feet and finally blurted out that he was a stranger in the city and asked whether I would have a drink or coffee with him. I suggested we go along to the cafeteria and we did. Afterward Jason told me it had been an instant attraction with him and it had with me too. It was like…like looking up and seeing something you've always hungered for and never found—the other half of a whole.

"We talked; we found we had the same taste in music, in books. Our backgrounds were not dissimilar. Jason's mother had kept him away from other young people and my mother's illness had done the same to me. While she was alive, I didn't dare take friends home. Her condition…it was too embarrassing. After her death, my father and I had to work so hard just to keep afloat. Father and I made a cozy little world for ourselves and I didn't feel the need for anyone else until he became ill."

"We were both so terribly lonely," Jason recalled. "So eager for love. We spent every moment we could together and that wasn't enough, so…we married." The mask fell away from his fine features and under it was sickness and horror. "I had fallen in love with and married my own half-sister."

"For a time you didn't realize that," Forsythe said.

"No," the girl said unsteadily. "For a time we didn't know. Jason and I decided to keep our marriage a secret because of his mother."

"She had so little time left," Jason said. "And Mama would have been heartbroken. She would have felt I had deserted her. I urged Susan to tell her father, but she wouldn't. She said there would be lots of time."

Taking out his jade holder, Kepesake stared down at it and then put it on the desk. "You were still registered in your hotel, Mr. Cooper."

"A place for mail and telephone calls only. Every afternoon, I'd wait for Susan to leave the store and we'd go to her flat. Time passed, a magical time, and then I was called back to Mousehole. As soon as I left Mama's room each evening, I'd go to a phone booth in the lobby of the hospital and ring up Susan. One night…"

"I had marvelous news for Jason," Susan said bitterly. "We wanted children, a number of them. We planned on a large family. I told him I was pregnant." The gray eyes fastened on Forsythe. "Did you know that?"

"Guessed. The cherub, the statue of a little girl, that remark you made about little Lucy that so upset Sandy."

"I was pregnant with my half-brother's child. A child who could be…it might have been a monster." A shudder shook her slender frame and she buried her face in her hands.

Kepesake gazed at her bowed head and his hands clenched into fists. It was Sergeant Brummell who asked, "When did you discover your relationship?"

Susan didn't lift her head and it was Jason who said, "The day that *he* came to the hospital to visit my mother. He'd seen Susan the day before. My mother was very ill and clinging to me and I hadn't been able to leave her to make my daily call to my wife…to Susan. After Mother introduced me to him, she asked me to leave them and so I went to the lobby and rang Susan up. I remember laughing when I told her about my long-lost father—"

"Who was *my* long-lost father." The girl's head jerked up, the flaxen hair spilled away from her face, makeup stood out starkly against her drained skin, making her look clownlike. "I can't tell you how I felt. I knew I *never* wanted to see Jason again, but I had to. After his mother's funeral, he came to my flat."

Jason reached out a hand toward her and she flinched away. "She was close to mad. The Christmas tree was still standing, but she'd taken off all the children's figures and smashed them."

"I first smashed the ones *he* had sent me for a bribe. You see, I'd aborted my baby." Her voice rose shrilly. "I'd murdered my own baby!"

"Susan had cut her foot on a shard of porcelain. It was covered with blood and she wouldn't…she wouldn't let me touch her to bandage it. I still loved her; I'll always love her." Jason looked from one man to another. "We *had* to do something."

It was Forsythe who said, "You accepted your father's invitation and came to Penndragon to kill him."

"No," Susan whispered. "We came to destroy something he loved as he'd destroyed us; destroyed our baby. Jason and I pretended to be strangers and we watched him closely. At first, we thought he loved his nephew—"

"You'd have killed Bunny?" Kepesake asked.

"If Winnie had loved him enough—yes. But we soon realized he loved nothing. He took us through his tower and we wondered whether he loved his paintings and jade and china. He didn't. He only collected; he had little feeling for beauty. In this entire world, there was only one thing he loved—himself."

Jason smiled, that wolfish grimace merely baring his teeth. "Then we hit on it. He told both of us about his grandfather's and father's long lives. He kept boasting he had thirty years left to enjoy his wonderful life. We took them away from him."

Brummell was as impassive as the younger man had been earlier. "Mr. Cooper, you loosened the brake connection on the Bentley."

"I did."

"Miss Vandervoort, you placed the marble statue over the door of the shed."

"Yes."

"Then why did you call to him and save his life?"

"While I was waiting for him to open that door, I realized it wasn't enough. The statue would fall and he would be dead. Never knowing why, never knowing he was losing his precious thirty years. He didn't deserve an easy death."

Kepesake stirred. "Had you made plans to kill him that night?"

Jason's lips pulled away from his teeth again. "We knew why Mr. Forsythe and Miss Sanderson were here, but we weren't going to let them stop us. We were watching for the first chance to finish him off. When Leslie asked for that sleeping capsule, it came. I lied about not having taken one. I did and it was powerful. As soon as Leslie was sound asleep, Susan and

I went to the tower. She wore Grace's Burberry and those red mitts—"

"I'd already decided to use the cherub," Susan interrupted. "He showed it to me so proudly and it looked…it looked like a beautiful baby. It seemed fitting. When we got to his bedroom, he was in bed, reading some papers. He was surprised but not alarmed. He made a joke about the coat and mitts, asked whether I was in disguise. Jason leaped on the bed and held him down. Then we told him all about our marriage and about our baby. We told him he was going to die. We expected him to beg, to plead for mercy, perhaps weep."

"He didn't," Kepesake said in a muffled voice. "Winslow Penndragon was many things, but he was valiant."

"He was," Jason said. "He didn't even struggle. Just lay back, smiled, and told us to go ahead."

"I struck his head," the girl told them. "Jason jumped back and I struck him again and again." One fist pounded her other palm. "Again and again until his head was a bloody pulp. That face of his was just a mass of bone and blood."

Kepesake was watching the fist rising and falling. "*Don't*. Was it worth it?"

Her hands stilled. "I destroyed his face and do you know what I see in my mirror? That face! I'd like…I want to destroy my own face. I'll never be free of him. Never!"

Jason sagged in his chair. "It changed nothing. All our memories…our lives are useless to us. God! I wish they still executed murderers. Oblivion…"

The chief inspector looked from the man to the girl— Susan's fair beauty, her brother's dark good looks, their different coloring, the same bone structure. "I'm *glad* it no longer is in effect. You've been punished enough already, but, yes, you'll always live with it. Even society doesn't practice that sort of torment. Miss Vandervoort, as soon as your statement is signed, I'll take you to your father."

Forsythe could stand no more. He rose stiffly and hobbled from the room.

Epilogue

When he reached the morning room, he found it cozy with lamplight, firelight, and heavy curtains drawn against the dark and the storm. Miss Sanderson huddled in an armchair on one side of the hearth and opposite her, perched on an armless chair, was Grace Penndragon. She was wearing a trim gray dress and steel needles flashed in her hands. Forsythe noticed the length of knitting suspended. The Argyle sock was nearly finished.

Without turning her head, his secretary said, "Are they...Have they left yet?"

"Not yet, but soon. Adam is taking the girl to the nursing home in London. I rang through for a rented car. Sandy, we're leaving. Would you go up and pack our cases?"

She got up and, as she opened the door, touched his arm. "Robby," she whispered and then she was gone.

"She's taking it hard," Grace said.

"Her emotions are still raw after that nightmare in Maddersley. Did she tell you about your niece and nephew?"

"She didn't have to. I already knew."

Forsythe sank down in the chair that Miss Sanderson had used. The cushions were still warm from her body. Putting her knitting aside, Grace poured brandy and handed the barrister a glass. "We can both use this, Mr. Forsythe."

"How long have you known?"

"From the evening that Susan arrived, I knew Jason and she weren't strangers."

"How?"

"Jason gave it away. When Evans brought Susan from the train, Winslow had all of us into the drawing room to meet his daughter. Jason and Susan went to elaborate lengths to show they had never met before. Winslow asked Jason to help him at the drink table and, while Winslow made up drinks to order, Jason poured soda in a glass, crossed the room, and handed it to Susan. She hadn't said what she wished and at that time none of us was aware she didn't touch alcohol. Winslow was excited, Leslie upset, Bunny fascinated by Susan. I was the only one who caught it. So I knew they were acting and waited to see what it was all about."

She paused and tugged on a ball of yellow wool. "They were good actors, but they did make another slip. I was hoping you wouldn't catch it."

"At the time I certainly didn't. Then today Sandy did something and I suddenly saw that silver cake plate piled with cherry cake and tarts. Sandy did this." He picked up a large ashtray. "She'd cut two kinds of sandwiches, salmon paste on this side, egg salad on the other. She served Adam and Beau and when she put the plate down in front of me, she turned it so the salmon sandwiches were facing me. Sandy knows I detest egg salad. Which is the point. When Susan put the cake plate down in front of Jason at tea that day, she did the same thing—turned it so the tarts were facing him. Yet, at that time, no one was supposed to know that he's allergic to cherries."

"And then you considered the information both of us had?"

"The questions that seemed to have no answers. Winslow told Sandy and me about his first meeting with his daughter. A happy, cheerful girl who appeared only amused to be told he was her father. The girl who arrived here later—depressed, ill, obviously hating him. Why the change?"

"I'd hoped you'd put it down to worry over her stepfather."

"I did...until today. But would worry account for her loathing for her real father? No, so something had happened, something traumatic. Something concerning her and Jason."

Grace sighed. "The same line of reasoning I took much earlier. Jason had been in London. Suppose they'd met, fallen in love, perhaps married..."

"Did you realize a baby had been conceived and been aborted?"

"Suspected it. Susan seemed so ill and that statue...such a charming figure of a small girl. The cherub was the picture of a fat little baby. Then the remark that so upset Miss Sanderson. Poor Susan, trying to persuade herself she'd made the right move in aborting her baby."

"Which you immediately tried to cover by diverting attention to yourself."

"Chiming in on the terrible state of the world? Yes, Mr. Forsythe, I dragged every red herring I could think of across your path, but I couldn't divert you."

He looked grimly at her. "You knew and you let them kill Winslow."

"Yes. You see Winslow had claimed three more victims. Susan and Jason and their unborn child. If he'd lived, there would have been more—Bunny for one, also Hobbs. Winslow would happily have ruined his own son. Not now. I know Bunny will save his cousin's restaurant. Do you understand? Winslow *had* to die."

"Under no circumstances can I condone murder."

"I can. Jason and his sister had nothing left to lose. Winslow had already taken any chance of a decent life away from them."

Setting down his glass, he said firmly, "And I can't sit in judgment."

"I can." She began to cast off stitches. When she'd finished, she held up the sock. "If you want it, it's yours."

He took it. "Yes, I want it. I've earned it." Her eyes fell and he asked, "Have you made any plans? Will you stay on here?"

"If Bunny does and if he wants me. If he doesn't, I'll take a flat or cottage somewhere."

"He'll want you."

She gave him a ghost of her wicked grin. "Happy ending, eh? Mother and son falling into each other's arms, vowing life-long devotion? Mr. Forsythe, there are no happy endings. But perhaps something can be saved from this tragedy. Perhaps my son and I can achieve a relationship of sorts." She rose. "I must go to Bunny. Tell him—"

"Be kind."

"I will. He loves the girl." Forsythe struggled up and towered over her diminutive figure. She smiled up at him and this time the smile was gentle. "For Bunny, I pray for a happy ending. Another girl he can love."

The door opened and Miss Sanderson stepped in. She was wearing a raincoat and Forsythe's topcoat was draped over an arm. "Time, Robby. The car's arrived and the driver's taking out the bags." Handing the coat to the barrister, she bent to kiss the older woman's cheek. "*Vaya con Dios*," Miss Sanderson whispered.

A smile of surpassing sweetness touched the lips of the old woman. "My friends, may you also go with God," Grace Penndragon said.

For Margaret J. Henricks,
who shared many a Christmas past

A Death for a Dietitian

Chapter One

Robert Forsythe cursed explosively and jabbed the bell connecting his desk with his secretary's. When Mrs. Sutter appeared, he transferred his glower from the brief before him to her placid face. "I asked for the Denton brief and you brought the Desston—"

"Mr. Forsythe, I could have sworn you meant the Desston one."

"I generally *mean* what I *say*. Kindly replace this and bring the correct one."

Hot color swept up her short neck, mantling the chipmunk cheeks of her no longer placid face. "It's not easy, you know, trying to replace Miss Sanderson. She has her own system, if you could call it that, and a right jumble it is. Everything helter-skelter—"

"It works for her." He thrust the folder out.

Without a word Mrs. Sutter seized it, spun on her heels, and stalked out. She didn't bother closing the door, and the barrister jumped up and pushed it to. Returning to the massive leather chair used in turn by his father and grandfather, he stared at the oaken panel. He had been harsh with his temporary secretary and the woman had a valid point. Not only did Sandy have her own mystifying system, but she was a hard act for anyone to follow. Abigail Sanderson seemed to possess an amazing amount of ESP and quite often handed him the material he needed without waiting to be asked. Of course, Forsythe thought, Sandy was not only his secretary but had once been his father's. And she was much more than a good right hand in chambers. Following the death of his mother, Sandy had assumed the maternal duties for a three-year-old boy. Through the years she had been friend, confidant, and at times, a sharp and exasperating spur. How, he wondered, could he have expected poor Mrs. Sutter, at short notice, to step into shoes such as those. And why had he practically forced Sandy to take the entire month off? Perhaps he had suffered momentarily from an overdose of Christmas spirit. All she had asked for had been a couple of days to do her shopping.

"Take the rest of the month," he had urged.

"But Robby," she protested, "it's only the first of December."

"Decembers are generally slow."

"Not always. This one might be hectic."

"Nonsense, we won't even know you're gone." He added grandly, "Consider it a Christmas present."

"I'd rather settle for an emerald pendant. Something small but elegant."

"You're talking to a barrister, not an oil magnate. Now scoot before I change my mind."

She had scooted, but her prediction had started to come true. The next week had been a nightmare, with briefs flooding in and his juniors, clerks, and office staff trying vainly to cope. Shifting in his chair, Forsythe banged open a drawer. It looked as though there was going to be a delay in getting that damn brief. Might as well do some work on the one he was leading young Peters in. Spreading the leaves of the folder, he bent his narrow head over it. The door squeaked open, someone moved across the room, and the Denton brief was slapped down over the one he was reading.

Without looking up he said, "Sorry I was so short, Mrs. Sutter—"

"What did you say to the poor thing, Robby? When I came in she was practically in tears."

"Sandy!" His head jerked up and he repeated with a rising inflection, "Sandy?"

"The new Abigail Sanderson." She pirouetted. "What do you think? And please close your mouth. You're managing to look like an idiot."

He closed his mouth but continued to stare. His Sandy had always been carefully groomed, with gray hair modishly styled, and the long lean body discreetly clothed in tailored suits and dresses. This Sandy…

She complacently patted her hair. Gray waves had been cropped into a cap of curls hugging a finely shaped head and, by some miracle of a hairdresser's art, turned a glossy silver. Makeup made her pale blue eyes look darker and discreetly softened the austere lines of her cheeks and chin. But that wasn't all. Layers of assorted shades of green chiffon wafted about her thin body. As far as Forsythe could tell, the layers began with apple-green and charged through the spectrum to a final emerald.

"What in God's name have you done to yourself?" he blurted.

"Come up to date and it's high time." She fingered a barbaric silver bracelet studded with what looked like chunks of jade. "And *I* didn't do it. This took time, energy, and an assortment of hairdressers and couturieres to accomplish. To say nothing of an appalling amount of money." She sat and crossed her legs, dangling a shapely limb covered with a mist of sea-green and ending in an emerald-shod foot. "Well? Do say what you think."

Her employer's mouth snapped open to do exactly that, and then he decided discretion might be the best part of valor. "Takes a bit of getting used to," he said weakly. "Rather exotic, but yes…you do look quite nice."

"*Nice*." Her lips curled. "You dote on quotes so here's one for you: 'It is a certain sign of mediocrity always to praise moderately.' As for you…" She critically eyed his dark suit, chalk-white shirt, and narrow striped tie. "Wouldn't hurt to change your own dull image. Here's a start." Picking up a parcel she had dropped on a chair near the door, she tossed it to him.

Paper rustled and he stared down at a hot pink shirt and a yellow and mauve ascot. "To measure up to these I'd have to have my hair tinted magenta and orange and buy a lavender velvet suit. Sandy, I'm a barrister, not a pimp."

She came out of her chair like a big green cat. "Are you implying I look like a hooker? And to think I was going to offer to come back and straighten things out here." In a swirl of chiffon she headed toward the door.

"Sandy!" He caught her arm. "Look, I'm abjectly sorry. You look wonderful, marvelous! I'll wear your gifts, I swear. It's simply I've never seen you looking so radiant, so—"

"Don't overdo it. You'll run out of adjectives." She smiled up at him and this was the gamine grin of the old Sandy. "Apology accepted. I'll even reconsider my intention of helping you out of this mess."

He was tempted to accept but successfully resisted. "Not necessary. We'll cope. Now, do sit down and tell me what your plans are for the remainder of the month."

"Ply me with drink and I'll tell all. Ah, whiskey. Not too much soda, Robby, I'm feeling rather festive." She took a long drink. "The day after tomorrow I leave for a remote island, or sort of island, where I will, unaided, solve the dastardly crime of murder. Rather stealing your thunder, eh?" She extended her glass. "Perhaps a touch more of your vintage stock."

He tilted the decanter over her glass. "I have a hunch you were imbibing whiskey, vintage or not, before you got here."

"Not so. I'm completely sober. On this sort of an island is a centuries-old inn filled with ghosts and brooding violence—"

"Just what is 'a sort of an island'?"

"A small chunk of land connected by a spur of land at low tide with the mainland. A sort of causeway. Are you, I hope, confused, barrister?"

"Not so," he echoed. "Sounds as though you've been invited to one of those murder parties that are so popular now. The ones where people spend enormous amounts of money to act out the plot of an ancient mystery novel."

"A modern one. Hot off the author's word processor." She waved airily and the bracelet glinted. "And my fellow guests will be celebrities, noted figures in the art world, and so on. And the celebrity sleuth will be none other than *moi*."

"Just how did they latch on to you, Sandy?"

"Slightly green-eyed, aren't you?"

"Certainly not."

"Well, somewhat disgruntled. To be truthful, you were the one they wanted, but they had to settle for me. As I explained, you'll be far too busy coping without me to—"

"I might have been able to arrange it."

"And that's why I haven't mentioned it before." Cool blue eyes examined him. "You're really getting hooked on this crime bit."

"You must admit the cases we've been involved with have been more exciting than receiving instruction from solicitors."

"*You* have been involved with. All I've ever done is trail along and make notes and let you bang ideas off me."

It was his turn to look searchingly at his secretary. "You did a first-rate job all on your own in Maddersley."

She said wryly, "And managed to get nearly killed because I couldn't figure out who had butchered that family. But this will be different. All playacting and fun and games."

The telephone shrilled and he lifted it. "I'm busy, Mrs. Sutter. Well...ask Vincent to handle it. No further calls, please. And Mrs. Sutter, sorry I was so abrupt earlier." Replacing the receiver, he said firmly, "Stop tantalizing and tell all."

"To do that I'd have to go back to my school days."

"The condensed version."

She settled back in her chair. "During those school days my best friend was Peggy Green. An awfully nice girl, gentle and loyal and affectionate. Peggy married young, and I was horribly jealous when I met her fiancé. Not only was Noel Canard a naval officer, but he was incredibly handsome. Looked exactly like my film idol of the time—Tyrone Power. I was Peggy's maid of honor and must confess spent most of the ceremony mooning over Noel. It wasn't long before I stopped mooning and decided better Peggy than me. Noel was as vain and selfish as he was handsome. After a time Peggy and I lost track of each other except for cards at Christmas and a birth announcement when their daughter, Nancy, was born. Then, last year..."

"Yes," Forsythe said gently. "I remember your attending Mrs. Canard's funeral. You mentioned her husband had died some years prior to your friend's death."

"And I wept all over your shoulder. Sheer guilt for not keeping in touch with Peggy. Of course Nancy was at her mother's funeral, and we spoke briefly. She told me about her father's death and also what had happened to him some years before it. There had been a fire aboard his ship and Noel was badly burned. Horribly disfigured, Nancy said. At the time the girl was fifteen, and after the accident she never saw her father again. And she rarely saw her mother. That's what I meant about Noel's being selfish. Nancy was bundled off to school and spent her vacations with relatives and friends."

"A grim life for a child," Forsythe said. "What about her mother?"

"Twice a year Peggy would come to London and visit her daughter, but the rest of the time she was holed up on that island I mentioned. Peggy's aunt owned the island and ran the inn there for years. Apparently at one time there was a fishing village on the mainland and the inn's clientele was drawn from there. Anyway, the aunt willed both inn and island to Peggy, and after Noel's release from the hospital, he insisted they live there." Miss Sanderson paused and then muttered, "It must have been a ghastly life. The only people on the island with them were an elderly couple who did the work. Noel wouldn't let them or even his wife see his face. Nancy said he wore some kind of mask."

"When did he die?"

"Five years ago. Either by accident or suicide. Noel tried to cross the rock causeway and was swept away by the incoming tide. His body was never found. For the first time Nancy went to the inn to persuade her mother to leave the place, to come to London and live with her. Peggy refused. She said her health was not good and she'd prefer to spend the short time left to her where she had lived so many years with Noel. Peggy was obsessively devoted to her husband."

"She must have been to desert her daughter like that." Forsythe shook a baffled head. "I take it the daughter, Nancy Canard, is the one who invited you to the celebrity murder party."

"Nancy Lebonhom now. Recently she looked me up. She's married to a writer—Gavin Lebonhom—"

"The name doesn't ring a bell."

"For a good reason. Gavin hasn't published as yet. Nancy says that's the reason for turning the old inn into—what would you call it?"

Forsythe shrugged. "A money-making murder house?"

"Close enough. Not only should they have gobs of money from guests, but Gavin is convinced after the publicity on this first party publishers will be beating a path to his door, begging for scripts. Nancy says he's been working for weeks on the mystery script for this party. Everyone but the detective will have a script with dialogue and movements and so on. The great detective will ad-lib and guess the identity of the murderer. Finally"—she made an extravagant gesture—"I will have my very own case. Abigail Sanderson's first case!" She held out her glass. "On that note I will have a stirrup cup and take my leave."

Forsythe pushed the stopper into the neck of the decanter. "The bar is closed. I am not having you reel through chambers convincing the staff we've been closeted getting stinking. I must consider morale. They're probably still in shock over your new image."

She snorted. "Nervous Nellie nearly keeled over."

"Stop calling young Peters that, Sandy. Although, admittedly, it does fit. But it doesn't take much to shake Peters."

"About the only thing that would shake Vincent is an earthquake, and his mouth was sagging open even farther than yours did."

"By the way, what are the names of your fellow guests?"

"Haven't the foggiest. Nancy wants to surprise me." She stood up and smoothed down chiffon. "Do you think I'll measure up?"

"Sandy, I promise you won't be overlooked no matter how scintillating your fellow guests. Have fun, but do keep in mind Christmas is being celebrated at the family house in Sussex and I'm counting on you for hostess duties."

She opened the door and struck a pose. "I shall be there though hell should bar the way."

"If you need help detecting," he said wistfully, "give me a ring."

"Find your own murder. Now, I go to solve heinous crimes, battle ghosts and things that go bong in the night. I go!" And in a swirl of multicolored chiffon, she went.

Forsythe tried to engross himself in the Denton brief, but his thoughts wandered back to his secretary. Ghosts, he thought, and one of them might be wearing a mask.

Chapter Two

Miss Sanderson's MG was the same shade as the final flimsy layer on her exotic new gown. But on this blustery afternoon she was sensibly attired in more prosaic clothing. The silver curls were concealed by a scarf, and chiffon had given place to wool trousers, a heavy pullover, and a jacket. As the small car darted over the dips and through the hollows of the narrow road, she gazed at the bleak countryside beyond the bare tangles of hedgerows. In summertime it might have had its own charm, but at present it was dreary, stretching away in monotones broken only by occasional copses of skeletal maples and alders. The only sign of life for miles was a huddle of sheep munching stolidly at browning grass.

She shivered, turned up the heater a notch, and glanced at the rearview mirror. At least she wasn't alone in this godforsaken country. The scarlet car still drifted along in her wake. It was closer than it had been, and she was now able to discern its make. A Lagonda. A fellow guest, she surmised. There was no other explanation for anyone's taking this road but for that reason. Then she grinned. Detecting already. Hedgerows dwindled and trailed off as the road widened into a graveled area.

The sea was directly ahead, a heaving, leaden mass the same hue as the lowering clouds. On the gravel surface three vehicles were drawn up in a line, and beyond them a stone pier pointed like an accusing finger at a low-lying mass that had to be her destination. Pulling the car to a halt, she hopped out. The island was larger than she had expected and close enough that she could distinguish a sprawling structure and something that looked like a boathouse. She had half expected to find a boat waiting on this side, but there was nothing but the lonely pier, the sky, and water. Well, at least some company was arriving. The fiery red Lagonda drew up smartly, and its sole occupant got out.

Miss Sanderson took one look and fought to control her expression. If she wasn't careful, she would be gaping with the same idiotic look that Robby had turned on her a couple of days ago. She had never seen the Lagonda's driver in the flesh, but that face had looked up at her from the sleeves of the albums she had purchased as Christmas gifts for two teenaged nieces. The clerk had assured her that this pop star was the current rage and her nieces would be ecstatic. Miss Sanderson had little knowledge of current rages and practically none about pop stars in general and had taken the clerk's word for it. On the record sleeve a golden-skinned person, attired in what looked like silk pajamas, reclined against a pile of satin pillows. Glossy black ringlets fell to silken shoulders, and from one earlobe a jeweled earring dangled. She couldn't decide whether the reclining figure was male or female. The face framed in ringlets was beautiful but completely androgynous. Any doubts were now laid to rest. He was beautiful but definitely male. The ringlets were topped by a knitted toque, the slender frame was attired in jeans and a white parka, and neither ear was adorned.

A hand was extended and his voice was melodious. "Reggie Knight," he told her. "And you are…"

She struggled for composure. If she wasn't careful, she would be begging for an autograph. "Abigail Sanderson. And you…you're the Black Knight."

White teeth flashed in a grin. "And you're Robert Forsythe's secretary." He glanced back at the narrow road. "Is he driving down by himself?"

"No. Robby is too busy to come. I'm substituting for him."

"That ruddy Felix! All but swore on the Bible that Forsythe would be here."

"Sorry. You'll have to settle for me."

Turning away abruptly, Knight stared out over the sea. "The only reason I'm here is because of Forsythe. Damn it to hell!"

Drawing herself up, Miss Sanderson said tartly, "I said I was sorry."

The beautiful face was suddenly contrite. "And I'm sorry too. Sorry I snapped at you like that. Put it down to artistic temperament." He turned up his collar and the white material contrasted as startlingly with the dark features as the flash of teeth had. "No sign of life on the island. Think they're going to leave us here to freeze?"

"I'm halfway there already." She glanced at the other cars. There was an elegant black Rolls, a white Cadillac, and a shabby brown Mini. "Looks as though some guests have already arrived. Are you acquainted with any of them?"

He pointed at the Rolls. "Only Felix and Alice Caspari."

"Caspari. Hmm...that rings a bell. Didn't he have a show on television a while back? Got it! Felix Caspari, the cook."

Flinging back his head, the Black Knight roared with laughter. "*Cook*. How I wish you'd said that to Felix."

"Well...a chef, then."

"Felix prides himself on being modest. As he will soon tell you, quite modestly, Felix Caspari is the chefs' chef. The gourmet genius whom master chefs turn to for advice."

"And Alice?"

His mirth faded. "Every genius requires a victim. Let's get out of this wind." He opened the door of the Lagonda. "I'll switch the motor on and at least we'll be warm."

Eagerly she crawled into the luxurious car. Soon the motor was purring and delicious warmth flooded out. She loosened her head scarf and unbuttoned her jacket. Her companion still huddled in his parka, rubbing his hands together. "Should have worn gloves. We Jamaicans feel the cold."

"You came from Jamaica?"

"My parents did. I'm a Liverpudlian. Ever been in Liverpool?"

"I've passed through."

"Wise thing to do. My happiest moment was when I left the place."

"You've come a long way."

"Riding the crest at present. Which means next week I may be a has-been. Pop stars have short professional lives."

"Some don't. Look at the Beatles."

He threw up his hands. "I *knew* you were going to say that. Name some others who are still popular."

"I'm afraid, Mr. Knight—"

"Reggie, please."

"Abigail, then. As I started to say, I know little about your field."

"Ah, but you know a great deal about your own." Opening the glove compartment, he pulled out a handsome silver flask. "Care for a nip?"

"Don't mind if I do." He poured into the silver cup that acted as a cap and handed it to her. As he lifted the flask to his lips, she studied his profile. Truly a beautiful lad and perhaps that beauty would prolong his professional life. He seemed bitterly disappointed that Robby wasn't here. She probed a bit. "My profession, if you could call it that, is legal secretary to a barrister. Rather dull, don't you think?"

"That's only part of the story. The other, exciting, part is being assistant to a man who has solved several affairs that the newspapers call 'impossible crimes.'" He quoted, "'Robert Forsythe, ably assisted by his secretary, Abigail Sanderson—'"

"Assisted," she said sharply. "A bumbling Watson."

"You sound resentful."

She was about to make a hot denial and then she said slowly, "I suppose, in a way, I am. Oh, not of Robby, but perhaps of his uncanny ability to take threads and knit them together. In every case I've had access to the same facts as he, and yet…"

"Forsythe puts them together and finds a solution and all you have are jigsaw pieces."

"Exactly. Afterward I always kick myself for not seeing it too."

He was gazing through the windshield at the island. "I'm interested in one particular case. I believe it was one of your earlier ones. Forsythe found the solution to a murder that had been committed many years before. Do you remember the one?"

"Vividly. It was our first case. And Robby solved it twenty-five years after the murder had been committed. It involved the Calvert family." She handed back the silver cup. "You're interested in vintage murders?"

"Not a murder…or maybe in a way it was." He swung around to face her. "Wouldn't you call the destruction of a name and a reputation a murderous deed?"

"It depends on the details—" She leaned forward. "Look. Signs of life. We're about to be rescued."

Switching off the ignition, he opened his door. "About time, Abigail."

They watched a figure on the island trotting down the path that led to the boathouse, and Miss Sanderson thought longingly of central heating, a good stiff drink, and a hot tub. Nancy Lebonhom had mentioned that her husband and she were looking forward to hosting parties for wealthy crime buffs, and the ancient inn had been renovated with this object in view.

The door of the boathouse opened and a trim speedboat nosed out. Behind the wheel was a figure muffled in what looked like a navy pea jacket, and behind the head strands of hair blew backward like a horse's tail. "That certainly isn't Nancy Lebonhom," she told Reggie.

"Felix mentioned you are a relative of our hostess. An aunt?"

"The chef was mistaken. I was a friend of Nancy's mother."

"Might better get out the luggage." While Miss Sanderson got her bag from her car, he lifted a case from the rear of the

Lagonda. Carrying both bags, he strode toward the pier. "Ship ahoy," he shouted as the boat nudged the stone pier. "We were afraid we were going to be marooned here."

The woman leapt from the cockpit and tied the rope to a stanchion. "I should have kept a closer watch on shore," she told them as she loped up the pier. "Only noticed you moments ago. Welcome to the Jester."

She was as tall as Miss Sanderson and appeared to have much the same build. She was younger, looking in her thirties. Light brown hair was strained back from a long narrow face and secured with a leather shoelace. Her brown eyes were warm and intelligent. "Miss Sanderson and Mr. Knight. I'm Fran Hornblower."

"A good name for a mariner," Miss Sanderson told her, and wondered if she should recognize the name. "Another guest?"

"A lowly retainer. A Jacqueline-of-all-trades."

"But Nancy said both her mother's employees were elderly."

"Too old to carry on. Peggy—Mrs. Canard—hired Hielkje and me when they retired. We've been here nearly two years. Hielkje is cook and housekeeper."

Reggie gave her his flashing smile. "And you're the handyman. Or should I say handywoman? Perhaps handyperson."

She smiled back. "Whatever, and much needed around the Jester."

"Is that the name of the island?"

"The inn. The island is nameless or was until recently. Gavin is now calling it Lebonhom Island."

"It's not actually an island, is it? Felix mentioned it has a connection with the mainland."

"Right at present it's high tide and the causeway is under several feet of water. It's not safe to use anyway. Quite rough and overgrown with mosses and lichens."

Miss Sanderson said, "Nancy told me the fishermen once used the causeway to get to the inn."

"Years ago, and it must have been in better shape then. There's no one left in the village now except an occasional transient. The cottages, like the inn, are built of stone and are still intact, but it's a ghost village. From the water you'll see it. And speaking of water, let's get underway. I imagine you're chilled."

"Clear through," Reggie told her. He waited until Fran was behind the wheel, and then he handed the cases down and helped Miss Sanderson into the boat. He unwound the rope and climbed down beside the secretary. The boat swooped around in a graceful curve and headed away from the pier. Fran waved a hand. "There's the village."

The cluster of stone cottages did look intact and so did their slate roofs. Reggie pointed. "Look. Smoke coming from a chimney. See? That house at the end of the street."

Fran shrugged. "Probably one of those transients I mentioned. Squatting for a couple of nights."

Miss Sanderson only glanced at the village. Her attention was on the inn. As they drew closer, she said, "It's much larger than I had pictured it, Fran."

"Gavin had that wing built on recently. Plans eventually to stick a matching one on the other side. His plans tend to be a bit grandiose."

"And you stayed on here after Peggy's death?"

"Nancy asked Hielkje and me to caretake until she was able to sell the place. But she married Gavin and he got a brainstorm going and decided to make his fortune here. Then they *really* needed us."

"Don't you find it lonely?" Reggie asked.

"I find it ideal."

Miss Sanderson huddled into her jacket. To take her mind off the cold she examined what she could see of the island. It didn't look ideal to her. A barren chunk of rock lunged out of the sea, and it was broken only by a few stunted trees and the sprawling building. The original inn was built of stone and was three-storied. Along the north side was a long addition in white clapboard, a single story. The recently added wing blended in surprisingly well with the inn. Small windows in both structures were bordered by black-painted shutters, and the only touch of color were red-tiled roofs. Fran expertly nudged the boat in against another stone pier, and in moments Miss Sanderson was following Fran up the steep path.

"It will be good to feel that central heating," Miss Sanderson said.

The brown ponytail bobbed as the woman turned to cast a sharp look at Miss Sanderson. "Exactly what did Nancy tell you about the Jester?"

"That it's been completely modernized."

"Hardly. I better warn you. No central heating, no electricity, no—"

"*What?*" Reggie gave an anguished howl. "And that bloody Felix lured me down to a primitive hovel without even indoor plumbing!"

"You and a number of others." Fran was laughing and her eyes danced. "There *is* indoor plumbing and that's about it. Gavin didn't waste money on nonessentials like comfort. Put every pound he could borrow into paneling and antique furnishings. Atmosphere, he claims, is most important. When the money comes flooding in, he hopes to add heat and light."

"But how do you manage?" Miss Sanderson asked.

"That's why the Lebonhoms need me. There's a cookstove in the kitchen, an old gas refrigerator, a few kerosene heaters, kerosene lamps—"

"Heat?" Reggie wailed.

"Fireplaces that require enormous amounts of coal hauled in to them."

Reggie had halted and now he lifted a fist and shook it in the direction of the inn. "I," he said decisively, "am going to kill that chefs' chef. I am going to carve him up with one of his custom-made knives."

"And I," Fran said heartily, "am more than willing to help you."

Chapter Three

O ver the inn door a weather-beaten board clattered in the wind. On it a capped and belled jester in faded tints disported. On the other side of that door the lobby spread out. Beside an oak desk was a door, a hall ran back into the inn's depths, and on the far side was a set of tall double doors. The lobby was floored in red and black tiles, and, rather charmingly, the red squares contained white-painted chess pieces, the black tiles, red ones. A red phone was perched on the desk, flanked by foot-high glass figures of the red and white queens. Miss Sanderson's first impression was that the lobby wasn't much warmer than it had been outside.

Fran Hornblower took Miss Sanderson's jacket and Reggie's parka and toque and hung them on brass pegs near the outer door. The other pegs were already crowded with an assortment of raincoats, parkas, one lustrous dark mink, and a short white fox cape. "Nancy," she called. "Your guests are here."

One of the double doors was thrown open and a chunky man popped out. Both his hands were outstretched and he was beaming. "Your host, Gavin Lebonhom," Fran said. "Gavin, this—"

"No need for introductions," he told them jovially. "Auntie Abby and the Black Knight. Welcome to Lebonhom Island and the Jester!"

"Reggie," the Black Knight said firmly.

"Abigail," Miss Sanderson said just as firmly.

"Righto. But Nan always calls you Auntie Abby."

"I prefer Abigail."

She did. Nancy Lebonhom was young enough that the auntie didn't jar, but her husband didn't appear to be much younger than Miss Sanderson. His thick dark hair was liberally salted with gray, and his upper lip was hidden under a salt-and-pepper waterfall mustache.

Shivering, Reggie clasped both arms over his chest. "Where's Felix?"

Their host raised a bushy brow. "Fran?"

"When I left he was in the kitchen venting his spleen on Alice and Hielkje."

"Tell him Abigail and Reggie have arrived and round up everyone for grog."

She shook her head and the ponytail bobbed. "I'm off on fuel detail. Those bedrooms are frigid. However, if you'd like to lug in coal, I'd be happy to oblige."

"You brought in fuel this morning. At least, every time I needed you that was your excuse."

"Any idea how much coal is needed to keep this place habitable, Gavin?"

"Very well, but if you see Nancy, tell her to bring the others." He took Miss Sanderson's arm. "Come into the bar and I'll stir up that grog and get you thawed out."

"That," Reggie told him, "will take some doing."

Gavin led them into the bar. "At one time this was the public bar. Saloon bar is back there. As much as possible I left it as it was when this place was actually used as an inn."

"Atmosphere," Reggie said.

"Precisely."

"I like it," Miss Sanderson said, looking around with delight. She felt as though she had stepped back in time. Here were the rough dark beams, the old oaken paneling, the wide polished counter, and the gleaming taps of an earlier century. In an alcove a stone-faced fireplace beamed heat. Spaced around the room were rustic tables and benches.

Reggie stretched like a cat and regarded their host more kindly. "Do those taps work?"

"Best of ale comes foaming out. But wouldn't you prefer grog?"

"Seldom drink anything stronger than beer. I can handle it myself. Put in a stint as a bartender at one time."

"As you wish. Abigail, come into the inglenook and I'll see what I can do for you."

The alcove was more a small room than the traditional inglenook. Cushioned benches almost ringed it, allowing only a narrow passageway to reach the outer room. Sinking on a bench, she stretched out her feet to the welcome heat and watched Gavin as he deftly mixed ingredients in a long-handled copper pot. "Did you ever put in a stint as a bartender?" she asked.

The waterfall mustache quivered as he smiled. "No, but I'm good with grog. Even Fran admits that, and she doesn't hand me compliments often. Simply can't understand a man who shuns manual labor. Ah, that should do it." He poured seething liquid into a pottery mug. "Careful, that's hot."

She inhaled the fumes and took a cautious sip. "Good! Nancy tells me you write."

"Been scribbling away for years with no result. Publishers are wary of taking a chance on an unknown writer. But I'm hopeful soon—" He broke off and bobbed to his feet. "Mrs. Montrose! Now, you probably recognize Reggie Knight, and here is Abigail Sanderson. Abigail and Reggie, may I present Sybil Clifton Montrose."

Swinging around, Miss Sanderson saw a short, wiry woman leaning across the counter, gathering one of Reggie's hands in both of hers. "What a pleasure! To think the Black Knight is right here. I've all your records and—"

"Care for a beer, Mrs. Montrose?" Freeing his hand from her grasp, Reggie reached for a pewter tankard.

"Thanks, but no. I prefer grog. I've so many questions to ask you I hardly know where to begin..."

Mrs. Montrose proceeded to ask questions and patiently the Black Knight answered them. While Gavin mixed hot water, whiskey, lemon, and sugar, Miss Sanderson studied the latest celebrity. Sybil Clifton Montrose, hostess *extraordinaire*, giver of parties and dinners that even the famous thirsted to attend. The photographs in magazines had been kind to her. In person she looked like an aging simian. Above a clever monkey face was a fluff of fine gray hair, and she wore gray slacks and a gray sweater, a padded red vest, and red sandals. The gray-and-red was echoed in a huge fluffy gray Persian with a red leather harness and leash linking it to its owner.

Reggie was drawing another beer and gazing, rather desperately, over Mrs. Montrose at Miss Sanderson. "Abigail," he called. "Do come and meet Mrs. Montrose." As the secretary approached, the monkey face swung toward her. Mrs. Montrose's nostrils flared as though she had just caught scent of dead fish. Bright black eyes swept from Miss Sanderson's sturdy shoes to her silver curls. "Where is your employer?" she demanded.

"Robby wasn't able to come, Mrs.—"

"How disgusting!"

The older woman turned back to Reggie, and Miss Sanderson was left staring at her back. Hot color flooded into her face and she thought wrathfully: Disgusting is right, Mrs. Montrose, what a disgusting old witch you turn out to be.

"Allow me to explain, dear lady," Gavin said, and brushed by the secretary. He was practically babbling. "We did think Mr. Forsythe could make it, but at the last moment..."

Putting down his tankard, Reggie winked at Miss Sanderson and lifted the flap in the counter. "Come have a look at this, Abigail."

The "this" he was pointing at proved to be a framed watercolor on the wall between two windows. In Miss Sanderson's ear he hissed, "A rude old girl, isn't she?"

"Obviously has no time for anyone but celebrities," she said tartly. "Hmm, that picture is charming."

"Think so? Take a closer look."

She took a closer look. It *was* charming. Three children, two girls and a boy, were skating on a frozen pond. The boy was falling, and the little girls, mittened hands clasped, were skating past him, tiny faces rosy and laughing. The pond was ringed by bushes and tall evergreens towering against a bright sky. Then she saw it. Behind a bush, merging with the shadows of the trees, was another, darker, shadow. Something misshapen, menacing, a feeling of malevolence. Innocence threatened by evil. She whispered, "What's that he—it—is holding?"

"At a guess I'd say an ax."

"Blimey!" She stood to one side and studied the scene. "Couldn't it be an optical illusion, the play of light and shadow? It's not all that distinct."

Lustrous ringlets shook. "Looks deliberate. Like a maniac about to use an ax on those kids. Wonder who painted it?" Swinging around, he called, "Gavin, who is the artist?"

Their host, who had been hovering over an irate Mrs. Montrose, looked relieved and hurried over. "My wife's father. Abigail, I understand you knew Noel Canard."

"For a brief time, long ago. I didn't know he painted."

"Nancy said her father had his heart set on an art career, but his family forced him into the navy. He did most of his painting after the accident. I've pieces of his work in all the guest rooms."

"Atmosphere?" Reggie asked.

"They do help." Fondly, Gavin regarded the watercolor. "A waste of talent, wasn't it? In the navy when he should have been—"

"Where is my grog?" Mrs. Montrose snapped.

"Coming right up."

Reggie watched the other man steering Mrs. Montrose to the alcove and said caustically, "He's lived with that horror and hasn't even seen it. Some atmosphere and some writer!"

Miss Sanderson dragged her eyes away from the picture. "I doubt I would have if you hadn't called my attention to it."

"Oh, *you* would have seen it."

Mrs. Montrose, now huddling near the fire, demanded, "Just where is Felix? I want a word with him."

"Yes," Reggie said. "Where is that bloody Felix?"

"Did someone mention my name?" a deep voice asked from the direction of the double doors.

Reggie strode forward. "Hiding, weren't you? Skulking around waiting for me to cool down."

"I rarely skulk. I've been working my fingers to the bone in that excuse for a kitchen, preparing a suitable dinner for all you lovely people. Gavin! Why haven't you done something about that primitive hole? How do you expect haute cuisine to appear from a nineteenth-century dungeon?"

An unbecoming flush mottled Gavin Lebonhom's face. "You know perfectly well the funds wouldn't stretch that far. Not after fixing up that VIP suite for you."

Reggie clamped a rough hand on Felix's shoulder. "Don't try to change the subject. You lied to both Mrs. Montrose and me. Assured us that Robert Forsythe would be here."

Felix sketched a cross over his creamy Aran sweater. "Only repeated what I'd been told. Nancy assured me that—"

"Like hell I did!" Nancy Lebonhom had entered the bar. "I told you what Auntie Abby said—Auntie Abby, you're finally here!" The girl rushed to embrace the older woman. "I'm so happy to see you!"

"You appear to be in the minority, Nancy." Fondly, Miss Sanderson gazed down at the round face, the short honey curls, the luminous hazel eyes. Nancy looked so much like her mother had at the same age.

Felix Caspari was trying to break loose from the Black Knight's golden hands. "Unhand me and let bygones be bygones. After all, we're gathered together for fun and games." He added plaintively, "Be a good chap and let me welcome Abigail." Reggie's hands fell away and Felix hastily walked over to Nancy and Miss Sanderson. "Despite this misunderstanding, I'm certain we are all delighted to meet you."

"I feel about as welcome as an outbreak of measles at a boarding school," Miss Sanderson told him bleakly.

"Then we'll have to make amends, won't we." Felix struck a pose. He was a handsome man. Tall and well built with a mane of chestnut hair, a short-cropped beard, sensual lips parted in a wide smile, shrewd eyes that weren't smiling. "I feel no need to introduce myself."

"Yes," Miss Sanderson said demurely. "I've heard about you. You're a cook."

Reggie made a sound much like the crow of a rooster and Felix gave a strangled one that sounded remarkably like a growl. "Dear Abigail, I am the chefs' chef, consulted by master chefs the world over. Although I am a modest man and often refer to myself as a dietitian—"

"Felix was never trained as a chef," Mrs. Montrose announced acidly. She had left the alcove and was leading her cat toward the counter. "The closest he came to it was the dietitian course I arranged for him when he was a young chap."

"Sybil," Felix confided to Miss Sanderson, "is my very dear friend."

"Patron," that lady corrected. "Felix's grandfather was our gardener, and Felix grew up as playmate to my son."

"Patron and friend," Felix said smoothly. "And the good angel who funded a catering business for me and sponsored me so I was able to get my start."

"At a price," a light female voice said.

Two women had entered the room from the saloon bar. The one who had spoken was in the lead. She was a small dowdy woman, possessed of a faded prettiness. In one hand she clasped a large tapestry knitting bag.

Thumping her mug on the bar, Mrs. Montrose told Miss Sanderson, "This is the cook's wife, Alice Caspari. And dear Alice, as *you* should know, everyone has a price."

Miss Sanderson was paying little attention. Mrs. Montrose had mentioned a son. Recently she had heard or read about that son. Yes, now she remembered, and a feeling of compassion for the elderly woman stirred. For years that son had been comatose, hooked up to a life-support system. After a great deal of effort his mother had won the legal battle and the life supports had been removed, the poor man allowed to die.

Miss Sanderson was polite to Alice Caspari and accepted a large flabby hand belonging to the tall woman who had accompanied the chef's wife.

"I might better introduce myself. No one else will bother. Hielkje Visser."

"Dutch?" Miss Sanderson asked.

"Frisian."

"Isn't Friesland a province of the Netherlands?"

"A true Frisian would hotly debate that, but as a half-Frisian—my mother was English—I'll answer yes."

"And you looked after Peggy Canard."

"Fran and I. We grew very fond of her. Peggy was a kind lady."

"Nancy is the picture of her mother, Hielkje."

"Perhaps when Peggy was young. When I met her, she had snow-white hair and was most frail. But yes, Nancy's eyes are like Peggy's were. Same color and as bright. You were Peggy's friend?"

"School friend. After Peggy's marriage we drifted apart."

"That happens." Hielkje gave a heavy sigh.

"I was wondering, Hielkje, if you would be kind enough to point me toward my room."

"You've had your fill of celebrities?"

"Completely sated, and I'd also like to freshen up."

"I'll check with Fran. She's trying to take the chill off some of the guest rooms."

Leaning against the edge of a long table, Miss Sanderson eyed the woman's broad back. Hielkje Visser was heavyset and her walk was brisk, but her skin had a yellowish tinge and purplish pouches sagged under her brown eyes. She looked far from healthy. Miss

Sanderson retreated to the alcove and found the little room unoccupied. She sank down near the hearth and rested her chin on a hand. She was gazing into the flames when she felt something soft brushing against her leg. It was the gray Persian, its smoky eyes glinting in the firelight. Bending, she rubbed the animal behind an ear. It arched its back and broke into a husky purr.

"Omar likes you, Abigail." Mrs. Montrose sank down beside the secretary. "An honor. He seldom takes to anyone. I feel I should…I really wasn't very nice to you earlier, was I?"

"No."

"In fact I was curt. I fear I don't take disappointment well, but I shouldn't have taken it out on you. As I grow older I seem to be getting more querulous." One monkey claw patted Miss Sanderson's knee. "Shall we start afresh?"

Lifting her eyes, Miss Sanderson saw the wrinkled face so close to her own lighted with a warm and engaging smile. She had been wondering how this irascible old woman had ever managed to become a sought-after hostess. Now she could see Sybil Montrose had two sides. This one was all warmth and charm, and Miss Sanderson warily wondered if Mrs. Montrose might have an ulterior purpose.

Omar left off purring and jerked away from the secretary's hand, giving vent to a loud and menacing hiss. Reggie Knight, carrying a foaming tankard, circled the cat and sat down opposite the two women. He told Omar's mistress, "I can see why you keep that animal leashed. Looks positively fierce."

She turned her smile on him. "What you're thinking is like pet, like owner. I was just apologizing to Abigail for my foul temper. Come to mama, darling." Scooping up the cat, she settled it on her lap and ran a soothing hand down the silky back. "When I get back to London, I'm planning a dinner party and I'm so hoping to have all of you there."

Reggie shook his dark head. "I seldom go to social deals."

"I've heard that. Which is why I was so anxious to meet you and Dolly and Mr. Forsythe—"

"Dolly?"

"You and Abigail haven't met her yet. She's spent most of the afternoon in her room. Said she had some work to do on her latest book."

"Another writer?"

"This time a famous one." The cat flexed claws against Mrs. Montrose's knee and she winced. "Don't do that, Omar! He has the worst habits. When he's happy he practically claws one raw. As I started to say, Reggie, the three of you are such retiring people it would be quite a feather in my cap if I could gather you at my table and introduce you to some of my friends—"

"How many friends?" Reggie asked.

"Only a select few. People who are mad to meet all of you." Mrs. Montrose turned her attention to Miss Sanderson. "I'd enjoy having your famous employer with us."

Honey, Miss Sanderson thought, definitely is supposed to attract more flies than vinegar. She noticed that an invitation hadn't been extended to Robby's humble secretary. "I have no idea what Robby's plans are, Mrs. Montrose. Christmas is such a rushed time." She added innocently, "But I should be happy to attend one of your dinners. I've heard so much about them."

"And I would be happy to have you," the older woman told her with no outward indication of happiness. "Do try to persuade your employer to attend too." She beamed another smile at Reggie. "And you must consider it too."

He stretched long, jean-clad legs toward the fire. "I understand you have some competition now, Mrs. Montrose. A lady named—"

"Eileen Carstairs. Don't believe all you read, Reggie. I'm positive Mrs. Carstairs must have bribed the columnist to write that gushy article. He had the unmitigated gall to say that woman's dinners outshone mine. She's nothing but an upstart!"

"She *has* managed to snag some illustrious guests."

"A couple of Arab sheikhs."

"Also a Russian ballet star and two astronauts. Then there was that Spanish tenor and that chap who writes the espionage books. Quite an impressive list."

205 ABR FOR A DIETITIAN 205

Her hand came down so heavily on the cat that it hissed and jumped down. After a moment it curled up on one of Miss Sanderson's feet. "An upstart!" Mrs. Montrose repeated. "A Johnny-come-lately!"

"You've been a hostess for many years," Miss Sanderson said.

Mrs. Montrose took a deep and apparently calming breath. "For most of my adult life. My husband, as you may know, was a career diplomat and I started to give little dinners to further his career…" Her voice trailed off and she gazed moodily into space. As though speaking to herself, she continued, "I did everything in my power to further Trevor's career. He had no ambition or drive. But *I* did and I pushed and prodded until it looked as though he would receive an ambassadorship…perhaps even be on the honors list. Then, shortly after our son's birth…Trevor died. Quite suddenly. All those years of work for nothing." She gave herself a little shake and her eyes snapped back to Reggie. "I sound dreadful, don't I? But I was raised in a much different world than you. A woman didn't have the same opportunity then as one does now. In my youth women almost always had to work through a man to accomplish anything. With my husband gone my dreams were shattered. For a time I had hopes for my son, but he was exactly like his father, and so I was thrown back on my own resources. It was then I found the flair I had for dinner parties coming to my aid."

Miss Sanderson had a remarkable memory. Robert Forsythe often compared it to a computer, and now a button clicked and she remembered the reason Trevor Montrose II had lapsed into a coma. She remembered the length of time that Mrs. Montrose's child had been just marginally alive, and her heart went out to the other woman. Sybil Montrose's life had been marked by tragedy. It was her turn to pat the older woman's bony knee and say sympathetically, "You have been remarkably successful in your own right."

Mrs. Montrose said bitterly, "And now that disgusting Mrs. Carstairs is taking that away from me."

Miss Sanderson's compassion was mirrored in the dark eyes of Reggie Knight. He said slowly, "Perhaps it is time to socialize a bit. I should be honored to attend your dinner."

"And I will certainly urge Robby to be there," Miss Sanderson assured.

"You're both so kind." Simian eyes blinked and Mrs. Montrose was on her feet. "Dolly! Over here, dear. You simply must meet our latest arrivals."

In the outer room, every person with one exception was heading toward the tall young woman. The exception was the chef's wife, who had settled on the bench directly under Noel Canard's watercolor and was serenely knitting. Pale blue wool cascaded from steel needles and she didn't lift her head. The others more than made up for Alice's indifference. Felix Caspari was holding Dolly's arm, Gavin was offering her a seat, Nancy was on her other side, and Hielkje Visser was trailing behind.

Miss Sanderson had no difficulty in recognizing this celebrity. That exquisite face and figure graced dust jackets on many of her own books. Dolores Carter-White, author of dozens of outstanding romances. She looks exactly the same as she does in publicity pictures, Miss Sanderson thought, all that is lacking are the French poodles, the white furs, the white Cadillac. No, she decided, only the poodles. The white Cadillac was parked near her own car on the mainland, a white fur hung near her own jacket on a peg beside the front door.

"Felix!" Mrs. Montrose bellowed. "Don't be greedy. Bring Dolly in here. I've hardly had a chance to say hello to her."

Obediently, Felix led the vision in the white silk jumpsuit toward the alcove. The rest of the entourage followed. Mrs. Montrose hurried to meet the small parade and possessively grasped Dolly's free arm.

"Shoo!" she told the others, and tugged the younger woman into the alcove. Introductions were made, Dolly was seated beside Reggie, grog was offered by Gavin and refused, and gradually order was restored. Miss Sanderson took a long and satisfying look at her favorite author. She noticed that Mrs.

Montrose, again perched at her side, was gazing transfixed from the Black Knight to Dolores Carter-White. Miss Sanderson didn't blame her. Apart both were eye catching, but together…

"I didn't catch your name," Dolly said, and Miss Sanderson realized she was being addressed.

"Abigail Sanderson."

"I'm afraid…"

"Robert Forsythe," Mrs. Montrose told her. "His secretary."

"Oh…so pleased."

Mrs. Montrose was hot on the trail. "You'll be even more pleased by my news. That little dinner party I mentioned to you earlier—well, the Black Knight has accepted and Abigail will have her employer there. Now, my dear Dolly, they are just as shy as you are and—"

"I am *not* shy," Dolly said sharply. "I merely value my privacy."

"As do Reggie and Mr. Forsythe. Please reconsider."

"I'll think about it," Dolly said vaguely.

Miss Sanderson realized that the famous author spoke rather hesitantly, her voice having a tendency to trail off. Except when she had been described as shy. There had been no hesitancy then.

"Mrs. Montrose mentioned you're working on a new book," Reggie said.

Dolly replied, but Miss Sanderson wasn't listening. She was drinking the younger woman in. A creamy blonde, she observed, a tinted oval face, eyes the same shade and brilliancy as one of Robby's cherished pieces of antique green jade. The jumpsuit looked as though it had been painted onto the slender but curvaceous body. With a start she realized that Dolly looked exactly like a Christmas present she had recently purchased for a small niece. Dolly was the picture of a Barbie doll, miraculously animated and life-size. She also realized that, spellbinding as the author was, she wasn't truly beautiful. Her being seated beside Reggie Knight made that only too apparent. The Black Knight's beauty didn't stem wholly from classic features, golden skin, glossy ringlets. It was the warmth and the expression of that face that lent it true beauty.

Forcing her attention back to the conversation, Miss Sanderson found they had worked through details on Dolly's current book and were discussing the difficulties public figures encounter trying to maintain privacy. "The public," Reggie was saying, "appear to feel we're their property, that we've no right to conceal any portion of our lives from them."

"I know," Dolly assured him. "Perhaps one should expect it. After all, we're packaged goods."

Miss Sanderson bent forward. "I don't understand."

"You're fortunate," Reggie told her. "Have you seen any of the sleeves on my records?"

"I bought a couple as Christmas presents."

"And just how was the Black Knight presented?"

"Silk pajamas, ringlets—"

"Just where is the famous earring?" Dolly asked.

His teeth flashed whitely. "Not with me, thank God. My press agent dreamed that public image up, complete with that disgusting earring. But you're familiar with all this rot, Dolly. The furs and Cadillac."

"To say nothing of poodles," Miss Sanderson chimed in.

Dolly shifted and crossed her legs. The cat immediately leapt off Miss Sanderson's foot and lashed out, its claws barely missing Dolly's slender ankle. Hauling the animal back, Mrs. Montrose scolded, "Bad Omar! Naughty boy!" She tightened her grip on the leash. "But then, Dolly, you must be fond of pets."

"I loathe animals. Those miserable poodles are my agent's idea."

"But why?" Miss Sanderson asked.

"Like Reggie's earring. A trademark." For the first time since Dolly had entered the alcove, she smiled, tinted lips exposing perfect teeth. "And because I'm a packaged deal. Completely phony. It wasn't always that way. When my first book was published I was living quite contentedly in a primitive cottage on a delightfully lonely moor. That book was published under my real name—Maud Epstein. An agent became interested and visited me there. He admired my writing but not *me*. I may not have been a beauty, but I wasn't exactly a hag and I became huffy. I informed him all that mattered was what I put on the printed page, and Rory proceeded to fill me in on success. Any number of writers, he said, could write romances as well as I could. What I needed was a gimmick, trademarks. He said if I wanted to be a best-seller, he would handle me, but I'd have to put myself totally in his hands." She waved a hand down her long body. "And this is the result."

Miss Sanderson was fascinated. "And you went out and bought a Cadillac and furs and—"

"At that time I could barely afford food. Rory rented the clothes and car and borrowed a couple of those horrible little dogs to have the first photograph taken. It appeared on the dust jacket of my next book, and that was published under a pseudonym. Rory came up with Dolores and I made up the surname. And *voilà*! Success arrived for Dolores Carter-White." Creamy blond hair brushed over white silk as she turned her head. "I'll bet my poodles against your earring that Knight is not your real name."

"And I'd lose my earring," Reggie told her. "Day is my name. Reginald Day. I suggested Night and *my* agent stuck a *K* in front of it. Do you ever feel, Dolly, that somewhere along the way you've lost Maud Epstein?"

"Occasionally. But somewhere under all the phoniness is the real me. That I'll never lose. Will you lose Reggie Day?"

"Never! I'll always be Damien Day's kid brother."

This time Miss Sanderson didn't have to search her memory. Her face glowing, she said, "I have one of your brother's records—"

"The one and only. Damien was killed in a car crash shortly after he cut that."

Mrs. Montrose nodded her head. "I remember. He was a friend of Felix's, wasn't he? That was...let me see. It was years ago."

The young man's head bent and thick lashes veiled his eyes. "Nine years, three months, eleven days."

"A tragedy," Miss Sanderson murmured. "He had the most marvelous voice."

"Was he a rock singer?" Dolly asked.

"Calypso."

Mrs. Montrose pursed her lips. "If I remember correctly, he was driving Felix's car when it happened. Felix was hurt, a leg injured, I believe. Wasn't there a child involved?"

"Both a child and a young woman. Damien was killed, they were killed. Felix had a broken leg and a concussion."

Dolly placed a hand on his knee. The hand was decorative, with pearly nails and a huge opal ring that blazed in the fire-light. "You must have been only a child at the time."

"Fourteen." Reggie lifted his head. "Damien was the only relative I had in this country. Our parents were dead and he was the one who got me out of that slum in Liverpool." He slanted a smile at Mrs. Montrose, but there was no humor in it. "You acted as patron for Felix, and after my brother's death, Felix acted in the same role for me. Took me in hand and arranged education and later took charge of my career."

"Felix has such a tender heart," Dolly said.

The man they had been discussing stepped into the alcove, plumped down beside Dolly, and took possession of a decorative hand. "Gavin's lighting up lamps now. Want me to have him bring one in here?"

"No," Dolly whispered. "Firelight's romantic."

"And so are you." He relinquished the hand and slid an arm around her narrow waist. She snuggled against him, making a sound much like Omar's purr. Felix nuzzled his lips against her hair.

Miss Sanderson's eyes widened and she glanced into the bar. Mrs. Caspari was still placidly knitting. Celebrities, she decided, are amazingly tolerant. Reggie, wearing a wide grin, glanced from Miss Sanderson to the chef's wife. He leaned across Dolly and told his patron, "Methinks you're shocking Abigail."

"Nothing to be shocked about." Felix's free hand caressed the opal in Dolly's ring. "We're engaged, Abigail. As soon as I'm divorced, this lovely lady and I will be married."

"*What?*" Mrs. Montrose shrieked in Miss Sanderson's ear.

"Calm down, Sybil," Felix said. "You're among the first to know."

"When? How?"

Reggie laughed. "To say nothing of where and why."

Gently, Dolly detached herself from Felix's arm. "Three months ago in Venice. We met, fell in love, Felix gave me this ring."

"But Alice?" Mrs. Montrose asked in a lower voice.

Felix shrugged a bulky shoulder. "She's dragging her feet, but she'll come around."

Still grinning, Reggie settled back. "So…a *ménage à trois.*"

"You," Felix said hotly, "have a filthy mind. Nothing like that. No hanky-panky. You know me. Wouldn't you say I'm a romantic?"

"With a touch of satyriasis thrown in."

Felix's thick lips twisted. "Such gratitude. You keep forgetting all I've done for you."

"No such luck. You keep reminding me."

Help, Miss Sanderson thought, I don't know if the Black Knight and the chefs' chef are going to come to blows or simply are sparring. If Robby were here, he'd have a quote from his beloved Bard that would cover this. He would also remind me of the new Abigail who has come up to date. But—she took another peek at Alice Caspari—it appears one can bring one's appearance up to date but the old mind sadly lags behind. I simply don't approve of a man bringing his wife *and* his fiancée to a party, murder or otherwise.

Apparently Mrs. Montrose, who was much older than Miss Sanderson, had no such scruples. "This is *wonderful*, my dear Dolly. Now you simply can't refuse my invitation. After all, Felix will be arranging the menu and has offered to supervise my kitchen staff. Do say you'll come."

"Don't push, Sybil," Felix told her. "Doesn't work with Dolly. Only makes her more obstinate."

Reggie said slyly, "Sounds as though you've tried pushing."

Tugging at his beard as though to rip it from his chin, the older man glowered at his protégé. Much to Miss Sanderson's relief, Fran Hornblower appeared at the far end of the bench. "Reggie and Abigail, your rooms are ready. I'll show you the way."

Reggie shook his head, but Miss Sanderson promptly rose. Felix stopped trying to destroy his beard and told her, "I'll be starting dinner shortly. Do come and watch." She was about to make an excuse but reconsidered. It would be foolish to lose an opportunity to see Felix Caspari in action. She accepted his invitation, and as they left the alcove, Fran muttered in her ear, "You should feel honored. That's practically a royal decree."

Felix called after them, "Fran, tell Hielkje I'm expecting her to lend a hand."

"Not tonight. When she's finished laying the table I'm sending her to her room to rest. Hielkje isn't feeling well."

"Trust Gavin to have an ailing cook! Well, I'll have to make do with Alice." He bellowed, "Alice, get out to the kitchen and prepare the vegetables."

Pushing her knitting into the bag, Alice rose and scurried across the room. Fran darted an amused look at Miss Sanderson. "You're looking rather stunned."

"In some respects I'm finding it awfully hard to come up to date."

They stepped into the lobby. There was only one lamp lit there, standing on the desk beside the white queen. The chill struck and shadows danced against the walls. She headed toward the door beside the desk, but Fran touched her arm. "That's the dining room. This way." She led the way down the hall. "This is the door. Notice the flashlights on the table. At night, never go into this wing without picking up one. Gavin had pretty little niches installed in the walls of the hall for lamps and then neglected to buy extras. I tried to sneak a few out of the bars, but he made me put them back." She opened the door and shone her flash around. Doors opened from both sides of the long hall and the air seemed even frostier than it had in the foyer.

"How many rooms?" Miss Sanderson asked.

"Ten. Five on each side. But the ones on the left are unfinished as yet. The guests are all on the right. This first door"—flinging the door open, she flashed light over a rough stone wall and steps painted Chinese red—"this used to be the outside staircase on the inn. Leads up to the other two floors. When Gavin built on this wing, he had it boxed in. Claims it would make a dandy fire exit." She banged the door shut. "Anyone caught in there during a fire would be barbecued."

Miss Sanderson stepped back. The rush of air from that narrow space felt as though it originated somewhere north of Iceland. She shuddered and Fran took her arm. "You'll soon be toasty. As you'll notice, the rooms are numbered. Dolly, of course, is number one. So she can dart out of her room and get to another heated area without chilling her little tootsies—"

"You don't like Dolly?"

"I don't know her well enough to like or dislike her. Saw her for the first time this morning when I ferried out the Casparis, La Montrose, and Barbie Doll."

Miss Sanderson laughed. "Odd. That's exactly how I think of Dolly. As a gorgeous, life-size Barbie doll."

"There certainly is a resemblance. No, it's not Dolly who puts my back up. It's her fiancé. Felix issues orders as though he owns the place and perhaps he does. Anyway, room number two belongs to wife Alice, number three to Reggie. Mrs. Montrose and Omar have four, and here is number five. Fitted up for that famous sleuth Robert Forsythe, and inherited by Abigail Sanderson."

"You were expecting Robby too? Nancy didn't tell you?"

"Nary a word. Gavin sent her out to snag your employer and perhaps she was afraid of his reaction when she didn't." She squeezed Miss Sanderson's arm. "I'm glad *you* came. As far as guests are concerned, with me you're *número uno*."

Miss Sanderson took a step toward her room, but Fran held her back. "Haven't finished your guided tour. Right beside your room is the lav. The bath is across the hall." A narrow beam of light settled on a door at the end of the hall. "The outside door opening onto a cold, windy night. Now, into your room."

"Blimey! I can see where a large chunk of Gavin's money went."

The room was spacious, the furnishings appeared to be antique, a fire blazed on the hearth, a lamp sat on the dressing table, another beamed yellowish light from beside the canopied bed. Miss Sanderson touched the mellow surface of a Queen Anne dressing table. "Are these reproductions?"

"Genuine. Even the lamps. Observe the hand-painted globes. Some items were already in the inn, and Gavin rummaged antique shops for the rest. He'd planned to furnish all ten guest rooms but could barely get five done. Scrimped on the construction of this wing to do that." Fran thumped a paneled wall. "Behind this pretty walnut is not enough insulation to stop a summer breeze."

"Didn't Nancy intercede?"

"Nancy has no say in the Jester. That's Gavin's baby. And Felix aided and abetted him. Until he realized there weren't enough funds left to cover the creature comforts he dotes on. Then Felix raised hell."

"Is Felix a partner?"

"No idea, but he must have put up some money. Gavin seems broke, and Nancy had only a little insurance from her mother's estate. And I rather doubt Gavin could have raised loans to cover what he's done here. Anyway, Felix was back and forth all the time this place was being tarted up, getting in the way and giving orders. Hielkje and I learned to detest the man." Grinning, Fran added, "Hielkje calls Felix a *sjoelke* and it fits."

"What is a *sjoelke*?"

"Frisian word meaning a spoiler. A person who grabs for himself. And Felix certainly grabbed the VIP suite for himself." Fran glanced around the room. "Couple of scuttles of coal over there, and I tucked a bottle of brandy and some glasses in that chest. Towels and so on in this drawer. Anything else you need?"

"Not a thing. Oh, where's my case?"

"In the wardrobe. I unpacked for you. That's a gorgeous chiffon dress, but better keep it for London. The fireplace in the dining room doesn't draw properly and I had to move in a kerosene heater. It's better than nothing, but the room is still on the chill side." Fran glanced at her watch. "I'd better herd Hielkje up to her room for a rest."

"She looks ill."

"She is. By the way, I'm driving her in to see her doctor tomorrow afternoon. Like to come along? Finchley's a pretty little place."

"Yes, I'd like that. And, Fran, thank you."

"Nothing but the best service at the Jester. Oh, better have this." She handed the flask to the older woman. "I noticed you brought one with you, but an extra could come in handy. I'll grope my way up the hall. I'll see you later." Watching the brown ponytail jauntily bobbing away, Miss Sanderson thought: That's one person who is also *número uno* with me. Quick moving, competent, overworked, and still finding time to be kind. Peggy Canard had been fortunate and so was Nancy. But it was a mystery why a woman with Fran's obvious ability would choose to close herself away in this desolate spot. She shrugged. None of her business. Wandering around the room, she felt content. Even if she hadn't been exactly a welcome addition to the party, she was glad she had come. She paused in front of the fireplace and glanced up at the gilded frame over the mantel. Another of Noel Canard's watercolors, and she regarded it warily. After a time she relaxed. Nothing in this one that jarred. He had exercised the same charm in this scene that he had used with his little skaters. A tawny-haired little girl, dressed in a blue dress and pinafore, was gathering daisies in a field. She was stooping, a few flowers clasped in one hand, the other reaching down into the grass for another. Sunlight glinted on her round face, and her hair looked as though a breeze was stirring it.

Then Miss Sanderson stiffened. Nearly hidden in the grass, its color and markings acting as camouflage, was a coiled snake. One eye glistened and it was reaching toward the dimpled hand. She sensed its bite would be poisonous.

Shaking her head, she looked for and found a towel and her sponge bag. As she opened the door, she felt curiously reluctant to step into the cold darkness of the hall.

Chapter Four

Closing the door of the bedroom wing behind her, Miss Sanderson placed the flash Fran had given her on the hall table. There were about a dozen lined up and they were an odd lot, large and small, new and old, cheap and expensive. Not unlike the guest wing. The bathroom sparkled with Dutch tile and extravagant fixtures, and the water flowing from the hot water tap was tepid.

Turning down the hall toward the rear of the inn, Miss Sanderson adjusted her black woolen skirt and pulled down the white angora sweater. She had taken Fran's advice and left her new gown on its hanger. Lucky she had brought this outfit. It wasn't spectacular, but it was warm. She pushed on a green baize door and found a stonefloored kitchen and Felix Caspari, resplendent in crisp white jacket and towering chef's hat, working at a long, scoured table.

"Abigail," he called jovially. "Take a chair and watch this cook at work."

Miss Sanderson took a chair near the other spectator. Dolly Carter-White, lavish in a floor-length gown and the fur cape, was perched on a high stool. The gown was split to the thigh and revealed a slender, shapely leg. The hand bearing the opal ring toyed with a pendant. Emerald, Miss Sanderson thought enviously, one perfect stone dropping from a platinum chain. The emerald was close to the color of the writer's eyes.

The third member of what Reggie had called the *ménage à trois* was darting around the kitchen, from the stove to the sink to the table where her husband presided. Alice had also changed, but she looked as dowdy in the long brown gown as she had earlier. If Dolly resembled a bird of paradise, Alice looked remarkably like a sparrow.

Felix said genially, "I'm hampered by these deplorable surroundings, but I did bring my own knives. Fortunately, I never travel without them." He waved at a pigskin case resting at one end of the table. Miss Sanderson peered at it, and the chef obligingly tilted the case. Nestled on green felt was an array of knives. The smallest was only about two inches long, and the largest looked as though it could hack its way through the toughest jungle. Selecting one, he held it up. "This is the most useful and my favorite. Six-inch blade of finest steel set into an ebony handle. It's a matching set and was made up especially for me. Now, I begin."

The knife blade flashed and he began. Miss Sanderson noticed another flash from the handle. She whispered to Dolly and was told that all the knives had Felix's initials in gold set into the ebony. As she watched, she marveled at the man's speed and dexterity. He didn't make a false move and seemed able to use both hands and his tongue at the same time. He lectured about the dishes being prepared, complained about the Jester's kitchen, and gave orders to and scolded his wife. It seemed Alice could do nothing right. Miss Sanderson marveled at the woman's forbearance. If it were I, she thought grimly, that chef would be wearing one of his sauces.

Time passed and Miss Sanderson had no comprehension of how much. Not only was it fascinating to watch, but the odors of food were making her mouth water. Lunch seemed a long time in the past, and her stomach was groaning audibly.

Finally, Felix carefully wiped his favorite knife, whipped off the towering hat, and spread his arms wide. "A feast worthy of royalty," he said modestly. Taking off the jacket, he threw it to his wife and held out a gallant hand to Dolly.

Miss Sanderson rose. "Can I help with the serving?"

"Of course not. Alice will handle it, and by this time that dratted Hielkje should be rested enough to help. Come along."

The dining room was as chill as predicted. The rest of the party members were waiting, and Hielkje was dispatched to assist in serving. Several small tables had been pushed together to provide one long enough for the ten diners. Felix sat at the head of the improvised table with Dolly on his right, Nancy Lebonhom on his left. Miss Sanderson selected a chair between Reggie and Fran and blinked when she saw the Jacqueline-of-all-trades. The ponytail had been brushed into long sheaves of shining brown hair, the jeans and pea jacket replaced by a knitted dress and matching jacket, her long face was touched with makeup. Fran Hornblower, she decided, was not only a fine woman but a fine-looking one.

Fran turned her gleaming head. "How did you enjoy your introduction to Felix's art?"

"He knows his business."

"That no one can deny."

"His knife set wouldn't look out of place in a jewel case."

"And probably cost as much as diamonds and pearls."

Reggie moved restlessly. "I'm starving."

"Rescue is at hand," Miss Sanderson told him as Hielkje trundled in the first course.

Miss Sanderson never forgot the menu for that meal. As she later told Forsythe, each course was not only superb but also couldn't seem to be topped until the next arrived. Chestnut soup was followed by ambrosia salad, salmon mousse with a lobster sauce, and then lemon sorbet to clear their palates. With those palates fresh and tingling they were regaled with stuffed trout and a dish modestly named *Viande de Boeuf* Caspari. The roast duck had a dressing that contained walnuts, apricots, and currants, and the sweet was a fluffy confection that smelled of brandy and tasted like heaven.

With dessert Hielkje and Alice took their places and started to catch up on their own dinners. Felix made no effort to be polite to the kitchen staff. He dusted off his mustache, threw down his napkin, and rose. Helping Dolly from her chair, he announced, "Hielkje will serve coffee in the saloon bar. This room is like a refrigerator." Fran's eyes shot sparks. "Not by Hielkje and not in the saloon bar. She's going to have her dinner, and I didn't get around to lighting a fire in there. You'll have to use the public bar."

"Alice," Felix snapped, "you handle the coffee."

Miss Sanderson had had enough. "I'll do it," she said, and stalked from the room. To her surprise, when she reached the baize doors she found that Alice Caspari was close behind her. "You should finish your dinner," Miss Sanderson scolded.

"I'm not hungry. Handling all that food rather destroys an appetite. This won't take long. Everything is laid out. You fill the creamer and sugar bowl and I'll put the coffee on." Alice measured coffee and confided, "This is the only job that Felix trusts me with except for preparing vegetables and that sort of thing." She lifted faded blue eyes to the older woman. "What did you think of dinner?"

"Any meal from now on is going to be an anticlimax."

"He's wonderful, isn't he?" Alice pinkened with pleasure. "An artist!"

Miss Sanderson resisted an impulse to kick the woman. It was obvious that Alice, despite her husband's treatment, adored the brute. Takes all types, she thought. For every tyrant there's a victim. Aloud she asked, "How long have you been married?"

"Nearly twenty years. But we've been together for much longer." Alice lifted the coffeepot onto a metal serving wagon and wheeled it toward a door Miss Sanderson hadn't previously noticed. "This way's shorter, Abigail. Through the saloon bar. Oh, I forgot. There won't be lamps lit in there. We'll have to go down the hall. Would you get the door, please."

Miss Sanderson held open the baize door and the wheels of the wagon clattered over red and black tile. Impulsively, she asked, "Aren't you…don't you…" She couldn't find the words. How do you ask a devoted wife whether she resents her husband's fiancée?

"You're thinking of Dolly Carter-White," Alice guessed, and then giggled. "You can't expect Felix to act like other men. He's had dozens of love affairs, but they never last long. Women just can't resist him."

This woman can resist him, Miss Sanderson thought. "But he intends to *marry* Dolly."

"That's just because he can't get into bed with her any other way," his wife said bluntly. They had reached the doors leading to the public bar, and Alice waited while Miss Sanderson opened one. As she pushed the wagon in, she whispered, "But first he must divorce me, mustn't he?"

The entire household was gathered in the bar. Gavin, looking rather self-conscious, was posted behind the bar, toying with a pile of cardboard folders. Mrs. Montrose, the gray cat perched on her lap, was seated at one of the tables, chatting with Reggie Knight. Near them Fran was talking to Hielkje. Miss Sanderson noticed that Hielkje's thick brown hair, earlier worn in a bun, had now been arranged in elaborate coronet braids. Nancy was perched on a barstool, and Felix and his fiancée were cuddling on a bench in the alcove. Their heads were close together and Felix seemed to be nibbling at a tinted cheek. His wife, assisted by Miss Sanderson, handed around coffee.

Balancing two cups, Miss Sanderson joined Nancy Lebonhom. She handed the girl one, climbed on a high stool, and glanced down the bar at Gavin and his folders. The one on the top was labeled "Confidential," and under it, in capital letters, was typed DOLORES CARTERWHITE. Ah, the scripts for the murder game. Alice Caspari returned from taking coffee to her husband and Dolly and, instead of filling a cup for herself, approached the counter. She whispered to Gavin and he turned and peered up at the rows of bottles. Alice pointed and he took down a bottle of jenever, selected a tulip-shaped glass, and handed them to Alice. The next time Miss Sanderson noticed the woman she was in her favorite spot, on the bench under the watercolor, knitting and drinking schnapps.

Miss Sanderson turned to Nancy. "Have your husband and Felix been friends for long?"

"Only since Gavin and I were married. I was the one who introduced them. You must remember—" Nancy gave a rueful little laugh. "I keep forgetting, Auntie Abby, you know little about me. Well, at one time I had aspirations for an acting career, with about as much luck as Gavin has had at writing. But I did get a job on a TV show as an assistant to Felix—"

"The cooking show?"

"Yes. Did you see any of them?"

"Unfortunately, no. You say you were his assistant?"

Honey-colored curls shook. "That was my title, but what I actually did was hand the great chef utensils, stand around looking decorative, and 'oohed' and 'aahed' when he gave me tastes of his creations. Felix called me his official taster." Nancy nudged the older woman. "Looks as though Gavin is ready to give his spiel."

"This seems most important to him."

Nancy laughed again. "He's been practicing his speech in front of a mirror."

Clearing his throat, the writer called, "Attention, everyone."

The hum of conversation faltered and then ceased and heads turned toward the counter. Shooting a look of annoyance toward the alcove, Gavin raised his voice. "Dolly, Felix! Would you please join us."

They stepped out of the alcove, but Felix looked bored and slightly resentful. "Couldn't this wait for a while?"

"No. After all, this is the reason for this party. I know the others are eager to hear what I have to say."

None of the others seemed overeager to hear his words. Mrs. Montrose appeared more interested in petting her cat than in Gavin, Reggie wasn't trying to hide the fact he was as bored as Felix, and Fran was yawning. Alice continued to knit, but the bottle and glass had disappeared. Miss Sanderson blinked. The only place those two objects could have gone was into the capacious knitting bag.

Clearing his throat again, their host fumbled with the folders. "Now, kindly attend. Any questions you wish to ask will be answered after I explain the…hem, the ground rules. To simplify this game I have used your own names as the names of the characters you will portray. Of course, that will be the only resemblance. I have a folder here for each of you, and in each is a comprehensive history of your character's background. There is also a script, showing the dialogue you will be required to give. The dialogue is important because it will display to our charming detective"—his mustache quivered as he beamed a smile in Miss Sanderson's direction—"certain clues. You must also memorize the details on your background because you must play fair and answer Abigail's questions honestly—"

"What did you cast me as?" Felix asked.

"Not as a chef, but you will enjoy your role. One point I stress is that under no circumstances are you to allow any of the others to see your material. In effect this might—"

"Do the murderer and the victim know that he or she *is* the murderer or victim?" Reggie asked.

"Of course." Gavin smiled slyly. "But that might be *victims*. That is the reason the folders must be protected from other people. Knowledge of either of these points would ruin the game. Now, as I call your name would you step up and—"

"Names," Mrs. Montrose said. "I feel you should have given us fictitious ones. It would be more interesting."

"As I said, dear lady, this will simplify things. And your own names are most interesting. As an example, take my name. I've never met anyone else having the same surname."

"It is unusual," Mrs. Montrose agreed.

"I believe it comes from Norman times. I have often fancied an ancestor might have been the Sieur le Bon Homme." Gavin proceeded to enlarge on his theory. "And you, Mrs. Montrose, must also be a descendant of a Norman conqueror."

"My husband was and better he than me. A pink mountain!"

Fran laughed. "I hate to blow my own horn, but my ancestor must have been the great Hornblower. Reggie, you may be a descendant of Sir Lancelot—"

"If you can picture that knight with a heavy tan," Reggie told her. He turned to Hielkje. "We know Abigail's the son of a sander. What about you?"

"Visser. A fisherman."

Fran seemed to be enjoying herself. "Caspari I can't do anything with, although it does sound a bit like a laxative, but Dolly... Ah, a cart and white horse."

"Or a carter with a white dog," Reggie chimed in.

Gavin pounded the counter with his fist. "Come to order! This is getting a bit ridiculous."

"No more so than considering you're a good man," Felix said.

Gavin pounded harder. "I call this meeting to order! Allow me to finish and then we'll have a nightcap." Gradually the meeting came to order and Gavin continued, "The only person without a script is Abigail. She will have to listen, observe, question, and attempt to outwit the author. And I must warn you, Abigail, that won't be simple. This script is a masterpiece of misdirection—"

"I hope," she interrupted, "you aren't going to spring facts on the last page I haven't had access to."

"Certainly not. I've played fair, but there are numerous red herrings."

"She'll solve it." Nancy put an arm around Miss Sanderson's thin shoulders. "Auntie Abby can smell out a fish at ten paces."

"We'll see." Her husband fingered his mustache. "Any or all of the rest of you may attempt to solve the case. If none of you do—"

"The great author will be willing to expound," Felix said caustically.

"True. Your expertise is in a kitchen, mine is behind a typewriter. Any questions?"

Reggie stretched his slender frame. "When is the game afoot?"

"I'd hoped to begin tomorrow." Gavin darted a sour look at Hielkje. "But Hielkje must be taken in to Finchley, so we'll start at lunch the day after tomorrow and—"

"Come now," Felix protested. "My time is limited."

"And so is mine," Reggie said.

This was one item Gavin obviously hadn't practiced in front of his mirror. He flushed, gulped, looked at his wife, and when she shrugged, said placatingly, "The game won't take that long. Abigail will have twenty-four hours to come up with a solution, and if she fails, I'll take over and then you all can—"

"Twenty-four *hours*," Miss Sanderson wailed.

"Boo!" Fran called. "Dirty pool."

"Robert Forsythe could have done it," Gavin said smugly.

A challenge, Miss Sanderson thought, and she picked up the gauntlet. "You're on."

"Now, folders and that nightcap." Gavin held one up. "Dolly."

In a swirl of silk skirts, white fox, and a heady perfume, the folder was gracefully accepted. "And a touch of cognac?" Gavin asked.

Felix's arm crept around his fiancée's waist. "My cognac and in my suite."

Reggie looked interested and ambled over. "I know the quality of that cognac, Felix, and I'm tagging along for a drink."

Gavin handed out folders and asked, "I thought you never drank anything but beer?"

"I said seldom, not never." Taking his folder, Reggie held out a gallant arm to Dolly.

As she took that arm, Felix scowled, and then his face relaxed. "Fine. Like me to carry your folders for you?"

"Dolly, Reggie." Gavin leaned over the counter. "Watch Felix and those folders. He's crafty."

Dolly waved hers. "Word of honor of a cart with a white horse he won't see mine."

"Nor mine." Reggie made a graceful and sweeping bow. "To take a peek at this he'll have to joust with Sir Lancelot."

As the three headed out of the bar, Miss Sanderson declined a drink and crossed the room to refill her cup. She noticed that Alice Caspari and her knitting bag had vanished. When she returned to her stool, the rest of the folders had been dispensed. She asked Nancy, "It's Felix that Gavin is concerned about with the scripts, isn't it?"

"None other, and Gavin has reason to be suspicious. Felix has a nasty sense of humor."

Gavin, carrying a brimming glass, joined them. "Felix is a confirmed practical joker. Nan, tell Abigail about that deal he pulled on the French chef."

His wife's hazel eyes glinted wickedly. "It happened on the TV show I was mentioning. A noted Parisian chef named Lebois was Felix's guest, and sly old Felix switched the paprika and the cayenne. The joke was supposed to be at my expense as I was usually the one who tasted and cried, 'Superb!' But this time Lebois raised a spoonful of a sauce laden with cayenne, told the studio audience and thousands of viewers, 'Zis will tempt taste buds,' and gulped it. He promptly spewed the stuff right across the counter at the camera."

Miss Sanderson howled with laughter, but Gavin wasn't laughing. He said grimly, "Tell her about the camera crew."

"This one was far from funny. The lads from the camera crew loved Felix's dishes, and after the show he let them devour the food he'd prepared. One day he made éclairs, which they were mad about, and the topping he concocted was that strong chocolate laxative. The poor devils bolted the éclairs, and some of them were off work for a couple of days. One of the older chaps was quite ill."

"Not funny," Miss Sanderson agreed.

"This one *was*." Gavin, now wreathed in smiles, leaned across the counter. "Nan says that after the Lebois debacle Felix tried to shift the blame to her by telling the irate chef it was her fault the bottles had been switched."

Giggling, Nancy took up the tale. "But Lebois had heard all about Felix's practical jokes and he wasn't fooled. He got a beautiful revenge. Lebois conspired with one of the camera lads and they dusted Felix's white jacket and chef's hat with itching powder. On the next show…" Hopping off the stool, Nancy pantomimed scratching at her head, digging into armpits, jumping and grimacing and squirming.

This time Miss Sanderson laughed until tears started to her eyes. "I should have watched that show," she gasped. "It *was* live?"

"Very much so. In fact, that was the liveliest show of the series. The viewers loved it."

"You can see," Gavin said earnestly, "why we can't allow Felix to see those other scripts. He'd figure out something devilish that would make me a laughingstock. I've worked hard and I'm damned if I'll let him ruin it, even if he is—" Breaking off, he called, "What's up now, Fran?"

"There's still the mess from dinner to clean up."

"Isn't Hielkje doing it?"

"She started to, but she was dropping in the traces so I bundled her off to bed."

Gavin swore and turned on his wife. "That ruddy woman! I told you we should have replaced her."

"But Hielkje was so kind to Mother."

"Kind or not, we simply can't keep on this way. If she can't handle the work, she'll have to go."

Pushing a strand of hair back behind an ear, Fran told him, "Gavin, she has no place to go."

"I'm not running a nursing home."

"After we get some medication for her tomorrow she'll be feeling better. Right now I'm looking for kitchen volunteers."

"Don't bother looking at me." Mrs. Montrose rose and picked up her cat. Over her shoulder she called, "And I don't do floors either."

Gavin glared at Fran. "You can be so embarrassing! Now you've offended Mrs. Montrose."

"Tough," she said, and looked hopefully at Nancy.

The girl sighed and climbed off her stool. So did Miss Sanderson. "I'll help," the secretary told her.

Gavin made no objection to this and sat, watching the three women gathering up cups and piling them on the serving wagon. Fran called, "Gavin, I'll expect you on fuel detail in the morning."

"You'll be disappointed. I've scads of work to do."

"You remember the bargain we struck? I told you we had to put on extra staff for this party and you said—"

"That we couldn't afford it."

"So we compromised. Nancy's to help Hielkje, you are to help me. Nancy's keeping her part of the bargain, but you haven't lifted a finger."

"All right!" He flung his hands up. "Don't nag. I'll help bring in the filthy coal."

Fran turned to her assistants. "Abigail, you finish up here and bring this stuff along to the kitchen. Don't forget the ashtrays. Nancy, we'll start washing up."

Miss Sanderson asked, "Shall I bring the dishes from the dining room?"

"Hielkje managed to gather them up." With Nancy in tow Fran briskly headed toward the lobby. Over her shoulder she called, "Gavin, no later than nine or your celebrities are going to be freezing."

He glared after her and told Miss Sanderson, "A regular Simon Legree."

"You're fortunate to have her."

"I suppose so. Fran does all her own work and half of Hielkje's. Funny, she can do anything. Not only runs the boat but fixes it up if anything breaks down. She can repair plumbing and does carpentry better than most of the high-paid carpenters we had in to build on the guest wing."

"I wonder where she picked it all up?"

Gavin poured himself another generous drink. "Somewhere in the Middle East. One of those bleeding heart liberals who went to refugee camps in Palestine and so on. A ruddy waste of time. Taking care of a bunch of terrorists!"

Miss Sanderson had piled the top of the wagon high. She bent to stack ashtrays on the lower shelf. "There are women and children there too. Hungry and sick. Perhaps if there were more people like Fran Hornblower, there would be fewer terrorists."

"Sounds as though you're another bleeding heart."

Shrugging, she changed the subject. "Nancy looks exhausted."

"She doesn't sleep well." Moodily, he gazed into his glass. "I had the devil's own time getting her to agree to keep this place on. Complains it's too isolated, but I know what's really wrong. Nan's frightened out of her wits of her father's ghost. Thinks—"

"*Ghost?*" She straightened and stared at him. "Noel Canard?"

"Ever heard such rubbish? When we came to live here, there was still an old couple in that fishing village on the mainland. A Sam something and his wife. They were moving into Finchley, but before they left they managed to fill Nancy full of their wild tales. Claimed a number of times they'd seen a black-clad figure crossing the causeway. They told her that's why they were leaving. Noel Canard, in his mask, was coming to get them."

For once Miss Sanderson agreed with Gavin. "Surely Nancy doesn't believe that superstitious nonsense?"

"She lets on she doesn't. But several times I've roused in the night and she's sitting straight up in bed, listening, white as a sheet. Always claims she's heard a sound." He tossed back the rest of his brandy. "Naturally she hears sounds in an old building such as this one. Creaks of timbers and that sort of thing. I keep trying to jolly her out of it. This morning I told Dolly and Felix about the old fisherman's ghost story and both of them were amused. Nancy was there and I was glad to see her smile." He thumped his glass on the wagon and stretched. "Well, I'm off now. If I'm going to lug coal in the morning, I'd better get some work done at my desk before I turn in."

They parted in the hall, Gavin heading up the staircase, Miss Sanderson wheeling the wagon down the hall. Only the single lamp in the foyer behind her was lit, and the hall was so dark she was tempted to snatch up a flashlight from the table. She was glad to reach the baize doors and nudge them open. The kitchen was warm and bright with three lamps lit. Fran was up to her elbows in steaming, sudsy water, and Nancy was drying dishes. "Bring the cart over here," Fran told her. "Then you can start sticking china in that cupboard. The cutlery goes in those two drawers. Hielkje and Alice must have washed up between courses, so we shouldn't be much longer."

Nancy hung a damp dishcloth and reached for a dry one. "If Gavin hadn't been so stubborn, we'd have electricity and could chuck all this in a dishwashing machine."

"And if pigs had wings they'd be soaring like gulls," Fran told her. "Cheer up, Nancy, it might be worse. Anyway, a couple of days and we'll be back to normal."

"And how long will it be before my dear husband decides to throw another murder party?"

"He'd better hold off until he can put modern conveniences in. The wealthy clientele he's hoping to attract will never stand for this. Atmosphere or no atmosphere."

They worked at top speed and finally Fran pulled the plug in the sink and reached for a sponge. "I'll finish mopping up here. You two trot along. Thanks for the help. If I discover any floors to be done, I'll bypass Mrs. Montrose and get you two. Abigail, remember to pick up a flash. You too, Nancy. I wasn't able to get that lamp at the top of the stairs lit and it's going to be blacker than hell up there." She called a cheerful goodnight, and Miss Sanderson and Nancy groped their way along the hall.

Nancy was clutching the older woman's arm, and Miss Sanderson squeezed the girl's hand warmly to her side. "I told your husband, Nancy, that you're lucky people. With Fran, I mean."

"Don't I know that! Mother was lucky too. At first she had no intention of taking either Hielkje or Fran on. Hielkje wasn't well, even then, and Mother didn't think Fran could handle the heavy work around here. Mother was looking for a couple, the woman for housework, the man for the boat and the other chores. But she liked both of them and took a chance. As Mother told me, Fran is worth two men and she's a wonderful nurse too. Mother couldn't have had better care than Fran gave her." They reached the table and groped for flashlights. Miss Sanderson found hers was long and heavy with a worn rubber grip.

At the foot of the stairs, she turned to say goodnight. Nancy still firmly clasped her arm. "I was wondering, Auntie Abby, if you'd like to come up to my sitting room. When I was sorting through Mother's boxes, I found some school pictures you might like to see. I recognized you in them immediately."

"It's been a long day. Perhaps tomorrow?" Nancy bobbed her head but retained her hold. Switching on her flash, Miss Sanderson beamed it up the staircase. She wondered if the girl was nervous about going up there alone. "Heck," she said. "No time like the present. Lead on."

They started up the stairs. Nancy switched her own flash on and shone it ahead of them. "Mother—" The girl broke off. As Miss Sanderson glanced at her, Nancy's mouth opened and she gave a piercing shriek. Her body went limp and she sagged heavily against the older woman.

Miss Sanderson beamed her flash upward. Standing at the top, motionless, was a tall figure in dark clothes. It was wearing a black mask.

Chapter Five

The figure moved, an arm lifted, in one hand something glinted. A knife? Taking her cue from Nancy, Miss Sanderson screamed.

"For God's sake!" the figure said. "Have you never seen a ski mask before?" He ripped off the mask and glossy ringlets tumbled to his shoulders.

Miss Sanderson hardly had enough strength to lower the girl to a step. Releasing the older woman's arm, Nancy wrapped both arms around her legs. "*Father*," she whimpered.

"The Black Knight," Miss Sanderson told her.

Their screams had been heard. Thrusting Reggie aside, Gavin raced down to his wife. A creamy blond head bobbed over the singer's shoulder. Gavin ordered, "Someone get that damn lamp lit up there." He bent over his wife's crumpled body. "What in hell is wrong with you, Nan? Did you fall?"

Miss Sanderson tried to detach the clinging arms, but Nancy held on to her legs like a limpet to a rock. "She's had a scare," the secretary told Gavin, and added shakily, "And so did I."

Felix Caspari had joined the group above them and the lamp was now showering a splash of yellow light over the landing. She could see that what she had thought a knife was actually Reggie's silver flask.

Gavin, now understanding the reason for his wife's collapse, cut loose at Reggie. "You damn fool! What in hell do you think—"

"Will someone explain what this is all about?" Reggie asked plaintively. "As soon as I know, I'll offer an apology."

"Forget it," Gavin rasped. He tugged at his wife. "Come on, Nan, I'll get you up to bed."

"I'll help," Miss Sanderson said. "Nancy, let go of my legs—there's a good girl."

Between them they got the girl up the rest of the stairs, down the hall, and into a small and cozy sitting room. Here there were not only lamps glowing, but a fire beamed warmth. Gavin lifted his wife to the sofa and Miss Sanderson scooped up an afghan and spread it over her. Pushing back his untidy hair, Gavin said, "I'd better get you brandy."

"No." Nancy's face was still colorless, but she managed a weak smile. "I'll be fine. Sorry to act like an ass, darling, but it was so dark and when I flashed the light up…You go along, Gavin. Auntie Abby, would you…"

"Of course." Miss Sanderson told Gavin, "I'll stay with her for a while."

"Well…all right, but she should be in bed." He paused by the door. "If you need me, I'll be in my study. And, Abigail, try and talk some sense into her. She's becoming a ruddy neurotic."

As the door closed the girl began to weep. Sinking down beside her, Miss Sanderson found her handkerchief and handed it over. "Gavin's right," Nancy sobbed. "I am becoming neurotic."

"That makes two of us. I panicked as badly as you did."

"It's this place. Not a neighbor for miles. Just rock and water and wind. I don't know how Mother ever stood it here." She mopped at wet eyes. "I'm used to cities and swarms of people and traffic and noise."

"I think there's more to it than that."

"Has Gavin…Yes, I can tell he has."

"He told me about the old fisherman's ghost story."

"And you think I'm *mad*." Nancy clutched her curly head in both hands and rocked back and forth. "Gavin thinks so too, and sometimes I agree."

"I do *not* think you're mad. Let's talk this out. Let's—" Miss Sanderson stopped abruptly. She had been about to suggest they lay ghosts to rest. Hardly tactful. "Surely, you're not frightened of your own father?"

"I never really knew him—"

"You must have memories. You said you were fifteen at the time of his accident."

"When I was a child, I didn't see that much of either Father or Mother. He was stationed in so many different places, and Mother always tagged along with him. She was devoted to him, and when it came to a choice between Nancy and Noel, it was no contest. Until I was old enough for boarding school, I was farmed out between a grandmother and a great-aunt. After Father was so badly disfigured, I never saw him again. All I knew was that he'd turned into a recluse and always wore that damn mask."

It would have been kinder, Miss Sanderson thought hotly, if the girl had been allowed to see her father's ravaged face than have to imagine what lay behind that mask. Aloud, she said gently, "You know there are no ghosts."

"Do you?"

"Yes." The older woman was glad that at that moment Robby wasn't with them. He was the one who always teased her about being fey. He was also the one who had tried to persuade her that there had been no ghost haunting the studio of Sebastian Calvert. She repeated firmly, "Yes."

"What if it isn't a ghost?"

"What are you trying to say?"

"His body was never found. He was a strong swimmer." Nancy was twisting the handkerchief as though trying to wring her tears from it. "What if he isn't *dead*?"

Despite the warmth of the cozy room, Miss Sanderson felt chill fingers running up and down her spine. There was more than a ghost to lay to rest here. This was nightmare land. She pulled herself together. Use logic, she decided. "What would be Noel's purpose in feigning death?"

"I'm certain he was…his mind was gone. After that horrible fire on his ship he was never normal. Does a madman have to have a purpose?"

"Even madness must, Nancy. Perhaps later in his life Noel was not normal, but I once knew him. Granted it was many years ago, but people don't change that much. Noel was very handsome and quite narcissistic about his looks. It must have been a terrible blow to him when his face was badly burned. But the man I knew was far too fond of comfort and ease to have voluntarily left the source of it."

"Mother?" Nancy nibbled thoughtfully on her lower lip. "That does make sense, Auntie Abby, but you must look at his paintings in order to understand how deranged he'd become. They're ghastly things. I keep telling Gavin that, but he refuses to see the horror in them. Gavin tells me it's my imagination." She continued to punish the handkerchief.

"It's not your imagination. I've seen it too."

"A man capable of that is capable of anything."

The girl's chin had set stubbornly, and Miss Sanderson resisted an impulse to shake her. Continue with logic. "Tell me this. How is a man with a mask covering a badly scarred face going to find shelter, food, fuel, around here?"

"I'd never thought of that! Father had no friends left, not one person to help him…" Flinging her arms around Miss Sanderson's neck, she hugged her. "I've been a fool! Father *is* dead and his ghost does *not* walk. Poor old Sam and Maggie were simply wallowing in superstition. Thank God you came down here!" Nancy glanced at the mantel clock and said contritely, "You must be exhausted. Look at the time."

Miss Sanderson was only too aware of the time. It was nearly two. She stood up and straightened her skirt. "I'm off to bed and you'd better head for yours. Want me to wait until you're settled?"

"Not necessary." Pushing aside the afghan, Nancy hopped up. "Gavin will soon be in, and I promise I'm not going to be a ninny anymore. That's over."

"Your husband will be glad to hear it. Gavin's been worried about you."

Picking up the heavy flashlight, Miss Sanderson opened the door. Nancy rushed to kiss her. She looked up at the older woman. "All Gavin is worried about is keeping me from selling this place. Goodnight, Auntie Abby, and thanks."

For a moment Miss Sanderson stood outside Nancy's room. Nancy and her writer husband had been married for less than a year. Judging by the bitterness in the girl's voice, it looked as though their honeymoon was definitely over.

Across from her a door banged open and light spilled across the floor. Felix Caspari, an arm anchored as usual around his true love's waist, said, "Still up, Abigail? I'm walking Dolly back to her room. That performance you and Nancy put on shook her up."

If Dolly was shaken, she certainly didn't show it. Not a hair was out of place and the oval face was serene. Biting back a sharp retort, Miss Sanderson asked, "Where did Reggie get the ski mask from?"

"I gave it to him." Felix murmured. "Careful on these stairs, Dolly. That lamp doesn't shed much light."

At the bottom of the staircase the lamp didn't help at all, and Miss Sanderson pressed the button on her flash. "You brought a ski mask with you?"

"Hardly. I found that one when I was rummaging around in the attic. Reggie's always complaining about Jamaicans feeling the cold, so I gave it to him." He added, "He also helped himself generously to my brandy. Even filled his flask."

Miss Sanderson held open the door to the guest wing. "Better take a flash," she told the younger woman.

Dolly shrugged. "I don't really need one. My room's only a few steps down the hall."

When Felix opened the door to room number one, light spilled out and the air from the room seemed delightfully warm.

It was also delightfully scented. Miss Sanderson peered past Dolly's shoulder. On an ornate dressing table flamed a huge bouquet of crimson roses. It would seem Dolly was number one in more ways than one. Felix and Dolly were now ignoring her. They were locked in a passionate embrace. She glanced from the lovers to the roses, smiled, and started down the hall. At that moment the door of room number two was flung open. Mrs. Caspari lurched into view. She managed to lurch into the doorframe, and the sharp juniper odor of jenever mingled with the fragrance of hothouse roses.

Alice was draped in a billowing nightgown and she had loosened her hair, holding it back from her face with a velvet band. Lamplight was kind to her, and Miss Sanderson realized that as a girl this woman must have been extremely pretty. Ignoring the secretary, Alice said, "So, Snow White and the seventh dwarf. Dopey!"

"I believe the one with the beard was Doc." Having corrected her rival, Dolly detached her lissome form from the chef's arms.

"Looks and brains both, eh?" Alice hiccuped and swayed. "Listen up, Snow White. You want to sleep with Dopey, feel free. He's slept with dozens of other sluts. But forget about trotting up the aisle in a veil. I am *Mrs. Caspari*, and I'm damn well going to stay Mrs.—"

"Alice!" Mr. Caspari roared. "You've had your bloody nose in jenever again. Why in hell—"

"Wasn't talking to *you*," Alice roared back. "Talking to Snow—"

"Shut your mouth, you bitch! Get back in that room or—"

"Or what, Dopey?"

Felix, his handsome face twisted with rage, took a step forward and raised his fist. "Want another taste of this?"

"I really wouldn't, Felix," a voice said. Reggie Knight was belting a robe around his slender waist.

The older man's arm fell and he muttered, "Well, *you* shut her up then. You know how she gets when she drinks."

Reggie moved up beside Miss Sanderson. "Never interfere in family fights. Not unless they get violent. Get it off your chest, Alice."

Alice tried to focus her eyes on her husband. "Not giving you a divorce. Not now or never. Paid a price for you, and I earned the right to stay your wife. You're *mine*."

For an instant it looked as though, Reggie or no Reggie, Alice was going to get her husband's fist in her face. Then Felix gave a deep sigh and gently pushed Dolly into her room. He closed the door and the lamplight was cut off. From the shadows his voice came and it was deathly quiet: "I belong to no one, Alice. Certainly not to you. Dolly and I will be married and you won't stop us. If necessary, I'll fake evidence against you."

Alice's voice was softer too. "You know all about that, don't you?"

There was no answer. A door creaked and Miss Sanderson decided that Felix had slipped back into the inn. Alice stood in the light shining from her room, tears pouring down her cheeks. Reggie stepped to her side. "Show time's over, Alice. To bed and sleep it off." As gently as Felix had handled his fiancée, Reggie handled Alice. Closing the door, he turned to Miss Sanderson. "Nasty, wasn't it?"

"I think I'm in shock. I never saw a mouse turn into a raging lion before."

"Only happens when Alice gets her nose in the schnapps. And she rarely does that. Never accomplishes anything either. Felix is something of a lion tamer."

"Using his fists?"

"On occasion. Not when I'm around."

He opened his bedroom door. "Care for a nightcap? I just happen to have some vintage brandy."

"So I heard. Purloined from the chef's private stock. Not tonight, Reggie. Like Hielkje, I'm stumbling in the traces."

"Is Nancy all right?"

"I hope so. That was a dumb thing to do."

"Still haven't the foggiest what I *did* do." He stretched. "I'll be off too. Been a long day."

Too long a day, Miss Sanderson thought, as she glanced in the mirror over the dressing table. Her silver curls were rumpled and her face looked as old as Mrs. Montrose's. She made record time in climbing under the down duvet. The sheets were icy, and she settled shivering into a little ball. Before she was warmed through she was asleep.

She roused once, heard what sounded like stealthy footsteps in the hall, and then settled back. That, she told herself firmly, is an example of the many sounds buildings make. Expansion or contraction. Definitely not Noel Canard, alive or dead, with a hideous face behind a black mask, coming to get me.

And then, drowsily, she remembered a plume of smoke funneling from a chimney in the deserted village across from the Jester.

Chapter Six

Morning arrived with light filtering between the curtains, a metallic clanking in the hall, a soft tap on the door. Starting up in bed, Miss Sanderson peered at her traveling clock. Only a few minutes after eight. The night had been as short as the previous day had been long. She thrust back the duvet and reached for her robe. Blimey, but this room was cold. She padded across the carpet and swung open the door. Fran, wearing jeans and her pea jacket, was bending over a serving wagon. Her hair was stuffed up under a navy watch cap. "Morning," she said cheerfully. "Sleep well?"

"Like a log. Breakfast?"

"Continental style. Which means coffee and a roll. Easier than setting up a table. You seem to be my only taker."

Miss Sanderson glanced down the hall. "Mrs. Montrose was the only one with sense enough to get to bed at a decent time."

"Bunch of nighthawks." Fran poured coffee from an insulated jug. "If they figure they'll make up at lunchtime, they're going to be disappointed. Hielkje is just going to stick something on the buffet. Better take more rolls, Abigail. Bran muffins this side, poppy seed the other. Ah, another customer. Morning, Reggie. How goes the knight-errant business?"

"Booming. What's in the pots?"

"Honey, marmalade, and raspberry jam. Better follow Abigail's example and load up. As I was just telling her, lunch will be light, and unless Felix handles dinner, it may come out of tins. Abigail and I are taking Hielkje to Finchley this afternoon. Care to come along?"

"Think I'll hang around the Jester. It may be cold, but we have great floor shows here." Taking a plate, he heaped it.

Fran pushed the creamer closer. "I heard about the show on the stairs. Seems you did a star turn. Gavin has cooled off now, but it's obvious he wanted to deck you last night. Why on earth did you pull a ratty trick like that?"

Miss Sanderson picked up her plate and mug. "Fran, Reggie knows nothing about the ghost of the Jester."

"But Reggie is going to find out and right now," the Black Knight said.

"Not from me." Fran set down the coffee jug. "I have to rout Gavin out for fuel detail, and that's going to be almost harder than doing the job by myself."

With a clatter of wheels against tile, she bounced down the hall. Miss Sanderson was turning toward her room when Reggie stopped her. "Come into my boudoir and tell all. I'm dying to hear about the Jester's ghost." He added coaxingly, "I've a nice fire going and I'll bet you haven't."

The fire was blazing and cast a circle of warmth around the hearth. Reggie put his breakfast down on a hassock and brought over a side table for Miss Sanderson's. Thinking of her own room, unmade bed, clothing thrown over chairs, she was amazed at the neatness of his. The bed had been made and everything was tidy. On a fine Regency chest his silver flask perched beside a ship's clock. He reached to the flask and poured a dollop into her coffee mug. "You look as if you could use a pick-me-up. Now, tell all."

She told him about Nancy's fears, and his dark eyes blazed. "That bloody Felix! Conned me again. His lousy jokes!"

"That one was a sick sort of joke." She took a gulp of coffee and lifted a muffin dabbed with honey. "How did he manage to get you to put on the ski mask?"

"He kidded about my Jamaican blood, brought out the mask, and said I should wear it to go down to the guest wing. Keep me from turning to ice in the halls." Reggie spread butter and marmalade and flung down the knife. "I'd had several tots of his booze and it sounded like a good idea. But this is a bit rough even for Felix. Maybe he didn't know about Nancy's—"

"Gavin told Dolly and him about it yesterday. Did he suggest you look up Nancy?"

"No. But he did say I should show the galley slaves in the kitchen the Black Knight's new look. And he probably suspected Nancy would be there. Abigail, I feel terrible. Poor Nancy. Seeing that figure looming over her on the dark staircase. God! She might have had a heart attack."

"She didn't," Miss Sanderson pointed out. "And perhaps in a way, it wasn't all that bad. We had a talk. I'm hoping I might have lanced that abscess of hers." She finished her last bite and settled back, flipping open her cigarette case. They sat in companionable silence, the only sound the hissing of coal on the grate. After a time she murmured, "Might better get it off your chest."

"How do you know I want to ask a favor?"

"All I know is that you're working yourself up to something. And I hardly think you get up early every morning to tidy your room. You were waiting for me."

He glanced at the neatly made bed and his teeth glinted. "Remind me never to try and conceal anything from Abigail Sanderson, girl detective. Very well, cards on the table. I want you to use your influence with your boss. Ask him, persuade him, I hope, to look into something for me."

Blowing a smoke ring, she regarded it. "That's one card. Turn over a few more."

"Can't you take me on faith? I know Forsythe will be intrigued. Tell you what, I'll autograph those record sleeves you bought for Christmas presents."

"This is connected with your brother's death, isn't it?"

"Perhaps the detective I need is sitting opposite me. Expound, Holmes."

"Watson. Bumbling along. Also elementary." On long fingers she ticked off points. "Your reaction to not meeting Robby—out of proportion. Mrs. Montrose's I could understand. She was hoping to snag off an illustrious and rather elusive celebrity. That remark you made about being interested in old cases. The look on your face when you spoke about your brother's death. More anger than grief."

"Remind me never to play poker with you." He pantomimed spreading cards on the hassock. "Damien and Felix went to a party at a country home. One of the swinging ones with lots of sex and booze and drugs. When they left in the wee hours, they got into Felix's car, a new Jaguar, and according to a maid, Felix was behind the wheel. His story was that before they pulled out of the driveway, he realized he'd had too much to drink, so Damien and he changed places. Felix also claimed that Damien had been drinking heavily and had been snorting nose candy—"

"Cocaine?"

"Yes. Felix said he dozed off in the passenger seat, and when he came to, the car was careening off the road and the next thing he knew an ambulance attendant was bending over him." Reggie's hands balled into fists. "Two people had been walking along that road. A young woman and a three-year-old kid. They'd been on their way home, their car had run out of petrol, and they were walking the rest of the way. According to the police, Damien crashed into them, killed them, lost control of the Jaguar, and smashed it against a tree. No witnesses and Damien was dead. They had to take Felix's word for the details." He looked directly into Miss Sanderson's eyes. "I *know* Felix was driving that car."

I'm too soft, she thought. I feel like patting his head and sympathizing. Just like Watson. Now, make like Holmes. She threw her cigarette butt into the grate and said evenly, "Your reasoning?"

It was his turn to lift a pink-palmed hand and tick off fingers. "Point number one—Felix's nature. No way he'd ever let anyone else drive his new car. Two—if Damien had been drinking and doping, why let him take the wheel? Three— Damien seldom had more than a glass of wine or a pint of beer. And he *never* took drugs—"

"You're certain? You said you were only fourteen at that time."

"When I was younger than that, I learned how my big brother felt about drugs. I was about nine and we were still living in a tenement in Liverpool. A gang of kids were in the alley behind the rattrap we lived in. One of them had come up with a couple of joints—"

"Marijuana?"

"Yes. We were passing them around, feeling like big men, when Damien came up behind us. The other kids took one look at him and took to their heels. Damien caught me and held me off the ground with my face on a level with his." Reggie rubbed an upper arm as though his brother had just released his grip. "Lord, but he was strong! He didn't raise his voice, told me in this level deadly tone that if I wanted to ruin my life, commit suicide, he'd finish me right there. Said he'd bash my head in. And he meant it." Reggie reached for his mug, found it empty, and put it back on the hassock. "Our parents had gone down the drain with alcohol. Both of them opened and closed the pubs. I loathed them, but Damien could remember when they first came here, and he kept telling me they should never have left Jamaica, that they simply couldn't adjust. He said they'd lost to alcohol, but we weren't going to lose to anything. Damien took me away from Liverpool and found a job in London. He was working as a dishwasher in a restaurant when Felix Caspari heard him singing in the kitchen. Felix took him up and it looked as though Damien was going to make the big time, but…"

But he had died before he had, Miss Sanderson thought. "You said Felix paid for your education—"

"I said arranged. When Damien started to work, the first thing he did was to take out an insurance policy on his life. He had a tough time making the premiums, but he said if anything happened to him, I'd be looked after. Felix took care of me in an impersonal sort of way, but once in a while he'd do something kind and rather touching for me. Funny, people have so many sides. Most of the time Felix is a selfish, egotistical monster, but occasionally he makes impulsive, generous gestures."

"And you want Robby to look into the accident, try to find proof that Felix was driving the car that night."

"Exactly. You see, Damien Day isn't remembered because he was a worthy human being with a tremendous talent. If he's remembered at all, it's as a drug-soaked swinger who ran down and killed a woman and a child. I want his name cleared. For once I want Felix to take his own medicine."

"That won't bring your brother back, Reggie."

"I know that only too well. But it's important to me."

She was tapping a thumbnail against a front tooth.

Reggie cocked his head. "What's that in aid of?"

"A bad habit, and one Robby complains about. It helps me think."

"And what are you thinking?"

She took another cigarette. "I've a feeling you're holding something back."

He slid to his knees and started to build up the fire. The ringlets fell forward, veiling his face. "I was saving this for Forsythe, but I'd better tell you. About six months after Damien's death I was visiting Felix and Alice for a few days. Felix's injuries had healed and he was back to normal. Had a hot new love affair going, and as usual, Alice was pretending to be ignorant of it. She bottles it up and then goes on a schnapps binge and all the venom comes spewing out—"

"Like last night."

"Similar. But this time Alice waited until Felix was out of the house, and then she called me down to his study. She handed me a letter she'd found while she was ransacking his desk." He poked at the grate and a lump of coal rolled across the hearth. "There was a check for a generous amount in it that Felix had had his solicitor send to the husband and father of the dead woman and the child. The man had returned it. He said he wouldn't accept blood money from his family's killer. He said he'd talked to the police constable who'd arrived first at the accident site, and the constable was sure that the driver of the Jaguar hadn't been Damien Day. He was a rural cop and rode a bike. The Jaguar had passed him moments before the accident, and although the visibility was poor, he'd had the impression the driver had a beard."

Miss Sanderson jerked forward. "Why didn't the police pursue this?"

Reggie looked bleakly up at her. "Put yourself in their place. When the car crashed, both Damien and Felix were thrown into the rear of it. They were jumbled up together, impossible to prove who had been behind the wheel. No witnesses, and Felix swore that Damien had been driving. The only evidence, the word of a lowly constable who admitted he'd only had a glimpse and the visibility was poor. But as far as I'm concerned, I agree with the man who wrote the letter and returned Felix's check. Conscience money!" He picked up the tongs and threw the lump of coal on the grate. "Will you speak to Forsythe?"

"I will, but I must warn you there's slight chance even Robby can prove your brother's innocence. About the only thing that can do that is a confession from Felix Caspari."

Reggie smashed the tongs down. "I'd like to choke it out of the bastard!"

"Easy." She rose, adjusted her robe, and patted his shoulder. "Violence won't help. Let's wait and hear what Robby says."

She left him, still kneeling, looking gloomily into the flames. He looks as though he's praying, she thought.

Chapter Seven

Miss Sanderson barely had time to dress and neaten her room before Gavin Lebonhom, without bothering to knock, came puffing in. He lugged two scuttles that pulled his shoulders down. His hair spilled over his brow, he had a black smudge on his nose, his expression resembled a thundercloud. His response to Miss Sanderson's greeting was a grunt.

"Shake a leg," Fran bayed from the hall.

Muttering a curse, Gavin grabbed up the empty scuttles and banged out of the room. Fran stuck her head into the room. "Lunch is laid on in the dining room, Abigail. Better have a bite. Happy boy and I will soon be finished, and after I wash up, we'll head for Finchley."

"Your assistant seems far from happy."

"It's good for him. Gavin's far too sedentary."

The buffet lunch turned out to be a savory beef stew and crusty bread. The long table had been dismantled, and the small tables had been returned to their places. Miss Sanderson dished up stew and made her way to the table where Mrs. Montrose and Nancy were seated. Nancy looked as fresh as a flower. The young, Miss Sanderson thought enviously, how resilient they are. Nancy has the nerve storm and I'm the one who shows its effects. Omar left his mistress's side and put a fluffy paw on Miss Sanderson's knee. She dipped a crust into the bowl and proffered it. He sniffed, gave her a disdainful look, and stalked back to Mrs. Montrose. "Omar," that lady stated, "is terribly fussy about food. Quite spoiled."

Glancing around, Miss Sanderson noticed that only Gavin, Fran, and Mrs. Caspari were missing. She knew what Gavin and Fran were doing. Alice…probably nursing a giant-size hangover. Her husband appeared to be in an expansive mood and was regaling Dolly and Hielkje with what, judging from their laughter, had to be a hilarious story. In a corner, Reggie, seated alone, was paying more attention to them than to his meal. As Miss Sanderson finished her stew, Fran came bouncing into the dining room. She'd taken off her watch cap, brushed her hair into a glossy ponytail, but was still wearing jeans and the pea jacket.

"Hielkje, Abigail," she called. "Captain Hornblower is ready to set sail."

Hielkje and Miss Sanderson headed toward the lobby. The cook bundled up in a moth-eaten fur coat and a heavy heads-carf, and as they stepped out of the inn, Miss Sanderson heartily wished she had a fur coat, moth-eaten or otherwise. Although the sky was clear and watery sunlight fell across their faces, the wind was even colder than it had been the previous day. As the speedboat cut through the choppy water, she looked searchingly at the deserted fishing village. No smoke funneled from the stone cottages.

The women made their way toward the cars, and Miss Sanderson asked, "Is the Mini yours?"

"Gavin's," Fran told her.

The little car was covered with dust and a fender was deeply dented. "Shall we take my car?" Miss Sanderson asked.

Fran dug into a pocket, extracted a ring of keys, threw them up, and caught them. "We ride in high style." She headed toward the Rolls, unlocked doors, flung a rear one wide. "In you go, Hielkje, and pull that rug over your lap. Abigail, you sit in front and help me navigate. Never driven one of these things before."

Fran handled the big car as she did most things, with quiet dexterity and ease. Miss Sanderson ran an admiring hand over the walnut dash. "Did you, by any chance, pick Felix's pocket?"

"Perish the thought! He pressed the keys in my hot little hand and told me we'd be more comfortable using this beauty. Odd chap. Drives one mad most of the time and then does something surprisingly kind. Felix also told me not to worry, he'd cook an informal dinner tonight."

That streak of impulsive generosity Reggie had mentioned, Miss Sanderson thought. Leaning forward, Hielkje touched Fran's shoulder. "What mood is Gavin in today?"

"Beastly. He was just recovering from the indignity of fuel patrol, and then he came storming out of his study and cornered me in the hall. Positively livid with rage. Accused me of opening a window and scattering papers all over his desk. I tried to tell him there was no way *I* would open his damn window. Not after working like a fool to keep the place warm, but he kept on ranting. Finally I shouted back. Asked how I could get into his ruddy study to do anything when he keeps it locked like a vault."

"And then he calmed down," Hielkje said.

"Wrong. He yelled something about Nancy having left the connecting door to their bedroom unlocked and went tearing off to give her hell."

Miss Sanderson opened her cigarette case and offered it to her companions. When they shook their heads, she lit one and observed, "Gavin is far from a model employer."

"You're seeing him at a bad time," Hielkje said. "Right now he's so tense and nervous. Trying so hard to make his party a success."

Glancing over her shoulder, Miss Sanderson noticed that Hielkje looked nervous and tense. Worried about her health or job? Probably both. She sighed and settled back to enjoy the comfort of the car, the scene unreeling outside her window.

Not that the view was inspirational. Sunlight didn't make the desolate downs any more attractive. Today she didn't even spot any sheep grazing, and it was a relief to turn onto a more traveled road. Here at least were signs of life. A petrol station and some cottages broke the monotony, and an Alsatian rushed from a drive to challenge the Rolls. Fran swung the car smoothly around a tractor trailer and pointed a finger. "There's Finchley, Abigail. Market town and not large, but seems a metropolis after the Jester. Now, battle plan. We'll drop Hielkje at the clinic and then—"

"Fran, it may take quite a while. Dr. Parker wants to make tests."

"Not to worry. I have to buy supplies and do some errands. You stay put in his office and I'll pick you up there. Abigail, what would you like to do?"

"Look around the shops. I still have a couple of presents to get."

"With all the party panic, I keep forgetting how close Christmas is getting. Oh, well, my list is short."

"So is mine," Hielkje said dolefully.

"Count yourselves fortunate," Miss Sanderson said. "I've scads of nieces and nephews, to say nothing of brothers, sisters, and in-laws."

Fran smiled rather sadly. "You're the fortunate one, Abigail. Now, where to meet. How about the local pub?"

"Rather a busman's holiday."

"At least they won't force you to help wash up. There's a tea shop that does a lovely cream tea."

"Sounds more like it."

The Rolls drew up in front of a square, ugly building and Fran hopped out and opened the door for her friend. Miss Sanderson noticed she hugged Hielkje before the stout woman started trudging up the walk. An elderly man with an elderly mongrel on a leash paused to admire the Rolls, and a boy with a Mohawk cut slowed his moped to make a rude gesture. Miss Sanderson promptly made it back and his eyes widened.

Fran slid back behind the wheel. "Think the locals had never seen a Rolls before." She caressed the walnut wheel. "Wish I owned this honey."

"And if pigs had wings—"

"They'd soar like gulls." Fran chuckled. "I'll drop you off here. Tea shop a block farther down. Don't spend all your money."

Miss Sanderson had no intention of being extravagant. Her new look had been too costly. A small gift for Mrs. Sutter, she decided, a slightly larger one for Robby. She glanced around the heart of the town. It didn't look as though progress had spread its ugly plastic and chrome and garish colors far in Finchley. The inn didn't look much younger than the Jester, and she was tempted to step inside and see if it had the same charm. You'll have enough atmosphere before you leave the island, she thought, and strolled on.

A window display caught her eyes and she stopped. There were twin pyramids of books, one a historical romance, the other a cookbook. She grinned. On the back of one dust jacket a dazzling Dolores Carter-White leaned against a Cadillac, hugging a white poodle to a furcovered bosom. Felix Caspari, handsome in jacket and chef's hat, beamed from the front of the other. The future bride and groom. At least if Felix could bully his wife into divorce, they would be. She was about to move on and then changed her mind. The perfect gifts for Mrs. Sutter, who doted on romance and history and cooking. Not only that, but for no extra cost the books would be autographed by their authors.

She loved bookstores, but she resisted the impulse to browse and was soon back in the street clutching a package. The moped breezed by and she stared at the rider, wondering whether they were about to enter the lists again. This time the boy turned his shorn head away and ignored her. Never let silver hair fool you, she told him silently. I give as good as I get.

Now for Robby. Ah, an antique shop with a tasteful display of chamber pots in the bowed window. Something small and not too expensive. Perhaps a smoking stand or bookends. A bell tinkled over the door, and at the desk a woman wearing a severe black dress and rhinestoned glasses raised a sleek head. She waved an expansive hand. "Do wander around. If you need assistance, give a call."

Miss Sanderson wandered around. She picked up a brass elephant, shook her head, replaced it, looked covetously at a fine Spode fruit bowl, and passed on. She examined a pipe rack made of bamboo and shook her head again. Then she spotted a case of jade ornaments. Keep away from that, she warned herself, though Robby loves jade and has quite a nice collection. No champagne tastes on a beer budget. Then she found herself leaning over the glass top, staring down at the piece in the dead center of the velvet lining. She tried to lift the top, but it was locked. Magically, the clerk appeared at her elbow, turned a key in the lock, and lifted the glass. "Which one are you interested in, madame?"

Miss Sanderson pointed, and the jade was placed tenderly in her palm. It was exquisite. Each limb of the tree, each green leaf was perfect. Pink flowers blossomed, and near the top a minuscule white jade bird threw back its throat in silent song. Silent? For an instant Miss Sanderson thought she could hear that song. Rhinestoned Glasses was now murmuring something about Han dynasty, and Miss Sanderson opened her mouth to tell the clerk to replace it in the case. To her horror, she asked the price, which was revealed in a mere whisper. Just as well not to shout *that* amount. Miss Sanderson saw Robby's face as he opened a Christmas parcel, peeled back tissue, glimpsed this beautiful thing.

"Will you take a check?" the disembodied voice that was her own was asking.

Not only was a check acceptable, but arrangements were made to send the jade tree to Miss Sanderson's London flat. When she reached the cold, windy street this time, she was deep in shock. Abigail Sanderson, she lectured herself, you're insane. Your bank account is depleted and you'll suffer the indignity of having to borrow from your ancient cook. And Aggie might be old, but she was canny and charged excessive rates of interest on her loans.

Anyway, that finished not only her bank account but her shopping. She trotted along and located the tea shop. By the time that Fran joined her, she was seated in a corner munching a Bath bun and sipping strong hot brew. Ordering the cream tea, Fran peered at her companion's plate. "Rather a frugal tea."

"Economizing. Good thing Christmas comes only once a year."

"I told you to watch your spending. But be of good heart. You'll be able to feast on Felix's cooking when we get back to the Jester." The younger woman shoved back her sleeve. "Lots of time. Those tests are drawn out. I hope Hielkje is bearing up."

"You're awfully good to her. Have you been friends for long?"

"We met when we were both interviewed by Peggy Canard. Less than two years ago. Answered the same ad. Hielkje was overawed that Peggy's daughter was the girl she saw on her favorite cooking show. But neither of us had much hope that Peggy would hire us. She wanted a married couple and didn't believe I could handle the maintenance work. When she found I had nursing experience, she decided to take both of us on trial. We made out fine and Peggy was quite pleased with us."

"At that time Peggy wasn't well."

"A heart condition. I could see that at a glance. All the signs. Bluish lips, shortness of breath. She lived only eight months, but we made her as comfortable as we could. Nancy came down to the island a couple of times and seemed relieved her mother was well enough looked after that she wouldn't have to concern herself. Nancy and Peggy weren't close." Fran cut into a cream-covered scone. "I had my hands full. Hielkje was ailing too. Finally Peggy and I forced her to go to Dr. Parker for treatment. Her problem was what I'd thought it was—thyroid. There was no reason for her to be ill, and medication put it right in no time. But Hielkje had neglected to take care of it herself. She has rotten luck. Last summer she had hepatitis and was terribly ill. She'd only started to pull out of that when she began to show her present symptoms." Fran sighed. "Practically a walking case history."

"You sound more like a doctor than a nurse."

"I'm not even a nurse. At least I haven't a degree to prove it. Picked nursing up the way I've picked everything up—by trial and error. I've even assisted with operations. Once David and I removed an appendix by the light of a couple of flashes."

"In the East?"

"Someone's been gossiping about my past."

"Gavin mentioned you once worked in refugee camps."

"And called me a bleeding heart. He was wrong. Those camps harden hearts. It's necessary or you'd bleed to death."

"And you worked with doctors?"

"One." Fran stirred milk into her tea. "David was an idealist…no, that's the wrong term. His was a practical dedication. Amazing man. Didn't care about race, religion, creed. All the world was his family."

"He's not heavy," Miss Sanderson said softly, "he's my brother." Fran nodded and Miss Sanderson asked, "Was?"

"He's dead. Killed in Beirut. There was a car bombing—"

"He was killed by a bomb?"

"David was shot. Gunned down by a policeman with an itchy trigger finger. David was running to help a child wounded by the bomb." Fran looked up. There were no tears in her brown eyes, only insufferable grief. "When he was killed I went berserk. Flung myself at the policeman and told him to shoot me too. Kill everyone! Kill the people who have come to nurse your sick, save your children!" Fran's voice had risen, and at the next table two plump women turned to stare. One, Miss Sanderson noted, had a smear of cream on a puffy chin. She stared coldly back and the women lowered their heads over their plates. "Sorry," Fran whispered. "David and I…we were lovers."

"So you came home and buried yourself on that godforsaken island."

"I have no home. I came back to England determined to give up the senseless crusade. Let them suffer and die. My heart bleeds no more."

Wrong, Miss Sanderson thought, your heart bleeds for David, who is dead, for Hielkje, who is alive, and must have for Peggy Canard. One cannot turn compassion such as that off like a tap.

Setting down her cup, Fran buttoned her pea jacket to the throat. "We'd better see if Hielkje is ready, Abigail." The Frisian hadn't waited in the warmth of the doctor's office. She was standing on the walk in front of the clinic, huddled in the ratty fur coat. As Fran bundled her into the car, she scolded, "Hielkje Visser, you have the makings of a martyr and try my patience something fierce."

"It looks serious, Fran."

Sliding in beside Miss Sanderson, Fran stared through the windshield. "How serious?"

"Dr. Parker didn't say. He has to wait for the results of the tests, but…what if he has to operate?" Hielkje started to cry. "What am I to do?"

"The obvious. If an operation is needed, you're going to have it. Did he give you medication?"

"Some pills. He said they'd help. Fran, Gavin will fire me!"

Fran switched on the ignition and the car purred away. "No, he won't. You'll have the operation and convalesce and your job will be waiting."

"But how? Nancy?"

"Nancy is right under his thumb. She can't do anything. But I can. If you go, I go. Think it's going to be easy to replace us? Most people would prefer the dole to living in that place. And how would Gavin enjoy using his delicate hands for manual toil?" Fran snorted. "He can't even get the ruddy boat started."

Hielkje blew her nose and wiped at her wet face. She managed a weak smile. "You're so good to me."

Miss Sanderson slanted a smile at Fran Hornblower. "The crusade goes on."

Fran said rather bitterly, "Old habits are hard to break."

Chapter Eight

That evening Felix served his dinner in the saloon bar. He had Gavin light a fire, and a number of brass lamps, shaped like ship's lanterns, cast a yellowish glow over the dishes spread the length of a refectory table. The saloon bar was smaller and more comfortable than the public bar. There were a number of side tables, and the faded brocade chairs were deeply cushioned. As Miss Sanderson joined the line to fill her plate, she reflected that the only informal part of dinner was its setting.

Alice Caspari wandered in and silently took a plate. The lion of the previous night had vanished and she was again a timid and subdued mouse. Taking a heaped plate, Miss Sanderson chose a chair near the fireplace and tucked in. As she dribbled lingonberry preserve over crisp Camembert fritters, she found she was regarding Felix more kindly. Whether it was the scrumptious food or the ride in his Rolls, she couldn't quite decide. He was also entertaining, amusing them with tales of his career. After a time Hielkje put in an appearance and carried her dinner over to the chair beside the secretary's. "Fran's battening down the hatches," she told the older woman. "It's working up to a storm and at this time of year they can be wicked."

Nancy joined them and perched on a footstool. "This is my first winter here and I'm not looking forward to it. It's bad enough in the spring and summer."

"Stop complaining," her husband told her tartly. He softened his tone. "There's nothing nicer than curling up in front of a roaring fire with a good book on a winter's night."

"Provided there's enough coal to keep that fire roaring." Fran Hornblower pushed past Gavin and stood on the hearth rug, rubbing her hands together. Her cheeks were glowing with color. "Foul night and it's going to get worse. By the way, Gavin, fuel duty at seven tomorrow morning if you want to start your drama on schedule."

Gavin took the order almost cheerfully. Smiling, he looked around. "Has everyone memorized their lines?"

"I haven't," Mrs. Montrose said flatly. She fed a bit of veal to her cat. "I've enough on my mind without doing that. I'll have to read from my script."

Hielkje colored faintly and glanced guiltily up at her employer but said nothing. Fran, who was bending over the buffet table, called, "I'll have to read too."

Gavin scowled and Felix clapped a hand on his shoulder. "Cheer up, old man. I've committed my role to memory and I'm certain Dolly has too. Writers have marvelous memories."

"We have to have," Dolly admitted. "But this time I don't have to use mine. I've no lines and—"

"*Dolly*," Gavin blurted.

"Sorry, Gavin, completely forgot my vow of silence."

And so much for Barbie Doll's marvelous memory, Miss Sanderson thought. Also, her first clue. She was mulling this over when Dolly rose, stretched her lithe body, and deposited a kiss on her fiancé's cheek. He hugged her close. "What's that for?"

"A thank-you for the wonderful dinner and a goodnight."

"Surely you're not going to bed so early."

Playfully she tugged at his short beard. "I'm going to put in a couple of hours on my book and then get some much needed beauty sleep."

Felix rose promptly to the bait and declaimed on the futility of beauty sleep for such a gorgeous creature. Smothering a yawn, Dolly slipped away from his grasp and called a general goodnight.

As the door closed behind Dolly, Nancy heaved a deep sigh and pulled herself off the footstool. "Hielkje, I suppose we better start the washing up."

Felix stopped being romantic. "Alice will have to help you, Hielkje. Nancy, I want to talk to Gavin and you."

Pouting, Nancy put a hand on Miss Sanderson's shoulder. "I was hoping to have some time with Auntie Abby. We haven't had chance for a decent chat."

"Sorry, but pleasure must give way to business."

"Business?" Gavin frowned. He brushed at his waterfall mustache. "What's this all about?"

"It may be a bitter pill but"—Felix laughed—"you can wash it down with some of my excellent brandy. We'll have our board meeting in my suite."

Gavin looked apprehensive and his wife was still pouting, but they followed the chef into the foyer. Sticking her knitting back in the bag, Alice started to clear the table and pile the dishes on one of the serving wagons. Hielkje rolled in another wagon and helped her. Mrs. Montrose, her cat curled peacefully up by her feet, bent her fluffy gray head over a book. For once Fran didn't whip around working. She sank into the chair vacated by Hielkje and draped her long legs over the footstool. She chatted with Miss Sanderson, and then the older woman glanced at her watch and rose. "I'd better get to bed before I fall asleep right here."

"Reggie already has," Fran said.

The Black Knight was sprawled on the sofa, his arms folded over his chest. Miss Sanderson said goodnight to Fran and Mrs. Montrose, patted the cat's head, and then paused by the sofa. In sleep Reggie looked so young, she thought, so innocent and so beautiful. His older brother, she recalled, hadn't possessed much claim to good looks. Damien had been taller and heavier than Reggie, and his skin had been darker, a blue-black. But his voice…ah, that had been as smooth and golden as his brother's skin was.

She trotted down the hall and picked up a flashlight. She opened the door to the guest wing and found the flash wasn't immediately needed. Strong light fell through the doorway of room number one. As Miss Sanderson stepped into the light, Dolly appeared in the doorway. She was draped in something diaphanous, and the lamps behind her silhouetted her figure and gilded the ends of her hair. Her face was in shadow. She jumped and gasped, "Who is it?"

"Abigail. Did I startle you?"

"A bit. This place is so…so spooky. Well, I'm off to the bath and then bed."

"I'll walk down with you." Miss Sanderson snapped on her flash and pointed the beam on the floor. Dolly thudded into Miss Sanderson's shoulder. "Sorry," she said, then asked brightly, "All ready to start detecting?"

"Ready as I'll ever be. Hey, that's not the bath. That's one of the unfinished rooms."

"So it is. Yes, here we are."

"You'd better take the flash."

"You'll need it."

"I have one I brought with me in my room."

"Ta-ta and goodnight."

Reaching past Dolly, Miss Sanderson opened the door of the bath. A lamp, the wick turned down low, sat on the tile sink, casting a dim light. Dolly walked in and managed to thud her shoulder again, this time on the doorjamb. Miss Sanderson stood in the dark hall wondering what was wrong with the woman. Could Dolly, like her rival, have had her nose in a bottle? There had been no smell of alcohol around her, but she'd acted tipsy. Drugs? Miss Sanderson shrugged and groped her way across the hall toward her own room. She came up hard against a door and found she was entering the lav. Trailing a hand along the wall, she located her doorknob by banging a hip against it. A fine person to mentally accuse Dolly of being in her cups. Here she was, sober as a judge, ricocheting off doors and walls. Well, I can certainly do something about being sober, she decided, heading toward the chest where Fran Hornblower had secreted the brandy.

As she sipped, she noticed that Fran's prophecy about the storm had come true. The shutters on her window were banging and clattering.

Miss Sanderson not only slept soundly that night but managed to sleep in the next morning. She had just finished tidying her room and was pulling a heavy cardigan over a rolled-neck sweater when a knock sounded at her door. It was Reggie, dressed as warmly as she was and wearing a wide smile. "Twelve o'clock high," he told her. "Force-ten storm raging and lunch is being served in that deep freeze they call a dining room. The game will soon be afoot. How is Holmes today?"

"More like Watson than ever."

"Try positive thinking. Think yourself into Holmes's clever shoes. Tell you what, I'll act as your Dr. Watson."

"For all I know you may be the murderer I'm trying to root out."

He waved his folder. "Aha, for me to know, for you to wonder."

As they wandered down the hall, she asked, "How is our host this morning?"

"Like a cat on a hot stove. Acts like the weight of the world rests on his shoulders. Gavin has opening-night jitters."

They passed the desk and she pointed at the glass queens. "Whimsical touch."

"They don't seem to fit the Jester. Clowns would be more suitable." He opened the door of the dining room and told her, "The orders are to take separate tables. Supposed to be a group of strangers."

With the exceptions of the host and hostess, who were seated at the table nearest the door, the guests were occupying their own tables. The tables were covered with snowy linen and each was ornamented by a crystal bud vase displaying one artificial carnation. The room was merely chilly, not frigid as it had been when Miss Sanderson had last dined there. She spotted the reason. Another heater had been moved in at the far end of the room. Hopefully she checked out the table beside it and found she was out of luck. Mrs. Montrose and Omar had snaggled that one, and Reggie had quickly taken the cozy table near the other heater.

Miss Sanderson pulled out a chair and plumped down at the table behind his. Behind her the wind and rain clawed icily at a windowpane. As Reggie pulled his chair closer to the heater, she shivered and muttered, "The days of chivalry have vanished. Knight-errant, indeed!"

"Blame it on my Jamaican blood. Either too thick or too thin for this climate. Never can figure out which—Hey! Look at Fran. Talk about figures. And legs. A shame she covers that shape up in denim most of the time."

Both of the Jester's employees were carrying sandwich trays and cheese and fruit plates. They were dressed as French maids from a drawing room comedy, complete with short black dresses, lacy aprons, and black net hose. Their hair was upswept and topped with jaunty lace caps. They wore flimsy black sandals with four-inch heels. The outfit suited Fran and displayed the trim figure and splendid legs that Reggie was admiring. Hielkje was less fortunate. With her stout torso and thick legs she looked like a sausage stuffed into a decorative casing. But she was handling the high heels more expertly than Fran was. Teetering over, Fran proffered a sandwich tray. Reggie leered up at her and whispered, "*Où là là.* And when do you get off work, *ma petite?*"

"Soon." She winked at him. "Wait outside the kitchen door for me. That should cool you off, *mon garçon.*"

Selecting a sandwich, Miss Sanderson asked, "When do we begin?"

"Anytime now." Fran held up her script. "But I haven't much to say. I think Gavin must have given Hielkje all the good lines."

As Fran moved unsteadily away, Miss Sanderson glanced around. The other guests seemed engrossed in their luncheons and their scripts. Gavin had a thick folder at his elbow, but he was bending over the table in what looked like a heated conversation with his wife. Reggie nudged Miss Sanderson. "Notice that two of the cast are missing?"

Mrs. Montrose was trying to interest her haughty Persian in a scrap of sandwich, and Alice Caspari was casting on stitches, this time using a dreadful shade of purple wool. "Ah, no sign of the lovebirds."

"Amazing, Holmes. I've no idea how you do it."

"Keep this up and you can do the detecting and I'll play your part."

At that moment Gavin Lebonhom swiveled around and called, "Hielkje, is Miss Carter-White not down yet?"

"You can see she's not."

Gavin thumped his script and Hielkje said, "Oh!" and hastily flipped her folder open. She managed to dip the bottom of it in a fruit plate.

"I think," Reggie said loudly, "that is the opening line in Gavin's opus."

Gavin turned to glare at the singer and Hielkje cleared her throat. "I believe, sir, the lady is still abed," she read, spacing her words.

"Perhaps," Gavin said, without consulting his script, "you had better check on her."

"Yes, sir. It will be faster if I use the lift—" Raising puzzled eyes, Hielkje said in her normal voice, "Gavin, we don't have a *lift*."

He ran his fingers through his unruly hair. "Can't you read, you idiot? In brackets, after 'lift.'"

She wiped peach juice off the page. "Dumbwaiter." She cleared her throat. "Yes, sir. It will be faster if I use the dumbwaiter."

Reggie made a muffled sound and Gavin spat. "Lift! The goddamn lift. Never mind, go on."

"Make your exit and wait in the hall for a few minutes," she mumbled, and followed the instructions.

Leaning back in his chair, Gavin wiped at his brow. Despite the cool air he was sweating. He asked his wife, "Where in hell is that..."

Nancy shrugged and his voice trailed off. "Take it easy," she told him. "You're getting too tense. He'll be along."

"He was supposed to be right here and you know it. I tell you, Nan, he's up to something and—Ah, Hielkje, did you wake Miss Carter-White?"

A more relaxed-looking Hielkje had returned. "I think you had better come, sir," she read in a flat voice. "There appears to be a dead body in the dumbwaiter—"

"Lift!" Gavin roared.

Miss Sanderson, her shoulders shaking, put down her sandwich. Reggie muttered in her ear, "I must be mad, but I'm beginning to enjoy this."

Gavin was looking expectantly at Mrs. Montrose and that lady said in ringing tones, "I strongly suspect, Mr. Lebonhom, that this play is foul!"

"Foul play!" he shrieked. "For God's sake, read it again!"

Mrs. Montrose looked affronted but obediently read, "I strongly suspect, Mr. Lebonhom, that this is foul play."

Reggie wiped tears from streaming eyes. "She was right the *first* time."

Miss Sanderson dug a sharp elbow into his ribs. "Gavin's glaring at you. I think you're on."

Paper rustled and Reggie blurted, "I think, Mr. Lebonhom, we had better have a look in that dumb—that lift."

"That," said Alice Caspari, "is a good idea. Hielkje, are you certain the person in the lift is dead? Could it not be a seizure of some kind?"

Alice must have read her lines correctly because Gavin gave her a look of pure gratitude. He said earnestly, "Yes, Hielkje, do explain. What made you think the body is dead?"

Hielkje seemed to have lost her place. She flipped pages rapidly. "There is blood all over, sir, all over her lovely white negligee. In her back is a jeweled dagger. I saw that dagger, sir, on her dressing table when I cleaned her room. Yes, Mr. Lebonhom, Miss Carter-White is definitely in bed."

"Dead! You flaming moronic cretin. You—" Nancy put a hand on her husband's arm, he took a deep breath, and said hoarsely, "Stage direction, Hielkje."

Hielkje raised her brown eyes. "'Faint'? Gavin, should I fall on the floor—"

"Collapse on a chair. Any chair." Gavin turned to his wife. "I should never have given her such a large part. She hasn't even bothered to read through the bloody script."

"Shh, darling. She's doing her best. She's sick."

"She's making *me* sick. Collapse, Hielkje, that you should have no problem with."

Hielkje promptly obeyed, throwing her heavy body on the nearest chair, which squeaked in protest. She seemed better at action than dialogue and sagged forward across the table in a most realistic manner. Stifling an impulse to applaud, Miss Sanderson gazed around. Mrs. Montrose was devouring a sandwich, Omar had dozed off, and Alice bent her mousy head over the flashing steel needles. Fran was leaning against the sideboard, sipping coffee.

"Fran," the harried author prompted.

She put down her cup and reached for the water pitcher. Pouring into a glass, she said, "I will give her a sip of water, sir. She has had a shock."

Carrying the glass in one hand, her script in the other, she hurried across the room. Gavin was nodding approval when Fran's ankle turned, and she lurched forward and delivered the contents of the glass over Hielkje's head and shoulders. With an outraged shriek the other woman jerked upright, and Gavin tore at his hair with both hands. Reggie had given up and sprawled across his table in what seemed to be hysterics.

"I'm sorry, Gavin. These damn shoes! I told you I hadn't worn heels this high in years." Scooping up a napkin, Fran swiped at the cook's face.

Her employer seemed speechless, and Nancy said sooth-ingly, "Darling, it will be better when we get to the next part. Fran, do carry on, please."

Dropping the napkin, Fran consulted her script. "The sip of water did revive her, sir. She is now able to show us the dreadful thing she found." She helped the sodden cook up and immediately staggered and grabbed the woman's thick arm. Muttering a curse, Fran kicked off both sandals.

Gavin now seemed numb. He mumbled, "Mr. Knight is correct. We will all have a look in the lift. Come along."

Nudging her cat awake, Mrs. Montrose led him past Miss Sanderson's table. Her script was stuck under an arm and she was nibbling another sandwich. Alice stowed away her knitting and tagged along behind. Reggie heaved himself up. "Abigail, Mrs. Montrose is a lady with much control. If I'd kept on eating through that opening scene, I'd have choked to death. I hope the next part runs smoothly, or I'm going to get a hernia from smothering my guffaws."

"Smothering! You sounded like a bull moose at mating time."

"I'm beginning to see why Gavin has never published."

"Mystery may not be his forte. Perhaps he should try comedy."

"If he did, he'd have a best-seller." Touching her arm, he pointed. "Behold, the dead body taking nourishment."

One of the doors to the public bar was ajar, and Miss Sanderson glimpsed Dolly Carter-White. She was perched on a barstool eating her lunch from a tray. She was wearing a fuzzy scarlet jumpsuit that was as form fitting as the white silk had been. "I should have thought she'd be curled up on the dumb-waiter posing as a corpse."

"Not so," Reggie told her. "Too messy for that lovely lady. Fran told me, in strictest confidence, the part of the corpse is being played by a mannequin." He chuckled. "A dummy in a dumbwaiter. Not bad, eh?"

"I wonder where her fiancé is?"

"Probably up to no good. Must remember there's a joker loose in the Jester."

"Gavin should have had you write his play. You have a certain way with words. Blimey, but I hope Felix isn't planning to ruin Gavin's play."

"Little late for that, Abigail. Fran and Hielkje, with Mrs. Montrose's able assistance, have handled that." He swung open a baize door. "Act one, scene two. The corpse in the lift-dumbwaiter."

Gavin, his color high and looking more cheerful, had taken up a post to the left of the stove. At his side a sulky looking Hielkje was trying to dry the bodice of her dress with a dish towel. Behind them were the wide double doors of the dumbwaiter. At that moment they were tightly closed. Alice, Mrs. Montrose and Omar, Nancy Lebonhom, and Fran were clustered around the host and his cook. Fran was standing on one leg like a stork, rubbing a black-net-covered foot against the calf of the other leg. Although the kitchen was warm with heat pulsing from the cooking stove, the stone floor must have been icy.

Waving the latecomers closer, Gavin declaimed, "Slide back the lift door, Hielkje. Don't be afraid, I'm right at your side."

Looking even more sullen, the cook grabbed both knobs and pulled the doors wide. Glaring at her master, Hielkje snarled, "There Miss Carter-White is, sir. I can't bear to look at her."

Instead of looking into the dumbwaiter, Gavin stared at his audience and said with great feeling, "By Jove, you are right! And the weapon that killed her is her jeweled dagger." Without looking away from his audience, he pointed a dramatic finger and gasped, "She has been murdered."

Someone gave a nervous titter and Miss Sanderson tried to see over Fran's shoulder. That shoulder went rigid. At the same moment Gavin swung around and looked down into the dumbwaiter. In a low, venomous voice he said, "Damn it to hell. Had to do it, didn't you? First ruin me, now ruin my poor play. Well…you've done it. Joke's over. Get the hell up."

Reggie hissed in Miss Sanderson's ear, "Sounds like Felix has struck again."

Miss Sanderson felt a stirring of pity for the beleaguered Gavin Lebonhom. She must try to rescue something from this debacle. Pushing at Fran's back, she ad-libbed, "I'm a detective. Let me through. Stand aside." There was a ripple of movement and the other guests cleared a path. Stepping up beside Hielkje, Miss Sanderson looked down. The platform was long and wide and came to her waist. On it a figure sprawled. It was face down with the legs drawn up and the right hand, palm up, at its side. The other arm was tucked up under the chest. Chestnut hair spilled over the collar of a tweed jacket. From the back of that jacket an ebony handle protruded. Tiny gold letters caught a glint of light and sparkled.

Gavin was now raving and cursing Felix Caspari. Some of the others were giggling. Miss Sanderson said curtly, "Shut up." She put down a hand and gingerly touched the inert hand on the splintery boards. The flesh felt like cold wax.

Turning, Hielkje bent to have a look. Then she gave a soft sigh and crumpled to the stone floor. This time her faint was done even more artistically than the one she had counterfeited in the dining room.

Chapter Nine

No attention was paid to the unconscious cook. Everyone was gaping at the still figure on the dumbwaiter. Miss Sanderson said, "Fran," and the woman stepped forward and shoved Mrs. Montrose to one side. She bent over Felix Caspari, her hands moving swiftly and competently. Then she straightened and pulled the doors closed. "We aren't acting any further. He's dead."

Dropping her knitting bag, Alice burst into tears. Gavin covered his face with both hands, and his wife had turned a sickly green. Alice was swaying and Reggie pulled up a chair and lowered her into it. He asked Fran, "Are you certain?"

"He's already starting to cool."

Clapping a hand over her mouth, Nancy sprinted to the sink. Bending over it, she retched. Mrs. Montrose dropped her cat's leash and dampened a dishcloth. She patted the girl's heaving shoulders and clapped the towel over her brow. Both Fran and Reggie were staring at Miss Sanderson. The secretary decided she must start playing her role in earnest. "All of you but Fran get out of here," she ordered. "Gavin and Reggie, you'll have to carry Hielkje. Mrs. Montrose, you take Alice and Nancy along."

Reggie nudged Gavin, and they bent and hoisted Hielkje up between them. Her head lolled back and Gavin grunted, "She weighs a ton."

Mrs. Montrose pulled Nancy away from the sink. "Someone must break this to Dolly."

"I'll do it." Alice pulled herself up and picked up her knitting bag. Tears were pouring down her face, but there was a faint note of satisfaction in her voice. "It's *my* place to do it. I'm Felix's widow."

The Widow Caspari was the first to exit the kitchen. Gavin and Reggie, panting over the cook's supine body, were last. Omar, dragging his leash, tripped Gavin, and he muttered a number of four-letter words.

As the baize doors swung into place, Fran turned and asked, "What do we do?"

"Get on to the police, of course. But first—have you any idea how long he's been dead?"

"I'm not a doctor."

"You're the closest we have to one at this moment."

"At a guess I'd say at least a couple of hours."

"Hmm. That would put it about eleven-thirty. Shortly before we had lunch."

"It's only a guess. The postmortem will pin it down fairly close."

Miss Sanderson led the way to the lobby and closed the doors to the public bar. A gust of wind rocked the front door of the inn, followed by a wild shriek from the direction of the bar. Fran winced. "Sounds like the widow has broken the news to the fiancée." She shivered and muttered, "Better get something on my feet before I get pneumonia."

Miss Sanderson headed toward the desk, and Fran fished around in a closet and found a pair of high rubber boots. As she tugged them on, she called, "Finchley is closest. Ask for Inspector James."

Miss Sanderson held out the receiver. "Dead."

"It can't be. Reggie was using it this morning." Taking the receiver, she held it to an ear and jiggled the bar. "Well, it's not working now."

"Could the storm—"

"Might have. Last winter during a storm like this the phone was out for a couple of days." She circled the bar and bent out of sight. When she rose, she held the end of a cord in her hand. "Not the storm. It's been cut."

The two women stared at each other. Miss Sanderson said, "What about the boat? Can you get to the mainland in this storm?"

Fran trotted over and opened the front door. The wind drove sleet into her face and nearly ripped the door from her hand. She struggled to close the door, and Miss Sanderson ran to help. Before it shut she saw whitetipped waves battering at the pier. "What do you think, Fran?"

The lace cap bobbed as Fran shook her head. "It's risky. Too heavy seas for a boat that size, even for a short distance. Under ordinary circumstances I wouldn't try it, but these are hardly ordinary. I'll give it a go. First, I better get these damn clothes off." She headed for the hall.

Miss Sanderson called after her, "Someone had better go with you."

"Who would you suggest?"

"One of the men."

"Gavin's hopeless. Probably gets seasick in the tub. But Reggie seems to have a cool head. Rout him out. Warn him it's dangerous. There are boots and waterproofs in that closet."

Miss Sanderson opened a door and peered into the bar. It looked like a battlefield. Hielkje was stretched out on a bench with a pillow under her head and her feet propped up. The widow was sitting under the watercolor, collapsed over the table, her face buried in her knitting bag. Dolly didn't look as much like a Barbie doll. Her creamy hair was hanging over a damp face with smudged makeup, and Mrs. Montrose was holding a glass to her lips. Omar was perched on the polished counter, nonchalantly washing his face with a fluffy gray paw. Beside the cat, Gavin perched on a stool, but he didn't seem to notice the cat or anything else. His wife had her back turned and appeared to be retching in the bar sink.

Catching Reggie's eyes, Miss Sanderson jerked her head toward the foyer. She explained the situation and then said, "You'll have to volunteer. Fran says it's risky. Do you know anything about boats?"

"Haven't the foggiest, but I'm a quick study." He burrowed into the closet, and by the time Fran had returned, he'd pulled an oilskin over his parka and located rubber boots. He tugged his toque down over his ears.

Fran eyed him doubtfully and pulled an oilskin over her pea jacket. As she jammed the watch cap down over her head, she asked, "Did Abigail mention that the boat could capsize?"

"She hinted at it. You do have life jackets I presume."

"Of course. But they'll be as much help as snowballs in hell if we're thrown into that water."

"Thanks. I needed that."

"All ready?"

"Ready, but far from eager. Let's go." He squeezed Miss Sanderson's arm. "Bear up. We'll be as quick as we can."

She told him shakily, "Reggie, I take back what I said about chivalry having vanished."

This time she had to fight to close the heavy door by herself. She glimpsed them struggling down the rocky path. Fran nearly fell, and Reggie grabbed her. Miss Sanderson shook a worried head. This was lunacy. They shouldn't try it. But they were both levelheaded, and if it looked hopeless, they would give it up and return to the inn.

Time to test her own courage by going into the bar. She decided not to tell the others about the severed telephone cord. They would panic. She straightened her thin shoulders and opened the door, trying to look confident. Mrs. Montrose was now trying to drain brandy into Hielkje's slack mouth. La Montrose, Miss Sanderson thought, was not only the oldest person there but the most composed. Heads swiveled toward the door, and Mrs. Montrose snapped, "How long will the police be?"

"I don't know. The telephone is out of order."

"What are we going to do?" Nancy threw down the damp towel and her voice rose with a raw edge of hysteria.

"It's being done. Fran and Reggie are taking the boat across to the cars. It won't take long for them to drive in to Finchley."

"Thank God for the boat," Gavin mumbled.

Alice jumped to her feet and the bag tumbled off the table, spilling purple wool and glittering needles. "Reggie? Reggie's leaving here?"

"To summon the police," Miss Sanderson said. "Fran couldn't go alone."

"He's escaping: He killed my husband! He hated Felix, blamed him for his brother's death."

"*Alice.*" Mrs. Montrose thumped down the glass. "Control yourself."

The widow turned on her. "If it wasn't Reggie, it was you."

"Just why would I kill Felix?"

"Because of Sonny. You always blamed Felix for Sonny."

"Don't be ridiculous. And stop making wild accusations." Mrs. Montrose paused and then made one of her own. "The police may feel *you* had an excellent motive for wanting your husband dead."

"Me? But I love…loved him."

"And there's your motive. Rather than lose him you might have decided you'd rather see him dead."

Felix's patron and his widow were glaring like Bengal tigers. "Both of you settle down," Miss Sanderson said. "Save your strength. You're going to need it."

Some Dutch courage may increase my own strength, Miss Sanderson thought, flipping up the panel in the counter. She took down a brandy bottle and poured a generous tot. The door to the foyer banged open and two bedraggled figures staggered in. Their oilskins dripped water, and Fran's ponytail clung damply to her neck. Heading toward the counter, they stretched out hands. Miss Sanderson promptly filled those beseeching hands with brandy glasses. "You decided not to try?" she asked.

Brushing a sodden ringlet away from his cheek, Reggie panted, "Someone decided for us."

"Used an ax and stove in the bottom of the boat," Fran explained breathlessly.

Gavin swung around and his eyes finally focused. "Exactly what happened to the telephone?"

"The cord was cut," Reggie said.

They panicked. Dolly came bolting out of the alcove, Hielkje let out a bellow and nearly fell off the bench, Nancy proceeded to have hysterics. Mrs. Montrose again rose to the occasion and cracked her palm across Nancy's face. Following the older woman's example, Miss Sanderson slapped her own hand on the counter. "Stop it! Stop it this instant. Losing your heads won't help."

"We're marooned," Gavin quavered. "Cut off from help with a murderer among us. We're all going to be murdered!"

"Keep that up and I'll oblige you right now," Reggie told him. "Listen. Abigail's right. We're *not* marooned. There's the causeway. As soon as the storm slackens, we'll cross to the mainland. At low tide, of course. Right, Fran?"

"If you happen to have suicidal impulses," she said, and refreshed her drink. "I must have, because when the storm dies down, I'll give it a go."

"You see," Miss Sanderson said. "It's only a matter of carrying on until the weather clears."

Hielkje seemed to be feeling somewhat better. She pulled herself up into a sitting position and said brightly, "Last winter a storm like this lasted for a week."

Nancy wailed and then subsided as Mrs. Montrose lifted a threatening hand. Pulling off the oilskin, Reggie draped it over a stool. "Hielkje, you're a great little help. Anyway, the weather is out of our hands. Fran says there's lots of food and enough fuel, so we'll muddle through. Right now I vote our detective get to work."

All eyes swung hopefully to Miss Sanderson. With a sinking heart she told them, "I'm a legal secretary, not a detective."

Giving her a wry grin, Fran repeated what the older woman had said in the kitchen. "At this moment you're the closest to one that we have."

Miss Sanderson lifted her chin. "Very well, I'll try. Now, about the mannequin that was supposed to be in the dumbwaiter. Who was supposed to put it there?" Fran raised a hand and the secretary asked, "When?"

"I did it after Gavin and I finished hauling coal in. That was…"

"We started at seven," Gavin said. "Finished up at exactly eight minutes after nine. I was watching the clock."

"I'll bet you were," Fran said. "When we'd finished I washed up, and then Gavin called to me and told me to fix up the mannequin in the dumbwaiter. I told him there was loads of time but he insisted, and I went up to the attic and did it." She paused. "Want to look around up there, Abigail?"

There was nothing Miss Sanderson wanted less, but she followed the younger woman through the lobby and up the staircase. "Better explain the layout of this floor, Fran."

"That's the VIP suite used by Felix. Two rooms and bath with only one door opening into the sitting room. Directly opposite that door is Nancy's sitting room, then the Lebonhoms' bedroom, then Gavin's study. All three rooms connected by interior doors. My room is beside Gavin's study, and Hielkje's is next to Felix's suite. The lav and bath are down this branch hall, and at the end is a door leading to the steps Gavin had boxed in." She swung open a door and Miss Sanderson saw a landing painted Chinese red with steps leading upward. "Now, Abigail, back to the main hall, and there is the staircase leading to the attic. Watch yourself, these steps are steep and narrow."

It was more a ladder than a staircase, and as they climbed, the air got progressively colder. When they reached the top, Miss Sanderson decided that the lower regions of the Jester were, in comparison, positively balmy. She tugged her cardigan closer and listened to Fran's rapid explanation. "Those are the doors of the dumbwaiter. The four doors opposite lead to storerooms and a lav no longer in operation. Originally this floor must have been used as quarters for the servants. Poor devils weren't exactly swaddled in luxury." She opened the door directly across from the dumbwaiter. "This is the room Gavin fitted up for his mannequins. Sort of a prop room. At first he planned to have the guest playing the part of the victim pose as the corpse, but Nancy talked him out of it. Said she didn't think Dolores Carter-White would agree to being crammed onto that platform and having her clothes covered with red ink—God!"

She had nearly tripped over a figure sprawled on the floor. The woman had long creamy blond hair and a jeweled hilt protruded from its back. The white silk was soaked with what looked like blood.

"Sorry," Fran said shakily. "I fixed it up myself, but it looks real, doesn't it?"

"A dead ringer for Dolly. Give me the details, Fran."

"After I spoke to Gavin, I came up here and dressed it." She waved toward a rack of clothing. Propped up against it, three other mannequins, two male and one female, stared with glassy eyes. On a bench beside them a number of wigs sat on holders.

Miss Sanderson's eyes ranged around the room. "Gavin did a thorough job on his theatrics."

"He got the stuff fairly cheaply from a shop going out of business. Anyway, I stuck the dagger in the back of the dummy, dribbled ink on it, and pulled it out here." She stepped across the hall and opened the doors of the dumbwaiter. "I arranged it on the platform and then let the dumbwaiter down to kitchen level."

Poking her head in the hole, Miss Sanderson looked at the system of cables and then bent forward. This part of the dumb-waiter was, like the kitchen opening, waist high. No danger of falling. She peered down into a black well. An icy current of air stirred her hair. At the bottom the earthly remains of Felix Caspari, master chef, huddled, separated from the kitchen by flimsy doors.

Fran must have been following the older woman's thoughts. "Neither Hielkje nor Nancy will go into the kitchen with…"

"We'd better bring him up." She turned away from the black well. "It's going to be heavy. Think we can handle it?"

"Stand aside. I can do it." Reaching up, Fran made an adjustment. "This thing was in bad shape when I came here. I had to completely overhaul it. Installed new cables and replaced the old platform with a larger one."

"What do you use it for?"

"Mainly for fuel for the bedroom floor. Believe it or not, but there are seven fireplaces to keep going on that floor. But"— she gave a heave and started to crank—"I've even used it to move furniture. Ah, here it comes."

All Miss Sanderson could hear was a muted rumble. "It moves quietly."

"I keep it well oiled. And if you're thinking it could be hauled up and down without being heard, you're right." Looking over Fran's shoulder, Miss Sanderson could now discern the shadowy shape of the platform. She braced herself. Then the platform was there and Fran locked it into position. She started to close the doors, but Miss Sanderson stopped her. "We'll have to take him out of there."

"Should we? Won't the police—"

"The police aren't here and we don't know when they will be. Fran, I know it's asking a lot, but I can't do it alone. We have to…to look him over."

For a moment Fran stood indecisively. Finally she nodded and her ponytail bobbed. "There are a couple of spare doors in the boxroom. Last fall I replaced the ones on my room and Hielkje's. We can use one as a stretcher."

They retrieved the door and placed it on the floor. Fran gave brisk instructions. "You take his legs. I'll handle his shoulders. Lord, he's stiffening up. Heave!"

They swung the grisly object off the platform, nearly dropped it, and then lowered it carefully to the door. Miss Sanderson stood back panting. "He must weigh over two hundred."

"Big man." Fran bent and grasped one end of the door. "You lift the other end, Abigail. We'll put this in with the mannequins."

They lowered the door in front of the clothes rack. As Miss Sanderson sank to her knees, she felt as though the glassy eyes of the three mannequins were watching her. She rolled the stiff figure back, and Fran braced it from the other side. Felix's eyes were wide open and his mouth gaped. From the corner of that mouth a worm of dried blood had seeped into his short beard. Tearing her eyes from that face, Miss Sanderson pulled the jacket clear of the barrel-like chest. "No blood on his shirt."

"No exit wound," Fran said calmly. "The knife is imbedded in his chest. Internal bleeding, and any blood from the entrance wound is soaked up by his shirt and this heavy jacket." Bending forward, she mercifully closed the staring eyes.

They eased him back on his face and Miss Sanderson studied the tweed-clad back. The ebony hilt protruded from between the shoulder blades. On it, tiny initials—FGC—sparkled. Custom-made for murder, she thought, and her eyes closed. Fran asked, "Abigail, are you all right?"

"Barely," she whispered, as Fran took her arm and hauled her to her feet. "Fine detective. But this is the first time I've actually handled…"

"I know. Takes a bit of getting used to. Take deep breaths."

Miss Sanderson took deep breaths and steadied. She forced herself back to her knees and ran her fingers over the tweed. A fingernail snagged and she said, "Take a look at this."

"A rip?"

"I don't think so. Looks as though it was cut. No jagged edges."

Fran examined the fabric. "A slit about an inch and a half long. About midway between the knife wound and the right armpit. Over a shoulder blade. Only the tweed cut; the lining's intact."

Miss Sanderson stood up. "Is there anything up here we can use to cover him?"

"A set of discarded curtains. I'll get one."

They draped the door and its burden with a rosecolored curtain. The velvet was faded and worn and dust billowed up from its folds. Miss Sanderson was thankful to leave the mannequin room and the staring glassy eyes. They stopped on the lower floor to wash up, and as Fran toweled her hands off, her companion perched on the edge of a claw-footed tub, her thumbnail beating a tattoo against a front tooth.

For once she wasn't asked what she was doing. Instead, Fran said, "When I think, I tug at my hair. Want to share?"

"That slit, deliberately cut. The positioning of it. What does it suggest?"

"I haven't the slightest idea." Fran's level brows drew together. "All I can say is, Felix Caspari was not a man to wear a damaged jacket. If he'd known it—"

"Oh, Felix knew all about that slit." Lifting cool blue eyes, Miss Sanderson smiled grimly. "He cut the slit himself. The last joke was played on the practical joker."

Chapter Ten

A certain serenity had returned to the public bar. Hielkje Visser had changed from her maid's costume and now looked like a sausage stuffed into a plaid shirt and jeans. Dolly had repaired her makeup and fluffed out her Barbie doll hair. The Widow Caspari was working on the dreadful purple wool. Omar had gone to sleep on the counter, and Reggie, swinging long legs, was perched on a stool near him. Nancy was huddled on a bench near the fire, and Miss Sanderson noticed the girl's color was better. Miss Sanderson checked her watch. Thirty-eight after three. Slightly over two hours since the discovery of the murder and it seemed like ten years. The room was shadowed and Gavin was moving around, lighting lamps, pulling curtains over windows, as though trying to shut out the storm. The sight of sleet slashing against glass disappeared, but the wind howled under the eaves and moaned against the hidden glass.

Reggie jumped up and offered brandy or beer, but Miss Sanderson shook her head. "Nancy, you and Hielkje make coffee. Reggie, the bar's closed. We need clear heads."

Reggie nodded. "Better rustle up some food too. I'm starving."

Setting down a lamp with a thud, Gavin pointed a dramatic finger. "Thinking of food with Felix in the kitchen stiff and stark."

"Fasting won't help Felix," Mrs. Montrose pointed out.

Nancy whimpered and Hielkje said, "I am not putting a foot in the kitchen. Not with that thing in the lift."

"Wonder of wonders," Reggie said. "She finally got her line right."

"The dumbwaiter is no longer in the kitchen," Fran told the two women. "It's now in the attic. Come along, I'll give you a hand."

Miss Sanderson climbed onto a stool and waited until a serving wagon was wheeled in and coffee and cheese rolls were distributed. Apparently Gavin had overcome his squeamishness as he helped himself generously. Even the widow managed to eat. The only ones with no appetite were Fran Hornblower and Miss Sanderson.

Gavin chewed, swallowed, and reached for the creamer. "And has the great detective come to any conclusions?" There was a sneer in his voice.

"I know how the murder was done," she told him. "But the identity of the murderer…who he or she is—"

"If you say X, I'll be sick," Gavin told her. "It's trite."

"This isn't one of your lousy scripts," Reggie said hotly. "This is real, so drop the great-writer bit."

Gavin flushed and Miss Sanderson asked him, "In your play, what was *your* murderer called?"

"The Jester."

"Aha!" Mrs. Montrose leaned forward, her simian face splitting into a smile. "A Freudian slip. And I'll wager Felix was cast as the Jester."

Gavin was now close to the color of Alice Caspari's knitting. Disregarding him, Miss Sanderson said, "Jester will serve. Now, we'll go back to yesterday morning. Gavin, Fran said you accused her of opening a window in your study."

"Either she did or Nan did. Neither of them would admit it." Gavin turned on his wife. "That was sheer carelessness.

Leaving that door to our bedroom unlocked. I've warned you repeatedly about that."

"Papers on your desk were disarranged?" Miss Sanderson asked.

"Blown all over the place. Even some sheets on the floor. The window had been closed again, but I could tell at a glance what had happened."

"Were these papers your script?"

"My master script. Everything was there, including a synopsis of the murder, how the mannequin was to be arranged on the dumbwaiter—" He stopped and his eyes widened. "Felix!"

"Exactly. While you were occupied helping bring in the coal, Felix got into your study and read your script. This morning he waited for Fran to finish in the attic—"

"You're right!" Fran jerked forward. "After I finished in the attic I was passing Felix's suite, and he popped out and asked how things were coming. I told him swimmingly and—"

"And he knew the coast was clear." Miss Sanderson lit a cigarette and gazed at the cloud of bluish smoke. "Felix must already have decided exactly how he was going to make Gavin look ridiculous. He must have cut a slit in the back of his jacket, and he took one of his knives…Gavin, come over here. Turn so the others can see your back. Now, Gavin is wearing a jacket similar to Felix's. On the dead man's the slit is right about here." She drew a finger down the rough tweed and felt Gavin's back muscles quivering. "The reason Felix cut into an expensive jacket is clear. The slit was intended to be a pocket to push the knife in, so at a casual glance it would look as though the hilt was sticking out of his back. But he ran into difficulty and had to ring in a confederate to help."

Reggie jumped off the counter for a closer look. "Why would Felix have needed help?"

"Hand me one of those swizzle sticks, Reggie. Now, Gavin, take this in your left hand and try to position it as though the pocket is right where my finger is resting."

He wriggled and twisted. "Can't be done."

"Ah," Reggie said. "A flaw in your reasoning, Abigail. Felix could have stuck the knife in the slit *before* he put the jacket on."

"No." It was Alice who spoke. "My late husband's knives were always honed razor sharp. He could have cut himself putting his jacket on. Felix would never have done that."

"Precisely," Miss Sanderson said. "And if Felix had cut himself, the joke would have been on him, not on Gavin. He found someone willing to help play the trick, and they sneaked up to the attic to prepare the scene. The mannequin was lifted off the platform, and Felix climbed onto it and handed his confederate the knife. Then he waited for it to be artistically tucked into the slit." She took a deep breath. "But the joker had unfortunately chosen the Jester. The Jester ignored the slit and drove the knife deep into Felix's back. Then the Jester lowered the platform again to the kitchen—"

"One moment," Mrs. Montrose interrupted. "Wouldn't that have taken a great deal of strength?"

Turning, Fran ran her eyes down Mrs. Montrose's frail body. "You could have done it. The way I've rigged the cables it would have been simple and easy. And it moves quietly. Abigail noticed that."

Gavin shoved his cup away so violently that it tipped and brown fluid flowed across the counter. "That bastard! First he ruins me, then he tried to ruin my play. I suppose he was going to jump up and laugh and shout something funny!"

"Gavin!" his wife cried. "He's *dead*."

"Then he's a *dead* bastard."

The Black Knight ignored Gavin's outburst. "The telephone. I used it at…let's see, it must have been—Fran, you came into the foyer while I was speaking with my manager. Any idea of the time?"

"I'd just finished in the attic. It was about—"

"The time doesn't matter," Miss Sanderson said flatly. "That foyer is so cold no one lingers in it. Anytime after Felix was killed the Jester could have slipped in there and cut the cord."

"Only between the time of the murder and the time we all were together in the dining room," Alice said rather shrewdly.

"The only person who wasn't in the dining room was..." She pointed a knitting needle at Dolly.

"And also Hielkje," Mrs. Montrose pointed out. "Remember, she left the dining room and shut the door."

Hielkje tugged at her plaid shirt and said indignantly, "I simply waited outside the door for a few moments."

"Quite long enough to have cut through the cord," Mrs. Montrose told her.

"This is a lesson in futility," Miss Sanderson said. "That cord could have been cut by any one of us before we gathered in the dining room."

"What about checking alibis?" Fran asked.

"Futile again. There are three entrances to the attic. From the main floor, from the guest wing, and a set of outside steps at the back of the inn. In a place this size it would have been easy to slip up there and back undetected. Unless two people were together constantly from about ten this morning until noon."

Brows furrowed in thought and eight heads shook. "You see," Miss Sanderson said, "I have no alibi either. I was alone in my room until Reggie came to get me for luncheon. I could have slipped up that boxed-in staircase to the attic and no one would have been the wiser."

Reggie nodded. "I could have too. I saw Gavin when he brought coal into my room and spoke briefly with Fran in the lobby after I'd finished my call, but that's it. What about the boat, Abigail?"

"No doubt done during the night. The noise from the storm would have covered any sounds the Jester made leaving the inn. Where was the ax kept, Fran?"

"Hanging from the wall of the boathouse. It wouldn't have taken long to chop a hole in the boat." Fran looked at Miss Sanderson. "But why go to these lengths? The Jester can't hope to escape. *All* of us are marooned here. Why delay having the police arrive?"

"There can be only one reason for that."

It was so quiet that all that could be heard was the shriek of the wind and a shutter banging. Slowly, sick comprehension showed on the faces of every person in the room with the exception of one. Gavin, his expression puzzled, looked from face to face. Hielkje dropped her cup to the floor and it splintered to pieces. It was Alice Caspari who whispered, "Because the Jester hasn't finished. He's planning on another victim."

"Or *victims*," Gavin blurted, and then proceeded to splinter into as many pieces as the china cup had.

"Brace up!" Marching over, Mrs. Montrose stood before him. He towered over her. "Stop that or you'll get what I gave your wife."

Reggie cursed and shoved Gavin onto the bench where Alice Caspari sat, her knitting neglected in her lap. The man crumpled down beside her, and over their heads, in Noel Canard's watercolor, the distorted figure holding an ax still watched the tiny skaters.

Her eyes locked on her father's painting, Nancy said hoarsely, *"Father.* He's the Jester."

Which proves, Miss Sanderson thought dolefully, that I'm about as good at therapy as I am at detecting. "Nancy, the only people on this island are in this room." Robby, she called silently, where are you in my hour of need? The answer was evident. In chambers going bonkers from overwork while she was going rapidly bonkers trapped in this inn with a group of people either in shock or having raving hysterics. She looked around for support and found it. Fran and Reggie had pulled themselves together, and Dolly's porcelain face was a serene oval.

"Abigail is correct," Fran said firmly. "Nancy, there are only two outbuildings—the boathouse and the coal shed. I promise you, anyone foolish enough to hide in them would die from exposure."

"I mean *here*. Somewhere in the inn. Hiding. He's mad, I tell you, mad!"

Hielkje gave a convulsive shudder and Gavin glanced apprehensively at the door leading to the lobby. Fran threw her hands up, and both she and Reggie looked at Miss Sanderson.

There was only one thing to do and Miss Sanderson proceeded to do it. "Nancy, we'll search the inn and the guest wing and prove to you once and for all that Noel Canard is *not* here. Fran, you and Gavin take the attic—"

"Not me." Gavin's head shook so violently that his mustache danced over his upper lip. "I am not setting foot out of this room."

Darting the man a contemptuous look, Dolly came gracefully to her feet. "I'll go with Fran."

Miss Sanderson said, "Reggie, you take this floor and the guest wing with…"

Mrs. Montrose stood up and tugged her quilted vest down. "I'll accompany Reggie."

"Good." Walking over, Miss Sanderson tapped Nancy's shoulder. "You'll help me search the bedroom floor and no arguments. We'll also lock all the exterior doors and the three entrances to that boxed-in staircase. Where are the keys?"

"We've never locked up," Fran said. "But there must be a ring of keys. Right, Hielkje?"

"In the kitchen. In the back of the drawer where the dish towels are kept."

Fran brought the keys and started distributing them. "They're labeled. Here's your lot, Reggie. Abigail, you take these." She tucked the rest in the pocket of her pea jacket.

Leaving Gavin, Alice, and Hielkje in the bar, the teams set out. Reggie paused to light the lamp on the desk in the lobby and then grinned down at Mrs. Montrose. "We'll check the dining room first. Nervous?"

She smiled up at him. "Not in the slightest." Thrusting a hand in the pocket of her red vest, she pulled out a small object and held it up. "Felix never traveled without his knives, and I always have my derringer with me. My husband gave it to me shortly after our marriage, and it's either in my handbag or pocket or, at night, under my pillow."

"How pretty," Dolly said. "The handle is set with mother-of-pearl."

Reggie laughed. "And how ferocious. A charming toy."

"Mock if you wish," Mrs. Montrose said, "but at close range this little toy will kill."

Reggie bowed to her. "In that case you go first and protect me."

They went to the hall for flashlights, and then Fran and Dolly preceded Miss Sanderson and Nancy up the staircase. Fran stopped to light the lamp at the top, and then her companion and she disappeared into the blackness of the hall.

"Where will we start?" Nancy asked in a quaking voice.

Terrified, Miss Sanderson thought, but with more courage than her husband was showing. "Right here. Felix's suite."

The chef's suite was totally different from the rest of the inn. It was furnished in a lavish modern manner. When the lamps were lit, they displayed a sitting room, bedroom, and bath decorated with pale blues and dove gray. The sole touch of vivid color was an abstract over the mantel. It too was modern, with swirls and blobs of reds, ambers, greens. On a chest were several decanters, an array of glasses, a pigskin case. Miss Sanderson lifted the top of the handsome case and eyed the one indentation. Felix's favorite knife, the one with the six-inch blade, was missing. Well, she knew the location of that. While Nancy remained in the sitting room, the older woman checked the bedroom and bath. She poked around in the huge wardrobe and found only an assortment of tailormade suits, a row of expensive shoes, a set of pigskin luggage. Draped over a chair was the creamy Aran sweater that Felix had been wearing when she met him.

In comparison with the luxury of the VIP suite, Nancy's sitting room and the bedroom she shared with her husband were shabby. Gavin's study was better furnished. He had a handsome desk and an onyx-and-silver desk set, a typewriter on a side table, two walls lined with books. Over the mantel another watercolor hung. Miss Sanderson glanced at it. For a moment it looked cheerful and innocent. It showed a beach scene, a child building a sand castle, two other children splashing through the waves. She had no difficulty locating what she was starting to think of as the artist's trademark. Behind the children a shark's fin sliced through the water. Gruesome, innocence again threatened with horror. She noticed that Noel's daughter was studiously avoiding looking at it.

When they stepped back into the hall, Miss Sanderson selected a key and locked the door leading to Felix's suite and his set of razor-sharp knives. As she headed down the hall, Nancy was so close that she walked up Miss Sanderson's heel. Swinging around, Miss Sanderson looked into the round face and wide eyes. "You're quite safe, you know."

"I'm behaving badly, Auntie Abby."

"We're all upset and nervous, my dear, but flying to pieces isn't going to help." She rested a consoling hand on the girl's shoulder and wondered if it was the shoulder of a murderer. Looking down at that face, so much like her childhood friend's, she couldn't believe it, but then Nancy Canard had once been an actress.

They moved down the branch hall, pausing twice to shine their flashes in the lavatory and the bath. At the far end of the hall Miss Sanderson opened the door and stepped out on the landing, flashing the beam of her light first down the Chinese-red stairs, then up. As the light hit the upper landing, it caught Fran's startled face and ponytail. Both women jumped and Fran called down, "Ahoy. Nearly finished up here. How are you doing?"

"Only your room and Hielkje's to do."

"Be sure to look under the beds. Wouldn't want a nasty surprise."

As Miss Sanderson locked the door, Nancy said plaintively, "Fran's making fun of me, isn't she?"

"No. She's only trying to introduce a lighter note." Silently Miss Sanderson added, And thank the Lord for that.

Both the remaining rooms were small, bare, and contained no hiding places. After Miss Sanderson had locked the rear door leading to the exterior steps, she turned to Nancy. "You do agree there's no one up here?"

"Yes, but—"

"All clear in the attic," Dolly called.

The other two searchers, Dolly in the lead, were making their way down the narrow steps. They walked in a group back up the hall and trotted down to the lower one. There they found Reggie and Mrs. Montrose, one hand jammed in the pocket of her vest, replacing their flashlights. Reggie's white smile flashed. "Nary a monster. We checked the unfinished rooms and all the ones that are occupied. The rear door and the one to the staircase are firmly locked. Hey, any one lock the front door yet?"

"You have that key," Fran pointed out.

"So I have. Wait a moment and we'll break the good news en masse."

The people in the bar had consoled themselves with a freshly fueled fire and a fresh pot of coffee. The searchers headed directly to the serving wagon and Dolly poured coffee. She handed a cup to Miss Sanderson, and her emerald eyes ranged past the older woman and settled disdainfully on Gavin Lebonhom. The news that there was no one lurking in the building didn't seem to be reassuring him. He rubbed his chin and said, "While you were gone, I was thinking. Any of you ever read that mystery about a group of people on the isolated island? They were murdered one by one, and the murderer turned out to be one of the victims who had only been pretending to be dead."

Reggie muttered a weary curse, and Fran spun around. "Are you insinuating that Felix Caspari is faking?"

"Well..."

"For God's sake, Gavin, stop being an utter ass! Abigail and I lifted him out of the dumbwaiter and he's not only dead but rigor mortis is setting in. If you think we're both in a conspiracy with Felix, you can go up and look at the body. He's in the mannequin room." She muttered, "And that's where you should be—among the other dummies."

"No need to be insulting. I'm only trying to help."

Miss Sanderson carried her steaming cup to the counter and climbed up on a stool. "That kind of help is doing more harm than good. Calm down and think constructively. If the Jester wanted to kill all of us, it would be simple."

The widow lifted her eyes from her knitting. "What do you mean?"

Miss Sanderson jerked her silver curls toward the serving wagon. "Poison in the coffee would do it."

Several cups were lowered, and Miss Sanderson lifted her own and took a drink. Dolly, casting a mocking look at Gavin, drained her cup. Gavin was gnawing at the end of his mustache. "Who is going to hold those keys? I vote Abigail does."

"You do trust me?"

"No reason not to. No motive. You only met us a couple of days ago."

"Perhaps," Reggie said in a sepulchral voice, "Abigail is a homicidal maniac with an aversion to celebrities."

Throwing back her head, Fran laughed. "Then I'm in no danger."

Miss Sanderson darted exasperated looks at them. "Act constructive and find something to put these keys in."

Folding back the counter flap, Reggie fumbled under the bar. "Got it." He pulled out a paper bag, swept the keys into it, and handed it to her. "Fran and I won't do further comedy turns. Carry on."

Miss Sanderson was tired and her head was aching dully, but she tried to carry on. "By now we're all agreed the only protection is to find the identity of the Jester. To do that I must question you about your pasts, your relationships with each other and with the murdered man. Do you agree?"

One by one heads nodded, and Mrs. Montrose said, "I've nothing to hide, but some of that may be…it will be painful to relate. I will not answer questions unless it is done in private."

Fran touched Miss Sanderson's arm. "I'll haul heaters into the saloon bar. You can set up quarters there. Gavin, you come help and no excuses. I'm not carrying both of them."

Gavin went along without protest, and Reggie jerked his head at Hielkje. "You and I will rustle up a hot meal. We could all use one. And we'll serve in the kitchen. Might as well be warm."

Miss Sanderson smiled at him. "Did you once do a stint in a restaurant?"

"As a busboy, but I'm a pretty fair bachelor cook."

Miss Sanderson glanced around. "Who's my first volunteer?"

"Might as well start with me." Mrs. Montrose came over to the counter and scooped up her cat. "Alice had better be there too."

"But you said—"

"You'll soon understand, Abigail. Alice has a starring part in this. Haven't you, dear?" she asked acidly. "Did you know our Alice was once an actress? Bit parts only, so this will be a nice change for her."

Alice was stuffing her knitting into the bag. "That's how I met Blanche Waggoner. She was always hanging around the theater, and I introduced her to Sonny Montrose—"

"That's quite enough. This information is for Abigail's ears only."

Fran looked around the door. "The heaters are in place. And I put a couple of pens and a notebook on the table. Need anything else?"

"No, that's fine."

"If you need me, I'll be in the kitchen giving Reggie a hand. Hielkje's comfortably ensconced in a chair watching him. Says she's too upset to work."

Miss Sanderson wondered if Fran was noticing her friend used her health as an excuse to dodge work. Hielkje certainly didn't look well, but the secretary had a hunch she traded on that appearance. Well, none of her business. Right now her business was unmasking a murderer.

In the saloon bar the heaters had been set at the ends of the refectory table and three lamps had been lit. One was on the table near a notebook and some pens. Miss Sanderson took a chair beside one heater, and Mrs. Montrose sank into the one beside the other heater. Alice Caspari glanced around and then pulled over the footstool and perched on it. She opened her knitting bag and Mrs. Montrose snapped, "Can't you leave that alone for a moment?"

"Knitting soothes my nerves, Sybil. A habit I picked up in the theater. While waiting to be called, you know."

Miss Sanderson flipped open the notebook and wondered how to begin. Mrs. Montrose took the decision out of her hands. "I'd better start from the first time I saw Felix. Don't look so glum, Abigail, I'll only give the highlights."

She marshaled her thoughts and then proceeded to give a concise account of her relationship with the dead man. Felix, it appeared, had been an illegitimate child, the son of the Montrose family's gardener's only daughter. "A loose woman," Mrs. Montrose said sternly. The loose woman had deserted her son when the child was five, and his grandfather had asked permission to raise Felix in his cottage on the Montrose estate. Mrs. Montrose was reluctant to agree.

"The boy's background," she explained. "My son was the same age as Felix, and I wasn't happy about old Simon Caspari's request until I met the boy. I'll admit I was charmed by him. Felix was a sturdy, handsome little fellow with chestnut curls and the nicest smile. He was also the opposite of my Sonny, an outgoing, confident, mischievous child. I gave Simon permission, and the two boys became playmates. Felix was always the leader, Sonny his faithful follower. Sonny was devoted to his little friend, and when the time came for him to go away to school, he was quite inconsolable. Felix, of course, attended a comprehensive. At sixteen Felix had had enough of school and begged me to send him to Paris to study cooking with a French chef." Mrs. Montrose gave a barking laugh. "Even at that age he had ideas far above his station in life."

"Felix had to settle for a dietitian course," Alice said indignantly. "He told me he felt Sybil had owed him more than that."

"I owed him *nothing*. But because of Sonny's attachment to the boy, I was generous enough to do that. When the course was finished, Felix took a job at a hospital in London and—"

"That's where I met him," Alice said dreamily. "I had a tonsillectomy and Felix came around to check my diet."

"And as soon as you were discharged from hospital, Felix moved into your flat and lived off you."

Alice glared at the older woman. "He hated that job and felt he was wasting his time at it. The pay was *terrible*."

"Mrs. Montrose," Miss Sanderson said. "Will you please continue."

"I will if Alice will allow me to. Where was I? Oh, yes. My son came down from Oxford and I was able to arrange a position for him at the Foreign Office. I was laying the groundwork for a career for Sonny. At the time I had high hopes for my son. He looked like his father, quite distinguished, and was well educated and beautifully mannered. All assets, and what he needed was a suitable wife. I started shopping around for the right girl. A wife with the proper background is so important, you see. At times I did despair of the boy. Sonny was so much like his father— dreamy, indecisive, rather weak. Then, rumors began to drift back to me. I checked and found he had resigned his position and was living with a—" It was Mrs. Montrose's turn to glare. "Alice, you'd better explain this part. After all, that girl was your friend."

"Blanche was never my friend." Alice turned her back to Mrs. Montrose and spoke directly to Miss Sanderson. "She was just a girl, much younger than me, who hung around the theater. When she wasn't there, she was on protest marches and sit-ins and things like that. Trying to save the world, you know. I didn't particularly like her, but I felt sorry for her. Blanche wasn't attractive and she seemed to have no friends or relatives. I took her in hand and gave her pointers on acting and her appearance." Alice preened. "I was quite pretty."

"She was." Mrs. Montrose gazed at the back of the mousy head. "An ash blond with a lovely skin and an excellent figure."

"Felix was always attracted by blondes—"

"I've noticed that," Mrs. Montrose remarked.

Without turning, Alice snapped, "Stop interrupting."

"Please," Miss Sanderson said wearily. "Alice, you said you introduced this girl to Sonny Montrose."

"I did. Sonny was still friendly with Felix, and they came around to the theater one evening. Blanche happened to be with me and I introduced Sonny to her." Alice looked past Miss

Sanderson's shoulder. "It was like one of those love stories you read. Love at first sight. Both of them just speechless and thunderstruck." She giggled. "Felix thought it funny. Blanche was such a drab and Sonny a real stuffed shirt—"

"If you mean my son was a gentleman, you're quite correct."

Alice ignored this. "Blanche stopped coming to the theater, and we heard Sonny had quit his job and moved in with her. I told Felix we really should tell Sybil, and he laughed and said she wouldn't hear about it from him. He said it served her right."

"About the reaction I would have expected from Felix." Patting her fluff of gray hair, the older woman continued, "When I did hear about my son, I went to London to get him out of that mess. The two of them were living in a dreadful loft over a garage, and when I saw it I was appalled. No real furniture, only a mattress on the floor and some cushions flung around. All the time I was there I was forced to stand. The girl was even worse than I'd feared. She was a common type for that era. What were they called? Flower children?"

"Hippies?" Miss Sanderson suggested.

"One of those unwashed creatures with hair dangling all over their faces. She was wearing a shapeless Indian print dress and had sandals on her grubby feet and strings of beads. She wore glasses, those odd ones—"

"Granny glasses." Alice added, "And she wasn't dirty. Blanche was always clean."

"When I saw my son I nearly had a stroke. Sonny had always been so immaculate, so well groomed. He'd grown his hair long, started a beard, and was wearing a fringed jacket, sandals, strings of beads. Do you know what the boy was doing when I arrived?"

Perhaps smoking hashish through a hookah, Miss Sanderson thought.

The old woman said tragically, "He was strumming a *guitar*. Sonny told me he was writing protest songs. I talked until I was hoarse. Generally I could handle him with little effort, but he'd changed…I couldn't sway him. Finally I appealed to the little tramp. I asked her if she wanted to ruin his life, told her if she truly loved my son she'd give him up. Sonny became furious and announced he'd found happiness and not only was he going to stay with the girl, but he intended to marry her. I can't even remember leaving them. I was completely shattered."

"What did you do?" Miss Sanderson asked.

"I went to Felix for help. He was shrewd and had influence with Sonny. Felix had been badgering me about funds to start a catering business, and I told him if he'd deliver my son back to me, I'd give him the money he wanted. As usual, Felix bargained and I agreed I'd also urge my friends to become his clients. I remember he laughed and said the price was right and he'd play the role of Judas—he'd break up the romance at once. All he wanted from me was to decoy Sonny down to our country home for a few days. I pretended I was ill and had our doctor summon my son to my side."

"And he came?"

"Yes. Sonny still had enough feeling for me to come." Leaning forward, Mrs. Montrose nudged Alice's back. "This is your first and only starring role. Tell Abigail all about it."

The widow didn't seem eager to begin. She fiddled with her wool, pulled down her skirt, tugged at the sleeve of her sweater. Miss Sanderson didn't prod, and at last the woman said huskily, "I suppose I should be ashamed, but Felix had his heart set on that catering business—"

"And he paid the price you demanded," Mrs. Montrose pointed out.

"Yes, he paid my price. He married me." Alice lifted beseeching eyes to Miss Sanderson. "Try to understand. We lived in my flat but…Felix always had other women. I didn't mind too much as long as he came back to me, but more than anything else I wanted the security of being his wife."

"I'm not here to judge," Miss Sanderson said crisply. "All I want are facts."

"It was so long ago anyway. Over twenty years and we were young and…" Alice straightened sagging shoulders. "At first Felix tried by himself. Women always went mad about him and he thought he could make Blanche fall for him and desert Sonny. So, as soon as Sonny returned home, Felix went to see Blanche. He turned on his charm and tried to seduce her. Much to his shock she threw him out of her loft. When he came back to our flat, he was furious. Then he calmed down and came up with another plan. For this one he needed my help. I'd heard him bargaining with Sybil and so I bargained with him. He gave me his word we'd be married."

"What did he need from you?" Miss Sanderson asked.

"Blanche wouldn't let Felix near her again, so he bought a bottle of her favorite wine and drugged it. I took it around to her loft, and at first she refused to let me in either. So I told her I'd come to apologize for Felix and then she did let me in. We sat on a couple of cushions and talked. I opened the wine and she drank a glass. The stuff worked quickly, and when she passed out, I unlocked the door and let Felix in. He carried her over to the mattress and undressed her. Then he stripped off his own clothes and got down with her. He made it look as though they were…well, you know. He'd brought the camera with him, and I took the pictures." With a touch of pride she added, "I'm awfully good at photography, and they were dandies. Clear as a bell. Felix had a friend develop them and then he gave the pictures to Sybil."

"There you are wrong," Mrs. Montrose said frigidly. "Felix didn't even bother showing them to me. He came down to our home, handed them to Sonny, and said something like, 'Take a good look at the little slut you want to marry.' Sonny looked at them and not a muscle in his face moved. Then he handed them back to Felix, got up, politely excused himself, and went to the library." She buried her face in her hands and her voice was muffled. "My son took his father's revolver and shot himself in the head. When we broke down the door, we found he was still alive. How I wish he'd finished the job properly!"

Miss Sanderson looked at the bowed head. "You buried him three weeks ago."

"I buried his shell." Her head jerked up. "You think me cold and unfeeling, worrying about a dinner party with my only child hardly in his grave. I suffered, Abigail, for years I suffered. But you must realize for twenty years my son was only marginally alive. His brain was so badly damaged that he never regained consciousness. Hooked up on a machine, tubes running in and out…When I finally won and he was allowed to die, I thanked God!"

"And you've always blamed Felix," Alice said bitterly. "Blamed Felix and me for doing what you wanted."

"I wanted my son back, alive and well, not as a living corpse. Yes, I blame you and Felix for what happened. Felix should have given those pictures to me, not to my son. I could have broken it gently to Sonny. He was such a sensitive boy, so much like his father."

Miss Sanderson was wondering how two such sensitive males could have borne a life with this woman. She asked, "What happened to the girl?"

The woman's simian face furrowed with displeasure. "She came storming into the hospital, demanding to see Sonny, making a horrible scene. She shouted she didn't believe me about his condition, that I was only trying to keep them apart. To quiet her I took her into his room, let her see him hooked up to that machine. I called in the specialist and asked him to explain Sonny's condition to her. Then she became quite calm. I told her to get out, never again to come near my son, never again to let me see her face. Before she left, she told me I was lucky he was still alive. She said, 'I'm certain, Mrs. Montrose, that we will meet again.' She quite upset me."

"The words don't sound threatening."

"Her voice was and so were her eyes. She had brown eyes, quite her nicest feature. Those eyes looked…inhuman. I must admit when I heard of her death a few years later, I felt relieved."

"She's dead?"

"I showed the article to Sybil." Alice had placidly resumed knitting and her needles flashed in the lamplight. "Only a short item on a back page. Blanche had gone to India with the Peace Corps or one of those things. She and another woman were taking a lorry loaded with medical supplies and food to a hill village when they had an accident. Some natives found them, took them to the nearest hospital, and Blanche died there."

"And how did you feel, Alice?" Miss Sanderson asked softly. "Relieved?"

"You *are* judging. I know it was a dirty thing to do, but to get Felix I would have killed."

Picking up the cat, Mrs. Montrose got to her feet. "Which you just did."

The younger woman leaped up and confronted her. "I know who the Jester is, Sybil. It's you! If I had been going to kill, I would have picked Dolly, not Felix!"

"Our Alice never did have any brains," Mrs. Montrose told the secretary. "Too bad she had to lose her looks. Well, any further questions?"

"Both of you sit down. I'm not finished. Do either of you know the names of the family involved in the accident that killed Damien Day?"

Mrs. Montrose shook her head. "I paid little attention to it at the time."

"Alice, you showed Reggie a letter from the child's father. Surely you remember."

"The child's name was Bonny. Yes, Bonny Wilson. I don't remember the mother's name. The father…I saw his name on the check he returned to Felix." Alice's low brow crinkled. "It began with a *C*."

"Charles, Calvin, Clifford?"

"No, something uncommon. I can't recall what it was. Why?"

Disregarding the question, Miss Sanderson asked, "What did Blanche look like?"

"I told you," Mrs. Montrose said impatiently. "Like a hippy. Except for her eyes, I don't remember anything but those awful clothes."

"Alice?"

"It's all so hazy. She was about your height, very thin, long straight brown hair. I can't even remember her features."

"Is there anything else either of you can think of?"

"One thing," Mrs. Montrose said with relish. "It probably is of no importance, but our hostess was once Felix's mistress. While they were both working on that cooking show. Alice, don't look at me like that. You know it as well as I do. Felix told me about it. Told me a joke about doing his interviews on the casting couch."

"Nancy?" Miss Sanderson was sitting bolt upright.

"Nancy Canard as she was then. Felix always had a weakness for pretty blondes."

"Does Gavin know?"

"I've no idea. And I've no further information."

"You can both go," Miss Sanderson said abruptly. "Ask Nancy and Gavin to step in."

"Both of them?"

"You heard me."

Mrs. Montrose picked up Omar. "No need to snap my head off," she said, and swept from the room. Alice, beginning to weep again, stumbled along in her wake.

Miss Sanderson was glad to see them go. That matriarch had enjoyed telling her about Nancy and Felix. Getting up, she paced around the saloon bar. She noticed that yet another of Noel Canard's paintings hung on the far wall. She refused to look closely at it.

The door from the public bar swung open, and the Lebonhoms entered. Miss Sanderson's eyes wandered past Nancy and settled on the man behind her.

Chapter Eleven

Both husband and wife appeared to be in better spirits. In fact, Gavin was more relaxed than Miss Sanderson had yet seen him, and Nancy had regained her fresh color. Gavin selected the chair at the far end of the table, and Nancy pulled the footstool over and slumped down beside him, one elbow braced on his gray-flannelled knee. He looked earnestly down the table at Miss Sanderson. "I've given this some thought…"

Lord, she thought, now we work through another plot of a mystery he has read or perhaps has written. "I've come to two conclusions," he continued. "There's no possible reason why the murderer—the Jester, as you've dubbed him—can wish to harm me. And there's no chance either you or the police can suspect me of having killed Felix. As you explained, the Jester was used to play a rotten trick on *me*." He gave a booming laugh. "Can you picture my helping to ruin my play?"

"You and Nancy told me about Felix's peculiar sense of humor. Perhaps it was perverse enough to enjoy forcing you to help him make you a laughingstock."

Gavin laughed again. "What a wild imagination you have! How could he possibly have done that?"

Not having that answer, Miss Sanderson turned to the young woman. "Nancy, I understand you and Felix were once…more than friends."

"Mrs. Montrose and Alice have been gossiping, I see."

The older woman's eyes wandered back to Gavin. He was placidly and rather messily charging a pipe. Dark grains of tobacco spilled down his shirt and littered the tabletop. "If you'd rather speak alone…"

"It's no secret, Auntie Abby, and Gavin knows all about it. For a few months Felix and I were lovers." Leaning forward, the girl confided, "My analyst tells me I'm attracted to older men because of my childhood. Seeking a father image, you know. And he's right. Since I was a child, older men have always attracted me, acted almost like a magnet. My first affair was with a history teacher. I was only fourteen at the time and he was—"

"For God's sake, Nan, Abigail didn't ask the story of your life!"

Miss Sanderson tapped her pen against the table. "Then Felix didn't force you into this…ah, intimate relationship?"

"Of course not! When Felix showed interest in me, I was delighted. He was so attractive and so good in bed."

Involuntarily, Miss Sanderson again looked at Gavin. He was now lighting his pipe. "Who broke this affair off?"

"Felix." She pouted. "As soon as the show finished, he lost interest in me that way. But we stayed friends. Don't look so stern. The world is much different now than when you and mother were girls."

"Chuck full of liberated women," Gavin agreed. "All living their lives as they please."

Wonderful new world, Miss Sanderson thought. And when Felix Caspari had been born out of wedlock, his mother had been branded a loose woman for doing exactly what these liberated women prided themselves on. She took a deep breath. "Gavin, were you aware of Nancy's relationship with Felix at the time of your marriage?"

"Not only that affair, but all her others. All with older men, of course. Shortly before we were married, Nan managed to keep me awake for hours confessing all. After the first couple of exposés I did doze off. Rather boring, like being forced to watch reruns on television."

His wife was now pouting charmingly. "Don't be beastly, darling."

"How old are you, Gavin?"

"I fail to see what that has to do with a murder." Apparently women weren't the only ones sensitive about their ages. Gavin reddened slightly and puffed out a cloud of aromatic smoke. Finally he grunted, "Old enough to be Nancy's father."

"I suppose," the girl said dreamily, "that's why I shamelessly threw myself at him when we met at a party. But you wouldn't be interested in that."

"I'm interested."

"It was shortly after mother's funeral. I was feeling so depressed that I decided I must cheer myself up, and I went to a party a friend was throwing. Allison was a makeup girl, and we'd become friendly while we were both working on the cooking show. It was a hectic affair, rock music booming and people shouting to make themselves heard above it. Really a crush too, Allison's flat is so tiny. I was sorry I went and then I spotted Gavin. He was so yummy I simply followed around after him but"—she turned and looked up at her husband—"he completely ignored me."

"I did notice her, Abigail. She was so pretty but so young. I steered clear of her."

"Not for long you didn't." His young wife smiled complacently. "When Gavin went to the drink table, I tagged along behind him. Allison came over to chat and she was teasing me about this inn. Asked what I planned to do with my white elephant. I told her the only possible thing I could do was sell the island and the Jester. Let someone else worry about the damn place. Then Allison asked about Felix, and I told her we'd broken up but were still good friends. Suddenly Gavin stopped ignoring me and he took me home and—"

"Nancy promptly took me to bed."

"I thought with Gavin it was only a passing fancy. But lo and behold, he asked me to marry him. In fact"—she looked around the saloon bar—"he proposed in this room. We'd come down for a weekend and he fell in love with this inn." She waved smoke away from her face. "I often tease him about falling in love with the inn, not with me."

Her husband made no effort to deny this, and Miss Sanderson flipped to a clean page. I feel ancient, she thought, quite out of tune. "Tell me how Felix Caspari came to be funding your renovations."

"It was Gavin's idea," Nancy said firmly.

"You're upsetting your Auntie Abby." Gavin chuckled. "She's struggling with the concept of a bridegroom borrowing money from his wife's ex-lover. But any port in a storm, and Felix was the only person I could touch for a loan. I'd made the rounds of the banks and so on, but the only collateral we had was this island and the inn, and they refused to lend a pound on them. So, I had Nancy invite Felix down here, and he saw the potential for turning this place into a fashionable murder-party house. I explained I'd be writing the scripts myself, and he became wildly enthusiastic. Felix put up what seemed to be an enormous amount of cash, and we had legal papers drawn up and then got to work."

"And you and Felix got along amicably?"

Nancy giggled. "At first. Gavin was kowtowing to Felix, yes sir, no sir, anything you say, sir. Then the money started to run out and it became a bit dicey."

"That was Felix's fault," Gavin said hotly. "Insisted on having that suite done over with the latest decorating and expensive furnishings. I told him it doesn't fit in with the rest of the inn and cost too much, but he had to have his way. Do you realize, Abigail, that with the money spent there I could have installed central heating and electricity?"

"Now who's getting off the track?" his wife asked.

Miss Sanderson said patiently, "Whose idea was this party?"

"Felix's," Gavin grated. "Another of his damn fool notions. I tried to get him to hold off, wait until we either got this place finished or have the first party in the spring. But no, the great man had spoken."

Nancy placed a chubby hand on his knee. "Don't rave on, darling. Felix was very good about it. Provided all the food, most of the booze, and arranged for the guests. How could you ever have gotten Dolores Carter-White, Mrs. Montrose, and the Black Knight down here?"

"I couldn't have," he admitted. "After I thought it over, it did sound like a wonderful chance for publicity."

Miss Sanderson dug out her cigarette pack and lighter. "Who suggested Robby as a guest?"

"Felix," Nancy told her. "I told him about you and Mother being such chums when you were girls, and he was excited. He said Reggie Knight wanted to meet Robert Forsythe and ordered me to go to London, see you, and make sure your employer came to the party. I failed, of course, and when I told Felix and Gavin, they were both furious. Felix said he knew Reggie would beg off if he knew Mr. Forsythe wouldn't be here, and also that Mrs. Montrose was frantic to meet him too. Finally Felix cooled down and swore us to secrecy. No one else knew about you, Auntie Abby."

"I noticed that," Miss Sanderson said wryly. She added silently, *And I devotedly wish Robby were right here instead of me.* "Tell me, Gavin, what was the board meeting about in Felix's suite last night."

Gavin had been knocking the dottle from his pipe. At her question he hit the glass ashtray so hard it bounced. "The absolute heartless bastard!"

His wife clutched his arm. "Let me explain, darling. You get so violent." The round face turned to Miss Sanderson. "This is one time I agree with Gavin. Felix took us up there, gave us a drink of his ruddy brandy, and told us he was in immediate need of money. The legal papers we'd signed entitled him to demand his money whenever he wished. Felix said we had to raise that money, and if we didn't, he'd foreclose and sell the inn."

Miss Sanderson was frowning. "I should have thought Felix made a great deal of money."

"He did," Gavin said bitterly. "And he spent money like water. On women and gambling and his lifestyle. Felix told Nan and me that he was stony and had to settle gambling debts and raise the funds to get rid of Alice and marry Dolly. I tried my best to reason with him, suggested he might borrow from Mrs. Montrose. Felix admitted there was a chance for a loan if he could persuade Dolly to attend the woman's bloody dinner party; he said Mrs. Montrose had hinted at it. But then he told us that Dolly was stubborn and he didn't think she'd agree. So...we left it at that. I could have *killed* him!"

Spinning around, Nancy stared up at him. Gavin patted her shoulder and gave a shaky laugh. "Of course, I didn't. Simply an expression all of us use. And Abigail, what I said earlier still goes. Felix would never have picked me as a confederate to play a lousy joke on myself."

Her cool eyes examined him. "What if he had offered to hold off on the foreclosure of the Jester for the price of your help."

"Ridiculous!"

But his wife was nodding. "Oddly enough, it sounds like the diabolic way Felix's mind worked. He might have been pretending to be broke just to force Gavin to—"

"Nan! What a lovely little helpmate you are."

"And what a sickening excuse for a husband you are!" Nancy burst into tears. "All you ever wanted was this horrible inn. I hope you do lose it."

"If I do, my child bride, you can get lost too!"

Nancy was sobbing, and her husband's hands had tightened into fists. Miss Sanderson snapped, "If you want to continue your family fight, go elsewhere. If not, let's get on with it."

Gavin sighed. "We'd better get this done. Nan, stop sniveling. You know I don't mean half what I say. I've been under a strain and so have you." He pulled out a handkerchief and handed it to her. "Next question, Abigail?"

"Tell me about your background."

"That I can do in one sentence. I want to be a writer, I've always wanted to be a writer, and I'm damned well going to be a writer."

"In the meantime you had to support yourself. Or did you inherit an income?"

"Hardly. All I inherited was a few sticks of furniture from a father who was a postal clerk. I've had so many jobs I can't remember all of them. Clerked in shops, tried to sell insurance, at one time worked for an estate agent. Earned barely enough to survive, but all I was interested in was writing."

"Was this your first marriage?"

"Second. Ann and I were divorced years ago."

"Any children?"

"One who died young. I suppose that's why my marriage broke up. After our child's death my wife was never the same."

Nancy was gazing soulfully up at him. "I never knew that."

"It wouldn't have interested you. Too involved with your own affairs, romantic or otherwise."

"That's a *beastly* thing to say. You—"

"That's enough, Nancy," Miss Sanderson said. "Among your numerous jobs, Gavin, did you ever act?"

"Not professionally. Ann and I were members of a drama society for a time. For amateurs we weren't bad and put on some fair shows. Why?"

"Only wondered." Miss Sanderson closed her notebook. "That covers it."

Gavin rose and his wife, wiping at damp eyes, got up too. Gavin asked brightly, "Any of the interviews thus far shed any light on Felix's death?"

"All of them. Four people—four motives."

He brushed at his mustache. "Doesn't take a detective to see Alice Caspari's. But what about Sybil Montrose?"

"Confidential information."

Nancy said rather shrewdly, "It might be connected with her son. Felix mentioned they were close friends. But what about Gavin and me?"

Gavin draped a long arm around his wife's shoulders. "Abigail is toying with the idea that I could have killed Felix to keep him from taking this inn away from me."

"Auntie Abby, that's *silly*. Felix's estate will be inherited by Alice. She'll probably do the same thing."

Her husband explained, "Felix's death does let me off the hook for a time. Perhaps give me a chance to come up with the money. And perhaps Alice will be more amenable than Felix would have been."

"Precisely," Miss Sanderson said.

"But what about me?" Nancy asked. "I certainly wouldn't kill Felix or anyone else just to keep this awful inn."

Her husband chuckled. "Woman scorned. Right, Abigail?"

"Right. Felix won your affection, Nancy, discarded you, and then turned up for your party not only with his wife but with the woman he intended to marry."

"That is nonsense!" Nancy's eyes blazed. "Come up to date. Women aren't like that anymore."

"My child, emotions don't change that much. Even in your brave new world, love and jealousy and hate still exist."

"You're horrible! So cold and not at all as I thought you'd be. I pictured you exactly like my mother. Gentle and kind."

Miss Sanderson rose and looked down at the vividly angry face. Rather sadly she said, "We were both disappointed. I had pictured you exactly as your mother was."

The girl bristled and Gavin pulled at her arm. "Come now," he muttered.

The door leading to the kitchen banged open and Reggie called, "Soup's on. Come and get it."

Spinning on her heels, Nancy stalked out of the saloon bar. Her husband followed, and as he passed the other man he said, "Women!"

Miss Sanderson's shoulders sagged and she rubbed at her brow. Reggie asked, "Little trouble?"

"Two worlds colliding. You go along. I'm not hungry."

"Seems to me you were the one mentioning keeping up our strength." He added, "You are eating if I have to—"

"My head is pounding and—" She smashed a fist down on the notebook. "It's no good. I can't be a detective. All I'm fit for is taking notes and asking stupid questions."

He put a consoling arm around her shoulders. "A couple of aspirin and some hot chow and you'll feel better. Abigail, you have no choice. The Jester isn't keeping us here to play parlor games with us. And you're the only one who can—"

"I know." She lifted her chin. "Lead on to that chow."

Chapter Twelve

The kitchen proved to be unexpectedly cheerful. The long table had been covered with a gay tartan cloth, and extra lamps had been brought in. Miss Sanderson, with aspirin provided by Fran and a heaping plate of shepherd's pie and vegetable salad dished up by Reggie, was soon feeling more cheerful. Her companions chatted determinedly, but by tacit agreement no mention was made of murder or Felix Caspari. Mrs. Montrose was exerting her considerable charm on Dolly Carter-White, and their host was being as charming to, and most solicitous of, the widow. Alice apparently was taking her new status seriously and had changed from her shapeless skirt and sweater to a shapeless black dress. Nancy Lebonhom bent her head over her plate, assiduously keeping her swollen eyes away from Miss Sanderson. Hielkje, despite her ill health, managed to tuck a copious supper away.

The first to leave the table was the Widow Caspari. Gavin jumped up to pull her chair back and murmured something in her ear. Alice said somberly, "Thank you, but no. I'd prefer to be alone." She looked around the table. "I suppose you people think I'm putting on an act. I know at times Felix could be…he did humiliate me and treat me badly, but…I wouldn't have stayed with him all those years if that was the way he treated me all the time. He didn't. Felix was often kind and thoughtful. I'm going to sit in the alcove and remember those times." She picked up her knitting bag. "This will soothe my nerves."

"We understand," Gavin said earnestly. "I'd better build that fire up so you'll be warm and—"

"No. You're kind, Gavin, but I'll do it. So many things to remember…"

On that trailing sorrowful note she made a stately exit. Conversation faltered and died. One by one the others drifted out of the kitchen until only the cook and Dolly were left with Miss Sanderson. Pulling her heavy body up, Hielkje started to clear the table. Then she thumped a stack of plates down and muttered, "Forgot completely about my medication." She sighed. "Have to go all the way up those stairs for it."

The baize door swung to behind her, and Dolly sat silently for a time. Then she reached for a plate of fruit and cheese and told Miss Sanderson, "I suppose it's my turn to be grilled. Let's do it here. Much warmer than in the saloon bar."

Miss Sanderson selected a piece of Brie. "Would you tell me about your background. Your family and so on."

"Family? I don't remember my father. He was a construction worker and was killed on the job shortly before my second birthday. When I was about eight, Momma remarried. My stepfather and I never got along. He was a nasty, miserable little man, obviously resentful of the child who had been foisted on him. Momma died of pneumonia when I was sixteen, and my stepfather made it clear I was no longer welcome in his house, so I struck off on my own."

Her eyes intent on the pear she was peeling, Dolly continued, "For nine years I held an assortment of jobs. Clerked in dress shops and bookshops and for a short and grim time, in a cardboard-box factory. When I was twenty-five my step-father died suddenly—heart attack. Rather surprised me. I'd never associated an organ like that with him." She raised brilliant emerald eyes. "Then I had another surprise. He'd left a legacy for me. Not a fortune, but sufficient to do what I'd always wanted. I rented the cottage on the moors and wrote my first book. As I told you, my agent, Rory, entered my life and Dolores Carter-White was born. And she has lived happily for the past twelve years. I suppose you'll want to hear about Felix?"

"Please."

Hielkje, who had quietly returned, dropped a pot and swore, but Miss Sanderson didn't look away from the woman opposite her. "You met Felix in Italy," she prompted.

"At a restaurant in Venice. I'd just finished a book and was exhausted. I was also irritable, and when I couldn't find the dish I wanted on the menu, I became quite curt with my waiter. I'd noticed Felix with a group of people at the next table, and I'd recognized him immediately. From his TV show and cookbooks, you know."

"Did he recognize you too?"

"From the way he was staring, I'd say yes. He heard me complaining to the waiter and came over to my table and told the poor man that if this lovely lady had her heart set on *ris de veau*, she must have it. I protested, but Felix said the chef wouldn't mind and made straight for the kitchen." Tinted lips parted over the perfect teeth. "From the roars issuing from that kitchen I assumed the other chef deeply resented Felix's invasion. Then Felix was back, bowing and kissing my hand, and put down the best dish of *ris de veau* I had ever tasted. He ordered champagne, and of course I had to ask him to have a glass. One thing led to another, and Felix escorted me to my hotel." The smile widened and became a laugh. "He had every desire to escort me into bed, but that was too high a price even for that dish. He took my rejection as a challenge and from then on was my shadow, showering me with invitations, flowers, gifts."

Hielkje had given up any effort at work and was staring at the author. "And you fell in love," she murmured.

The blond head turned and Dolly laughed again. "Been reading my books, Hielkje? Sorry, no romance in this story."

She turned back to Miss Sanderson. "Felix really wasn't capable of love, but he was terribly obsessed and infatuated. As for me…frankly, I felt it time to marry and he seemed suitable husband material."

"Despite the small fact he was already married," Miss Sanderson said dryly.

An elegant shoulder moved in a tiny shrug. "According to Felix, merely a marriage of convenience. One he kept on with only because he'd never found a woman he wanted enough to bother divorcing for."

"You felt no pity for Alice Caspari?"

"Not a whit. She's such a doormat. The only time Alice showed any spirit was when she downed jenever, and that was only bottle courage. But Alice shouldn't have worried. By the time we arrived for this so-called party, I was having second thoughts."

Miss Sanderson lifted a bunch of green grapes onto her plate. This then was the author of her favorite books. Warm, passionate tales of love and sacrifice, of man and woman working through all the obstacles one could imagine to find happiness ever after. Dolly must have been following her thoughts. She said lightly, "I think I've disillusioned you, Abigail. But I only write the plots, I don't live them. Where was I?"

"Having second thoughts about your not-so-true love."

A wrinkle appeared between the startling eyes. "At first Felix seemed ideal. He was handsome, physically appealing, a public figure. He seemed an asset, but I soon found he had faults. He was a spendthrift, carelessly tossing money around. I didn't care for that. I value money. And that sense of humor of his! It was cruel, at times verging on sadistic."

Miss Sanderson pulled off a grape, then put it down on her plate. "Did he tell you about the joke he was planning to pull on Gavin?"

"Not a word. But then, he knew well how I felt about his jokes."

"I take it you aren't mourning him?"

"I feel badly about his death, yes. But his widow is doing enough mourning for both of us." She rose gracefully. "Any further questions?"

"One. Have you ever done any acting?"

"No." Dolly smiled down at the older woman. "But writers are supposedly closely allied to actors."

As Dolly left, Miss Sanderson followed her with her cool gaze. And are you an actress? she asked silently. Could it have been Felix Caspari who was having second thoughts?

Hielkje bustled over and started stacking plates. "She isn't a bit like I thought she'd be," the cook confided. "But none of these celebrities are. Mrs. Montrose isn't even polite, and Reggie is much nicer than I thought a rock star would be."

"And Felix Caspari?"

"He was a *sjoelke*." Hielkje paused and then added piously, "But he is dead and may his soul rest in peace and go to *himel*." She gestured at the mounds of dishes, cutlery, and pots. "So much to do all by myself. It will take a long time before I finish up and you can interview me."

Taking the hint, Miss Sanderson rose. "I'll give you a hand and we can talk while we work."

When she reached the sink, she found she was the one faced with the washing up, while Hielkje, clutching a dish towel, waited. Rolling up her sleeves, Miss Sanderson plunged her hands into the hot soapy water. Hielkje was able to talk faster than she worked and a gush of words flowed from her. Patiently, Miss Sanderson washed dishes and separated the wheat from the chaff. Father Visser had been Frisian and his wife English. Their only child, Hielkje, had been born in Leeuwarden, and shortly after the child's birth Mrs. Visser and her daughter had deserted father Visser and returned to England and a stern Chapel family.

"I was never told why we left my father," Hielkje confided. "Mother simply called him 'that rotter,' and she didn't care much for me either, always said I looked just like 'that rotter.' The only times she was decent to me was when I was sick. As soon as I could, I left home and went to London to look for work."

Miss Sanderson rinsed the last dish and started on the cutlery. It appeared that Hielkje had had as many jobs as Dolly and Gavin had had. Her health was "not robust" and her employers too demanding. She was close to thirty before she had her first suitor and seized the opportunity to marry and retire to a life of ease. It hadn't quite worked out that way. "Eric had a farm in Kenya," Hielkje explained. "I thought it would be a good life with oodles of servants, but when I got there, I found all he'd been looking for was unpaid labor. Eric turned out to be a slave driver." Her brown eyes indignant, she recalled those days. "I've always had a heavy build and look strong, but my health is poor and I simply couldn't stand it. Finally I appealed to my mother, and she did send me my return fare, but she told me I'd made my own bed and when I came back would have to make my own living. So I drifted from job to job, and then I spotted Peggy Canard's advertisement and came down here to apply."

Miss Sanderson was doggedly scouring a pan. From then on, she thought, Hielkje had had an easy life, an understanding employer in Peggy and with Fran to do most of the work. "And you've been happy here, Hielkje?"

"It's been the best part of my life. Peggy was wonderful to me and Fran…Fran's been like a mother. In fact, much more motherly than my own ever was."

The secretary lifted her head and gazed at the other woman. Hielkje looked years older than Fran Hornblower. She put her thoughts into words. "You're younger than Fran?"

"Only a few months younger. I know I look older than my age, but that's because of my health, you see. Poor health ages one dreadfully. Yes, we were all very content until Felix Caspari came down and started to boss us around."

"Did Felix ever bring his wife with him when the inn was being renovated?"

"He always came alone. Neither Fran nor I liked the man. Always ordering us around and complaining. But he could be thoughtful. Felix brought me Dutch chocolate a couple of times and bought that pea jacket for Fran. All she had was a thin

jacket, and he said she needed something warmer. Strange man."
Draping the towel over a rod, Hielkje stretched. "Thank good-
ness that's done." She sank on a chair and watched her companion
scrubbing out the sink. "Many hands make light work, Abigail."

Miss Sanderson rolled down her sleeves and picked up the
notebook and the bag of keys. "Shall we turn off the lamps?"

"Better leave them. Fran is probably gathering up the
others to clean and fill."

After the warmth of the kitchen the hall seemed even
colder than usual. Shivering, Miss Sanderson picked up a flashlight, wondering if she'd ever be truly warm again. Then she
cocked her head and asked Hielkje, "Did you hear anything?"

"Only the wind." Hielkje yawned. "Well, I'm off.
Goodnight."

Miss Sanderson paused at the door leading to the guest
wing and then changed her mind and wandered down the hall to
the lobby. The door of the dining room opened and Fran pushed
one of the metal wagons out. "No rest for the wicked," she told
Miss Sanderson. "You look exhausted. Should be in bed."

"That's where I was going when I heard some kind of thud.
Did you drop something?"

Fran pointed at the wagon. Both shelves held rows of
lamps. "Nary a one. Must have been a shutter banging. I'll
gather up the lamps in the public bar and that should do it."

Miss Sanderson held open a door, and Fran pushed the
wagon into the bar. She stopped abruptly. The secretary peered
over her shoulder. Then they both knelt beside a figure crumpled near the counter. "Nancy," Miss Sanderson moaned. "Fran,
is she…"

"She's fainted. Get a couple of cushions from the alcove
and I'll prop her feet up." Fran lifted her head and her nostrils
quivered. "Do you smell something burning?"

"Smells like cloth." Pulling herself up, Miss Sanderson
headed toward the alcove. As she reached the narrow passage
between the benches, she could see the source of the smell. A
ball of purple wool, badly scorched, rested on the hearth rug.

Miss Sanderson's eyes traveled from the wool to a foot shod in a heavy black brogue and then followed the leg up to the hem of a black dress. Stepping into the alcove, she stood over the figure huddled on the bench, the mousy head turned toward the dying fire. Alice Caspari, looking deep in sleep. Miss Sanderson put out a hand and touched a shoulder. The head sagged forward, and from an ear something long and thin and shiny stuck out like an obscene antenna.

"Abigail," Fran called. "Be quick with those cushions."

Gulping, Miss Sanderson backed away from the hearth. "I think," she said unsteadily, "you'd better come here." Dimly she was aware of Fran beside her, of the ponytail of brown hair falling over the shoulder of the pea jacket.

"Get yourself a drink," Fran ordered. "Can't have you passing out too."

Miss Sanderson found herself behind the counter, a glass clutched in one hand, a bottle of Glenfiddich in the other. Funny, she had no memory of reaching for the bottle or glass. Then Fran was on the other side of the counter. "You'll have to see to Nancy. I'm going to get...I guess it better be Reggie. Gavin is useless."

When Fran returned with the singer, Miss Sanderson was seated on the floor, Nancy's head in her lap. Nancy was moaning, rolling her head from side to side. Reggie looked down at her. "Is she all right?"

"She will be." Miss Sanderson's voice had steadied. She held the glass to the girl's pale lips and Nancy's teeth chattered against its rim. "I'd better get her up to her room."

That was easier said than done. Most of the girl's weight sagged against the secretary's thin body. At the top of the staircase she let the girl sag to the floor, ran down the hall, and banged on the study door. From the other side of that door a voice quavered, "Who is it?"

"Abigail. Get out here and look after your wife."

Without waiting for the door to be unlocked she sped back down the hall to Nancy. Gavin joined them, and he seemed more annoyed than anxious. "What in hell is wrong with her now? Did she see another ghost?"

"She saw Alice Caspari with a knitting needle driven into an ear," Miss Sanderson said brutally.

Gavin Lebonhom collapsed beside his wife. He grasped at his thick hair as though about to wrench it out by the roots. "This is a *nightmare*. I keep hoping I'll wake up and—"

"Wake up and look after Nancy," Miss Sanderson snapped, and raced down the stairs.

When she panted into the public bar, she found Fran and Reggie perched on stools, gulping Glenfiddich. Reggie was wearing striped pajamas, a heavy robe, and sheepskin slippers. Taking the bottle, Miss Sanderson poured a hefty drink. She told her companions, "This time we know exactly how long the Jester had. From the time supper was finished until Nancy came in here. She must have come for a drink. This bottle and a glass were on the counter."

Fran nodded. "Probably smelled burning wool as we did and went over to fish the ball from the coals. She must have thought Alice was asleep, and then she saw that needle—"

"Ran to get help and fainted." Miss Sanderson propped her back against the counter. "That must have been the thud I heard." Leaning around Reggie, she asked Fran, "Would it be difficult to kill a person like that?"

"Easy and fast." Picking up a swizzle stick, Fran grabbed Reggie's chin with her free hand and pushed the stick into his ear.

He wrenched away. "Find another model. What do we do now?"

"Cope," Miss Sanderson said morosely. "Do the best we can until this bloody storm dies down and we can get help."

"What will we do about…" He pointed at the alcove.

"We certainly can't leave her there," Fran said. "We'd better put her on the dumbwaiter and take her up to the attic."

The nightmare that Gavin had mentioned came alive in the next hour. Armed with flashlights and lamps, the three went up to the attic where the pathetic remains of Alice Caspari rested on the platform of the dumbwaiter. Mercifully she was lighter and limper than her husband had been, and Reggie was able to lift her unaided onto the door that Fran and Miss Sanderson brought from the boxroom. The eyes of the mannequins glittered eerily as the door was lowered and a rose velvet curtain draped over the small figure in the black mourning dress. Motes of dust billowed up from the curtain and lamplight danced against the walls.

Fran looked down at the two doors and their dreadful burdens and scrubbed her palms down her jeans. "The Jester had better call a halt. Run out of doors and old curtains." She began to laugh, a shrill and ragged sound that alerted Reggie and Miss Sanderson.

Putting a comforting arm around the woman's shoulders, he guided her from the room, and by the time they reached the bottom of the ladderlike stairs, Fran's laughter had dissolved into tears. As they moved past Gavin's study, the door creaked open and he peered through the crack. "Everything under control?" he whispered.

"Just ducky." Fran began to laugh again. "Instead of building on another guest wing, you'd better enlarge the attic. It's cold enough for a mortuary but not big—"

"For God's sake," he snapped. "You're acting as neurotic as Nan is."

"You must excuse us poor females," she said shrilly. "Cracking up just from finding and disposing of bodies."

Gavin snarled, "Snap out of it—"

"You'd better get that door shut," Reggie told him evenly. "One more asinine word and I'll knock you down."

The door slammed so hard it rocked on its hinges. Pulling herself away from Reggie, Fran wiped the sleeve of her jacket over her eyes. "Tantrum all over, folks. Sorry about that."

"Don't be," Miss Sanderson told her warmly. "You're a tower of strength, but even crusaders have limits. Can I give you a hand getting to bed?"

Fran managed a smile. "Not that far gone yet, Abigail. Anyway, I have to get those lamps cleaned up."

Taking her shoulders, Reggie steered her down the hall toward her room. "Not to worry. This knight will attend to the night lights. And no, Abigail, I never did a stint in a lamp factory, but we used them a number of times in Liverpool when my parents neglected to pay the electric bill."

As Fran stepped into her room, Miss Sanderson told him, "You're a man of many talents, Reggie Knight."

He waved toward Fran's door. "And that's one wonderful lady." He smiled down at Miss Sanderson. "And you're another one."

"Flattery will get you everything. I'll give you a hand." They retrieved the wagon loaded with lamps from the public bar and took it to the kitchen. They worked quickly with Miss Sanderson wiping the globes and her companion trimming the wicks and filling the bowls. As Reggie put the last one on the table, he asked, "Care to talk or too tired?"

"I don't feel tired at all. Strange. Earlier I was reeling with fatigue. Now I feel quite keyed up."

"Adrenaline flowing. My room or yours?"

"Mine."

He opened the door of the guest wing. "I'd better stop off and get my flask."

"I have supplies of my own." She opened the door of her room. "You stir the fire up and I'll pour."

He picked up a coal scuttle. "Wonder how brandy will sit on top of Glenfiddich?"

"We'll soon know."

He raised his glass. "Cheers." Then he gave her a wry grin. "Are you thinking you may be drinking with a murderer?"

"The thought has occurred to me." Leaning forward, she touched her glass to his. "Here's to good hunting."

Chapter Thirteen

Sinking to a chair, Reggie turned an unsmiling face on her. "You're taking one hell of a chance. It would be simple for me to finish you off and none the wiser."

"Using what for a weapon?"

He glanced around. "The Jester seems to use anything handy. Felix's knife, Alice's knitting needle. Now, down to cases. Allow me to read your mind, Sherlock. After our conversation about Damien's death you think I may have despaired of meting out punishment to Felix by legal means and decided to give it to him myself."

"It's possible."

"Poor Alice had nothing to do with my brother. Why would I kill her?"

"To cover up the first murder. Felix could have let slip to his wife the name of the person who was going to help him play the trick with the dumbwaiter."

"Explain this. When you were describing the way her husband was killed, why didn't Alice spring to her feet and point an accusing finger at me?"

Miss Sanderson gazed into the flames. "She didn't strike me as an intelligent woman. Felix may only have hinted at the identity of his confederate and she wasn't certain it was you. But later Alice could have come up with the answer, perhaps mentioned something that alerted you and—"

"And I followed her to the public bar and rammed a knitting needle into her dull little brain." He pushed back a ringlet. "I'm about to blow your theory into smithereens. Alice would have had to alert me *after* Felix's murder. Right?" Miss Sanderson nodded, and he asked, "Then why did I sneak out and put the boat out of commission the night *before* Felix was killed?"

"You wouldn't have had the slightest reason to do that. And that's why we're here alone. Do you think I'd have been foolish enough to be alone with you if I'd thought you are the Jester? As a matter of fact you are the one person in this inn I feel I can trust."

He held out his glass. "Let's have a drink on it. Much more of this and I may switch from beer to spirits. Abigail, my offer to be your Watson still holds. Want to bounce ideas off?"

She jumped up and started to pace. "Can you recall the names of the family members who were involved in your brother's accident?"

"Those names are practically engraved on my mind. Wilson—mother Jean, daughter Bonny, father Cuthbert."

"Did you ever see Cuthbert Wilson? Even a picture of him?"

He shook his head. "Only picture I saw was in a newspaper, and that was only of Jean and her daughter. Pretty blurry at that. You're toying with the idea that Wilson is the Jester. But there's nobody in this place who suits the bill. Except…"

"Yes," she said. "Except a man who seems a quivering mass of fear. A man who admitted he once appeared in amateur theatrics. A man who also admitted he had once been married, his child is dead, and his wife 'never was the same after the child's death.'"

"Gavin Lebonhom! No, that's too much of a coincidence. Being right here on the spot when Felix…Abigail, I don't believe in coincidences."

"Neither do I. Try this out. Gavin met Nancy at a party. He showed no interest in her until he overheard one of her conversations. Nancy has a suspicion that the mention of this inn was the reason for his sudden attention. But the woman she was talking to had also talked about Felix Caspari and her relationship with him."

"Got you again, Holmes! Felix was back and forth to this place any number of times this year. Seems to me if Gavin was Wilson, he had ample opportunity to avenge his family long before now."

"Numbers."

"Huh?"

"Normally there are only four people here. Gavin, Nancy, Fran, and Hielkje. Right at present we have four more people to cloud the issue."

"Again, Gavin had no reason to harm poor Alice. Oh…same reason you gave for me. Felix let drop a hint about his helper…No, it won't wash. Why maroon us all if Gavin had got his target?"

Miss Sanderson made a swift turn and dropped back into her chair. "I might be able to answer that if I could figure some way Gavin could get off this island."

"Make his escape, you mean?"

"Right. Let's face it, Reggie, all we have to go on is what these people have told us. Any of them could be lying through his or her teeth. But the police…Lord! How I wish I had their facilities. They can dig into backgrounds and find out in a short time whether Gavin Lebonhom and Cuthbert Wilson are one and the same. If Gavin is the Jester, his only hope is to run for it."

"I take your point." He rubbed his jaw. "But the only way I can see to get off this island is either by the causeway, and that certainly can't be used until this storm dies down, or by flying." He lifted his dark eyes. "You think any one of the others might be the Jester? What about Nancy Lebonhom?"

Tersely she explained what she had learned about Nancy and her affair with Felix. His teeth flashed whitely and he said,

"Hell has no fury and so on. Possible, but weak. La Montrose?" He listened intently and then said, "Stronger motive for her. And one that does include Alice. If Mrs. Montrose blamed Felix for her son's attempted suicide, she'd also blame his wife. What a rotten thing the Casparis did to those young lovers." Leaning forward, he thumped his glass down on the hearth. "How do you work Dolly Carter-White into this?"

"Her motive is even weaker than Nancy's. Dolly gave me to understand she was changing her mind about marrying Felix. What if it had been the reverse? Dolly is highly intelligent and seems to have a huge ego. Somehow I don't think she'd take kindly to having that ego bashed."

"Possible, but…" It was his turn to desert his chair and pace. Finally he swung around and spread his hands. "It simply won't work, Abigail. With the exception of Mrs. Montrose there's no earthly reason to harm Alice Caspari. And remember that boat and the telephone line. The only purpose for marooning us here must have been to finish off both the Casparis." He peered down at her. "You're holding something back."

"Something I hate to even contemplate." She bent her head.

The Black Knight stared down at her silver curls and then one word was wrung from him. "*Fran.*"

"Fran Hornblower, who might once have been a girl named Blanche Waggoner."

"*No.*"

"I feel exactly the same way." Miss Sanderson stared down at her folded hands. Fran of the warm, intelligent eyes, of the gentle capable hands, of the swift movements, and the rare compassion. She felt tears spring to her eyes and blinked them back. "Reggie, this is one time I'm *begging* you to poke holes in my reasoning."

Sinking cross-legged on the rug, he said somberly, "Give me your reasoning."

Miss Sanderson reported to him as she often had to Robert Forsythe. He listened as intently, interrupted twice, nodded once, and when she had finished, he said softly. "This emotion Fran felt when she spoke of David…it did seem genuine?"

"Heartbreakingly so. That wasn't faked. However, David could have been Sonny Montrose, and Lebanon, England. Reggie, two women were in that lorry accident in India where Blanche was supposed to have been killed. What if their identities were jumbled? What if Blanche came back as Fran Hornblower?"

"And years later took a backbreaking job on this island because Peggy Canard's daughter was a friend of Felix Caspari's." His golden fingers tore at the nap of the rug. "Why *years*? Why wait so long?"

"Fran doesn't seem a truly violent woman. Perhaps she fought back that hatred for years and then something happened to make it explode into murder." Miss Sanderson placed a hand on the young man's shoulder. "Reggie, three weeks ago the life supports were removed from Sonny Montrose and he was allowed to die."

White teeth nibbled at his lower lip. "It seems so…airtight. That description you were given of Blanche, it's sketchy, but it does fit Fran. Tall, thin, brown eyes and hair. Alice Caspari told you the girl was younger than she was. Alice was in her mid-forties. Fran must be in her late thirties. Damn it! That fits too." He moved restlessly. "And I can *see* Felix getting Fran to help him in the attic. She's kind of a servant and he had nothing but contempt for menials. Give them a few pounds and they'd do anything. Abigail, if anyone ever deserved a knife in the back, that bastard did. Let's forget this. If the police unmask Fran, all right. If they don't, let's keep our ruddy mouths shut. I happen to sympathize with this murderer."

She said wearily, "I'd like to agree, but we can't."

"*Justice*," he said scathingly.

"She has to be stopped. Reggie, who is responsible for Sonny Montrose's actual death?"

"Christ!"

"Sybil Clifton Montrose is the next one on Blanche Waggoner's list." She reached for her flash. "We'd better warn her."

"About Fran?"

"We've no real proof. We'll tell her of Alice's death and also tell her to keep her door locked and not to let anyone in."

It took some time to rouse the old woman. When she finally opened her door, the fine fluff of gray hair stood up like a ruff. But her eyes were alert and she pointed the tiny derringer, not at Miss Sanderson, but at the man beside her.

"I've been doing some thinking," she told them. "I'm not worried about you, Abigail, but that man is not entering my room."

Reggie tried to sound jovial. "Fine treatment for a knight."

"The proper treatment for a man with good reason to hate Felix. Now, what do you want? I'd just nicely dozed off when—"

Miss Sanderson took a step forward. "It's about Alice Caspari—"

"If she has her nose in the jenever again you can handle her." She started to close the door.

"Alice is dead," Reggie told her.

The derringer wavered and she clutched the door for support. The color drained from her face and she swayed. Reggie put out a hand and she stepped back, jerking up the weapon. "How?" she whispered.

"A knitting needle," Miss Sanderson said. "Thrust through her ear into her…" She pulled herself together. "For your safety you must keep your door locked and let no one in. In the morning I'll stop by for you. Understand? *No* one."

The gray head bobbed and the door shut. Reggie and Miss Sanderson heard a bolt being shot into position. Reggie jerked his head. "Better let Dolly know too."

Dolly took it better than the old woman had. She still wore her red jumpsuit, and behind her Miss Sanderson could see a table with a portable typewriter and piles of yellow sheets. On the dressing table the roses were shedding petals that looked like bright drops of blood. Dolly agreed it was a sound idea to keep her door locked, thanked them, and turned back to her worktable.

"Lucky devil," Reggie said. "At least she has something to keep her mind busy."

"Tomorrow," Miss Sanderson told him, "one of us has to be with Mrs. Montrose all the time."

"Or with Fran."

"Yes," she said brokenly. "Or with Fran Hornblower."

Chapter Fourteen

When Miss Sanderson escorted Mrs. Montrose into the kitchen for breakfast, they found most of the others already gathered. The only person missing was Fran. Reggie, a towel pinned around his narrow waist, was at the stove turning bacon in sizzling grease. Nancy was toasting bread, and Hielkje was laying the table. Perched side by side on tall stools, Gavin Lebonhom and Dolly watched.

"Where's Fran?" Miss Sanderson asked Hielkje.

"Lighting the fire in the saloon bar. She hasn't brought fuel in yet. Said you had the keys. But she said there should be enough coal to last until this afternoon." Setting down a plate, Hielkje rubbed a broad hand across her brow. "I don't know where Fran gets all the energy from. I feel like a wet rag."

Fran popped in from the saloon bar and gave Miss Sanderson a cheerful smile. "You've a smudge on your cheek," the secretary told her.

"But I've a song in my heart."

Gavin said peevishly, "You're perkier than you were last night."

"With good reason." Fran cocked her head. "Hear anything?"

He listened and then said, "Nothing."

"And that's the answer." Striding over to a window, she pulled back cotton curtains. Weak sunlight streamed into the room. "Early this morning the storm blew itself out."

"Thank God!" Dolly sagged on the stool. "The causeway?"

"I'll have to wait for low tide." Fran pushed up a sleeve and consulted her watch. "Four hours, give or take a few minutes."

With knees that felt like jelly and a pounding heart, Miss Sanderson dropped onto the nearest chair. Reggie cracked an egg and deftly dropped it into bacon grease. "You all right, Abigail?"

Unable to speak, she merely jerked her head. Fran glanced around. "Any volunteers to go with me?" She turned to the Black Knight. "How about you?"

"Uh-huh. One stint I never put in was that of a tightrope walker. I'm afraid it's up to you."

Everyone started to talk at once, but Miss Sanderson moodily watched Reggie. She knew why he hadn't offered to go with Fran. The Black Knight was hoping she would make a run for it. Miss Sanderson found she was hoping the same thing. Take a car, she told Fran silently, get away from here and never let yourself be found. In the meantime…Reggie lowered a hot platter of bacon and eggs on the table and the sight and smell made her stomach lurch. She reached for a slice of toast.

Hielkje, as usual, had a hearty meal, but as soon as her plate was emptied, she got to her feet. "You'll have to make do without me—"

"As soon as this business is settled," Gavin growled, "I'm going to make do without you permanently."

"I don't care! Fire me if you want. I…I can't stand any more. I'm going up and lock myself in and take one of those pills Dr. Parker gave me."

Fran called after her, "Make sure that's only one pill." She smiled at Miss Sanderson. "Hielkje has a tendency to overdo medication. Waits until she gets a cold and then gulps half a bottle of vitamin capsules."

"She's still on the right track." Dolly stretched her long frame like a cat. "Jester or no Jester, I've a deadline to make, and I'm going to barricade myself in my room until the police get here."

Mrs. Montrose hesitated and then scooped up her cat. "Sounds like a good idea."

"I think," Miss Sanderson said quickly, "you should stay here. It's safer."

"I'm quite able to know where I'll be safest." Her black monkey eyes gleamed. "I suppose most of us have ways of calming our nerves. Poor Alice always knitted and I read Austen. Right at present I'm rereading *Emma* and I find it most relaxing. I'll take along this last rasher for Omar. He's wild for bacon." The huge cat reached out a paw and she scolded, "Naughty boy. When we get to our room mama will break it up for you."

The next one to rise was Gavin. He told them expansively, "Going to get all the facts down while they're still fresh."

"Facts?" Fran's dark brows pulled together. "You mean about the murders?"

"Of course. I've made notes on Felix's and now must fill in Alice's death. There's a book here, you know. Possible best-seller." Jauntily, he made his departure.

"Not if you write it," Fran muttered. She said quickly, "Forgot you were still here, Nancy. Spoke out of turn."

"I happen to agree with you. I've always known Gavin is simply dreaming about being a writer." Taking Miss Sanderson's hand, the girl squeezed it. "Auntie Abby, I'm sorry I said those horrible things to you yesterday. When I found Alice—" Nancy gulped and flung both arms around the older woman's neck. "I knew then what you were trying to do. Trying to stop things like that from happening and doing it all alone. You're not cold, you're very brave."

"I didn't prevent Alice's death."

"You tried. And if you were gentle and soft like Mother, you couldn't do things like that." Honey curls brushed softly against Miss Sanderson's cheeks and the girl whispered, "I'm sorry I disappointed you."

Holding the girl away from her, Miss Sanderson gazed down into the hazel eyes. "Nancy, I'm sorry too. Sorry I confused you with your mother. You do look like her, but you're Nancy, she was Peggy. I can never really understand your world, any more than you can mine, but surely we can try. We can be friends."

"We can, Auntie Abby." Nancy, her face radiant, stepped back. "I'm going up to Gavin now. Try to make amends to him for what I said yesterday."

Reggie was mopping grease off the stove. He said disgustedly, "Rats deserting the sinking kitchen. I'm going to have dishpan hands. Fran, how about grabbing a towel?"

She laughed. "The Black Knight's fans should see him now! It's my turn to say sorry. Must be catching. You and Abigail will have to cope. I'm off on fuel detail. Abigail, I'll need the keys."

Reggie shot a look at Miss Sanderson and she said firmly, "Both fuel and washing up can wait. Fran, while you're gone this afternoon, Reggie and I will handle the coal. I vote the three of us take a holiday."

"And I second the motion." Pulling off his improvised apron, Reggie threw it on the counter. "You two make yourselves comfortable in the saloon bar and I'll bring coffee."

Miss Sanderson took the younger woman's arm and led her into the next room. It was as warm as the kitchen, with a fire blazing on the grate and two heaters beaming warmth. They had barely taken chairs when Reggie wheeled in a metal serving wagon. A wheel squeaked dismally. "Handy things, these wagons," Reggie said.

Jumping up, Fran bent over a front wheel. "In some ways, but..." She spun the wheel and it squeaked again. "The wheels on these ruddy carts always need oiling. Well, that can wait too. Anyone care for a touch of brandy with their coffee?"

"Fine idea," Reggie said. "I'll get it."

Fran glanced after him. "That lad missed his calling. He'd have made a dandy butler."

Reggie came trotting back and extended the bottle. Both the women nodded and he tilted it over their cups. Leaning back, Fran asked, "I understand you told La Montrose and Dolly about Alice last night. How did they take it?"

"Nothing seems to ruffle our romance writer." Pushing the footstool over, Reggie sat down between them. "It hit Mrs. Montrose hard. She positively blanched, and I thought she was going to pass out." He pointed at the picture over the mantel. "Noel Canard wasn't quite as grisly in that one. Noticed it yesterday."

Fran looked up. "Nancy said her mother told her that was one of Noel's earlier works, painted shortly after Peggy and he came to live here. Maybe he wasn't so morbid then."

"Have you looked at it, Abigail?" Reggie asked.

"No. I've had quite enough of Noel Canard."

"Take a look. You're going to be pleasantly surprised."

Miss Sanderson put down her cup and rose. Reggie was right. This watercolor was fairly mild. It pictured only one child, a towheaded boy who looked around eight. He was forlornly squinting down at his feet. Half buried in the grass was a pair of wire-rimmed glasses. Both lenses were shattered. "For Noel this is almost poetic," she remarked. "All I can see is a little chap, terribly shortsighted, who has broken his glasses and will have to find his way home without them."

Fran nodded. "Nary a monster in sight. Not even a cliff the boy might fall off. The only mishap I can see is that he's thumping a shoulder against that tree."

Sliding back in her chair, Miss Sanderson rested her head against the back of it and closed her eyes. As though from a distance she could hear Reggie's voice, sounding determinedly cheerful, and Fran's, sounding quite naturally cheerful. Reggie was asking Fran if she planned to stay on at the inn, and she was telling him she never made plans, simply went with the tide. Fran, go with the tide, Miss Sanderson silently urged. We'll keep Mrs. Montrose safe and you get across that causeway and disappear. She wondered how Robby would feel about her emotional involvement with this murderer and then found she didn't care. For the first time in days she relaxed, allowing her mind to wander aimlessly. That weary mind fell effortlessly into a light sleep and no nightmare disturbed it. The dream that formed was only puzzling. She watched a chubby boy, squinting with myopic eyes and rolling a serving wagon along that had a squeaky wheel. The boy lurched into a doorjamb and banged his shoulder. Something fell, and at first the dreamer thought it was the child's broken glasses. Then she saw it was an ornate emerald pendant.

Shaking her head from side to side, Miss Sanderson roused. Blearily, she saw Reggie and Fran staring at her. "Napping?" Reggie said. "You were mumbling something about a cart."

Miss Sanderson didn't reply. She jerked up, her thumbnail drumming against a front tooth. Reggie started to speak, but Fran shushed him. Both of them stared at the secretary. Her hand fell away from her mouth and she pointed. "Fran, what do you always call that?"

"A serving cart. Abigail, are you all right?"

Miss Sanderson was on her feet. "Dear God! I've been a blind fool. As blind as that—" She waved toward the painting and then she was running. When she reached the foyer, she found Reggie and Fran were pounding along behind her.

"Wait," Reggie called. "Where in hell are you going?"

"To keep Mrs. Montrose alive."

Fran gasped, "She's locked in. She won't let anyone in."

Miss Sanderson tore open the door to the guest wing. "There's one person she'd open that door for."

They raced past closed doors. Dolly's, the one that Alice Caspari had slept in, the Black Knight's. Miss Sanderson thudded to a stop. She flung open the door of Mrs. Montrose's room and then stretched out an arm to halt Reggie and Fran.

Sunlight streamed through the window, highlighting the simian face of the professional hostess. Mrs. Montrose sat stiffly, a hand on each bony knee. Beside her a tall woman stood. A hand bearing an opal ring held a tiny derringer. Sunlight sparkled from the inlaid handle. The muzzle was jammed against Mrs. Montrose's fluffy head. Creamy hair brushed the younger woman's shoulders as she turned an oval face in their direction. From the face of Barbie Doll, the dark brown eyes of Blanche Waggoner regarded them.

Chapter Fifteen

For moments all that could be heard was the hiss of coal on the grate, a deep intake of breath from behind Miss Sanderson, and Omar's ragged purr from the rug near Reggie's feet.

Blanche's voice broke the silence. She squinted and asked, "Who is that behind you, Abigail?"

"Fran and Reggie. It's all over, Blanche. Put down that toy."

"As Sybil Montrose told us, this is not a toy. Granted, there's only one bullet, but that will be enough. If one of you move, she's dead. That I can see enough to do."

"Contacts," Fran whispered. "Green contacts."

"I used to wear glasses, but Rory decided they didn't fit my glamorous new image. When I had my hair bleached, he insisted on green contacts. They've come in handy. Mrs. Montrose never guessed my identity. Not until I took them out so she could recognize me."

Mrs. Montrose said in a monotone, "I knew her *then*. I never forgot those eyes. She was the one person I didn't fear. When she tapped on my door, I was…I was so happy to see her."

"And I was happy to see you alone." Blanche smiled down at the old woman. "Happy to talk with you before I send you to join the Casparis in hell." She peered at Miss Sanderson. "I saved her until last. Of the three, she was the most important to me. You know, legal secretary, I'm curious. I would have been afraid of Forsythe, but I didn't think you could figure this puzzle out."

"A few moments ago the pieces fell into position. Fran always calls those serving wagons *carts*. Reggie said when we told Mrs. Montrose about Alice's death, she positively *blanched*. And he meant she went *white*. Then I remembered that silly business about names the second day we were in this place, and I realized that Blanche Waggoner was now Dolly Carter-White. I also remembered that Blanche wore 'granny glasses.'"

The blond head bobbed. "And doubtless you recalled my bunting you all over the hall the other night when I was going to the bath. I'd taken out my contacts, and although I managed to keep my face in shadow, I couldn't see properly. It would appear, Abigail, that you're a sleuth!"

"And a realist. There's no use in harming Mrs. Montrose. Fran and Reggie and I will have no problem holding you for the police."

A dreadful smile touched the tinted lips. "You work with a barrister. Tell me, will my sentence be any longer for three murders than for two?" Mrs. Montrose moaned and Blanche glanced down at her. "Don't make me impatient. The old value life, and if Abigail can keep me talking, you'll have a few more precious moments. Anyway, I want to tell you how I did it and why—"

"I know why," Mrs. Montrose whispered. "You're *mad*."

"She's not mad," Fran said evenly. "She's coldly, horribly sane."

"And you should have been a doctor," Blanche said mockingly. "Now, Abigail, try to stall me with questions."

"I have no questions. I know how you became Maud Epstein. She was the woman killed in the lorry accident. Your

IDs must have become mixed, and you decided it was a good idea to change your identity—"

"Wrong. I'd taken out an insurance policy and made Maud the beneficiary. I'd no one else to put down for that, and I was fond of her. Maud had no one waiting in England for her either, so I simply let them think it was Blanche Waggoner who had died so I could collect the money. After all, it was *mine*. I'd paid the premiums. I'm not a thief!"

A moot point, Miss Sanderson thought numbly. This woman had killed two people and was holding a gun to a third and was worried that her honesty might be in question. "Did you come back to England to take your revenge on—"

"No, I'll admit I still hated the three of them. Felix and Alice and Mrs. Montrose had taken Sonny away from me, ruined his life and my own, but he was still alive and..." Blanche's voice trailed off and she stared down at the top of Sybil Montrose's head. "That was why I started to write romances. Critics claim that although my plots differ, the hero and heroine always remain the same. They're correct about that. Sonny was always the strong, stalwart hero, and I was always the beautiful heroine. You see, as long as he was alive, there was hope we'd find *our* happy ending and—"

"My son was *not* alive," Mrs. Montrose rasped. "After he shot himself he was only medically—"

"Shut up, you old fool!" Blanche dug the barrel of the tiny gun into gray hair. "Look at the advances in modern science. There was still a chance for a miracle, that Sonny would be cured—"

"No!" Mrs. Montrose's voice rang out. "His brain was destroyed. He was only a shell—"

"Be quiet!" Miss Sanderson ordered. The older woman's life hung by a thread and she seemed to be deliberately goading Blanche. She said hastily, "When you went to Venice, did you plan to meet Felix?"

"It happened exactly as I told you." Blanche laughed. "I couldn't believe it. I thought Felix would surely recognize me, might even remember my voice, but I'd changed too much. He was obviously infatuated, and although I loathed him I played along. It amused me and I decided to play a joke on the joker. After he divorced his faithful Alice and announced our engagement, I planned to break it off, as publicly and messily as I could, and then tell him who I actually was." The laughter faded and the oval face became blank again. "Three weeks ago Mrs. Montrose won her court case and Sonny…she *murdered* him. I knew I'd never write again. With Sonny dead there was nothing left—no warmth, no passion, no dreams."

"And you came here for revenge."

"Yes. You see, they'd taken Sonny away from me, my writing away from me. Oh, I pretended I was writing, but I knew I'd never write again. There was nothing left for me but this. And it was so easy. Last evening, Abigail, I lied to you. Felix believed I enjoyed his jokes. He asked me to help him with the joke he planned to play on Gavin. After he read Gavin's script, he came to me and I agreed to help. That night I went down to the boathouse and put an ax through the boat's bottom."

"And the next day you cut the telephone cord while the rest of us were in the dining room." Miss Sanderson touched Reggie's arm and pointed down. He followed her eyes and gave a small nod. "Did you tell Felix your identity before—"

"Of course. I would have liked to have done it the same way as I did with Alice, face-to-face, looking into his eyes. But Felix was too big and powerful for that, so I had to wait until he'd arranged himself on the dumbwaiter. Before I drove that knife into his back, I told him. Now, my dear Mrs. Montrose, time for you to follow those lovely friends of yours. Do say hello to Felix and Alice for me."

Now or never, Miss Sanderson thought, and she ran into the room. Blanche whirled, automatically twisting the derringer away from the old woman. Its barrel pointed at the secretary. At the same moment, Reggie stooped, seized the cat, and hurled it at Blanche. Omar landed on her arm. He hissed with fury and raked her flesh with talonlike claws.

Fran leapt past Miss Sanderson and grappled with Blanche. The derringer gave a tinny little bark and the secretary staggered back. It's true, she thought, you feel the bullet before you hear the sound.

She was aware that Mrs. Montrose, with remarkable speed, was heading to shelter behind the bed. Reggie was helping Fran Hornblower, and they were tying Blanche to the desk chair. It looked as though they were using tights as ropes.

Miss Sanderson lost interest. She slid down and braced her back against the wall. The wall felt cold, but something warm was welling from her upper body. I'm bleeding to death, she thought drearily. Abigail Sanderson's first case is her last one. Now I'll never see Robby's face when he opens his jade tree at Christmas.

Reggie was shouting, and then Fran was kneeling beside the secretary. "Get the first-aid box," she told the singer. "Under the desk in the lobby. Hurry!"

"I'm dying," Miss Sanderson said without much interest.

Gentle capable hands were cutting Miss Sanderson's sweater away from a shoulder. "Like hell you are," Fran said inelegantly. "One of those flesh wounds you read about in thrillers. Painful but certainly not fatal." She said over her shoulder, "Stop wringing your hands, Reggie, and make tea. Strong, and throw in lots of sugar."

Mrs. Montrose had retrieved her cat and was joyously hugging him. "Good Omar," she told the animal. "You saved your mama's life!"

Fran grinned wryly at Miss Sanderson. "How does it feel to join the club? That's the gratitude crusaders generally get. *You* get the pain, and the ruddy *cat* gets the hero badge."

She pressed a bandage against the wound. Miss Sanderson got the pain and promptly passed out.

Chapter Sixteen

There were times when Robert Forsythe wondered why he kept his rambling costly home in Sussex. Tonight, as he looked around his study, he knew. Meeks had kindled a wood fire, and the smell of fruit wood mingled pleasantly with that of pine needles. On the Aubusson carpet near the desk used by generations of Forsythes was the tree erected for his private enjoyment. The tall tree in the drawing room easily outshone this one both in size and decoration. The baubles on his study tree showed their age, gilt flaking from fragile glass, an angel at the top with a mended wing, a bluebird missing most of its tail feathers. But each shabby object represented a memory, a moment that would never come again.

Reaching out, he gently touched a small object. "You brought this for me on my fifth Christmas," he told his companion.

"Frosty the Snowman? That happened to be your fourth Christmas. The same year that your father gave you the electric train."

"Right. I was recovering from measles—"

"Whooping cough," Miss Sanderson corrected.

He turned to look at her. "Sure you're not too tired?"

She shook her silver curls. "We always see Christmas day arrive, Robby." She glanced up at the mantel clock. "Not long now. The evening went well, didn't it?"

"Enjoyed by all. And your new image proved to be a sensation. Colonel Barton was practically goggling at you. Better watch it. He's shopping around for a third wife."

"Some of the guests found the sling intriguing. Inspired idea to use silk to match my dress."

He glanced at the green sling that did match the final layer of chiffon and turned away. The shock of that telephone call from Inspector James of the Finchley police force was still too recent, too harrowing. He said gruffly, "Sandy, that was the stupidest move you ever made."

"How did I know a murder party was going to turn into the real thing?"

"You know what I mean. Walking right into a gun!"

"Only a derringer, Robby, and I didn't think the woman could see well enough to even hit the wall. Anyway, I was only trying to distract her." She squirmed into a more comfortable position and changed the subject. "Bubbly ready yet?"

The cooler sat on his desk and he turned the long-necked bottle. "Just about there. But you get only one glass. I noticed the amount of punch you were downing."

"Four cups, but who was counting. Aren't you curious about who rang me up?"

"I know. Mrs. Meeks told me it was the Black Knight. She was all aflutter. Believe it or not, but she adores him, says she has all his records. When you came back, you looked like a cat full of cream. Good news?"

"Excellent. Nancy Lebonhom is finally convinced that her father, dead or alive, does not roam the Jester, and Gavin and she are keeping it on. Mrs. Montrose, who seems as canny about money as my Aggie, is funding the rest of the renovations and paying for central heating and so on."

"Ye gods! They're going to continue giving parties after having two murders and an attempted third enlivening their first?"

Lifting shapely legs onto a hassock, Miss Sanderson grinned impishly up at him. "I understand Gavin has written that plot into a new play. I wonder who will play my role? Reggie says the Lebonhoms and Mrs. Montrose think they have a gold mine on that island."

"No doubt they have. I wonder whether they plan to have a ghost in a black mask wafting down the corridors?" He bent and poked at a log, and orange and red fire devils spiraled up. "I overheard part of your conversation with Gene Emory, Sandy. Something about having already made your New Year's resolutions."

"Two resolutions, and don't look so dubious. These I intend to keep. Number one—never ever again will Abigail Sanderson accept a second case, and—"

"You certainly proved your ability on this one!"

"And found out exactly how glamorous it is to carry the full detecting load. From now on, you're the detective, and I'll happily bumble along making notes and asking asinine questions."

He shook his head. "On that one I'll wait and see. What's your second resolution?"

Her sound arm made a sweeping gesture, starting at the cap of metallic curls, wafting down the chiffon dress, and pointing at the extravagant emerald shoes. "All this goes."

He cocked his head and looked down at her. "I'll admit I wouldn't mind seeing your hair back to normal, and those heels are treacherous, but Sandy, do hang on to that dress."

Her eyes narrowed. "You're up to something."

How, Forsythe thought, do you try to conceal something from a person who remembers you had whooping cough on your fourth Christmas? It was his turn to hastily change the subject. "Did the Black Knight have any other tidings of joy?"

She was diverted and her eyes sparkled. "That was what made me so happy. Fran is leaving the Jester for good. As soon as Gavin got back to normal, he fired Hielkje and—"

"Where is Fran going?"

"If you give me a chance, I'll tell you. Reggie Knight has decided to do something constructive about his brother's memory. He's investing in a small nursing home near Finchley, and Fran Hornblower is going to manage it. It's to be called the Damien Day Home."

"And the ailing cook?"

"Hielkje goes with Fran. In what capacity I don't know."

"From what you said about Hielkje Visser, my guess would be as resident patient." He glanced at the clock. "Uh-oh, time for champagne and present opening."

He hurried over to the tree and carefully detached two presents. They were small, one wrapped in red paper, the other in silver. The red one had a silver bow, the other a large green bow. Under the opulent tree in the drawing room were mounds of gaily wrapped gifts, but opening their special gifts to each other had become a tradition. Always in the study, always alone. As he handed the silver package to Miss Sanderson, the clock majestically struck midnight.

"Merry Christmas, Sandy." He kissed her brow and she smiled up at him.

"Merry Christmas, Robby. You open yours first."

"You go first."

"Let's do it at the same time!"

Paper and ribbons and bows flew, and Miss Sanderson held up an emerald pendant set into antique gold. "Robby," she whispered.

He was staring down at the tiny jade tree. "I can hear the bird singing," he said rapturously.

"So could I. I heard it in the shop."

Carefully, he carried the tree to his desk, situated it dead center, covered it with the glass domed lid from a candy dish. Then he took the pendant Miss Sanderson was extending and clasped it around her neck. Standing back, he beamed. "I *knew* it would look wonderful with that dress." His secretary's eyes were moist and he said huskily, "One glass of bubbly and I'm bundling you off to bed. Big day tomorrow. Sixteen dinner guests, crackling goose, plum pudding, and..."

He pulled the cork and poured. Handing a glass to Miss Sanderson, he knelt at her side. "To Christmas past, Sandy."

"And to many more to come."

"Amen." Robert Forsythe touched his glass to hers and they both drank.